D0058672

COLD, COLD BONES

A TEMPERANCE BRENNAN NOVEL

KATHY REICHS

SCRIBNER

NEW YORK   LONDON   TORONTO   SYDNEY   NEW DELHI

Scribner

An Imprint of Simon & Schuster, Inc.

1230 Avenue of the Americas

New York, NY 10020

First Scribner hardcover edition July 2022

SCRIBNER and design are registered trademarks of The Gale Group, Inc., used under license by Simon & Schuster, Inc., the publisher of this work.

For information about special discounts for bulk purchases, please contact Simon & Schuster Special Sales at 1-866-506-1949 or business@simonandschuster.com.

The Simon & Schuster Speakers Bureau can bring authors to your live event. For more information or to book an event, contact the Simon & Schuster Speakers Bureau at 1-866-248-3049 or visit our website at www.simonspeakers.com.

Manufactured in the United States of America

1   3   5   7   9   10   8   6   4   2

Library of Congress Cataloging-in-Publication Data has been applied for.

ISBN 978-1-9821-9002-6
ISBN 978-1-9821-9004-0 (ebook)

33614082950295

This one is for the sisters neglected up until now:
Sue Weber
Laurel Toelle
Renate Reichs

Coming back to where you started is not the same as never leaving.

—Terry Pratchett

COLD, COLD BONES

1

It began with an eyeball.

The pupil was wide as a Texas prairie, the iris the color of faded denim. Crimson vessels spiderwebbed the yellow-white sclera.

More on that later.

SUNDAY, JANUARY 30

"Don't hurt yourself."

"I've got this." Despite the cold and damp, my palms were sweaty. My everything was sweaty.

The carton slipped from my hands as the words left my mouth. *Thunk!*

"Damn."

Sighing in irritation, Katy set down a lamp, a peculiar Alice-in-Wonderland arrangement with a long, crooked neck.

"Did you notice the word on top?" Assuming I hadn't, she spelled it out. "B.O.O.K.S. What do you suppose that means, Mom?" We'd been at this for hours and, in addition to clammy, we were exhausted and sick of the whole bloody thing. And cranky as hell.

"The box contains books." Terse.

"And what is one property of a box of books?" Lips barely moving.

I said nothing.

"They're heavy!"

"Let's break for lunch."

"Let's."

We hopped from the back of the truck. Grabbing the lamp, Katy crossed a small patch of winter-dead lawn fronting a mid-century brick bungalow whose entrance was standing wide. I followed her inside, for the zillionth time that day, and closed the bright red door behind me.

As Katy climbed the stairs with Alice's curious illuminator, I continued down the hallway to the kitchen. Which, given the home's aged exterior, was astonishingly state of the art. Marble countertops, College of Surgeons–level lighting, built-in coffee extravaganza, adult beverage center, top-of-the-line stainless-steel appliances.

Crossing to a Sub-Zero refrigerator the size of a boxcar, I withdrew two cans of cream soda and placed them on the island beside a white takeout bag. I was adding paper towel napkins for flair when Katy reappeared.

Seeing the bag, she beamed. "Please tell me you hit the Rhino."

"I hit the Rhino," I said. "Got your deli favorite."

"The Stacked High?"

"Yes, ma'am. A Sicilian for me. Cold."

Hands washed, we unwrapped our sandwiches and popped open the sodas. Were messily chewing when Katy asked, "How's your back?"

"Dandy." Though my lumbar was registering displeasure with the morning's activities.

"You really should leave the heavy stuff for me."

"Because I'm a nerd scientist and you're a badass combat veteran?"

"Was."

"Hallelujah!"

"What? You didn't approve of me serving my country?"

"I approved of your service. I hated that much of it was done in a war zone."

"That's generally what serving your country is all about."

Following a post-college period of, I'll be kind and call it "uncertainty," my naive and reckless daughter went full circle and answered Uncle Sam's call. Awesome, I told myself. She'll find direction. Self-discipline. Being female, she'll be in no peril. Sure, my attitude was sexist. But this was my twentysomething golden-haired child who was boarding a bus for boot camp.

Then the regs changed to allow women in the trenches. En masse, the ladies shouldered their M16s and marched off to fight alongside their brothers-in-arms.

Following basic combat training, the golden-haired child chose her occupational specialty, 11B. Infantryman. Katy's time in uniform re-introduced me to military acronyms and jargon I hadn't heard since my ex, Pete, was a Marine.

In a nanosecond, or so it seemed to me, Katy was deployed to Afghanistan to join a brigade combat team. Not so awesome. Lots of anxious days and sleepless nights. But her tour went well, and twelve months later she returned home with only a small scar on one cheek.

Life in the field artillery agreed with my daughter. When her enlistment ended, to my dismay, she re-upped. To my greater dismay, she signed on for another Middle East deployment. Hello darkness, my old friend.

All that was past, now. The tossing and turning was over. Well, mostly.

Last fall, Katy had decided to hang up her boots and camos and return to civilian life. She was honorably discharged and, to my surprise and delight, decided to settle in Charlotte. At least for a while. Why? She won't say.

Katy also refuses to talk about her time in the army. Her friends. Her overseas duty. The scar. So, we're playing it like her former employer: don't ask, don't tell.

We ate in companionable silence for a while. Katy broke it.

"Is the nerd scientist currently working on any rad bones?"

"A few."

Katy curled her fingers in a give-me-more gesture. They were coated with shimmery creole mustard.

"Last week a barn in Kannapolis burned to the ground. When the rubble cooled, firefighters found the remains of two horses and one adult male, all charred beyond recognition."

"Shitty deal for the horses."

"Shitty deal for everyone."

"Let me guess. Farmer Fred was a smoker."

"The body wasn't that of the property owner."

"Did you ID the guy?"

"I'm working on it."

"The horses?"

"Chuckie and Cupcake."

"Were they valuable?"

"No."

"Weird."

"What's weirder is that the man had a bullet hole right between his eyes."

"Whoa. Someone went kinetic."

Katy fell quiet again, thinking about bullet holes, maybe horses. Or creole mustard.

I am a forensic anthropologist. I consult to coroners and medical examiners needing help with corpses unfit for standard autopsy— the decomposed, dismembered, burned, mutilated, mummified, and skeletal. I help recover those with the misfortune to die away from home or a hospital bed. I give names to the nameless. I document postmortem interval and body treatment. I consider manner of death, be it by suicide, homicide, accident, or natural causes.

Mine was not the job of any parent Katy encountered growing up. But she was good with my being different, and in her teens began asking questions. Some things I shared, others I didn't. *Many* others.

In my experience the world divides into two camps: those fascinated by my profession and those repelled by it. Katy, never squeamish, has always been a member of Camp Fascination.

I glanced up. Katy's eyes were looking past me, focused on a point elsewhere in the room. Elsewhere in time? I didn't ask what she was thinking. Waited until she spoke again.

"What's the sitrep with *Monsieur le détective*?"

"Sitrep?"

"Situation report."

My daughter was asking about Lieutenant-détective Andrew Ryan, a former Sûreté du Québec homicide cop with whom I currently was living. In Montreal and Charlotte. *C'est compliqué.*

"Ryan?" I asked.

"No. Inspector Clouseau," she said, rolling her very green eyes.

"We're good."

"*That* sounds convincing."

"Really. Ryan was here at Christmas. You two just missed each other."

"He's retired, right? Working as a PI?"

"Yes."

"Where is he now?"

"On a case in Saint Martin."

"Tough duty."

"The guy blisters if he even looks at a beach. Canadian skin, you know."

"He's gone a lot?"

"He is."

"What's he privately investigating?" she asked, hooking air quotes.

"It has to do with a grounded sailboat and an insurance claim."

"Sounds boring."

"Many of his cases are."

I took another bite of my sandwich, blotted red wine vinegar from the front of my tee. Stole a peek at Katy. She'd asked about *my* love life. What the hell?

"So." Casual as a Sunday stroll on a boardwalk. "Any romance in your life?"

Katy gave what some might call a guffaw. I've never been clear on how one sounds.

"*Ro*-mance? Did you really use the word *'ro*-mance'? Like, do I have a suitor? A sweetheart? A beau?"

"People still say romance."

"People over eighty."

"What about—"

"Let it go."

Katy's altered tone triggered a warning. But we'd been joking. Hadn't we?

I was about to change the subject, when Katy's eyes narrowed in a way I didn't like.

"I've been in the army for eight years, Mom. I've been to war. I've seen people with their limbs blown off, their heads shattered, their organs spread around them as they bled out. I've seen little kids die. The last thing I believe in is romance."

"I didn't mean to upset you," I said, unsure how I had. But I think you're getting the picture. My daughter came home touchy and I was treading softly.

Katy leaned back and ran both hands down her face. "Sorry. I'm just tired from this friggin' move."

"It's amazing how much a small truck can hold," I said lightly.

Katy raised a palm toward me. Despite the greasy yellow coating, I high-fived it.

"Let's wrap this bastard up," she said.

"Let's do," I agreed.

We bunched our wrappers and stuffed them into the bag, and were heading down the hall when Katy asked,

"Have you ever met one?"

I was lost. "One what?"

"A cold Sicilian."

I could think of no response.

"I've dated two," she said. "Each was hotter than a steak on a grid-dle."

I definitely didn't follow up on that.

The remaining boxes and household items took more than three hours. One oversized chair almost didn't make the cut. With a lot of cursing and maneuvering, and a little muscle from a sketchy-looking guy passing by on the sidewalk, we finally managed to force the thing through the door.

Since we looked and smelled like escapees from some subter-ranean chamber, dining out wasn't an option. Having no idea of the location of her soap and towels, Katy accepted my invitation to clean up and eat dinner at my home, called "the annex," but insisted on sleeping in her new digs.

Remembering my first apartment with its mattress on the floor and Salvation Army Papa-san chair, I understood and didn't try to dissuade her. She'd hang back to lock up and follow in her own car.

Long before the era of zip codes, the fine citizens of Charlotte loved to distinguish the sectors making up their town. Each area was endowed with a name and set of stories. Plaza-Midwood. Tryon Hills. Eastover. Dilworth. Cherry. Perhaps this practice wasn't always for the purest of reasons. Nevertheless, old ways die hard. As the city grew and new developments appeared or old areas gentrified, the new neighborhoods were also tagged with catchy, realtor-friendly labels. NoDa. South End. Piper Glen. Ballantyne.

Katy's house was in Elizabeth, an older section composed of a hodgepodge of bungalows trimmed with expansive front porches and interspersed with enormous brick mansions, and high-priced condos resulting from the demolition of the quaint but outdated. Mature pines, willow oaks, and magnolias shade the here-and-there charmingly root-buckled sidewalks.

But Elizabeth isn't strictly residential. The hood's main drag is home to the Visulite, the city's first movie theater, recently converted to a live-music venue. Its streets host a suitably eclectic collection of restaurants, bars, boutiques, and food trucks frequented by the well-to-do and the barely doing.

No description of Elizabeth appears without the word *trendy* or *hip*. It's that combo of soccer practice and carpool by day/partying and merrymaking by night—plus a location just a bump east of uptown—that accounts for the area's appeal to young professionals.

Point of information. Some Charlotteans say uptown, others prefer downtown. Positions on the issue are unshakable and have nothing to do with geography.

I live in Myers Park, another bump out from the city center. Its shaded streets boast a mix of old Georgians and Colonials elbow-to-earlobe with new Italianate, Neo-classical, and brutalist monstrosities resulting from the replacement of knockdowns on undersized lots. Meticulously manicured lawns all around.

Myers Park has a price point only slightly higher than Elizabeth, but its residents tend to lean conservative. More lawyers and bankers, fewer artists and poets.

The drive took all of ten minutes. It was dark by the time I pulled onto the circle drive at Sharon Hall.

A word about my home, which is somewhat unconventional.

Sharon Hall is a nineteenth-century manor-turned-condo-complex lying a spit from the Queens University campus. My little outbuilding is called the annex. Annex to what? No one knows. The diminutive two-story structure appears on none of the estate's original plans. The big house is there. The coach house. The herb and formal gardens. No annex. Clearly the little outbuilding was an unimportant add-on.

I once sought the help of an architectural historian at UNCC. She dug but failed to learn anything useful. Kiln? Tackle shed? Smokehouse? She had other suggestions that I've forgotten. I don't really care. Barely twelve hundred square feet, the arrangement suits my needs. Bedroom and bath up. Kitchen, dining room, parlor, and study down.

I rented the annex when my marriage to Pete imploded, and, eventually, I bought the place. Made no changes until the past year. Then, major renovation. The Ryan story. Later.

Arriving home, I let myself in and set my purse on the counter. Called out to Birdie. No cat appeared.

Not up to dealing with a feline snit, I climbed to the second floor, stripped, and took a very long, very hot shower. When I emerged, smelling of goats' milk and chai body wash, the cat was regarding me from atop the vanity, round yellow eyes filled with reproach.

"I know. I was gone longer than anticipated. It couldn't be helped." No response.

"You wouldn't believe how much stuff she had." Jesus. I was apologizing to a cat.

Birdie hopped to the floor and exited without comment.

"Whatever," I said to the haughtily elevated tail.

I was pulling on sweats when a voice called up the stairs. "I'm here."

"Coming right down."

Katy was standing in the kitchen, face tense.

"There's a box on your doorstep."

"No," I said, laughing. "Not another box."

I stepped outside and scooped up the package.

"Who's it from?" Katy's voice sounded odd.

"No idea."

"Is there a return address?"

I shook my head no.

"Were you expecting something?" Back rigid, Katy maintained her distance from me. From the thing in my hands?

Suspecting that the unexplained parcel was the source of my daughter's uneasiness, I set it on the counter, got a Heineken from the fridge, and handed the beer to her.

"Chill," I said, wary of whatever dark memory had been triggered. And wanting to calm her. "I get lots of deliveries. Half the time I've forgotten what I ordered."

Digging a box cutter from a drawer, I cut the brown paper, then sliced through the tape. After laying back the flaps, I peered inside.

My breath caught in my throat.

My hand flew to my mouth.

2

mpaled like a bug on a pin, the thing was fixed in place and gazing straight at me.

Katy's reaction was more verbal than mine.

"Holy fuck!"

Slowly, I lowered my hand.

We both stared.

You guessed it. This is where the eyeball comes in.

When detached from its owner, an eye looks like a macabre Halloween prop. This one's iris was blue, its pupil dilated and dead black. The whole glistened with a hyaline sheen.

The muscle at the eyeball's base was the color of raw beef, the vessels feathering its exterior an anemic red. The paper toweling on which it lay was white with turquoise patterning along the edges.

Colorful. That was my first reaction. Funny the things your brain offers when shocked.

Katy voiced my second thought.

"It looks fresh." The words came out strained. Odd. Katy had never been squeamish.

"Very," I agreed.

"Could be from a cow," Katy suggested after a brief pause. "Cow parts are easy to buy."

"Cows have brown eyes," I said absently, my attention focused on anatomical detail.

The small sphere was about one inch in diameter. Too small for a bovine.

"Some animals have blue eyes. Dogs, cats, horses, swans, owls—" Realizing the awful implications, Katy let the thought go.

I noted that the pupil was round, not oval.

Retrieving my recovery kit from the pantry, I withdrew a flashlight and two latex gloves. Shining the beam into the pupil, I observed the area just below the retina, at the level of the choroid.

Saw no blue-green sparkle.

A cold knot began to form in my gut. Ignoring it, I leaned closer to the box. Smelled no preservative. No hint of putrefaction. This enucleation was recent.

I swallowed.

Katy is genius at interpreting my body language. Always has been. Even as a kid she was never fooled by my evasions or diversions.

Katy sensed a shift from genial to grim.

"What?" she demanded, voice sharp and far too loud.

"I think it's human," I said quietly.

"Why?"

"Size, shape of the pupil, number and arrangement of the muscle attachments, absence of a tapetum lucidum."

"What's that?"

"You know how some creatures' eyes appear to glow when caught in your headlights at night? That's because of the tapetum lucidum, an area of pigment at the back of their eyeballs. The tapetum lucidum amplifies light entering the eye, thus improving the animal's night vision."

"And this bad boy has none?"

I wagged my head no.

"This is fugazi."

I had no clue the meaning of that, but based on her delivery, had to agree.

"Now what?" she asked.

"Now I call the ME."

"Seriously?"

"It's the law if this is a human body part." I nodded toward the box.

"It's Sunday night."

Good point.

The current Mecklenburg County medical examiner was hired when her predecessor, Dr. Margot Heavner, got the ax due to unprofessional conduct. For almost a year, Heavner, who liked to be called Dr. Morgue, had made my life pure hell. Don't get me started.

But Heavner was history. Her replacement, Dr. Samantha Nguyen, was both competent and congenial.

Still. It *was* a weekend.

I was reaching for my mobile when Katy demanded, "Call the cops."

I turned to her, brows raised.

"Who leaves a fucking eyeball on a porch? This could be a threat."

Another good point.

"Christ, Mom. Who did you tick off?"

Too many candidates.

Birdie chose that moment to make an appearance. He looped my ankles, then lifted his gaze, eyes full of hope that a treat might be forthcoming.

I ignored him.

"What if this person was murdered?" Katy jabbed a thumb toward the box.

"Isn't that a bit melodramatic?"

"Is it? Living people don't get eyeballs removed and do nothing."

"Why don't you have a shower while I sort this out," I suggested.

A full ten seconds passed. Then, "Fine." Tone clearly indicating that it wasn't.

After locking the back door with a resolute flick of her wrist, Katy disappeared into the dining room. As her footsteps receded up the stairs, I sat at the table, removed my gloves, and dialed a familiar number.

Thumbing more keys, I worked my way through the directory. Eventually, a human voice answered. One I'd heard for more years than I want to admit.

I explained the situation to Joe Hawkins, the death investigator working morgue intake. A job he'd held since before the invention of the wireless.

"An eyeball in a box."

"Yes," I said.

"On your back stoop." Hawkins speaks in clipped phrases. And at the rate a slug navigates mud.

"Yes."

Behind me I heard the soft *thup* of paws.

"Human."

"Probably."

"Just the one?"

"Does that matter?" Not fully managing to hide my annoyance.

"Nope."

There was a very long moment of dead air.

"Are you still there?" I asked, unsure if we'd been disconnected.

"What would you like?"

"Send transport?" Slowly.

"Could do. It's just me here now."

"Do you know when?"

Hearing rustling behind me, I turned.

Birdie had hopped onto the counter and overturned the box, sending the eyeball rolling free. Uninterested in the main prize, he was clawing at the toweling, scattering the Bounty with wild abandon.

"Bird! No!"

Horrified, I clicked off and rushed to lower the cat to the floor.

He sat, shot a leg, and began licking his nether regions.

I was re-gloving when Katy joined me.

"Holy shit." She summed up the situation.

Gingerly, I collected the towels and returned them to the box. I was reaching for the eyeball when Katy yelped, "Stop!"

My hand froze.

"What's that?" She was pointing at the eyeball's left side, between the parts that had faced the world and the tissue that had held the orb in its socket.

I leaned sideways for a better view.

Katy was right. There was an irregularity in the eyeball's white outer layer. A defect? A scar?

Curious, I got a lens from my kit and raised and lowered it over the anomaly. Eventually, found the correct level for focus.

Under magnification, a pattern emerged. Maybe?

"It looks like the sclera is scratched," I said.

"Scratched how?"

"It could be lettering. If so, it's unbelievably small." I handed her the lens. "Maybe your superhero eyes can read it." Unlike me, my daughter has been blessed with uncannily crisp vision. Ophthalmologists always marvel. And score her a bilateral 20/15.

"Jesus, this is teeny. Must have been done with a needle of some sort." Pause. "They're numbers. Three. Five. Period. Two. Six. One. Six. The last one's a letter. N."

I grabbed paper and pen and jotted as she deciphered. When she'd finished, we looked at the string, then at each other. Neither of us had a suggestion as to the meaning of the sequence.

Katy was repositioning the lens when my phone rang. I crossed to the table to pick up. It was Hawkins. A transport van would be by within the hour.

When I returned to the counter, Katy had rolled the eyeball. I didn't reproach her for touching it with bare fingers.

"There's more on the right side."

I picked up my pen and tablet.

"Eight. One. Period. Zero. Four. Three. Three. W."

Katy's head snapped up.

"GOFO." Slapping her forehead with her free palm.

My face must have registered confusion.

"Grasp of the fucking obvious," she translated. "Those are probably GPS coordinates."

I read what I'd written. "Thirty-five point two six one six north. Eighty-one point zero four three three west."

"That's beyond freaky," she said. "Why would someone carve coordinates into an eyeball?"

"To indicate where it came from?"

"Tell me the carving was done after the owner was dead."

"Certainly after the eyeball had been removed."

I didn't go into detail. Katy didn't request it.

"Now what?" she asked.

"Now we eat dinner and wait for the ME van."

"No black-eyed peas."

"Not a chance."

"And you call the cops."

She was right.

"Fine." Mimicking her tone from earlier. "There's spaghetti sauce in the freezer, pasta in the pantry."

I was punching another auto-dial number when the device rang in my hand. My eyes went to caller ID. Mixed feelings.

Bracing myself, I clicked on.

"I see you're having a wild Saturday night," I said, hearing a frenzied sports announcer in the background.

"And I'm catching you between sets at the Roxbury?"

Erskine "Skinny" Slidell, for decades a detective with the Charlotte-Mecklenburg Police Department, had recently retired and gone into a cross-border PI partnership with Ryan. The strategy was that Slidell, being barely fluent in English, would work cases in the States while Ryan, fully bilingual, would handle those in which French would facilitate communication. So far, the concept was working. Business, though not exactly booming, was steady enough.

But, unlike Ryan, Slidell couldn't totally cut the cord. A cop since emerging from the womb, and having zero outside life of which I was aware, Skinny continued to volunteer with the CMPD cold case unit. Also, unlike Ryan, the guy had the personality of a canker sore.

"What's on your mind?" I asked, ignoring Slidell's comeback to my opening dig. And astounded that he'd heard of the Roxbury, a hip nineties dance club.

"I got something I want to roll by you."

"OK." Hiding my surprise.

Katy had finished pressing buttons on the microwave and was watching me. I mouthed the name Slidell, then shrugged.

"I got a guy I'm tailing," he began.

"Why?"

"Let's call it indiscretion. I hear there's some gizmo I could put on his phone without me physically having the phone. You know anything about that?"

"You need a techie. I can send you some names."

"That'd be good."

Katy pointed at the box. I shook my head. She nodded hers.

"I have something I'd like to roll by *you*," I said, knowing I'd regret it.

Slidell made a sound in his throat. Which I chose to interpret as agreement.

I explained the eyeball, the minuscule writing.

There was a silence so loud it screamed. Then, "How do you get yourself into this shit, Brennan?"

I said nothing.

"So, it's like one of these freaks who carves Paris on a grain of rice?"

I hadn't thought of that. "Could be."

"You sure it's human?"

"I think so."

I waited out more empty air.

Then Slidell asked the same question that Katy had. I'd had time to consider who I might have angered.

"I have a neighbor who's annoyed with me."

"What'd you do? Pee in her pansies?"

"The man dislikes my turtle." Icy.

"I thought you had a cat."

"It's garden art. Cement. He claims it scares his kid and wants me to remove it."

"Just take the damn gewgaw inside."

"I don't want to."

"You think this shitbag could be eyeball-level pissed?"

"I doubt it."

I could picture Slidell wagging his head. Then, "I'll call over, see if someone can check this out. I'm guessing they'll bump it to the newbie, a maybe human eyeball not being high priority."

"Who's the newbie?"

"Henry. A real piece of work."

Three beeps, then I was listening to dead air.

"Skinny's up to form," Katy said.

"You heard that?"

"You were holding the phone away from your ear. Do you really think your neighbor is capable of this?"

"Not really."

"You got a laptop?" Katy asked.

"Does a duck have a bill?" I replied.

"Only when it dines out."

"Bada-bing. We're on the same page, right? We run the GPS, see what pops."

As Katy set water to boil, I booted my Mac Air and entered the eyeball coordinates into Google Earth. The globe had just stopped whirling and zooming in when she crossed to peer over my shoulder.

We both stared at the screen.

"What the hell?" Katy voiced our mutual astonishment.

3

"That was fast." The kid looked about ten minutes out of high school. His hair was blond and badly cut, his cheeks mottled with alarmingly inflamed zits. The Belmont Abbey College campus cop uniform hung like an older brother's hand-me-down on his thin frame. A big one.

"I'm sorry?" I phrased it as a question.

"Y'all are here about the privy, yeah?" Even filtered through the blue cone covering his nose and mouth, the kid's voice was unexpectedly resonant.

Random thought. At first, I found masking outside the autopsy room quite bizarre. Now I slap on my N95 and hardly notice that others are similarly garbed.

Slidell drew air to speak. The paper rectangle riding his lips sucked into a deep concavity.

Taking pity on the kid, I jumped in. "The thing in the privy?" I said, again raising my voice to indicate a question.

"You're cops, right?" Looking from Slidell to me and back. "I mean. We just got the call."

"What call?"

"To check out an old privy behind MV."

"Who called?"

"Someone at MV, I guess."

"What's MV?"

"MiraVia."

"Which is?"

"Housing for girls that get knocked up."

"Excuse me?" Beyond chilly.

"You know. They get pregnant without waiting for that ring on the finger."

"They're students?"

"Yeah. They're a quiet bunch, don't bother us much. Since I've been here, we've had only one other call from out there. Residents said they'd had a break-in. Appeared they had, so I rolled it over to you guys."

"Did you ask the name of today's caller?"

"No."

"Don't you keep a log?"

"Yes. But I got distracted because something was going on." The kid's brows dipped in thought. Which seemed to be a new experience for him. "Right. A moron ran his car into the gate out front. Did you see the whack in the brick?"

"What's the story on this privy?" Slidell was out of patience.

"Beats the shit out of me." Goofy grin. "Get it?"

"Hilarious. You know what ain't hilarious? You wasting my time."

The kid's hand rose to pick at his cheek. A decidedly bad idea.

"Take us to this privy," Slidell demanded.

"I'll have to—"

"Now!"

The kid swallowed, sending his Adam's apple hopping. "Do you have your own vehicle?"

"No, genius. We was beamed out here by—"

"What's your name," I asked, smiling kindly.

"George," he offered, sullen now because of Slidell's bluster. Or due to Skinny's failure to treat him as one of his brethren in blue.

"You lead, George," I said. "We'll follow."

George pulled on a battered leather jacket, then donned a hat that made me think of Barney Fife. I half expected him to say, "Let's nip this in the bud."

Outside, George slid behind the wheel of a golf cart displaying the school's emblem on its front hood. We got back into Slidell's 4Runner.

Throughout the early-morning drive west on I-85 and across Belmont-Mt. Holly Road, Skinny had remained uncharacteristically quiet. Thankful, though curious, I'd taken his cue and focused on answering and, mostly, deleting emails on my phone. I exchanged a series of texts with Katy on the joys of unpacking.

The previous night, when I'd shared with Slidell my plan to check out the GPS coordinates carved into the eye, he'd launched his usual salvo of protests. Typical Skinny performance. Then, seeing I wasn't to be dissuaded, he'd insisted on accompanying me.

I wasn't sure of Slidell's motivation. Slow day in the gumshoe business? Bad feeling about the eye? Maybe Skinny's goddam paternalism was simply surfacing again.

Full disclosure. I was glad Slidell was with me. I wasn't sure where the coordinates would lead. Or what we'd find there. I was on the same page with Skinny. A human eyeball did not bode well. *Maybe* human eyeball.

The sky was gloomy and overcast, the air late-January cold. I'd brought gloves and worn boots and a parka. Still, I hoped we wouldn't be outside long.

I took in the view as we looped a small perimeter road. I knew little about Belmont Abbey College, the bulk of which I'd learned via the internet the previous night. Including the following:

The seven-hundred-acre campus contains a Benedictine monastery, home to about twenty-five men committed to prayer, work, and virtue. It also contains a Catholic liberal arts college, home to about seventeen hundred students presumably committed to similar pursuits. Perhaps not in the same order.

The complex was impressive. The monastery dating to 1876. The basilica. The student dorms and administrative and academic buildings. Most of the architecture was true to the original Gothic Revival vision.

The road, undoubtedly named for some kindly dead abbot, passed between tennis courts and a soccer field that would have made any Ivy League school proud. Just beyond the athletic facilities, George turned right. So did Slidell.

Straight ahead stretched a long one-story redbrick building whose front facing rose into four triangular peaks. George circled to a lot at the rear and parked. Slidell pulled the 4Runner up beside the cart.

We all alighted. George paused to get his bearings. A moment of scanning, then he flapped a skeletal arm toward a heavily wooded area behind the building, which I assumed was MiraVia.

George spoke into a handheld radio that looked like something from the pilot for *Starsky and Hutch*. Received a response full of static. Then, without a word, he set off.

I shouldered my backpack and followed. Behind me, I could hear Slidell's muttering. Thanked the gods I wasn't close enough to catch the commentary.

George crossed to an indistinct thinning in the vegetation at one edge of the asphalt. The area was so overgrown I doubted anyone would spot the trailhead without prior knowledge.

I followed George onto the path, pushing aside low branches and periodically adjusting the straps on my pack. Behind me I heard weighty footsteps, the snapping of twigs, and the rustling of dead leaves.

The privy was a brief walk from the parking lot, deep enough into the trees that, even in winter, the thick tangle of limbs overhead obscured most daylight. Being in perpetual shadow, the terrain was muddy and devoid of ground cover.

I took a deep breath. The air smelled of mold and rot and things organic. Despite the cold, I was glad it was winter. Most insects were dead or hunkered down, waiting for spring.

George held back at a discreet distance, arms crossed, face ruddy from his windy ride. Which was actually an improvement. The heightened pigment camouflaged the war raging on his cheeks.

Slidell joined me and stood with feet spread, right arm cocked inside his unbuttoned overcoat. Which was brown with torn lining hanging below the hem in back. I wouldn't say the man was panting, but he was breathing hard.

The privy fit the image my mind had conjured. Built of wood now weathered by decades of rain and wind, the tiny hut looked large enough to accommodate a single user. The roof was flat and sloped downward, front to back. Clearly past its prime and probably long abandoned, the shanty leaned at an angle that didn't inspire confidence.

The tilt of Slidell's shoulders told me he'd gone into cop mode. After assessing the privy, he did a three-sixty scan, eyes alert, weapon hand still at the ready.

The woods were silent save for the scraping of limbs above us in the occasional breeze. Now and then, a bird threw out an opinion, perhaps commenting on the drama unfolding on the ground below.

I checked the GPS app on my phone. It told me we were dead on with the coordinates. I nodded to Skinny.

Gesturing for George and me to hold back, Slidell stepped to the privy and peered closely at the gap surrounding the door, at the handle and hinges. I knew his thinking. I'd been lured to this spot. Was there a chance the shed was booby-trapped?

Seeing no wires or other indicators of an explosive device, Slidell picked up a rock, stepped back, and hurled it at the door. Nothing.

Turning to me, he said, "Let's do this."

I snapped pics of the privy and its surroundings. Circled it. Snapped more. Like Slidell, I stayed alert for anything suspicious.

I was starting to have qualms. Hoped I hadn't dragged Skinny out on a "fool's errand," as he'd labeled it.

My thoughts were definitely conflicted, though. Would I really prefer that we find another gruesome token? A note saying *Gotcha!* Nothing at all?

Tamping down my misgivings, I dug into my pack, then, gloved and masked, thumbed on my flashlight. Stepping forward, I gingerly pulled the rotting handle on the privy door.

A shriek rent the air.

My heart leapt into my throat.

Behind me I heard the *slup-slup* of Slidell's shoes moving fast. Sensed him at my back.

"Just a rusty hinge," I said, voice far calmer than I felt.

"Let's see what's in this goddam shitter so we can get outta here."

Ignoring the shrill squeaking, I levered the door as far back as it would go. Slidell placed a beefy hand on the wood to hold it open.

The shed's interior was lighted only by fuzzy rays oozing through cracks between the crudely nailed boards. I shined my light around. It crawled over a lidless, one-hole wooden bench spanning the back, a broken toilet seat leaning against its base, and an angled peg, absent TP, jutting from the wall.

Spiderwebs clogged each of the shed's corners and trailed in billows across its sloping ceiling. Brittle leaves and yellowed newspapers lay mounded at the point where the walls met the floor. As outhouses go, this one scored zero for ambience.

I banged the handle of my flashlight against the shed's exterior. Did it again. No small furry creature skittled out in alarm.

Deep breath, then I stepped up into the privy. Despite the cold, my nose detected a pungent odor. Familiar. Strong.

"*No,*" a voice in my primitive brain protested.

"*Yes,*" my olfactory lobe countered.

With growing dread, I inched forward and shined my beam into the heart of the beast.

My stomach went into a tuck.

Over the years, the privy must have served as a depository for trash deemed unsuitable for normal disposal. The mound in the pit topped out at a full six feet below the level of the hole. Protruding from it I could see a toaster, a segment of garden hose, a very badly treated umbrella. The rest of the fill I didn't want to consider.

The item that I assumed triggered the gut-tuck lay atop the heap, brilliant white in the beam's small oval dancing along its surface. The object was spherical, its outer surface glossy and crinkly and bearing a logo.

I was staring at the thing when I felt the shed teeter and heard the thud of Slidell's feet on the floor. The tobacco and sweat smells emanating from his overcoat mingled with those already tainting the air.

I moved sideways. Slidell stepped forward and peered down through the hole.

"Sonofafreakingbitch!"

"I thought you'd say shit."

"What? The whole world does standup now?"

"Can you reach it?"

"Oh, now that *is* funny."

Slidell backed out without turning around. I heard him shout a command, then he reappeared at the open door.

"The boy genius is going to find something to reach down in there."

The boy genius took almost forty minutes. During his absence, I shot pics and recorded notes. Slidell butt-leaned a giant pine, alternating between checking his phone and thumbnailing some intruder troubling his molars.

George returned carrying a long wooden pole capped with a small brass hook.

Flashback. A nun at St. Margaret's Elementary reaching to lower the upper half of a very large, very old window.

Yep. Weird where your brain takes you at times.

But George hadn't fully thought his plan through. There was no way the pole would fit into the shed. Believe me, we tried.

Cursing, and flushed so deeply I feared a cardiac episode, Slidell strode to the 4Runner, stripped off the malodorous coat, and opened the back. After a great deal of furious gophering around, he rejoined us with a small handheld saw.

"Cut the goddam handle!" Thrusting the tool at the boy genius.

Clearly, George wasn't a do-it-yourself guy. The process took a full seven minutes.

No one made a move.

"Fine. I'll try to snag the thing," I said to George, not wanting Slidell's sweaty bulk with me in the small space. "You provide lighting."

Looking like I'd told him he was needed at a leper colony, George pulled his Maglite from his belt and stepped into the privy. I followed with the truncated pole.

While George had been away, I'd viewed my new images by spreading each with a thumb and forefinger. When enlarged, they'd shown knotted handles at the top of what I guessed was a plastic pharmacy or grocery bag. My plan was to hook one or both of the loops.

Deep breath. Ill advised, given the circumstances.

I stepped to the bench and inserted the pole into the opening. Compared to his sawing, George's flashlight skills were top-notch. I quickly found the handles and maneuvered the hook, testing and re-testing until I felt resistance.

Bit by bit, I altered the angle of the pole. The bag was heavier than I'd expected.

Or was it?

A human head weighs roughly ten pounds.

Inch by inch, I levered the bag toward the opening. I felt like an angler reeling in a fish.

A clumsy angler. My fingers were stiff from the cold and, halfway up, let the pole roll in their grasp. The bag swayed wildly.

"Crap!"

George startled and the beam veered.

I adjusted my grip. The bag remained firmly snagged on the handles.

"Sorry," I said.

The light settled.

When the bag was finally level with the hole, George set down his flashlight and dragged my catch two-handed onto the bench.

Way to go, boy genius.

"Shit, that stinks."

"It does," I agreed.

"That's a Target bag," George observed while wiping his hands on his pants. "I can see the red bull's-eye."

Again, I agreed. Then, "To get decent photos I need better light."

"Right." This time the boy genius didn't reach out.

I lifted our booty between my palms as George had done.

Jesus, it stank.

Careful not to stumble, I carried the bag outside and set it on the ground.

Four eyes watched as I changed gloves, filled out a case identifier, then shot more pics. When I'd finished, Slidell produced a Swiss Army Knife, thumbed open the blade, and handed it to me.

I kneeled beside the bag.

Heart drumming, I slit the plastic.

4

The stench was enough to flatten a greenhorn.

And did. Or maybe it was the sight.

George landed with a sound like a dumbbell hitting a mat. His Maglite rolled across the mud with a soft *tic-tic-tic*. Settled between the roots of an oak, beam still shining gamely.

"Christ, the fucknuckle's out cold."

Ignoring Slidell's callous remark, I hurried to George and checked his carotid and breathing. Both were good.

"Lift his right leg," I ordered, rolling George to his back.

"No way." Slidell looked like I'd asked him to lick the floor of a holding cell.

"Just do it!"

He did. Grudgingly.

Together we raised George's legs above the level of his heart. After eight seconds the kid opened his eyes. Slidell dropped the skinny limb as though he'd been scalded.

Rising on knees popping in protest, Slidell stepped back. Mercifully, he said nothing.

"Are you OK?" I asked.

"I think a spider bit me," George said, reaching for his hat.

"That's probably it," I replied, knowing there'd been no spider. "Why don't you relax for a while? Detective Slidell and I will deal with this."

Nodding, George got to his feet and withdrew to what he considered an odor-free distance.

Slidell and I returned to the bag and its grisly contents.

With the handles untied and the plastic laid back, the smell of putrefaction was overwhelming.

I looked at Skinny.

He pulled out his phone and hit a preprogrammed key.

"Homicide," he barked.

By three-thirty I was in an autopsy room. The remains, designated MCME 213-22, lay on a stainless-steel table, snugged between two rubber bolsters. The plastic bag sat on a counter labeled and packaged for transport. X-rays glowed on a computer screen. The back porch eyeball waited in a nearby cooler. Its label read MCME 210-22.

Slidell and I had killed the hour waiting for a crime scene unit by searching the immediate area. Found nothing else of interest. When the team arrived, we left. Nguyen had authorized me to bring the remains to the MCME, so we'd tucked the bag into the back of the 4Runner and headed to Charlotte.

Throughout his tenure with the CMPD, Slidell's vehicles had always looked and smelled like rolling dumpsters. Since he was driving his own SUV, Skinny now insisted on lowering every window. The ride was chilly. On many levels.

I'd just finished viewing the X-rays when I got a call from reception. A detective named Henry was asking to see me. I directed Mrs. Flowers to issue a pass and send him to my office.

Slidell had been right about prioritization. The case was being assigned to the newbie of whom he'd spoken so highly.

I threw blue plastic sheeting over the remains, removed my protective gear, and washed up. Then I headed out through the bio-vestibule and crossed the lobby to the other side of the building.

Detective Henry was not what I'd expected. She was at least six feet tall, blond and blue-eyed, and totally ripped.

Yeah. She.

Henry was sitting in the chair facing my desk. Popped to her feet when I came through the door.

"Temperance Brennan." I smiled and extended a hand.

"Donna Henry." Her grip was in the range of an industrial vise.

I circled my desk and sat.

First impression. Detective Henry spent a lot of time in the gym. And a lot of money on clothes. She wore ankle boots, black skinny jeans, and an Alexander McQueen blazer over a cream silk blouse. A Burberry scarf and puffer lay across her lap.

Second impression. Detective Henry had logged far too much time in the sun. Or needed a higher SPF blocker. Her face was tan. That looked good. The skin was wrinkled beyond what it should have been at her age. That didn't look good. I guessed she was hovering on either side of thirty.

Henry smiled but remained seated and waited for me to speak.

"I understand you've just joined Homicide/ADW." I referred to the CMPD unit that investigates murders and assaults with a deadly weapon.

Henry nodded.

"Why did you want to work violent crimes?" I asked to be friendly.

"Doesn't everyone?"

No.

Seconds passed. Henry's smile held.

"What was your previous unit?"

"Domestic violence."

"And before that?" Jesus. This was starting to sound like a job interview.

"I've been in Charlotte about three years now. Before that, I lived in LA. That's where I grew up. But I came to hate the whole SoCal vibe. Except for the ocean, of course. That was awesome."

"You were a detective with the LAPD?"

"Yup."

"Why did you leave?"

"Who can live in LA on a cop's salary? Besides, I'd been waiting forever for an assignment to the Robbery Homicide Division. So was everyone else on the job. Anyway, I had a marriage go south, and I have a cousin living in Myrtle Beach. I heard through her that Charlotte was recruiting, applied, and here I am."

First LA, then three years here. Yet Slidell still considered her a newbie.

"Do you like living in Charlotte?"

"I do. Instead of a studio apartment I have a whole house to myself. A whole goddam block." She spread her arms.

"What have you got?" I nodded at a brown envelope lying atop the Burberry.

On the frosty drive from Belmont Abbey, at Slidell's insistence, I'd reluctantly shared my first take on our privy find. Female. White. Adult. Postmortem interval (the PMI) probably less than two years. Given the plastic bag and the protected environment in the perpetually shaded privy, a precise PMI estimate was impossible.

You can imagine Skinny's delight at those vague descriptors. Nevertheless, he'd passed them on to Henry.

"I ran a search using your time of death range and bio-profile. Found some possibles."

Henry pulled a printout from the envelope and scanned three lines of data.

"Eve Lott, age thirty-eight. Reported missing February 23, 2020. Lucille McFarland, age forty-three. Reported missing June 16, 2021. Ariadne Bruce, age forty-four. Reported missing December 18, 2021."

Henry looked up expectantly. "Do you want the sitch on each?"

"Sitch?"

"Situation. Backstory."

"Not now." OK, newbie. Let's see how you do. "Shall we view the remains, Detective?"

Not waiting for a response, I rose to retrace my path to the "clean" side of the facility. Looking somewhat less than keen, Henry followed.

In the autopsy room, I handed out gloves, a surgical mask, and an apron and we both suited up. Then I stepped to the table and threw back the sheeting.

Peering up from between the bolsters was a human face. Or what remained of a human face. Decomposition had converted the features into a death mask bearing little resemblance to the person it had presented to the world in life.

Beside me, I sensed Henry tense. But she didn't draw back. Or pull a George and pass out. Believe me, I've seen well-seasoned cops hit the tile.

The facial tissue was a blanched and soggy wrapper fast losing its grip on the underlying bone. The nose was compressed, the nostrils flattened against what little flesh remained on the cheeks. The lips were curled back in a rictus grin, exposing teeth yellowed by age or by contact with liquified brain and muscle. A sparse tangle of hair clung to the largely bare skull, its color leached to nothing by the by-products of decay.

But it was the eyes that held Henry's attention. As they had Slidell's and mine.

The right one was shriveled and constricted, the iris discolored to a milky violet. What remained of the pupil was hidden behind a half-closed lid. A paring knife jutting from its center.

The left eyeball was gone.

"Some freak cut out her eye." Barely audible. Muffled due to Henry's unfamiliarity with the mask?

I turned. Recognized the look. Could this be the first time the newbie had seen violent death up close?

Wordlessly, I went to the cooler. Returned with the back-porch eyeball, now sealed in a Tupperware container labeled MCME 210-22.

"This was delivered to my home," I said.

"Delivered?"

"In a box."

"What happened to the box?"

"It went to the crime lab," I said matter-of-factly. "As will the plastic bag that contained the severed head. And the knife."

"You suppose this eye came from that head?" She glanced back and forth between the two.

"If not, we've got one hell of a coincidence. But of course, I'll order DNA testing on both."

"Why's the head so grody while this eyeball looks perfect."

"Decomp—"

"I get the ashes-to-ashes bit. But why is the eye so well preserved?"

"I intend to figure that out."

"And why would someone leave a body part on your back porch?"

"That, Detective, is a question for a cop. Which brings us to your next task."

"Dental records."

"Yes."

"Which MP?" Missing person.

"All three."

"On it, boss," she said, and snapped a somewhat less than crisp salute.

I worked until seven.

Once I'd shot photos and videos, I gently removed and bagged the knife. While packaging the plastic sack I considered the Sharpie writing on its surface: *"Here's Johnny!"* A bad pun about the privy? A reference to late-night TV? To the skull? To something unrelated to the bag's contents?

Finally, I prepared the head for maceration. Since there was nothing more I could tease from the putrefied flesh, I'd have Hawkins remove it to allow me a better look at the bone.

Before leaving the MCME, I phoned Katy to see if she wanted to catch a quick dinner. She was entangled in sorting kitchenware. Said if she quit, she'd dump everything in drawers and never arrange things properly. I understood.

On the way to the annex, I stopped at the Harris Teeter for a few basics. Exited with a full cart and $246 additional on my credit card.

I was unloading my trunk when my least favorite neighbor came flying out of the main house. With long, angry strides he arrowed straight toward me.

I considered darting into and not re-emerging from the annex.

"Ms. Brennan." Pointing one long finger in my direction. "Do not avoid me."

Too late.

Crap.

Alasdair Campbell is a fully owned subsidiary of Snarky, Inc. The man is loud, egotistical, and combative. Campbell has lived at Sharon Hall for about three years, and throughout that time has committed his life force to tormenting me. His current complaint involves a garden sculpture allegedly upsetting his son.

Shifting the grocery bag to my left hand, I turned and smiled with a warmth I didn't feel.

Campbell bore down, face red as the squares in the scarf wrapping his throat. Disloyal, I thought, knowing the Campbell tartan was green.

"Finlay had another episode today," he declared, breathing hard. His features were a combo of fury and exertion.

"I'm sorry to hear that. I hope he's still seeing Dr. Chee." I'd recommended the child psychologist. Was surprised when Campbell had followed through on my suggestion.

"It's that cursed turtle. Every time we pass it Finlay has an attack."

"Dr. Chee thinks Finlay's distress is caused by my garden sculpture?" She doesn't. Chee and I are old friends and had spoken. Strictly in hypotheticals, of course.

"That's not the point," Campbell snapped.

"That is precisely the point."

"You must remove that obscenity."

"If you bring me a note from Dr. Chee stating that the turtle is causing Finlay emotional discomfort, I will be happy to do so."

Campbell's eyes narrowed in a menacing way. I braced for further demands.

"I'll gie ye a skelpit lug!" he spit, then whipped around and stomped off.

WTF?

Exhausted by my long day in the field and at the autopsy table, I didn't have the energy to jot down the phrase.

After baking and eating my frozen lasagna, I tried phoning Ryan. Got his voice mail. Left a message.

I showered. Then Birdie and I climbed into bed and watched CNN for a while. He likes Don Lemon. I prefer Anderson Cooper.

I turned off the lamp and TV and lay in the dark, images swirling in my head. A small brown box. A severed head. A weather-beaten privy. A very fresh eye.

Again, the cells in my id nudged those in my forebrain. *Pssst!*

What?

Try as I might, I experienced no cerebral breakthrough.

The house seemed very empty without Katy. Very quiet. Except for the running toilet in my bathroom. I thought about waterfalls. Floods. Plumbers.

I considered getting up to jiggle the handle.

The cat fell asleep long before I did.

5

January turned into February.

I heard nothing from Ryan. Zilch from Katy. Zip from Henry or Slidell.

Wednesday dawned without drama. It wasn't warm or cold. Wet or dry. Cloudy or clear. It was a morning of non-weather.

A groundhog in Pennsylvania saw his shadow. I've never been clear on whether that's good news or bad. Six more weeks of winter seems long to me.

The phone rang as I was preparing to leave the annex. I was still baffled by the lack of decomp in the eyeball. Nguyen had green-lighted me to dissect, so I wanted to get slicing. And I needed to collect samples from it for DNA testing.

"Dr. Brennan." Squad room sounds crowded in behind the greeting.

"Detective Henry."

"I have the files."

"X-rays?"

"Yes."

"Good work. I've given the dentist a heads-up. I'll text him to say

37

that we're heading to him now." I believe in flexibility. The eyeball could wait. "Meet you at his office in twenty."

I gave Henry a name and address, then disconnected.

Dr. Ari Leshner has been drilling and filling since Hammering Hank started belting them out of the park. The old guy isn't ABFO certified, but he can determine a match or an exclusion as accurately as any boarded forensic odontologist. Over the years, Leshner and I have examined scores of periapical, panoramic, and cephalometric images.

Leshner's office is in Myers Park in a single-story *L*-shaped building on Queens Road. One of many so-named streets meandering through Charlotte. My advice to newcomers and out of towners: if you blunder onto any road named Queens, get off.

A black Ford Explorer was parked on the small patch of asphalt enclosed by head-high hedges behind the building. Henry was in it, got out when I arrived. Today the skinny jeans were brown, the blazer a soft-as-Bambi tan suede.

A bell jangled us into the waiting area, a small space rimmed with lattice-back chairs. Straight ahead, a fish tank burbled and glowed a calming welcome. Of course, it did. It was a dental office.

The receptionist greeted me with a smile. Lucy? Lacey? "He's expecting you."

Lucy/Lacey buzzed us through to a hall lined with treatment rooms on the left, offices and supply closets on the right. Leshner was at a desk in the last in the row. On hearing us, he scooched from his chair and crossed to greet us.

"Tempe. So nice to see you," he said, raising a hand in my direction.

"I wish it wasn't always under such bleak circumstances," I replied, gripping his stubby fingers in mine.

"Indeed." Leshner's eyes shifted to my companion. Who was trying hard to mask her surprise.

"This is Detective Henry," I said. "She's recently transferred into violent crimes." Three years. Jesus, I was thinking like Slidell.

"My pleasure," Leshner said, again reaching up.

Henry nodded, shook his hand.

Ari Leshner's limbs are short, his torso and head of average size. When wearing his beloved elevator shoes, the man stands approximately four feet one. Achondroplastic dwarfism, he once explained. No biggie. He'd chuckled at his own joke.

Leshner crossed to a free-standing light box, climbed onto a high stool, and flicked a switch. The top surface lit up.

I handed him an envelope. He shook a set of small black squares onto the viewing screen and arranged them in proper anatomical order.

Leshner's nose swoops downward then curves up again, and white curls frame his broad forehead and cheeks, giving him the air of a mischievous gnome. He nurtures the look and often acts the part.

Face solemn, Leshner turned to Henry. "You know the proper term for these?"

Henry shook her head.

"Dental pics." Then the chuckle.

Unsure of the proper response, Henry produced a tiny brown envelope from the first of three files she carried. "Eve Lott," she said.

Leshner arranged Lott's periapicals below those Hawkins had taken of the privy skull dentition. Compared the two sets, square by square.

"Nope," he said, returning Lott's X-rays. "Next?"

Henry dug out another batch. "Ariadne Bruce."

Leshner repeated his actions. A beat, then, "Nope. Next?"

Henry handed him the third set of radiographs. "Lucille McFarland."

Leshner leaned forward a full minute, finally sat back. "Sorry. Strike three."

"Thanks for looking," I said. "While you're at it, care to comment on age for the unknown?"

Leshner was quiet longer this time.

"I'd say forty, with a plus minus range of five years."

"Anything else jump out at you?" I asked.

"She had a lot of work done."

"Distinguishing features?"

"Looks high quality. American. Standard materials. Otherwise, not really."

Leshner pushed from his elevated seat and landed with both knees bent. Straightened, bringing his face to boob-level on me. "Need a full workup?"

"Yes, please."

Thirty minutes later I had detailed charting and a technical description of the privy skull dentition. A missing upper-right first premolar. A rotated canine. Three restorations. One root canal.

As we headed for the door, Leshner asked, "You know why they call me the king of dentists?"

I bit. "Why?"

"I specialize in crowns."

Outside in the parking lot, Henry and I discussed our next move.

Using the newly acquired dental data, the descriptors white and female, and an age range of thirty-five to forty-five years, she would search local, state, and national databases listing missing persons.

I suggested she start with NamUs. Funded and administered by the National Institute of Justice, the National Missing and Unidentified Persons System serves as a clearinghouse for missing, unidentified, and unclaimed person cases throughout the United States.

I also suggested she give the key word *decapitation* a whirl.

While she did that, I'd go to the MCME and proceed with my slicing and sampling. Assuming Hawkins had completed the maceration, I'd take a close look at the defleshed skull.

Traffic was clogged in uptown. Big surprise. While alternating between stopped and lurching forward a yard at a time, I mentally rehashed the previous night's slide show and the morning's conversations.

A head in a plastic bag.

An eyeball in a box.

A woman who took care of her teeth.

I was pulling through the MCME gate when my id finally confided in my forebrain.

A head lacking parts.

A torso lacking parts.

What year was that? Where had those remains turned up? Was this case connected?

I hurried across the parking lot, already hitting a speed dial key on my phone. Was surprised at the quick pickup.

"Yo." Slidell's usual. Background noises suggested he was driving.

"I hope your day is going well." To bait Skinny into some form of greeting. A hobby of mine. As expected, the ploy didn't work.

"I'm kinda busy here. You got something to say?"

I told him about our visit to Leshner. When I'd finished, "So it's back to square one."

"Henry's running the profile from here to Sheboygan."

"Why Sheboygan?"

"It's a manner of speech. I could have said Peoria."

Slidell did that thing he does in his throat.

"Listen." I changed tacks. "I've been thinking."

"God help us."

I ignored that. "Do you remember the severed ear that came in a few years back?"

I climbed the steps as Slidell flipped through his mental file cabinet.

"We tracked it to a corner boy who decided to go freelance," he said at last. "The kid's entrepreneurial ambitions dropped him low on certain popularity charts."

"The body turned up later missing some organs." I entered the building and waved to Mrs. Flowers.

"Bingo. Organs. This head thing's a whole different puppy. First off, it was chucked into a privy behind a convent for preggies."

"It's not a convent." I entered my office and hung my purse on the hall tree.

"Whatever. I'm chasing that down."

"You're on your way to MiraVia?"

"As we speak. Gotta focus on my driving."

Dead air.

Asshole, I didn't say.

I sat down at my desk, booted my computer, and ran a search. Quickly found the case I'd mentioned to Slidell. MCME 356-19. MCME 363-19.

The vic was nineteen-year-old Miguel Sanchez, street name Scrappy. The day before Christmas 2019, Scrappy's ear was found nailed to a tree outside his Beacon Hill apartment in South Charlotte. Three days later, the rest of Scrappy turned up in a Wendy's dumpster, sans liver, kidneys, and heart.

No one knew anything. Though the murder was thought to be gang related, no arrest was ever made. The dossier remained open.

Slidell was right. The two killings had little in common.

Still, the id guys persisted.

I returned to the same autopsy room I'd utilized on Monday.

The skull now sat on a rubber ring, bone gleaming white in the light from the overheads. Two squares of tissue floated in a labeled vial beside it.

Damn, Hawkins was good at his job.

I clamped a case form onto a clipboard and, carefully rotating the skull, began filling in data.

I noted small brow ridges, slender cheekbones, a delicate mandible, and gracile muscle attachments.

Sex: *Female*.

I observed a skull shape that was neither short and round nor long and narrow, minimal projection of the lower face, sharply angled nasal bones and a narrow nasal opening with lipping and a tiny spine at its lower border.

I took cranial measurements and ran the metrics through Fordisc 3.1. The program agreed with my assessment.

Ancestry: Caucasoid/White.

Simplistic view of race. I get it. But I don't go into the complexities of ancestral origins, gene flow, and population boundaries with cops. Most just want to know how a vic or perp would be viewed by other people.

I assessed the state of closure of the sutures, the squiggly lines at which the individual cranial bones meet. The amount of arthritis in the mandibular joint. The condition of the teeth. Was in agreement with Leshner's estimate.

Age: Thirty-five to forty-five years.

I double-checked everything on the X-rays. Saw no surprises. Was pleased that Henry was working with good parameters.

I scanned for anomalies, scars, lesions, deformities, and evidence of disease and unhealed trauma. Saw nothing.

My stomach growled loud enough to be heard in Taiwan.

I glanced at the wall clock.

One-forty.

I set aside the clipboard, cleaned up, and returned to my office. Pulling a lunch bag from my purse, I laid a soggy tuna sandwich and dispirited clump of grapes on my blotter.

I craved a Diet Coke but resisted. I was trying to cut back on caffeine. On whatever it was that made the stuff capable of dissolving an iron nail in four days, a tooth in twenty-four to forty-eight hours. Or were those urban myths?

Note to self: Fact-check tales of Coke's corrosiveness at Snopes .com.

While eating the sandwich, I looked up plumbers on the internet. Friendly Dale's Plumbing Service got five stars. I dialed.

Friendly Dale said he could help me the following week. I wondered if, in the meantime, he'd help with my water bill. Didn't ask.

The grapes were at least half a decade past their prime. And warm from the hours spent cuddling the sandwich. But I was still hungry.

I popped the greenest of the lot into my mouth. It was mushy and somewhat flavorless. I tried another, idly gazing at the survivors remaining in the bunch.

Snap!

An idea sent me upright in my chair. Plucking another grape, I sliced through the skin with my thumbnail and observed the pulp.

Bunching and tossing the bag, wrappers, and uneaten fruit, I shot to my feet. Totally pumped, I hurried across the building and into the bio-vestibule, snagging the eyeball from its cooler on my way.

In the autopsy room, once again properly garbed, I clamped a movable magnifying lens to one side of the autopsy table, then positioned a cutting board below it. After illuminating the fluorescent ring, I transferred the eyeball from its Tupperware container to the board.

Selecting a scalpel from a surgical kit, I made my first delicate cut.

My second.

Almost shouted hallelujah!

I understood why the eyeball was so much better preserved than the skull.

6

Nguyen killed the saw in her hand. The blade stopped oscillating and the whining cut off. The small room hummed with sudden silence.

Nguyen's eyes studied me from over her mask, the irises a brown so deep they almost blended with the pupils. Her brows, drawn with surgical precision, were canted in concern. Or confusion.

"Please repeat that?" she said.

The guy on the table said nothing. His face was peeled down to his chin, the top of his skull gaping wide.

"The eyeball was frozen," I said. "The tissue is milky and—"

"This makes sense." Soft accent. Mostly Boston, with a hint of something more exotic.

"I was eating defrosted grape—"

"One mustn't freeze grapes."

"I know. Do you want details?"

"Later, please. Right now, I must finish with this gentleman."

"What happened to him?"

"He fell from a zip line."

"Cause of death?"

"Acute numerical assumption."

I just looked at her.

"His number was up. His heart had stopped."

I returned to my own tile, glass, and stainless-steel chamber. Cut slivers from the eyeball, sealed them in a vial, and labeled the cap. Placed the vial in the cooler beside tissue taken from the privy head before maceration.

The knife and plastic bag had already followed the box and paper toweling to the crime lab. After jotting a note to Hawkins concerning DNA processing of both sets of samples, I returned to my office.

First, I called Henry. Got voice mail.

My iPhone showed the time as five-fifteen.

What the hell?

I hit a speed dial button.

"You got nothing better to do than harass my ass?" Again, it sounded like Slidell was on the road.

I laid out my theory concerning preservation of the eye.

"You're saying some mope mined an eyeball and popped it into his Frigidaire?"

"Yes."

"What about the head?"

"I'm unsure. It's possible that was also kept for a while."

"Taken from who?"

"I don't know," I said, fighting the urge to correct Slidell's grammar.

"How'd he get hold of a human head?"

"Maybe he got hold of a whole body."

Slidell spent several seconds mulling that gruesome possibility. Not for the first time, I was certain. Then, "Why deliver the eyeball but chuck the head to rot?"

"Maybe the eye was meant as a message."

"Ya *think*? What message?"

"I don't know."

"Why you?"

"I don't know." I was saying that a lot. "Did you learn anything useful at MiraVia?"

"That crew's like one big bleeding-heart Sunday-school choir. They think the world's gonna be all kittens and bunnies if they just—"

"The privy head?"

"One kid, Sandra-Leigh Keyler—belly's now bigger than her IQ— went to the crapper to off-load a jar of cigarette butts."

"She didn't want others to know she was smoking."

"I didn't query her motive. Sandra-Leigh sees the plastic bag with writing across the front. It said, '*Here's Johnny!*' Apparently, she'd seen a movie called *The Shining* and was totally creeped out."

"The Stanley Kubrick film with Jack Nicholson?"

"I look like the *Hollywood Reporter*? Anyway, Sandra-Leigh fessed up, an exploratory committee was formed, took a gander, dimed security. Not sure why these bimbos found a bag with writing so unnerving, but the rest is history."

I could imagine how Slidell's visit had gone. Felt enormous sympathy for the "bimbos."

"The whole friggin' lead dead-ended." Slidell activated his turn signal. It clicked softly, as if to punctuate his list. "No missing staff, no AWOL baby mamas, no angry boyfriends, no hostile mean-girl rivals, no miffed teachers or priests. Nothing but sunshine and butterflies."

"Did the women offer any suggestions as to who might have ended up in their privy?"

"None."

"Any ideas who might have used the privy to dispose of a head?"

"Someone who knew it was back there."

Valid point.

"Any guesses who that someone might be?"

"Got one name. Some of the brain trust thought a gardener was weird. Otherwise, nada. They all agreed the crapper's been abandoned for decades."

"Except for occasional trash disposal."

"Except for that."

Slidell's engine cut off. I figured he was headed for lunch.

"I pulled the file on that old case I mentioned." Wanting to discuss Sanchez before Skinny moved on to his Whopper or Big Mac.

"Scrappy." Followed by an impatient sigh.

"I see parallels. Scrappy's ear was found in one place, the rest of him in another. His body was missing its heart, liver, and kidneys."

"Like I said. Organs. Not an eyeball. And Scrappy was a banger. Different MO. Different COD. Remember the fifteen stab wounds?"

"Both cases involve knives," I said.

"Are you listening to me? Scrappy was a gang hit."

I hated to admit it, but I suspected Slidell was right.

"Shall I brief Detective Henry, or would you prefer to do it?" I asked.

"I'm not sure about that dame."

"Because she's a dame working homicide?"

"Because she acts like a goddam rookie."

"Henry spent several years with the LAPD."

"Doing what? Traffic busts?"

"She was a detective. I didn't ask what division."

"Did you know that besides her issue, the dipshit packs a .380 ACP backup, hides a sap in her waistband, and wears a knife strapped to one ankle? Regular Dirty Harry."

"She told you that?" I didn't point out that Dirty Harry carried a Smith and Wesson Model 29.

"Yeah."

"That makes her a dipshit?"

"No. The fact she told me makes her a dipshit."

Katy phoned as I was descending the front steps of the MCME.

"Hey, sweetie. What's up?"

"A clock, a spice rack, a bed, and two shelves."

"Progress."

"Dad came by. He's hopeless with anything mechanical."

"I know." God, did I know. "But he's a good lawyer."

"He installed the cordless vac charger upside down. Are you aware he's leaving for the Seychelles tomorrow?"

"Mm." I wasn't. Wondered which bimbo of the month would be diving with him. Really didn't care. "Got the kitchen in order?"

"That's why I'm calling. Want to come for dinner and help organize?"

"Sure," I said, not really wanting to do the second part. "What time?"

"Whenever."

"I'll catch a quick shower and feed Birdie, then swing by. Say, thirty minutes?"

"OK. And can you bring dinner?"

"Make that forty-five."

The shower was great, the cat indignant. The wait at Maharani took half an hour. By the time I got to Katy's house it was after seven.

"What did you get?"

"Chicken tikka and lamb korma. Naan. Raita."

"Hot damn." Practically ripping the bag from my hand.

Katy had a bottle of Decoy Pinot Noir going. She refilled her glass. I got a soda from the fridge.

We split the entrees, each of us grabbing a piece of naan. After adding the cucumber and yogurt sauce to our paper plates, we tore the cellophane from the plastic knives and forks and dived in.

As we ate, I looked around the kitchen. Saw little progress since moving day.

"I assume you focused your efforts elsewhere?" Jocular tone.

"I needed a place to sleep, Mom." Defensive.

"Exactly where I'd have started."

The bedroom took three days? I didn't say it.

"Where shall we launch our mission, boss?"

Katy pointed at two cartons stacked beside the Sub-Zero. "I think that's kitchen stuff."

While I cleared the dinner debris, she got out a box cutter and sliced through tape.

Good call. The top box held a jumble of pots and pans, Tupperware, and cheap cooking utensils. Very few in any category. Apparently, the culinary arts held no appeal for my daughter.

The bottom box contained dish rags and towels, plastic tumblers, and an incomplete set of melamine dinnerware. Pottery Barn, I guessed. The bottom layer was composed of an odd assortment of mugs.

As we placed items in cabinets and drawers, I took a stab at conversation.

Easy, Brennan. Keep it light.

"I imagine you'll be relieved when all these boxes are gone."

"Fuckin-A."

"Have you contacted any of your old Charlotte friends?"

"Not yet. I've been balls to the wall with this move."

As we began on the mugs, I asked, "Any plans for what's next?"

"Attacking the jungle my landlord calls a backyard."

"I was thinking a bit longer range."

I waited for the blast. It didn't come.

"I'm considering a few things."

"At one point you talked about nursing school."

Katy shelved a mug. It said: *Don't make me use my Army voice.*

"I saw a lot of nasty shit in Afghanistan. Abused women. Dead babies. Legless civvies. Raped schoolgirls. Had they been *allowed* to attend school, which they weren't before we got there."

She unwrapped another mug. *All American Shitkicker.*

"Everywhere, masses of people with no place to go. No homes. Hell, no villages. Some of that was our fault, some of it wasn't."

More mugs went onto the shelf.

"I met a few bad actors while in service, but any joe in my unit would have taken a bullet for me."

She paused, perhaps thinking of someone who had.

"What I mean is, someone always had my six. We were a team. Then these guys return stateside. To what? I'm lucky. I have you and dad. And, thanks to Gran, and Coop, I can afford this place."

A little backstory. My almost octogenarian mother, Katherine Daesee "Daisy" Lee Brennan, had the foresight to provide my daughter, Katy, and my sister Harry's son, Kit, with modest but respectable trust funds. Katy's postcollege love, Aaron "Coop" Cooperton, had the lack of foresight to drive over an IED while en route home from a Peace Corps mission in Kabul. To his family's shock, Coop left all his earthly wealth to Katy. That wealth turned out to be substantial.

I've always suspected that Coop's death was the impetus for Katy's joining the army. And the motivator for her volunteering for duty in Afghanistan. Twice.

"—and now we just pack up and haul ass. And how does our government thank its troops for their service?" Katy was still on a roll. "They end up jobless and homeless. I'm not saying *all* of them. But way too many."

I didn't interrupt.

"Do you have any idea how many homeless we have in this country?"

I waited for her to answer her own question.

"Over half a million. Roughly nine thousand right here in North Carolina. Around forty thousand of that national number are vets."

"That's deplorable." I meant it.

"You remember the passerby we ambushed to help get the chair through the door?"

"A fond moment."

"His name is Calvin Winkard. Goes by Winky."

"Of course, he does."

Katy gave me The Face. "Winky served in the Gulf War. Got a purple heart for taking a bullet in the leg. Now he sleeps in a tent on the grounds of the Roof Above Day Services Center. Do you know the shelter?"

"It's just outside the beltway, right?"

"Yeah. Mustn't have the unwashed and unkept mingling with our Armani and Chanel-spritzed uptowners."

I knew Roof Above from personal experience. Due to the COVID pandemic, and requirements for restricted indoor occupancy, a small tent city had grown up outside one of its two buildings. When a tenter died and someone finally noticed the odor, I was tasked with accompanying Hawkins to make sure none of the decomposed corpse was left behind.

"They deserve better. All the homeless, not just vets. I want to do something!"

"What?" I asked, stunned by her vehemence.

"I'm not sure. Open a soup kitchen? A pantry? Fund a private shelter? Start a charitable foundation?"

While impressed with my daughter's passion, I was wary of her apparent naïveté.

"Do you know how to go about doing any of those things?"

"I've talked to a lawyer."

That surprised me.

"Everything's just so fucking complicated," she said, groaning.

Katy reached for the last mug. Its base hit the shelf with a loud crack.

"Sometimes I just can't stand it."

7

Nothing much happened for the next four days.

Ryan called on Saturday. The Saint Martin case was more complicated than anticipated. Turned out the spinnaker bag held, not a sail, but the motherlode of blow. The boat owner was now "whereabouts unknown." Ryan wasn't sure how long he'd be in the islands. Had yet to feel the sand between his toes.

Slidell and Henry went radio silent. I assumed neither had news.

Katy and I emptied boxes, positioned and re-positioned furniture, hung pictures. The hours spent with my daughter weren't always pleasant. One day she'd be warm and appreciative of my company, the next she'd take issue with everything I said. The mood swings were worrying, the constant need to weigh my comments exhausting. But Katy researched shelters, made a choice, and offered to volunteer. The director was delighted to have her.

The groundhog must have issued a memo. Temperatures plummeted and Wednesday's non-weather became a fond memory. On every station, the talking heads began drawing diagrams and breathlessly uttering the "S" word. Snow!

Charlotte is a Sunbelt city. We have winters, sure, but they're short and reasonable. Some years we don't even break out the woollies. But every now and then the climate gods collude to produce the white stuff.

As with hurricane warnings, mention of snow sends the town into hyperdrive. Schools and courts close, supermarkets empty of staples, and generators disappear from hardware stores. Liquor sales skyrocket, but shovels remain readily available. Usually, we toss salt on our driveways and walks, then build snowmen or go tobogganing on the golf course. After the frenzy, we just wait for the melt.

Monday morning, I drove to the MCME under clouds so dark and bloated they appeared to belly-scrape the earth. A snow sky. I planned to wrap up a few loose ends and head back home early.

My assumption concerning Slidell proved incorrect. Skinny had been busy over the weekend.

I'd barely removed my parka when Nguyen appeared at my door.

"I fear we're in for a blizzard," she said.

"Looks that way."

"I don't like snow. Snow and ice are the reasons I left Boston."

Knowing my boss hadn't come to discuss the weather, I waited.

"Do you have a moment?"

"Of course." I gestured at the chair facing my desk.

Nguyen came in and sat. She held a paper in her right hand.

"Detective Slidell phoned me early this morning." Raising the page. "Though retired, he is a very diligent man."

"He still works with the cold case unit."

"That explains his interest. Detective Slidell managed to get to the bottom of the Belmont Abbey situation." In case I was unclear, she added, "The remains you recovered from the outhouse."

I nodded.

"The victim was not a pregnant student as Detective Slidell first suspected. In fact, he has been unable to find any link to the monastery, the college, or MiraVia. But he is still investigating that angle."

Nguyen has one annoying trait. She speaks very precisely and approaches topics in her own way. OK. That's two.

"Actually, once Detective Henry had the dental information, it was she who got the match through NamUS. Detective Henry gave the name to Detective Slidell, and he carried on."

I felt like employing a prod. Finally, Nguyen got to the ID.

"The woman's name is Veronica Justine Kwalwasser. Your age estimate was quite accurate. Kwalwasser was forty-two at the time of her passing."

"Which was when?"

"August 18, 2020."

"How did she die?"

"Metastatic breast cancer."

I didn't see that coming.

"Yes." Nguyen read my face. "I was surprised, too. Until I heard the whole story."

Nguyen glanced at her scribbled notes.

"Do you recall an exposé about a crematorium found to be improperly handling bodies?"

"The Tri-State Crematory in Georgia?"

"No. Right here in Mecklenburg County. The story made the news about two years ago. The incident occurred before I was hired."

"Right. Happy Trails Cremation Services. Their ads promised the cheapest rates in town."

Nguyen nodded. "That's the one. Instead of cremating, the owner was simply stacking the bodies in his garage. When the EPA finally investigated, they found forty-seven corpses in varying stages of decomposition. The man claimed his cremator had stopped functioning properly."

"Wasn't Happy Trails located off Monroe Road?"

"Yes."

"It was shut down."

"Yes. The owner was charged with theft by deception, giving false statements, abusing a corpse, and various burial service–related frauds."

I was out of the country at the time, so members of the re-

gional DMORT—Disaster Mortuary Operational Response Team—
convened to sort through and identify the deceased. Can't say I was
sorry to miss that one.

Nguyen again consulted her notes.

"I'm unclear about his process, but Detective Slidell ran the name
Kwalwasser through his cold case database. When he pulled and read
the file, he found mention of Happy Trails."

"No shit."

Censorious glance due to my language?

"It seems Ms. Kwalwasser's brother, Mr. Kenneth Kwalwasser,
engaged the services of Happy Trails following his sister's death. As
next of kin, he was contacted concerning the malpractice at the crematorium. Furious, he visited the facility frequently throughout the
DMORT operation. Much to the annoyance of those involved in the
process. On two occasions, the man had to be forcibly removed."

I had no idea where this was going.

"The investigation took four months. One of the dead in the
garage was, indeed, Ms. Kwalwasser. The initial ID relied largely on
fingerprints but was later confirmed with DNA."

"Why not dentals?"

The deep brown eyes locked onto mine.

"Ms. Kwalwasser's head was not with her body."

"Where was it?"

"The head was never found."

"Had other corpses suffered the same kind of trauma?"

"No."

"How did her head become detached?"

"You know what I know, Dr. Brennan. For anything further, you
must speak with Detective Slidell."

I dialed Skinny as Nguyen was disappearing through the door.

Got voice mail. Left a message.

Then I sat, agitated, a zillion questions spinning in my brain.

How had Kwalwasser lost her head? Did her neck give out due
to gravity following decomposition? How was her body positioned?

Did rodents or other scavengers have access to the garage? Were the cervical vertebrae gnawed? Note to self: ask Slidell if there are pics of the scene.

An uglier possibility. Was Kwalwasser intentionally decapitated? If so, by whom? Why? Note to self: ask Slidell the current whereabouts of the owner of Happy Trails.

How did Kwalwasser's head end up behind MiraVia? Why remove it from Happy Trails? Why put it in a privy? Why *that* privy? Why stab the head in the eye with a paring knife? Why was the other eye frozen?

Who removed Kwalwasser's eyeball? Why? Why *her*?

Why deliver the eyeball to *me*?

Again, that subliminal nudging.

What the *hell* was my subconscious teasing?

To settle my nerves, I went to the kitchen for coffee. I know. Caffeine was probably counterproductive. But all the talk of snow was making me cold. And I needed to stay focused.

I was wrapping up a prelim on the eyeball when the chief reappeared at my door. Hot damn. A visit from the boss twice in one day.

"I've just received a call." I didn't like the look on Nguyen's face. "I truly hate to ask you this, given the weather."

Then don't. I didn't say it.

"A body has been discovered in the state park up near Troutman. According to the ranger, the remains are not fresh, and the situation requires an anthropologist."

While I appreciated the ranger's respect for my discipline, I was less than thrilled to be going out on a recovery with a snowstorm threatening.

"He suspects it's a suicide and fears evidence might be lost once snow starts falling," Nguyen continued.

"Who's going?"

"Mr. Hawkins."

"Fine," I said with the enthusiasm I typically reserve for plunging a toilet. "I'll meet him outside in twenty."

I rode in the transport van with Hawkins. A CSU team followed in their vehicle.

During the hour-long drive, Hawkins and I mostly discussed baseball. He's a fan, has kept a signed photo of DiMaggio on his desk for as long as I've known him. When the MCME moved to our new digs, the pic of Joltin' Joe was the only personal item Hawkins brought along.

In the early part of the last century, to create hydroelectric power, Duke Energy began damming the Catawba River from just above Morganton, North Carolina, down to where the river joins the Santee-Cooper in South Carolina. Norman was the final and largest of seven lakes created. Its massive shoreline now touches four counties—Mecklenburg, Iredell, Catawba, and Lincoln.

Locals still talk about what lies under Norman's waters. A textile mill. A housing community. A two-hundred-year-old estate called Elm Wood. Part of US Highway 21, which connected Charlotte and Statesville.

To appease those who lost property, and anyone else irate about the power plants, or not, some of the newly created reservoirs and their surroundings were turned into recreational areas for all to enjoy. Our destination was one of these playgrounds.

Lake Norman State Park is a nineteen-hundred-acre hunk of land at the mouth of Hicks Creek on the lake's northern shore. The amenities include the usual boat ramps, swimming beaches, picnic shelters, campgrounds, and hiking trails.

A ranger was waiting for us at the main headquarters building when Hawkins and I entered. His name tag said *T. Edy.*

T. Edy was dressed all in green. Made me think of the old nursery rhyme and its similarly attired anti-hero, Hector Protector.

"Ranger Edy." Hector proffered a hand.

I introduced myself, then stepped back slightly as Hawkins reached in and shook Edy's hand.

"I was afraid it might be you," Edy said to me.

Oh?

"I'm sure you don't remember me."

He was right. I didn't.

"Terrence Edy. Back at the gray dawn of history, I took one of your classes at UNCC."

"I'm sorry." Not appreciating how old Edy was making me feel. "I've had so many students over the years."

"Not surprised. Frankly, you screwed me on my grade."

"It's nice to see you." A vague image was rising from the gray dawn mist. A tall gangly kid trying but failing to grow facial hair. Last row in the lecture hall, dirty sneakers propped on the chairback in front of him.

"Background?" Hawkins asked in his typical terse manner.

"This park allows dogs," Edy said. "A hiker was walking his beagle when it started barking and acting goofy. The dog's name is Ruggles. The man's name is Clayton Carter. Those are Carter's words, not mine. Anyway, when Carter let Ruggles run, the dog veered off into the trees and started yowling by a big oak. Carter spotted the body, hustled here, and led me to it."

"Any health or safety hazards we need to know about?" I asked.

"Beast of a wind in that area. That's why no one goes up there. Which is why Carter did. He said Ruggles had grown bored with the more popular trails, wanted to see new territory. Ask me, Ruggles was hoping Carter would freeze his nads off and they could both go home."

"Anything else?"

Edy shrugged. "Best you see the scene for yourself. I touched nothing, won't vouch for the wildlife."

"Can we get a vehicle in there?" Hawkins asked.

"Part way. The dead dude's just off the Lake Shore Trail."

"Let's do this," Hawkins said.

Edy retrieved a broad-brimmed gray hat and positioned it carefully on his head. Donned a green parka. Made me think of George, the young security guard back at the MiraVia privy.

Flakes had begun testing the air as we'd entered the building, diaphanous crystals seemingly ambivalent about whether to linger. That changed quickly and, by the time we climbed up to Ruggles's oak, the snow was fully committed. It coated the branches above us and whitened the ground in patches at our feet.

For a moment we all stood staring, snowflakes stinging our cheeks and layering the brim of Edy's hat.

Hawkins summed up our collective shock.

"Well, I'll be jitterbugged."

8

Four hours later, I was back at the MCME.

With Ranger Edy's "dead dude."

And Slidell.

Happy day.

CSU was still working the scene but had forwarded pics taken at my direction.

Skinny had come by my office to discuss Veronica Kwalwasser. Upon learning of the state park vic, he'd joined me in the autopsy suite, thinking there could be a link to one of his cold case files.

We were in a room outfitted with special ventilation. The stinky room. Every morgue has one. Didn't need it. The remains were giving off almost no odor. Not so for Skinny. I guessed he'd enjoyed a brat with kraut and onions for lunch.

Hawkins had videoed, photographed, and undressed the "dead dude." His clothes were hanging on a drying rack, his boots sitting side by side on the counter. His corpse lay naked on the floor-bolted table.

I'd briefed Slidell. He and I were now viewing the scene photos. Which required us to stand shoulder to shoulder at the monitor. In addition to onions and kraut, I was enjoying a tsunami of stale coffee and cheap drugstore cologne.

"The bonehead offed himself," Slidell summarized.

"It has all the signs of a suicide."

"How the hell did he get out there?"

"Edy said he could have arrived by foot, bike, or vehicle. Or come by water. The lake's just over that rise." I pointed to a small hill in one of the photos. "The park's not enclosed or patrolled back there."

"Yeah? Then where's the boat? The Schwinn?"

"I agree. He probably walked."

"How come no one spotted this guy?"

"The body was camouflaged by vegetation and extremely hard to see. Besides, Edy said no one goes back there."

"Ruggles and his pal did."

"They did. And Ruggles used his nose, not his eyes."

"No ID?" Slidell asked for the second time.

"None," I repeated. "And no note."

"That's hinky."

"It's odd," I agreed.

"Go again." Slidell twirled a beefy finger at the screen.

I returned to an image taken somewhere along the trail and worked through a series leading up to the oak. And the kudzu-wrapped bundle hanging from it.

Introduced from Asia as a garden novelty, kudzu quickly became the bane of the south. And the source of much myth. The vine is reputed to be unkillable. It's said that kudzu's growth is so rapid one must lock the doors at night to bar it from invading your house. You get the idea.

The vines we were viewing were winter black and leafless. Still, the subject resembled a giant nest, the outer tangle thick enough to obscure the thing wrapped inside.

The next series was taken after the kudzu had been snipped and stripped. The pics showed a corpse that looked like something from an Egyptian tomb.

The man was wearing black work boots, jeans, and a plaid shirt so faded the colors were unrecognizable. A yellow polypropylene rope around his neck ran to a branch above his head. He wore no hat. No belt.

Bad planning on the latter. Gravity had done what gravity does. As dehydration shrunk the man's muscles and fats, his boxers and jeans had slipped to mid-thigh, revealing genitals in which he'd undoubtedly taken much pride. Determining the victim's sex would not be a problem.

The final close-ups showed a face transformed to an Amenhotep horror. Unlike determining gender, assessing ancestry would be tough. And the man's next of kin would be doing no visual ID.

After the final image, I stepped to the table. Sighing behind his mask, Slidell followed.

Immediately after death, regardless if the deceased is an egret or an emperor, nature sets to work recycling the atoms composing the organism, returning its energy and matter to the universe. That process is accomplished via one of two processes: putrefaction or mummification.

The hanging site provided a perfect combination of elevation, sun exposure, and constant air movement. These factors, along with the man's protective clothing, resulted in minimal animal scavenging and invasion by necrophagous insects. Edy's "dead dude" was transiting through door number two. His flesh was brown and leathery and tightly molded to his bones. His eyes were shriveled peas peeking from below half-mast lids, his nose a distorted and compressed isosceles. His scalp retained perhaps a dozen tenacious sun-bleached strands.

The man's withered upper lip was recurved against the few bristles that remained of his mustache. His lower lip was frozen in the drooping position it had assumed when his jaw dislocated. Instead of a tongue, a brown mass filled the space between.

"What the hell's in his mouth?"

Having no answer to Slidell's question, I reached out and applied pressure to the mandible with both my thumbs. Felt no movement. Pressed harder. The jaw yielded not a micron.

Choosing a very sharp scalpel, I made linear incisions from each corner of the man's mouth back to the level of each ear. This cut the masseter muscle bilaterally and opened the face.

Next, I picked up forceps, grasped the obstruction, and tugged gently. Slight resistance, then the thing slid free with a soft crackling sound.

The mass was approximately three inches in diameter, papery light, and composed of small, pentagonal cells. We both recognized it immediately.

Slidell lurched backward from the table. "Goddam. Anyone alive in there?"

"The wasps are long gone," I said, admiring the geometry of their creation. "But it's a beauty."

"What's it doing inside the guy's mouth?"

"Wasps and hornets often build nests in empty or partially empty skulls."

"You gotta be kidding me."

"So do some bees. A hollow sphere suits their architectural needs."

"Can we get back on track? How long since the guy strung himself up?"

"Hard to tell. Once a body mummifies it can last a long time."

"That's real helpful."

"Prelim estimate, two to three years. Could be more. Could be less."

"Got a profile?"

"Male."

"Yeah, we know that 'cause of Mr. Whoopee hanging out of his pants."

"Middle age." I'd observed the teeth and sutures before Slidell arrived.

"Not that shit again. Can't you gimme something else?"

"When I've cleaned the bones."

"He white?"

"Same answer. But unofficially, I'd say that's likely."

"Great. I'll run a search for a middle-aged *maybe* white guy hung like a—"

"The man was short, maybe five-five tops." I shifted topics. "Did you want to tell me something about Veronica Kwalwasser?"

"Nguyen filled you in?"

"She told me what she knew."

"There ain't much more at this point. Silas Tannen, that's the genius who owned Happy Trails, struck a plea deal and is doing a twelve-year jolt. Not sure how eager he'll be to get out. He's also facing a gorilla of a class-action civil suit. Anyway, I talked to Tannen. He's got no idea how Kwalwasser's head went AWOL. Never heard of Belmont Abbey or MiraVia."

"You believe him?" I asked.

"The guy's one fry short of a Happy Meal, but yeah. He probably don't have enough gray cells to lie."

"Did anyone else work at the crematorium?"

"It was strictly a one-man operation. I did learn that there were other complaints over the years, a couple police visits. I plan to run that down."

I was about to ask another question when Hawkins popped his head through the door. Did I mention that he's tall and gaunt, with thinning black hair slicked back with shiny goop. Very Halloween-esque.

"Need help cutting?" Hawkins nodded at the table.

"Shortly," I said.

"X-rays are ready. He's logged as MCME 224-22."

"Thanks."

Hawkins withdrew. Slidell took a step to follow him.

"How about we check the films together?" I suggested, entering the case number into the system. "We might spot something that could narrow your search."

Slidell returned to the monitor.

The radiographs started at the man's head and worked toward his feet. A bright white track, a zipper, indicated they'd been taken while the body was still dressed. SOP. Good to know if there's anything in the clothing that could be dangerous.

"What's that?" Slidell indicated a dense white circle on the right side of the man's forehead."

"Looks like an osteoma."

"Which is?"

"A benign bone tumor."

"You're talking a big bump that people would have noticed?"

I got calipers and measured from the screen. "It's two and a half centimeters, so, yes."

The next anomaly appeared in one of the man's hip joints.

"At some time in the past he fractured the neck of his right femur. The break healed but at an odd angle, so his right leg appears to be slightly shorter than his left."

"He woulda limped?"

"Probably."

"Jesus. This guy was a mess. No wonder he killed himself. What the frick is that?" Slidell asked when we'd moved to the next plate.

We both studied the object glowing white at the femoral midshaft.

"Must be in a pocket," I said.

Crossing to the drying rack, I lifted the jeans and tested for a lump. Felt nothing. Moving slowly, I inserted forceps into the right back pocket. Empty. The left.

Deep down, wedged against the bottom seam was something rigid. Using the tweezers, I flicked the object upright, teased it out, and walked back to show Slidell.

In my palm was a metal cylinder with a decaying wooden handle at one end. The cylinder was roughly two and a half inches long and a half inch in diameter. Attached to the handle by a half-rotted lanyard was a flat piece of metal, curved and serrated at its tip.

I looked a question at Slidell. He shrugged.

"No idea at all?" I asked, perhaps a bit too sharply.

"What am I, Tim the Tool Man?"

I placed the object under the magnifier. Thumbed on the ring light.

"There's a logo on the handle, but the lettering's toast."

Wishing for Katy's visual acuity, I readjusted the lens. "Maybe *QO* something? *CC? AC?*"

"Gotta hit the pavement." Slidell's heels squeaked across the tile. "I'll use what I got on this guy, see if anything pops."

I straightened.

Slidell was already pushing through the door.

I spent a few more minutes with a hand magnifier. Eventually gave up in frustration.

I spotted nothing else unusual in the skeleton. No abnormalities, no other healed or fresh fractures, no surgical inclusions. No bullets.

After shooting pics with the lab Nikon and my iPhone, I bagged and tagged the cylinder. Was placing the Ziploc beside the boots when my id tossed the same caution flag as when I'd processed the eyeball.

What?

There was absolutely nothing linking the two cases. Kwalwasser and Sanchez, maybe. Both bodies were found missing parts. But these remains were complete. A suicide by hanging.

An *apparent* suicide, I corrected myself.

My subconscious stayed vigilant but offered no help.

I checked the time. Six-ten. Suspecting the snow was having its way with the streets, I knew I should head home.

I decided to send the CSU pics to my iPhone. Was finishing when the id guys piped up again.

I looked at the image currently on the computer screen. Taken from the point at which the trail began seriously rising in elevation, it provided an overview of the body dangling from the oak. I paid closer attention than I had earlier with Slidell. Or when Hawkins and I had been freezing our asses in the snow.

The man's head was slumped sideways toward his right shoulder. His jaw was displaced but clinging to his skull by dry and shriveled ligaments. Nothing wrong there.

The rope was knotted just below the man's mastoid process on the left. OK. A side-positioned knot was more consistent with suicide than one located at the nape of the neck. Wasn't it? And what about the knot itself? Having no expertise beyond Girl Scout level, I vowed to contact a knot expert. Wasn't there one at the Laboratoire de Sciences Judiciaires et de Médecine Légale? A knotologist? Then it struck me.

The man was hanging with his toes approximately six feet above terra firma. The rope, not counting the noose, was eight feet long. I'd measured it. The man had stood five-foot five. I'd measured him, too.

I did some quick math. That put the branch at almost twenty feet above the ground. How the hell did he get up that high? The tree had small knobs projecting from its trunk. Enough to get footholds? Maybe. The "dead dude" was wearing boots.

I searched the views of the surrounding area. Saw nothing in the background that the man could have used to enable him to grasp the branch. No dead trees to drag over. No stumps to stand on. No collapsible stepladder to climb.

I considered possible scenarios.

Might he have scrambled up an adjacent tree, then swung over, Tarzan style?

With a limp?

Might he have lassoed the branch, then scaled the trunk, rock-climber style?

Was I creating drama where none existed? Injecting unwarranted suspicion?

I was leaning in that direction when my iPhone buzzed on the counter.

I glanced at it to check caller ID.

Smiling, I clicked on. Was about to open with something light and witty but wasn't given the chance.

"Where are you?" Katy's voice was shaky and much too loud.

"At the ME office." My heartbeat kicked up a notch. "What's wrong?"

"Have you looked out a window?"

"I'm in an autopsy room."

"It's snowing like a sonofabitch."

"Right." Relief triggered a laugh. "I was doing a recovery when it started. The woods were pretty—"

"It's a fucking blizzard!"

That stopped me cold. Katy's alarm seemed way out of proportion to what she was saying. I pictured her standing at a window, eyes roving, radiating anxiety.

"Has something happened to upset you?" I asked cautiously.

"Yeah. I'm away from home and up to my ass in snow."

"Where are you?"

"At the shelter."

"Where's your car?"

"Here." In the background I could hear institutional sounds, muffled voices, clangs and scrapes, maybe an elevator bonging.

"You don't feel comfortable driving?"

"No."

That seemed out of character.

"You can't call an Uber?" I knew that was dumb as soon as I said it. In blizzards, Uber cars became as rare as trout on the tundra.

"I don't feel safe." Voice rising. "You don't get it."

"Tell me."

I waited out a very long silence. When Katy spoke again it was clear she was forcing her voice calm.

"I spent the better part of the last eight years maneuvering jeeps through one goddam desert or another. Snow and ice aren't in my skill set."

"I'll come get you."

"Please."

"No problem. And, Katy?"

"Yes."

"I'll bet you're a crackerjack on sand."

"A lot of good that'll do me with this creep."

"What creep?"

"Never mind. I shouldn't have said that."

She disconnected.

What the hell? Katy was never this fragile. I couldn't imagine my daughter spooked about driving on ice. And who was the "creep"?

Uneasy, I secured the body, grabbed my things from my office, and set out.

9

In 2019, the Urban Ministry and the Men's Shelter of Charlotte merged to form Roof Above, an organization offering shelter and aid to single adult males.

The original facilities stand within a stone's throw of each other. Well, a small stone. Both are on the wrong side of a beltway circling uptown. Neither will ever appear in a Christie's luxury real estate spread.

Katy had been assigned to the facility on N. College Street. Driving to it, my emotions went aerial, rising and falling like a kite on a summer wind. It was dark. And cold. And snowing hard.

Lights glowed in apartment and condo windows I passed on the way. TVs flickered blue. I envied the occupants their cozy domesticity, wished I could go home and shed my dirty scrubs. Share defrosted beef stew with Birdie. Sleep.

I dreaded facing Katy's prickliness. Where would her moodiness take her tonight? I worried that her irritability was symptomatic of something more serious.

My thoughts pinballed. Frustration over the "dead dude." Concern for my daughter. Annoyance at having to venture into a sketchy part of town at night. Didn't taxis operate in blizzards? I thought so. Anyway, it wasn't a good mix.

I arrived at the shelter a half hour after leaving the MCME. Twice the time it normally took. Despite the snow, business was booming. Perhaps because of it.

Men in baseball caps and ratty jackets lingered on the walks or leaned against the building's high stone foundation. A few talked, some to others, some to themselves. Many stood with shoulders hunched, hands thrust deep into their pockets. Most smoked.

Katy was waiting just inside the door. A dozen eyes watched her hurry to the curb and climb into my car.

"Have you ever thought of dumping this heap?" she asked, buckling her seat belt with unsteady hands.

"All the time," I said.

"Does this car have snow tires?"

"What do you think?"

I could sense Katy trying to control her breathing. For a very long moment she said nothing.

On a bench up a small hill on the shelter's grounds an old man arranged a bundle and dropped onto it, one hand cupping the stub of a cigarette clamped in his lips. I watched his smoke drift up and dissolve among the flakes.

The silence in the car was deep enough to drill for oil.

"Good first day?" I asked to break it.

"Good enough. Let's get out of here."

The tires crunched softly as I turned onto Twelfth Street and began wending my way toward Elizabeth, hands white knuckling the wheel, speed topping out at a blistering twenty mph. The snow was giving the wipers a run for their money.

Despite my cautiousness, now and then a rear wheel lost traction and we fishtailed. Each time, Katy's hands flew forward to brace on the dash.

No one spoke until I pulled to the curb in front of her house.

"Sorry I overreacted," Katy mumbled, sounding not all that sorry.

"Driving in snow freaks me out, too."

"But you did it."

"I did."

"Old-lady style," she added.

I cut a sideways glance at my daughter. She was grinning. Her sense of humor was restored now that she was home and felt safe? I noticed that she wasn't reaching for the door handle. Maybe she, too, sensed that more needed to be said.

"What's up, kiddo?" I asked.

"What do you mean?"

Tread carefully, Brennan.

"You don't seem yourself."

"And what is myself?" The last word indicating we were back to prickly.

"Self-assured, tough, confident. A woman with a bring-it-on attitude."

Katy said nothing. Seconds passed.

The car grew chilly. Or so it seemed to me.

I tapped a button to pump up the heat.

Inside, the only sound was the hum of the blower. Outside, several streets over, an engine growled and metal scraped concrete. Hot damn. Who knew our fair city owned plows?

The silence seemed to last forever. Then, Katy said something completely unrelated.

"I really think I'll like working with the homeless."

I took the hint and went along. "That's good."

"It will be rewarding."

"What services does Roof Above offer?"

"The usual. Food, clothing, housing, counseling."

"What will they have you doing?"

"A little of each." Her mouth twisted up on one side as she snorted. "Except counseling. I'm hardly the one for that."

Snow was falling hard now. Knowing I should keep moving, I decided to stay. As long as Katy was willing to open up, I'd linger and face the consequences later.

"Just curious," I said. "Why have you chosen to work with men?"

Katy shrugged. "I know women have major problems. Especially those with kids. And those with asshole spouses or ex's who smack them around. But, in general, I think abused and homeless women get more attention. As a result, they have more options."

"Could be." Not sure I agreed with that.

"Most of these men have absolutely nothing. Many are sick. Many are addicted, either to drugs or alcohol. Many are totally alone with nowhere to turn."

"Can't they—"

"And a lot of them are vets. They did their service and now society treats them like shit." Intense wouldn't do justice to her tone.

She reached for the door handle. I noticed that her hand was still trembling.

I'd helped Katy through skinned knees and science projects gone bad. Walked her through puberty. Counseled her during crises of academics, friendship, and self-esteem.

Like any mother, I'd consoled my daughter in matters of the body and the heart. It was challenging, often exhausting. The breast lump that turned out to be benign. The fenderbender that ended up costing a mere $300 for repairs. The lost ID that we found in her bathrobe pocket. All these calamities would be followed, within a day, by Katy's bouncing back to her cheerful, unruffled self. Coop's death had been the exception, of course. But this time also seemed different.

Much as I longed for solitude—the stew, the bath, the judgmental cat—Katy didn't look as though she should be alone.

"Remember our snowed-in parties?" I asked. Chirped? "Would you like to stay at my place tonight? Have one of those?"

She said nothing.

When I turned sideways, intending to repeat my offer, Katy was staring past me, her spine rigid and angled toward the dash. Her body was motionless, her hands tightly clenched in her lap. The Mazda's interior was black due to the snowy accumulation on its windows. Only Katy's eyes were visible, dark and wide and full of fear.

Her altered demeanor stopped my breath. She seemed to be somewhere far from the car and the snow. From Charlotte. From me.

Was she reliving some horror I would never understand? Or perhaps she *had* heard my invitation and was considering options.

When she spoke again, her voice was low and calm.

"You must think I'm royally fucked up."

"Of course, I don't." I did. "But I am concerned about you."

"You sound like a therapist."

I said nothing.

"I overreacted," she said, offering a small, self-deprecating laugh. "The big bad soldier freaked out by a storm."

I waited for her to go on. Across Kenmore, I could hear two kids arguing about the best way to roll a snowball on their lawn. Stage one of Frosty, I assumed. Their voices were muffled by the shrubbery and the curtain of flakes between us. Far off, a siren wailed softly.

I sensed more than saw a change in Katy's body language. She debated with herself, decided. That decision was another exit ramp.

"Not tonight," she said, unbuckling her belt. "Thanks for coming to get me."

Maybe it was fatigue, or frustration, or all her evasiveness since returning home. I lost it.

"Oh, no you don't, young lady. I want to know what's going on!" I exploded. "You phone me at work in a panic, say you don't feel safe, and mention some creep who's scaring you. I drop everything and race to the shelter. When I arrive, you bolt through the door like the place is on fire. In the car, you act as jumpy as a cricket on a fry pan. Then it's, 'Thanks for coming to get me' with no explanation of why you can barely goddam breathe!"

The force of my anger shocked her. She sat paralyzed inside our dark cocoon, a catatonic cut-out against the opaque glass beside her.

"I'm guessing this isn't totally about snow." Now I was the one fighting for control. "What's the deal with this creep, as you labeled him?"

She held a moment, then settled back into the seat. The tension seemed to drain from her shoulders. As before, she turned inward, hosting another session with herself. Choosing a starting point? Weighing alternatives? Considering more evasions? The truth?

I waited.

Finally, she began. Her first words indicated the path she'd chosen. She'd share, but only so much. It was a tactic she'd used since learning to talk.

"Some odd characters frequent the shelter."

I considered that an understatement.

"'Odd' meaning rough?" I asked.

"I guess you could say that." She was selecting her words with torturous care.

"Violent?" My pulse kicking up again.

"I don't think so. The homeless are like any subculture. You have to learn the jargon, the etiquette, the rules about personal space, belongings, that kind of thing. Basically, if you can avoid pissing folks off, you're fine."

She went quiet again. Closing it down? Doing more mental triage: what to give, what to hold back, what to keep for possible future discussion. I decided to prod.

"So what's the story with this 'creep'?" Hooking air quotes. Which was largely pointless in the gloom. "Is he threatening you?"

"Not directly."

"Is it Slinky?"

"Winky. Let's not talk names."

"Why not?"

"Seriously, Mom?"

Right. Etiquette.

"Why does he make you nervous?"

She didn't deny it.

"I think he was following me today. At lunch, I went into JJ's for a hot dog. I saw him on East Boulevard when I left. Later, when I took my break, I spotted him on a sidewalk, walking in the same direction behind me. I tested whether I was being paranoid by varying my pace, speeding up and slowing down. He did the same. I tried dodging him by darting into a CVS. When I came out, he was loitering in the parking lot."

"You're sure it was always the same man?"

"Yes."

There was another long silence.

Up the block, a dog barked, either protecting his turf or confused by its sudden change in appearance.

"That's not all."

Katy's chin dropped, I assumed to stare at her hands. Which were again clasped in her lap.

"He's talking some really jacked-up shit. All day I tried to avoid him, but . . ." She left the sentence unfinished. "The dude's disgusting."

"Creepy."

"Yeah."

I couldn't read her expression, but the tautness of her body revealed her fear.

"Does he sleep at the shelter?"

She shook her head. "Sometimes he eats there."

"Has he ever been violent?"

"Not that I've heard."

"Is he into drugs?"

"I don't know. But he smells of booze."

"What else can you say about him?"

"Nothing."

"Do you know where he lives?"

"There are things we don't ask. I'm told that now and then he pitches a tent outside on the grounds. I assume the rest of the time he bounces around on the street."

Etiquette.

A vehicle crept past on Kenmore, its headlights slicing through gaps in the white-out covering our windows. Slowly, the slices moved across us, making their way toward the back seat. Katy's face looked pale and drawn in the brief slash of light.

"You know what?" Her voice startled me. "I really am acting section eight tonight. This guy's probably not a predator. It's an instinct you develop in a war zone where you're constantly gauging the locals. Is this kid a friendly or will he shoot my ass? Is that granny hiding a gun under her burqa? Does that goat have an IED up its butt? This guy is just trying to get my attention, maybe to prove he's tough, maybe to shock me. If I see him again, I'll just tell him to fuck off."

She leaned over and hugged me.

"In more diplomatic language, of course. I really am sorry for being a jerk. Nice metaphor, by the way."

I was lost.

"The cricket in the fry pan."

"I think it was a simile."

"Later gator!"

I watched until she was inside her house.

All the way home our conversation replayed in my head. Katy's mood swings frightened me. How could she be scared, surly, evasive, witty, loving, and apologetic all within the span of an hour? It was clearly not snow that had set her off.

Sudden stab of guilt. Had I increased Katy's fearfulness by discussing my work? Was she being melodramatic, falsely linking a set of harmless coincidences?

Or had she run across a genuine psychopath? Someone who could hurt her.

Should I phone the police?

And the question I'd been avoiding since Katy's return. Was my daughter suffering from PTSD?

Should I phone the army psychologist?

At the annex, I shared the stew with Birdie, then soaked in a tub while Coltrane blew sax in the background.

Sleep was a long time coming, but eventually my mind yielded. I went down hard and deep.

Good thing. The next day would be a nightmare.

10

K nowing the storm would put Charlotte in lockdown, I hadn't bothered to set an alarm. May as well have. Birdie started nudging me well before seven.

I kept my eyes closed, my body still, pretending sleep. The cat didn't buy it. Or didn't care.

I spent a short time playing Freud with a dream my brain had offered sporadically during the night. More like dream fragments, the snippets a disjointed montage involving a head and torso I couldn't fit together, a mummy singing "I Will Survive," and Katy driving a jeep through dunes. Didn't need ol' Sigmund to explain any of that.

By seven-thirty the head-butts had grown aggressive. I got up, did a brief morning toilette, and headed for the kitchen.

First off, I fed Birdie as he absolutely expected. While making coffee, I checked the situation outside. The sky still glowered gray and unfriendly. The snow had stopped, but I estimated that at least fourteen inches had managed to stick.

The grounds around the annex were an undulating field of white. I could see no gardens, no shrubbery, no porches or stairs. My car looked like a frosty hippo hunkered down on the driveway.

79

I poured myself a generous helping of Cheerios, then settled at the table with my mug and bowl. And the TV remote.

Confession. I am a news junkie. Of the old order. I still subscribe to the Charlotte *Observer*, the hard-copy version, delivered to my door daily. Katy makes fun of me, but I like the feel and smell of news-print. I enjoy spreading and slowly leafing through the pages.

It's said that nothing new ever happens. To some extent, that's true. It's like rotating items on a blackboard menu. Monday: hur-ricane. Tuesday: good/bad jobs report. Wednesday: mass shooting. Thursday: uprising in small foreign country. My obsession is know-ing what item is on the board on any given day.

That morning there was zero chance that a kid on a bike would toss a paper on my porch, so I turned on the tiny countertop TV and chose CNN. The regulars were bringing me "the latest news, weather, and high interest stories to start my day."

Birdie jumped onto the chair beside mine. Apparently, I was being forgiven for the late breakfast service. More likely, he had hopes of scoring the milk dregs left in my bowl. He circled twice, then dropped and began cleaning his paws.

At eight o'clock, wanting an update on driving conditions, I switched to the local ABC station. Not that I was going anywhere.

My fourteen-inch estimate was spot on. Unfortunately—the weatherman looked sincerely sad—that total fell short of the county's all-time best. On February 15, 1902, Mecklenburg got smacked with a mind-boggling fifteen inches. But no state ribbon. On March 13, 1993, Mount Mitchell in Yancey County had recorded a whopping three feet.

It was more information than I needed, but confirmation that I'd be spending the day at home.

I crossed to Mr. Coffee to refill my mug. Was offering my bowl to the cat when the hour's lead news story caught my attention. I froze, cup in hand, eyes focused on the small Sony.

Like the weatherman, the newscaster looked appropriately grim.

And anchorlike: surgically bobbed blond hair, teeth that were a testi-
monial to braces and regular brushing.

"—unidentified body found at Lake Norman State Park, just off
the Lake Shore Trail. The victim is a white male, forty, six feet in
height. He was found by park ranger Terrence Edy."

The station switched to footage of Edy being interviewed by a
reporter with a handheld mike.

"How did you find the body?" The voice pitch suggested a female
journalist.

"I do regular patrol."

What?

"How long had the man been in the park?"

"Maybe a year, maybe three. Hard to say. He was really dried out."

I felt a spark flame in my chest.

"Dried out?"

"Yeah. Like a mummy."

"What did you do?"

"Called the ME. I've had training in forensic anthropology, so I
suggested they send one."

The heat roared up my throat and blasted my face.

I'm no rock star at anger management. And what I was feeling
now wasn't minor irritation—an upset over the plumber not showing
on time or the car trunk refusing to open. No. It was true, nerve-
frying, fiery, lava-red fury. I don't often lose my temper, but when it
happens, I go full-on Kilauea. Call it a character flaw.

"Damn!"

Birdie coiled at the ferocity of my expletive. Held a beat, then
relaxed, radiating disapproval.

"And did they?" the journalist asked.

"Yeah. Brennan. She's the only game around here."

A new visual aid appeared. Taken in the late nineties, the tired
old video was kept on file and trotted out as needed. It showed me at
an exhumation, derrière up, head down in the pit. Not my best angle.

The reporter reappeared. Bundled and snow covered, she now spoke directly to the camera.

"This is Chelsea Willis at Lake Norman State Park for ABC News. Back to you, Dana."

Willis handed off to the anchor, warm and toasty behind her desk.

"According to Ranger Edy, the unidentified man died wearing work boots, a plaid shirt, and jeans," Dana Whoever said. "At this time, there is no indication of foul play. Anyone with information is encouraged to contact the Charlotte-Mecklenburg Police Department or the Mecklenburg County Medical Examiner's Office."

Both numbers appeared on a chyron at the bottom of the screen.

"Sonofafreakingbitch!"

That was over the line for the cat. Birdie jumped to the floor and departed the room.

Unable to stay still, I began to pace.

Why had Edy tipped ABC? Did the jackass hope to be a TV or internet star? Did he think he could score some coin? Who else had he phoned? What else had he leaked?

Edy took credit for discovering the body. Claimed he was trained in forensic anthropology.

"Jesus!"

He'd told ABC that the vic was in his forties. Six feet tall. Bullshit! I'd bet my life he was much shorter than that. Or had the journalist misread Edy's comments?

Either way, what damage might these potential inaccuracies cause?

The ol' Brennan temper had me crisscrossing the kitchen.

Enough!

I grabbed the phone and dialed Slidell.

He answered by saying he couldn't talk. I launched in anyway. Was cut off after two sentences.

Now what? Call Henry? Nguyen?

And tell them what? I'd allowed a former student to overhear confidential information?

Deep breath.

Another.

Calmer, I decided that shoveling snow might dissipate some of my anger. Properly jacketed, booted, and mittened, I ventured outside.

I saw no neighbors. No confused dogs. Not a single car turned in at Sharon Hall or passed by on the street. A block over, across Selwyn, muted laughter and squealing broke the stillness. Snowball wars were being fought on the Queens University campus.

I bent to work with a broad-bladed shovel, images tumbling inside my pom-beanie-warmed head. An hour and a half later all I'd produced was a partially clear porch and a path down the center of the walk leading to the drive. And a gallon of sweat.

But the physical exercise did help some. Still, I felt tense and out of sorts. Frustrated. Not in control.

Another character flaw. I'm a control freak. I can't rest until I've cracked a case, solved a puzzle, or fixed a problem. I told myself the privy head was no longer my concern. I'd done my job with Kwalwasser. I would finish analyzing the mummified remains as soon as the bones were cleaned.

Besides, neither case was urgent. Neither appeared to be a homicide.

On a cerebral level, I had to acknowledge that my arguments had logic.

So why that persistent whisper from down under? I couldn't shake the feeling that I was overlooking an important clue. Some tiny element that my subconscious was noting but my conscious self was missing.

A link between the cases? Slidell was adamant that none existed.

No harm in looking. I was trapped anyway. If I found something, I'd just have to convince Skinny.

Back in the annex, I re-filled my mug, a decidedly lousy idea, booted my Mac Air, and brought up five case files.

After opening a blank spreadsheet, I labeled the rows with names and the columns with descriptors. Then I clicked on MCME 210-22 and MCME 213-22, Veronica Kwalwasser's eyeball and head, and started entering data into the grid:

Sex: female
Age: forty-two
Ancestry: Caucasoid
DOD: August 18, 2020
COD: Natural/metastatic breast cancer
Body type: eyeball/severed head/no ME analysis of torso. Head stolen 2020 (probable date)
Body location: eyeball delivered to private home (mine), head dumped in privy (MiraVia), torso left at Happy Trails crematorium (later cremated)
Postmortem body treatment: head detached (manner unknown), left eye removed, right eye stabbed with paring knife
NOK: brother, Kenneth Kwalwasser

I recalled that Slidell had said the family was of Dutch origin. That Kwalwasser never married, had no kids, worked as a paralegal, and lived the last ten years of her life in Dillworth.

I added those facts, then moved on to MCME 356-19, and MCME 363-19, Miguel Sanchez's ear and body:

Sex: male
Age: nineteen
Ancestry: Dominican
DOD: December 24, 2019
COD: Homicide/exsanguination due to multiple stab wounds
Body type: ear/eviscerated body/liver, heart, kidneys missing

Body location: ear at Beacon Hill Apartments/body in dumpster behind Wendy's at Park Road Shopping Center

Postmortem body treatment: ear nailed to tree/body's abdomen opened, organs removed (not recovered)

NOK: mother, Maria Sanchez

I cruised through the old police dossier, added that Sanchez was Latino and in the drug trade, and that the murder was thought to be a SUR 13 hit.

I studied the grid. Slidell was right. A middle-aged white woman who'd resided in Dillworth and died of breast cancer. A Latino kid who'd lived in southeast Charlotte and been killed by a rival gang.

I began a new row. MCME 224-22. No reason except for that nagging voice:

Sex: male

Age: thirty-five to fifty

Ancestry:

DOD:

COD: suicide (?)/ligature strangulation by hanging

Body type: full corpse/mummified

Body location: Lake Norman State Park

Postmortem body treatment: none

NOK:

I had nothing else.

Again, I considered the grid. Kwalwasser and Sanchez lived far apart, on many levels. It was unlikely their paths had ever crossed. Kwalwasser died of natural causes. Sanchez was murdered. Sure, the two corpses were missing body parts, but what were the chances both were targeted by the same person? And why include the hanging man? He'd committed suicide. And was missing nothing.

Yet my subconscious kept hinting these cases were linked. Or was I misreading the messages?

I vowed to finish my analysis on the mummified remains. And to view the original police file and scene photos from Happy Trails.

Call Henry?

Why not? Slidell was obviously preoccupied.

She answered after three rings. "Detective Henry."

"Dr. Brennan, here."

"Oh." Flustered? "Sorry to go dark on you. I'm OOT."

"Hope it's somewhere nice." Assuming she meant out of town.

"We got a credible tip on a terrorist threat. LT sent me to Asheville."

"Lots of snow up there?"

"Shitbuckets."

"Listen, I'd like to get a look at the hard copy and scene pics from a 2019 homicide."

"An open case?"

"Yes. Sanchez, Miguel. Street name Scrappy." I gave her the police file number.

"Never hurts to take another look, eh? I'll call in, let them know what you want. By the way, I haven't forgotten your eyeball."

"Slidell briefed you on Kwalwasser?"

"Yes, ma'am."

"Anything new on your end?"

"A preference for burial over cremation."

"Stay on it. I caught a suicide that'll keep me busy for a while."

Ten minutes later the house phone rang.

The voice was one I'd never expected to hear again.

11

harles Anthony Hunt was a classmate at Myers Park High. He'd lettered in three sports. Of course, he had. His father, who was African American, played guard for the Celtics, later for the Bulls. His Italian mother was a champion downhill skier.

But Charlie was more than three-pointers and a pretty face. He'd led the debate team and served as president of the Young Democrats. Our senior yearbook predicted him as the grad most likely to be famous by thirty. I was voted most likely to do stand-up.

Following graduation, I'd left Charlotte for the University of Illinois, gone on to grad school at Northwestern, then married Pete. Charlie had attended Duke on a hoops scholarship, then UNC–Chapel Hill law. Over the years I'd heard that he'd married and was practicing up north. Then, following the tragic death of his wife, he'd relocated to Charlotte and taken a job as a public defender.

For clarification, I wasn't a total slouch in high school. Like Charlie, I played varsity tennis. He was all-state. I won most of my matches.

I'll admit. I found Charlie Hunt attractive. Everyone did. With his emerald eyes, curly black hair, and skin a pleasant combo of Africa and Italy, the guy was leading-man handsome.

Change was sweeping the South back at the "gray dawn" as Edy would have phrased it. Still, old mores die slowly. Charlie and I didn't date. But the Labor Day weekend before our collegiate departures, he and I swung a bit more than our rackets. The match involved tequila and the back of a Skylark.

To this day I blush recalling that episode. Embarrassment? Or? Never mind.

I recognized the voice immediately.

"Charlie Hunt?"

"The one and only. How are you, Tempe?"

"I'm good. How are *you*?"

"Excellent."

"Wow. Charlie." I knew I was babbling. Couldn't help myself. "How long has it been?"

"Years. Let's leave it at that."

"Let's. Are you still working at the public defender's office?"

"No, ma'am. In private practice now."

"I'm still doing my thing with bones." An expression he and I had loved to mock.

Charlie laughed. "I know. I've kept tabs."

Oh?

"Still living in the same townhouse?"

"I am. I think about you often, Tempe. Do you remember that time, when was it, Labor Day weekend, right before we both headed off to college?"

As if lying in wait, the memory cells fired a volley. Me in shorts and a tank with bling on the front, hair doing a flippy Farrah Fawcett number, upholstery stinging my sunburned back.

Alone in the kitchen, my cheeks flamed.

"Mm," I said.

During her period of "uncertainty," Katy had clerked at the public defender's office. For Charlie. Learning her boss was widowed, she'd tried fixing us up. Ryan and I were on the outs at the time, so Charlie and I had tried dating. Too much water under whatever. It hadn't worked out.

To change the subject, I started to brief Charlie on Katy's recent past and current status. He cut me off.

"I know. Katy's the reason I'm calling."

Was Charlie also keeping tabs on my daughter?

"Oh?"

"Your daughter is one impressive young lady."

I said nothing.

"She phoned me last week." Cadence suggesting he'd clicked into lawyer mode. "She explained her desire to start a charitable foundation and wanted to know if I could offer legal advice."

"Is that something you do?"

"If she's serious, my partner can definitely help her. But first I'd like to get a better feel for where her head's at." He paused, as if debating whether to expound. Didn't. "Could we have coffee, exchange a few thoughts?"

"Sure." Relieved that Charlie wasn't a stalker. Concerned that he'd detected something amiss with Katy.

"Great. I'll have my secretary get back to you with details as to when and where."

"Sounds like a plan."

"Stay home and off the roads."

"They're bad?"

"Unless you're driving a Zamboni. It won't last. The snow's already beginning to melt."

"And Charlotte has plows."

"We do?"

"I heard one."

"I'll be damned. Ciao."

"Ciao."

I sat a minute, bombarded by images from our high school years. Charlie in a tux at the senior prom, Sallie Banderman at his side. Charlie in math class, pencil-tapping his temple, deep in thought. Charlie on the cafeteria floor, sweaty and pale from a reaction to a cookie. Charlie flying high for his signature slam-dunk.

Mixed in with the oldies were a few more recent recollections. Charlie across the table at the Beef and Bottle, face more lined and a widower, but still lady-killer handsome.

Jesus. Enough.

What to do next?

I had to think about something other than Charles Hunt. Other than eyeballs and heads and mummies. Anything.

Grabbing a Terry Pratchett novel, I moved into the study. Birdie joined me on the couch and was soon snoring.

Though I tried, my brain refused to chill. I couldn't concentrate on happenings in the Discworld.

I ran through options. Found few. Agitated, I gave up on the wizards and returned to the kitchen. Booted my Mac and transferred the latest batches of pics from my phone.

The screen was offering a magnified image of the strange object I'd extracted from the hanging man's pocket when a fist pounded on the back door. I looked up, startled.

A hooded figure stood on my porch, tall and hunched, back turned toward the window. I rose and crossed to open the door.

My neighbor's glasses were fogged by breath rising from inside the non-tartan scarf wrapping his face. Bushy brows filled the space between the black frames and the lower edge of his tuque.

"Finlay has had another setback," Campbell launched, going right to full throttle.

"I'm sorry to hear that." Chilly as the air oozing through the gap between us.

"That abominable creature terrifies him."

"He can't see the turtle. It's buried in snow."

"He knows it's there. Don't you see?"

I didn't.

"We'd barely ventured out to build a snowman when Finlay started to cry. That's not right."

"No. It's not."

"He's a sensitive child."

He's a nutcase. Or you are.

"Have you secured the note from Finlay's doctor?" I asked.

"I will."

"I look forward to seeing it."

Firmly but quietly, I closed the door.

Thirty minutes later it happened again.

"Goddam it!" Glancing up, then sheepishly hurrying to open the door.

"Oh my god, Katy."

"You don't sound thrilled to see me."

"Campbell just came by."

"He still being a jackass?"

"That's not fair to donkeys. How did you get here?"

"I walked."

"Are you serious?"

"A few streets are cleared. Not many. But, hey, there's no such thing as bad weather, right?" We spoke the last sentence together. "Only improper clothing."

"Come in."

She stomped each foot to shake off the snow, then bent to unlace her boots.

"Want lunch?"

"Hell, yeah."

Katy's face was flushed from exertion and cold, her hair tousled from yanking off her hat. The mix of red and gold looked spectacular. As did her smile.

My heart soared to see it.

"Ham and cheese or tuna?" I asked.

"I have choices?" One corner of her mouth lifting slightly. "I'm stunned."

"I buy groceries." Faux offended.

"Once a year, whether they're needed or not."

"You're getting what you get, soldier."

"Former soldier." Indicating her civvie jeans and UVA sweatshirt.

As I assembled sandwiches, Katy took a chair at the table. Her drumming fingers suggested this wasn't an idle visit. She had something on her mind.

I set two placemats and centered a plate on each. Added napkins and went to the fridge for sodas.

When I sat, Katy checked the contents of her bread. "This is ham," she said. "I wanted tuna."

One of my fingers saluted her proudly.

We ate in congenial silence. She got to it when we'd finished.

"Listen, I'm sorry about last night." Eyes avoiding mine. "I acted mental."

"It's all right." Not disagreeing.

"No, it's not. You were helping me, and I was bitchy."

"Want some fruit?"

"No, thanks."

I took a banana from the basket I'd displaced to one side. Peeled it.

"Preparing for the apocalypse?" Katy asked, idly observing my laptop.

"What does that mean?"

"Armageddon. The end of life as we know it." Waggling splayed fingers.

"I know what apocalypse means. I don't understand your question."

"The firestarter." Cocking her chin at the screen.

"Hold on." I pointed at the image. "That little thing is a firestarter?"

She nodded. "Are you compiling a kit?"

"A kit?"

"A survivalist kit." The green eyes rolled. "Jesus, Mom. I was asking if you're becoming a prepper."

"Let's back up. That's a firestarter?"

Katy nodded.

"How does it work?"

She pointed to the cylinder. "That's a ferro rod." The flat piece. "That's a multifunction tool. You use the ruled edge to measure stuff, calculate scale on maps, that sort of thing. The cutout is a hexagonal box wrench. It'll also remove bottle caps. The serrated end is for making tinder shavings from sticks."

"Then you scrape the rod to ignite the shavings."

"Roger that."

"Who owns these things?" I asked.

"Campers, preppers."

"What's a prepper?"

"Really?"

I circled a wrist. Go on.

"A person who prepares for a major disaster or cataclysm."

"Like what?"

"War, worldwide economic collapse, global epidemic, the zombie uprising, you name it. Doomsday preppers gather materials into kits to survive the end of the world. Some create entire locations."

"Underground bunkers?"

"Maybe."

I sat back, wondering if MCME 224-22 might have been a prepper.

"What's the deal on this?" Katy asked, again indicating the firestarter.

I briefed her on the hanging man.

"Any chance you can read the logo on the handle?" I asked.

Annoyingly, she did not need to lean closer to the screen. Or zoom the image.

"COS."

Our eyes met. She shrugged. I shrugged.

"A survivalist outfitter?" she suggested.

"Let's give it a go."

I swiveled the Mac to face me and googled COS. Got links to a company offering contemporary design in women's clothing, College of the Sequoias, and a zillion office supply outfits.

"Add the keyword survivalist."

I did.

Got links to wilderness survival programs all over the country. Several to Edward Michael Grylls.

"Who's—" I started to ask.

"Bear Grylls?" Sounding incredulous at this gap in my knowledge. "You need to get out more, Mom."

Ignoring that, I added North Carolina to my search parameters.

Katy and I cruised the Google offerings. Lots of action in the Blue Ridge Mountains, in the western part of the state.

We saw the link simultaneously. I clicked over to the website.

"Fucking A," Katy said.

Wordlessly, I picked up the phone.

12

Cougar's Outdoor Survival
The end of the world is coming!
Be prepared for natural and man-made disasters
Learn to survive mass carnage, looting, and chaos
Master the skills needed to save yourself and your family

I read the web page opener to Slidell. Explained how we'd made the connection via the firestarter.

"The guy's name is Cougar Piccitelli," I added. "He operates a survivalist camp in Gaston County."

"What the hell's a survivalist camp?"

"Preppers."

"What the hell are preppers?"

"Think about what I just read to you. Or google it. Piccitelli's camp is near High Shoals. Which isn't far from Lake Norman."

"I know where High Shoals is."

Bully for you.

"You're thinking this Piccitelli could be the hanging vic?"

"Yes."

"You say the guy was dangling for years. How's the website still running?"

"Maybe there's new ownership but they kept the same name."

As expected, Slidell had a long list of reasons why the visit had to wait a day. Topping it was the road conditions. I hated having to admit he was right.

We made plans for the morning, then disconnected.

WEDNESDAY, FEBRUARY 9

Slidell picked me up at eight. By then, the temperature had clawed to within grasping distance of 32 degrees F. Still, getting to High Shoals was frustratingly slow.

Somehow, Skinny had managed to finagle a CMPD ride, a Ford Explorer, probably using his violent crimes/cold case creds. Guess he didn't want to endanger his precious 4Runner.

As Slidell maneuvered around plow-mounded snow and the mishaps of drivers unaware of the concept of pumping the brakes, I rode shotgun. Gazing out the window, I took in the overburdened trees and bushes, some bent almost to the breaking point. The dripping gutters and downspouts. The meltwater-darkened streets and sidewalks. Not many takers for either of those, pedestrian or wheeled.

Waiting out the light at Randolph Road, I watched the drivers of a Corvette and an Optima argue beside their accordioned vehicles, breath billowing from their mouths in small white clouds. Corvette was a chunky dude wearing enough leather to upholster a sofa. Optima was a white-haired woman with earmuffs and a red wool coat hanging to her boot tops. My sympathy lay with the Kia lady.

Slidell took I-85 west, then 321 north, eventually turned onto a two-lane winding through pine forest.

Silent the whole trip, Skinny now turned to me.

"Remind me of the exact name of the place."

"Cougar's Outdoor Survival."

"It don't come up on my navigation."

"I'm guessing Cougar's not a hospitable guy. Did you run a background check on him or the camp?"

"Of course I did. The guy's got no sheet and I came up empty on a photo search. There's no record of a 911 or complaint about the camp. Hospitable or not, the asshole better be flying his welcome flag today."

"The kid at the gas station said it's along here." Despite Skinny's protests, I'd insisted on stopping.

"Yeah. That yak won't be opening no acceptance letter from Yale."

We went slowly, watching for the gravel road and swinging gate mentioned by the yak. Spotted the landmarks five minutes later. Slidell made the turn.

We both lowered our windows. Assessed, ears alert, eyes scanning.

A chain secured one end of the gate's horizontal iron pole to one of two vertical uprights anchoring barbed wire running to the left and right. A sign hung from the pole's center: *Keep Out. Trespassers will be shot. Survivors will be shot again.* The artwork consisted of a capped figure holding a long gun.

Mounted high on a tree was a single security camera. I glanced toward Slidell. He'd spotted it, too.

I saw no one. Heard nothing but the soft drip of reluctantly yielding snow.

Slidell got out and strode to the gate. I noticed he was carrying heavy.

When Slidell yanked the chain, the links slid free in his hand. So much for tight security. He kicked the barrier. It swung inward with a harsh grating sound.

We both froze.

No salivating dog rushed forward. No gorilla with a twelve-gauge emerged from the woods.

Slidell retook the wheel and we crept forward. Fifty yards farther, a man cradling an AK-47 blocked the road. He wore head-to-toe camo and, beneath his unzipped parka, a black tee that said: *A gun in the hand is better than a cop on the phone.* Scruffy beard. Skin once fair, now looking like decades spent in the Kalahari. Acre-wide chest providing plenty of room for the tee's slogan.

In a clearing beyond AK, I could see crudely built lean-tos, a rock-bordered firepit surrounded by stumps, one large yellow tent, and what looked like a small corral. Except for the assault rifle, the setup reminded me of the pioneer unit at Camp Pinewood.

AK raised a hand, palm out. It was not a friendly hand.

Slidell rolled to a stop.

"That's as far as you go, pal."

"And you would be?"

"None of your fucking business."

"Police." Slidell said. "I'm gonna raise my badge now, real slow."

I doubted AK would be impressed.

Slidell held his shield out the window.

Never lowering his firearm, AK took a step closer and glanced at the shield for half a heartbeat. "You got a warrant?"

"Do I need a warrant?"

"You're treading on private property. Got it posted, real clear."

"We're here about a guy named Cougar Piccitelli. You must know him, this being *his* posted property."

AK looked startled. Or not. Hard to tell with the low-brimmed cap and all the facial hair.

"What do you want with him?" AK was nervous, his finger jittery on the trigger.

"Mainly, we want to know if he's still breathing." Slidell's voice was getting that edge.

"What the fuck?"

"Last week, a stiff turned up over in the state park. We got reason to believe it could be Piccitelli."

"What makes you think it's him?"

Slidell cocked his chin from the envelope in my lap toward the man in the road. I withdrew the firestarter and held it up.

Now AK looked surprised. And puzzled. "Yeah? So?"

"The man had this in his pants," I said.

"Big fucking deal. We give those to everyone who takes the course."

"We?" Slidell asked.

Realizing his mistake, AK scowled.

"You work here?"

"I work for no man."

"That would make you Cougar Piccitelli?"

Sullen nod.

"So, this little entrepreneurial triumph is yours?" Slidell's gesture took in the gate, the barbed wire, the woods.

Not wanting to antagonize Piccitelli further, I leaned my head out the window. "Is there any way to trace the owner of this?" I asked, dangling the firestarter by its lanyard.

Piccitelli crossed to me. "Lemme see it."

I held the firestarter out. Piccitelli took it. He was relaxing somewhat, realizing that he and his camp weren't the focus of the inquiry, that our visit had to do with a corpse in a park. A corpse that wasn't his.

Tossing the firestarter back—I made the catch—Piccitelli shook his head no.

"OK," Slidell said. "Let's take a run at it this way. Our vic was short, had a knob on his head the size of a bowling ball, and maybe walked with a limp. That ring any bells?"

Something flicked in Piccitelli's eyes, then was gone. He didn't respond.

"I'm sure this man's family is wondering where he is," I said.

"The fella hung himself?"

"Yes."

A beat, then, "Frank Boldonado."

"Boldonado fits that description?" I asked, wanting to be sure I understood.

Piccitelli nodded.

"What can you tell us about him."

"Can't tell you jack shit. He came here once for the course. Never saw him again."

"When was that?" I asked.

"Hell if I know. Three, four years ago?"

"You got contact info?" Slidell barked.

Piccitelli's frown held.

"Do you know how Mr. Boldonado found you?" I asked.

"He hangs with a guy named Bobby Karl Smith, or used to."

Slidell looked at him hard, probably wondering the same thing I was. Could Piccitelli be lying to get rid of us, or were these people real?

"Who's Bobby Karl Smith?"

"A real piece of work."

"Meaning?" Slidell snapped.

"Mean as a snake."

"Smith also attended your little play school?"

"More than once. The guy's hard-core. Enrolls in camps all over the country."

"What's Smith look like?"

"A snake."

"We could have this little chat at the station."

For a very long moment the two scowled at each other. Piccitelli broke first.

"Smith's got a scar running his jaw."

"Tall? Short?"

"Tall enough."

"That it?"

"The guy lost his eye to an IED."

"Does he wear a glass eye? A patch?" I asked.

"Nope. Lets it all hang out."

"Smith a vet?" Slidell asked.

"Yeah. A bitter one."

"When's the last time you saw Boldonado?"

"I don't keep a calendar."

"Smith?"

"Same answer."

Slidell glared. Piccitelli glared back. So did the AK.

"Do you know how we can find Mr. Smith?" I asked.

Lifting one hand from the AK, Piccitelli gestured toward the two-lane at our backs. "Keep on keeping on," he said. "When you come to a *Y*, split right. About a quarter mile more, you'll see a dirt road cutting downhill on the left."

"Smith lives there?" Slidell snapped.

Piccitelli glared again. He was very good at it.

"Can we expect other company?"

Piccitelli shrugged.

"Don't plan no trips," Slidell said, tossing out the old cliché. With that, he threw the SUV into reverse and gunned backward, spewing mud and gravel onto the shape-changing patches of snow.

"What do you think?" I asked when we were once again on the blacktop.

Slidell snorted. "Real affable guy."

"Think he's on the level?"

"Or maybe he's busting his balls laughing at us right now."

That was it for conversation until we'd made the split, then the turn.

Piccitelli wasn't kidding. The road, if it even qualified as one, dropped at about a thirty-degree angle, two frozen tire tracks running the center of a strip of grudgingly softening mud.

Lurching slowly downhill, vegetation scraping both sides of the Explorer, Slidell spoke without turning to me.

"Stay alert."

"Always." Then, "Why?"

"I got a bad feeling."

"Sounds like Boldonado fits the profile for the hanging man."

"I don't like these pricks."

I was about to query which pricks when Slidell hit the brakes so hard I had to brace on the dash.

Just ahead, the road rose a few degrees, then dropped even more abruptly. We both studied the bizarre sight in the small valley below.

To the left was a partially filled pit. To the right was an enormous mound of soil. Sloping at the sides, square at the corners, and flat on top, the hillock looked like a smaller version of Cahokia Mounds, a burial site in Illinois where I'd worked as a grad student.

Unlike the pre-Columbian ceremonial structure I'd excavated, this mound had been created with a backhoe. Conical bumps from individual front loader bucket dumps rippled its surface. A raw wound, suggesting ongoing pirating of soil, gouged its southeastern corner.

The sequence of events was clear. A hole had been dug; the dirt heaped nearby. Now the heap was being mined to re-fill the hole.

It was the open half of the pit that riveted my attention. More accurately, its contents.

Placed deep enough to eventually be buried by a thick layer of soil, maybe four meters below ground level, were two bright yellow buses parked side by side.

"What the fuck?!" I was with Slidell on that.

"They're school buses," I said.

"No shit. But why?"

"To provide living space following a doomsday event."

I was recalling an article I'd read the day before while studying up on preppers. A story about a survivalist in Ontario who'd buried forty-two buses. Over the decades, the man had outfitted his underground compound with LED lighting, food, tools, even a dental office.

"This is some messed-up shit," Slidell said.

"Piccitelli said Smith was hard-core."

"If Smith and his pal Boldonado are so hot to survive, why would one off himself?"

Excellent question, Skinny.

"Based on size, it looks like Smith dug the pit, then buried four buses," I said. "He's positioned another pair and is planning on two more."

"Why not grab any old crate?"

"I believe school buses are required to have extra reinforcement in case of a rollover."

"Safety first."

Neither of us laughed.

We both considered the layout again. The buried buses. Flattened rectangles to either side of the mound, probably parking areas. A crude enclosure constructed of logs. Deer carcasses hanging from trees. Here and there, a footpath straggled into the trees.

The forest ringing the little valley was interrupted at only two points. One was the road we were on. The other, a break across the clearing, looked large enough to access heavy equipment.

There wasn't a living thing in sight.

Slidell eased down the hill and drove to the edge of the pit.

"Here's how we're gonna play this," he said, opening his door. "You stay in the car."

"Not happening."

Slidell twisted to face me. "Christ on a cracker! For once, just once, will you do as I say?"

Taken aback by his vehemence, I didn't protest.

Irritated, I watched Slidell stride to the pit and disappear down a set of makeshift stairs. A full minute passed. Two.

I was debating a move to join Skinny when I caught motion in my peripheral vision.

Glancing sideways, I saw a hooded figure running toward the woods, head bent, legs pumping hard. Perhaps sensing eyes on its back, the figure turned its head.

For an instant a terrified gaze met mine.

Without thinking, I flew from the car and gave chase.

13

Winter is a mean bitch.

Unprepared for the icy ground, I almost face-planted. Whatever-planted.

Pinwheeling to regain my balance, I struggled to keep my eyes glued to the spot where the figure had vanished. If I lost sight of the thin gray sliver, I knew I might never find it again.

Cursing the lack of tread on my boots, I pounded across the valley, alternately sinking into mud and skidding on ice. At the break, I veered into the woods.

The temperature dropped and the world dimmed. The trees around me—mostly loblolly pine and, high up, still laden with snow—blocked what little daylight was managing to peek through the clouds.

I halted, listening, scanning. Panting.

I heard no thundering boots. Saw no hooded figure lurking behind a tall trunk.

Scrambling onto a fallen tree, grasping a nearby branch for stability, I raised up on tiptoes for a better view.

The figure was nowhere to be seen. Not surprising. He had home-court advantage and had used it well.

Was it Smith? If so, why had he run? If not Smith, then who?

Above me, a bird trilled some avian warning. Or maybe he'd spotted a buddy.

Suddenly, twenty yards up, I made out an elbow or shoulder disrupting the outline of the bark shielding it.

Sudden thought. Could the guy be armed? Was he waiting for me to present an easier shot?

Screw it.

I jumped down and, using trees for cover, wove forward, trying to keep my quarry in sight. That proved impossible. Setting a course toward the place where I'd last seen him, I followed the path of least resistance through the brambles.

I'd gone almost fifty yards when a mittened hand wrapped my face from behind. My hair was yanked down sharply, and my jaw shot skyward. Something popped in my neck.

The hand reeled me in. I heard heavy breathing close to my ear. Took in a skunky smell, like sweat and rancid fat.

My heart raced and blood pounded in my ears.

The hand let go. Another joined it and both shoved violently on my back. I threw my arms out to break my fall, but the downward momentum was too great. I hit a rock, scraping my cheek and forehead and rattling my brain. Black spots danced in my vision.

As I attempted to push up, a boot slammed my spine, sending me flat once more. I could see only pine needles and breathe their scent and dust.

Eyes watering, I rolled to my side and again tried rising onto all fours.

Another pile-driving kick sent me back into the needles. Air exploded from my mouth. I struggled to turn my head. To breathe.

Finally, I managed to sit up. All was quiet. I was alone.

Minutes passed as my paralyzed lungs relaxed.

I gulped oxygen.

When I got back to the bunker, Slidell was still inside the first bus. Hearing my footsteps, he turned, prepared to lambast me for leaving the car. Stunned, he paused to look me over. To take in my bleeding cheek and chin and one swollen eye.

Instead of bellowing, Slidell tugged a hanky from his pocket and gestured at my face. Hand still shaky, I reached for his offering. Locating a reasonably clean section, I folded the dingy square of polyester and held it against the abrasions.

"You OK?" Casually shifting to block a doorway leading into the next bus.

I nodded.

"What the fuck happened?"

I explained my little romp in the woods.

"Any idea who?"

"No."

"Smith ain't here."

"Is anyone?"

"No."

Why wasn't Slidell chastising me?

"It was probably one of these fuckwad preppers who scrambled you."

"Whoever was in the woods knows his way around here," I said. "But why would he run? Attack me?"

Slidell shrugged a beefy shoulder.

"Don't look like anyone actually lives in this dump," Slidell said, feet spread, arms crossed on his chest. "I'm guessing you're right and this is some sorta safe house for the end of the world."

"Did you find anything to suggest a potential suicide?" I readjusted the cloth on my cheek, refusing to host thoughts of the microorganisms calling it home.

"Whose suicide?"

"This Boldonado guy."

Slidell's nonresponse came too quickly. "Let's get you to some first aid."

"What's up, Detective?" Raising both my brows. Which hurt.

"What?" Defensive.

"Whatever you're not telling me."

"It's nothing you need to worry about. I took pics."

"You don't have a warrant."

"I got an unnamed dead guy and a wit that ties him to this place."

I wasn't sure of the legality of Slidell's reasoning but didn't pursue it.

"Show me what you're blocking."

"Goddammit, Brennan. Can't you ever—"

"Show me." Daring him to refuse with my one good eye.

Muttering some imaginative profanity, Slidell pivoted and crossed a platform leading into the next bus. I followed.

Like the first, the second bus had two bare bulbs hanging by cords from the roof, jointly providing about two watts of light. The windows were boarded over, the rounded sides outfitted with shelving on the right and a long work counter on the left. The shelving held rolled sleeping bags, collapsible chairs, burner stoves, Coleman lanterns, and an assortment of items about whose functions I was clueless.

Unlike the first, this bus had a jerry-rigged desk spanning most of the width of its rear end. The crude arrangement consisted of a thick piece of plywood balanced across a pair of sawhorses. A metal swivel chair sat between the sawhorses, a torn bed pillow cushioning its seat.

On the desk, a small monitor projected a live video feed from a camera somewhere high up outside. Behind the desk, a large bulletin board stood layered with paper.

"Smith must have seen us pull up," Slidell said.

"If it *was* Smith."

"Whatever. Asshole could've capped us the second we got out of the car."

Slidell left the next thought unsaid. And I, like a moron, had chased an unknown person into the woods while unarmed.

My face throbbed and my digits had grown numb from the cold. Ignoring the pain and incipient frostbite, I walked to the desk and began perusing the bulletin board. Thumbtacked to it were dozens of news articles, some clipped originals, some photocopies.

I stepped to the right. As I skimmed headlines, the tiny hairs on my neck tingled.

Some names I knew. We all knew. Edmund Kemper. Jeffrey Dahmer. John Wayne Gacy. Ted Bundy. Wayne Williams. Charles Manson. Gary Ridgway. Others were less famous. Ronald Dominique. Patrick Kearney. John Norman Chapman. The theme was frighteningly clear.

"Jesus." I swallowed. "He collects stories about serial killers."

Slidell said nothing.

"Maybe he's some sort of weird hobbyist," I said, not really believing it.

"Or could be he's researching for his master's thesis."

"And you accuse me of trying to be funny?"

I moved to the left side of the montage. This mix was more diverse and included murder in all its glory. A boy kidnapped and buried alive in Newport, Rhode Island. A co-ed raped and killed leaving a party in Austin, Texas. A family slaughtered in Durham, North Carolina. Solo players were featured, both modern and historic. Lizzie Borden. Drew Peterson. Andrea Yates. Casey Anthony. Robert Durst. Susan Smith. OJ. Some pairs. Bonnie Parker and Clyde Barrow. Leopold and Loeb. Erik and Lyle Menendez.

"Jesus Christ!"

"Don't have a thrombo."

Even in my outrage, the irony didn't escape me. Normally I'd be saying that to Skinny.

I sensed Slidell cross to stand by my side. Felt his eyes on my face.

Deciding I wasn't about to keel over, or simply drained of patience, Skinny yanked his black L.L.Bean gloves tight onto his hands and stomped from the bus.

I stood staring at the ominous display.

The ride home was as anticipated.

Slidell castigated me for not following orders. I replied that I wasn't a cop. He preached about taking unnecessary risks. I said I was a big girl. He insisted I visit an ER. I refused. He commented on deficiencies in my personality. I thanked him for sharing his disappointment. The discourse made the Israeli-Palestinian peace talks look like parlor games.

At home, Birdie's reproachful stare was not what I needed.

After cleaning my face with wet cotton balls, I showered and applied antiseptic. Both stung like hell. Next, I downed a barely heated can of Campbell's tomato soup and followed that with two Advil. Then I climbed to the bedroom and closed the shutters.

I tried Katy's number. Got voice mail.

Switching my iPhone to silent mode, I crawled into bed.

14

I slept the rest of that day and night and late into the next morning. Birdie managed to break through at eight-fifteen. I went straight to the bathroom mirror. My face had crusted over and my right eye looked like fruit going bad. Great.

Also, if I turned my head too sharply, pain shot from the base to the crown of my skull. More Advil and a coffee chaser helped some. Or maybe it was the bagel with blueberry cream cheese.

A glance out the window revealed sunshine and a melting world. That was good news.

I left the annex at nine and twenty minutes later was at the MCME. As I passed Mrs. Flowers, she warbled that Detective Slidell had phoned. Glancing up and seeing my face, her eyebrows rose, and her mouth reshaped into a perfect *O.* I kept moving.

My computer screen showed that two requisition forms had landed in my in-box. Ignoring them, I phoned Hawkins's extension to ask about MCME 224-22.

The hanging man's bones still weren't ready.

"When?" I asked.

"Soon," Hawkins said.

"Why is it taking so long?"

"Had to get prints. Mummies are tough."

"Fair enough."

Next, I dialed a number at the violent crimes unit.

"Detective Henry."

"Tempe Brennan here."

"Wowza. How *are* you, Doc?"

"Peachy," I said.

"I figured you'd take a couple days off."

Great. Henry knew about yesterday. That meant everyone did.

"It was no big deal. Free dermabrasion."

"Ha! Good one. Detective Slidell said you looked like—"

"Did he tell you to run the guy who buried the buses? Bobby Karl Smith. Looks like he's a prepper."

"Yes. And I did. Nothing popped."

"Nothing?"

"Zip."

"Find out who owns the property. Track the buses. Where they were purchased, who—"

"I'm on all that. Not sure why he wants it. I guess he thinks Smith's the douchecanoe who cracked you in the noggin?"

"Mmm."

"You figure this Boldonado's your hanging dude?"

"It's a possibility."

"As soon as Hawkins shoots me the prints, I'll run them through AFIS." She referred to the Automated Fingerprint Identification System database."

"Keep me looped in."

"Roger that."

After disconnecting, I checked my mobile for missed calls. Slidell had phoned at seven-forty, again at eight. Left no message either time.

That made three calls, two to my cell, one to the switchboard.

I sat a moment, fingers massaging the sides of my noggin, resisting the urge to poke at my cheek. Then I opened and read the requests.

Two pathologists needed anthro expertise. The first case, MCME 239-22, was in the morgue. I read the synopsis twice, not believing the story the first time through.

The facts were as follows:

A woman in Mount Holly was struck by a falling object while wrapping burlap around shrubs in her yard. The object was a small sack. The woman opened the sack. Inside were charred bone fragments and other debris. The woman called the police. The police traced the sack to a crematorium offering aerial scattering over the locale of your choice.

Winds were erratic on the day of the shrub wrapping. Up above, as the plane's hatch opened to release the contents of the about-to-be-untied sack, the aircraft was caught in a sudden updraft. The sack slipped from the grip of the person holding it, and the dearly departed plummeted to earth.

The family was not happy, and litigation loomed.

The remains were human, so the Mount Holly cops had sent them to the MCME.

I was to verify that the loved one was inside the sack. And alone. As stipulated by contract.

I love my job. New day, new adventure.

The second case, MCME 237-22, had come from Burke County, and sat under plastic sheeting on the counter behind me. Which occasionally happens if animal remains are suspected and no odor threatens.

This synopsis was short and meticulously uninformative: bucket with suspicious contents.

I peeked under the plastic. Yup. One bucket. I was about to take a closer look when Slidell thundered through the door.

"Where the goddam hell have you been—"

"Good morning, Detective."

"You look like crap."

"Thank you."

"That hurt?" Cocking his chin in the general direction of my face.

"Not at all." Smiling. Which was painful.

"I'm going to get the cocksucker. When I do, he'll wish his mama had died in preschool."

"Please sit down." Craning up at Skinny was killing my neck.

Slidell sat. Unbuttoned his jacket. Which was puke green with something brown going on in the weave. Loosened his collar and what passed for a knot on his tie. No guess on the color there.

"This Smith is a nutjob," Slidell began. "He had fucking carcasses dangling from trees."

"He's a prepper."

"Just a prepper, eh? What about that archive on serial killers? Howdy doody! Slaughter and carnage!"

"The man seems to have an interest in true crime."

"Seems to?"

"I appreciate you looking into Boldonado and Smith," I said.

"Eeeh." Flapping a hand at my face. "What's *your* thinking on that?"

"Whoever knocked me down undoubtedly saw me as an intruder."

"That was one jackass move."

"What have you learned about Boldonado?" I asked, anxious to change the subject.

"Piccitelli's lead looks solid. I found an MP report from 2019. Profile fits. White male, forty-nine, five-foot-four. Hawkins is sending Henry prints he lifted off the corpse."

"Who filed the report?"

"Angelina Boldonado. Frank's gramma."

"Oh?"

"Apparently Boldonado was in the habit of taking the old lady to Mass every week, him being her only living relative. One Sunday little

Frankie stopped showing up or answering his phone. Grannie gave it a month, then filed the report."

"Did you interview Angelina?"

"She died last year."

My phone rang. I ignored it.

"You say Smith's a nutjob. Do you think he could have dropped the eyeball on my porch?"

"That seems a stretch. What's his connection to you?"

"He clipped and saved articles about murder. I often work murder cases. Those cases often make the news."

A moment of very tense silence crammed the small office. Then I posed the same question my subconscious had been forcing on me.

"Do you see any connection among Sanchez, Kwalwasser, and Boldonado?"

"Yeah. They're all dead."

"Shrewd."

"You got any idea who this prick eyeball fairy could be?"

"I'm confused. Is Smith the cocksucker and the eyeball fairy is the jackass-prick?" I knew better than to goad when Slidell was in outrage mode. But his blasé attitude was pissing me off.

Slidell pushed to his feet.

"You're going through the pics you took inside the buses?" I asked.

"Me and Henry. Keeps the dimwit outta my hair."

"Would you like help?"

"I got it covered." Slidell strode toward the door. Turned. "And I better not get word you've gone cowboy and—"

"Hee-haw," I said.

"Jesus Christ. How about you stick to what you do and let me catch the bad guys?"

"Is Smith?" I asked.

"Is Smith what?"

"A bad guy."

Slidell stormed out grumbling comments I was mercifully spared.

I sat a moment, head throbbing, ants crawling under my skin. Knowing Skinny was right about the stupidity of me chasing a stranger into the woods.

As usual, when frustrated, I couldn't sit still.

I glanced at the request form on my screen. The bucket on my counter.

I pictured the hanging man. Boldonado?

Screw it.

Dropping into my chair, I dialed a Montreal area code.

"Laboratoire de Sciences Judiciaires et de Médecine Légale," a robotic voice said.

"Célia Quintal, *s'il vous plaît.*"

"*Qui appelle?*" Who's calling?

I told her.

"*Un instant, s'il vous plaît.*" One moment, please.

The line went hollow. Waiting for the connection, I pictured the *T*-shaped Édifice Wilfrid-Derome, the LSJML, my twelfth-floor lab with its view of the city and St. Lawrence River, my empty desk.

Ryan.

Why had Ryan gone silent?

Before I could launch a self-pity party, Quintal picked up.

"Tempe. How lovely." Thickly accented English. "Have you returned to Québec?"

"Soon," I said.

"*Bon.* To what do I owe this long-distance pleasure?"

"I have a knotty problem," I began, knowing Célia had heard that one ad nauseam.

"Amusing," she said in a tone that suggested it wasn't. "How can I help?"

"Aren't you researching the differences between knots in suicide and homicide deaths?"

"*Mais, oui.* My colleagues and I are developing a checklist of characteristics to aid in distinguishing between the two."

"I'm interested in learning about neck ligatures," I said. "Do you have something in print?"

"Sadly, our publication is still in the works."

Damn.

"Can you quickly run me through the major points?"

"But of course."

I grabbed a tablet and pen.

"We should start with some basic terminology."

I had a feeling I was about to learn much more than I needed to know about knots.

"Most people who tie knots produce ordinary configurations like the overhand and its variants, the half-hitch and half-knot, which have *S* and *Z* mirror images. These are called chiral knots. That just means mirror-image knots."

Why not just call them that? I didn't say it.

"The *S* variety is more common and is weakly associated with right-handedness."

I jotted that down.

"Some knots, like the overhand and half-hitch, are tied with one working end. That's called a wend. The knots typically seen on parcels usually incorporate two or more components called half-knots. Half-knots require the person making them to work two wends simultaneously. Are you with me?"

"Yes."

"Tying two half-knots produces one of the four cardinal knots. *S/S* and *Z/Z* granny knots, *S/Z* and *Z/S* reef knots. Would you like me to explain chirality consistency among tiers?"

"I'm really interested in homicides versus suicides in hanging deaths."

"*Bon*. First off, let me say that hanging is much less common in homicides."

"Tough to pull off with the victim wriggling and all."

"*Pardon?*"

"Never mind."

"Most hanging suicides involve either partial or total suspension."

"Partial is definitely not the situation with my case," I said.

"Double neck ligatures are involved slightly more frequently in homicides than in suicides. A single ligature and a single neck wrap are present in most of the latter. Sliding knots, like slip knots, occur more frequently, and suicides usually have a single-factor knot.

"Fixed, or immovable, knots are more prevalent with homicides, and the knot is more frequently positioned at the back of the neck. In suicides, the knot is more frequently in front or at one side."

Quintal sounded like she was cherry-picking relevant data while skimming.

"In the homicide cases that I observed, the ligature was tight, usually smaller than the circumference of the victim's neck and often deeply embedded in the soft tissue. Suicides were more frequently characterized by loose ligatures and an inverted *V* mark in the neck tissue at the point of suspension."

"Let me summarize," I ventured, wanting to be sure I understood. And to move this along. "In suicides by hanging there's usually only one neck wrap, the ligature is loose and may leave a *V*-shaped mark, the knot is usually one factor, sliding, and less frequently placed in back."

"*Tres bon, madame.* But keep in mind, our sample wasn't large, and the differences we observed were not statistically significant. These are very rough guidelines."

"Thank you so much. This has been enormously helpful." Maybe.

"I'd be happy to view images, should you wish to transmit them."

"I may do just that."

I was opening the hanging man's file when Nguyen appeared at my office door.

"Oh, my!" she said upon seeing my bruises and abrasions.

"Just a wee mishap. I'm fine."

Nguyen didn't press. Which I appreciated. "I trust you've found the latest requests."

"Yes."

"The bucket is not urgent. But the Mount Holly police officer has rung me twice."

"That case was just logged in yesterday."

"Officer Condor is a very impatient man."

"That's his name?" Fighting back a smile.

Nguyen nodded.

"Then he should allow us at least six days."

"I don't understand."

"It's a book title. I'll head over to look at Condor's cremains now."

That's not what happened.

1 5

The sack was lavender. Stitched onto the silk were the words *Until we meet again*. Seemed more in line with a Happy Trails pitch, but who am I to judge.

I typed all relevant data into a case form. The decedent's name was Edgar Seymour Stokely. He'd died of prostate cancer at age seventy-two.

"Paperwork" completed, I poured the contents of the sack onto the plastic-backed sheeting I'd spread across the autopsy table. There wasn't much to pour.

The cremation process is quite thorough. A cremator—a high-energy furnace fueled by propane gas—reaches a temperature of 1800 degrees F. Which is damn hot. After burning, the bone fragments that remain are allowed to cool, then magnetically scanned to extract metals, things like melted bits of dental restorations or appliances, surgical implants, or casket hardware. Following scanning, the fragments are ground into what looks like gray or white sand.

I once had a client who expected actual ashes and, upon finding the grainy material, suspected she'd been scammed by her husband's family. She'd asked me to determine if the cremains they'd given her were, in fact, kitty litter. They weren't. Hubby was in there.

On average, human cremains weigh about five pounds. Due to greater bone density, those of men may weigh slightly more than those of women. Cremains equal roughly 3.5 percent of one's body weight in life.

Everything looked good for Edgar. Except for the cancer, of course.

I was wrapping up when Mrs. Flowers rang to say that Detective Henry was at reception. I told her to pass along that I'd be there in ten.

My office has a window. I consider that one of the triumphs of my career. Throughout my tenure at the previous facility, I'd had none. I'd camouflaged the unbroken walls with a pair of blowups, one a street scene in Old Montreal, the other a wide-angle shot of the dunes and Atlantic Ocean on Isle of Palms. I'd captured each image by shooting through an open window. Crafty.

I was surprised to find Henry in my office. She wasn't admiring my precious view but studying a picture lifted from my desk. Katy and Charlie Hunt at some social function years back.

Hearing my footsteps, Henry turned.

"Holy shit, your face. Does it hurt?"

"No." It did.

"Good." Wagging the framed photo in her hand. "Is this your daughter?"

"It is."

"She looks heavy-duty. What does she do?"

Heavy-duty? "Katy is just out of the army, temporarily volunteering at a homeless shelter."

"You two look so much alike. Who's the studly fella next to her?"

"Charlie Hunt. Post-college, my daughter worked for him at the Public Defender's Office."

"The dude looks smoking *hot.*"

"He's an old friend." Inexplicably, I was finding Henry's comments annoying. Maybe her tone.

Henry sensed my irritation.

"Sorry, Doc." Gently replacing the photo. "Touching your stuff was over the line."

"Not at all. I'm a little off today."

"I get it. Have you seen a doctor? Did you need stitches?"

"What can I do for you, Detective?" As I circled my desk.

"There I go again." Tight shake of the head. "Sometimes I suck at boundaries. But I do recognize that I suck."

I indicated that Henry should sit. She took the chair facing me. Today she wore a cropped black leather jacket over a red silk blouse.

"Kwalwasser's going nowhere, and things are quiet, maybe because of the friggin' cold, so I asked if I could help Detective Slidell with the suicide and the bus sitch. The guy's a legend. My LT was good with it."

Skinny?

"Any news on Frank Boldonado?" I asked.

"When I leave here, I'll run the hanging dude's prints. If Boldonado's in the system, easy peasy. If not, I'll pay Cougar Piccitelli a visit to see what else he knows about Smith or the B-man."

I raised both brows.

"Boldonado. For what it's worth, my gut says these guys are just two more creepoid preppers."

"Why would Smith run from Slidell and me?"

"Preppers aren't fond of unannounced company."

"Have you seen Slidell's pics from inside the buses?"

Henry nodded. "Mondo beyondo."

"I visited the first two. What's in the others?"

"The third is outfitted as a kitchen. The fourth has tables and chairs, probably a dining area. The last two hold rows of bunk beds. I'm guessing any future additions will also provide sleeping space. Nothing to get crunked up about. But Detective Slidell is giving the images a deeper stroll."

"Will you be able to trace the buses' point of purchase?"

"I'm working on it, but not optimistic. Retired school buses aren't exactly a rare commodity. They're available through classifieds, government auction sites, school systems, Craigslist, eBay, the Facebook Marketplace, govdeals.com, publicsurplus.com. Did you know there's a whole world of fruitcakes who buy and convert old school buses? Call themselves Skoolies."

Henry stood. Rolled her shoulders while absently adjusting her weapon. The Glock on her belt. The others would have been awkward.

"Keep me posted," I said.

"Will do."

When Henry left, I went to the kitchen and downed a carton of yogurt and a banana, drank a can of LaCroix sparkling grapefruit as a chaser. While eating I considered phoning Katy again. Would calling two days in a row piss her off? Maybe. What didn't these days. I took the chance and dialed. Still no answer.

Twenty minutes later I was back at my desk, trying to concentrate on my report on Stokely's cremains. The ants were again partying under my skin, so I was having minimal success. Unlike Henry, the *Formicidae* were "crunked." Every time a phone sounded anywhere along the hall, I reached for mine. It was never my line ringing.

At two I dialed Slidell.

"Yo."

I briefed him on what I'd learned about knots.

"So?"

Unsure myself of the significance of Quintal's comments, I switched gears. "Anything on Smith?"

Slidell snorted. "Right. Smith."

"You don't think that's his real name?"

"If that's his real name, I'm Frank Sinatra."

"Henry was here."

"Ms. Left Coast have some case-cracking epiphany?"

"No. But she thinks Boldonado—the one who fits the hanging-

man profile—and Smith are probably harmless, albeit creepy, preppers."

"Based on her vast experience working domestic violence." I
could picture him rolling his eyes.

"Did you spot anything tying Boldonado to the buses?"

"I'll tell you what I spotted in there. Fuck all. No photo of a proud
hunter smiling over a gutted deer. No rambling manifesto authored
by Smith. No good-bye note signed by Bodingo. Zip."

"Boldonado. What about the rest of the compound?"

He repeated what Henry had said. Added, "No personal effects.
No clothes. No toiletries. Oh, except for a box of surgical gloves."

"That's odd."

"Maybe the guy worried about chipping his manicure."

"Doesn't sound like anyone lives there," I said.

"If they are, they ain't big on hygiene. Or eating."

"Henry said you were going through the pictures you took. Find
anything enlightening there?"

"Not yet."

"How do you read it?"

"Could be what we said, the little freak set the place up as a
doomsday hidey-hole. Or could be he uses it as a getaway for his serial killer/true crime hobby. Maybe he shares a crib with an old lady
don't like his pastime. Maybe she don't let him run around naked at
home. Or smoke his Cubans. How should I know?"

"You'll stay on Smith?" I asked.

"He ain't Smith."

"Whatever."

"I'm on it."

"Will you ask for a warrant?"

"Based on what? Old news and stories about Son of Sam and his
pals?"

In the background I heard squad room noises, pictured Slidell at
the long table in the center of the cold case unit.

"What about Boldonado," I asked. "You'll check for corroboration he spent time with Smith?"

"I gotta tell you, Doc. This hanging guy being a suicide, he don't top my list."

Knowing the reception it would receive, I voiced the thought that was bothering me.

"I can't shake the feeling Kwalwasser, Sanchez, and Boldonado, if that's who the hanging man turns out to be, are somehow linked."

I found myself listening to a dial tone.

I spent the rest of the afternoon finishing the report on Edgar Seymour Stokely. Still couldn't bring myself to look at the damn bucket.

At four-thirty, my phone rang.

"Bingo. Eighteen-point match."

I waited for Henry to continue.

"Your suicide vic is Francis Leonardo Boldonado."

"Why were his prints in the system?" I asked.

"Boldonado did a stint in the army." She paused, probably doing mental math on the dates. "Must have been right out of high school. He was reported missing August 29, 2019, by Angelina Boldonado."

"His grandmother."

"According to Angelina, Frank was a forty-two-year-old short guy who limped due to issues arising from a lead foot. I'm paraphrasing."

"Any relatives or known associates?"

"Grandma has passed, there's no spouse, ex, or other fam in the area. So, sadly, that's it for now. But I'm digging. I figured you'd want a heads-up on the positive."

"Does Slidell know?"

"Yes, ma'am. He seemed underwhelmed."

After disconnecting, I swiveled my chair to face the much-appreciated window, put my feet on the desk, and encouraged my mind to wander. It didn't. Instead, my thoughts boomeranged back to Slidell's mulishness.

Skinny refused to consider the possibility that the Kwalwasser, Sanchez, and Boldonado cases could be connected. He was right about the varying victim profiles and manners of death. There was no common MO.

What if the nagging voice in my subconscious was wrong? What if I was seeing associations that weren't real?

Questions rode the boomerang.

Where did Bobby Karl Smith and his buses fit in? Slidell felt certain Smith wasn't the man's real name. Who was he? Why use an alias? *Did* they fit in?

Was Smith some sort of voyeuristic hobbyist interested in serial killers and true crime? Film and TV producers make millions off violence. Publishing houses crank out thousands of books featuring rape and killing. Might Smith derive some grotesque pleasure merely from researching and charting murders?

Boldonado was an apparent suicide by hanging, so Slidell wasn't interested in the case. Fair enough. But Piccitelli said Boldonado palled around with Smith.

Slidell wanted me to back off from Smith and his buses. What did he say? Stick to what you do and let me catch the bad guys.

What is it I do?

I recover and analyze human remains.

I resolved to do precisely that.

Once Boldonado's bones were clean, I'd scrutinize every millimeter of his skeleton. I'd review the Kwalwasser file and reexamine the skull. I'd pull everything still available on the Sanchez case.

I was punching Hawkins's extension when a ping indicated an incoming text on my mobile. Hoping it was Katy, I picked up the device.

Charlie Hunt.

CH: Hope u r well.

TB: Terrific.

CH: Still up for coffee?

TB: Sure.

CH: Know Waterbean Coffee on N Tryon?

TB: Yes.

CH: 10 am Saturday?

TB: U R on.

CH: Have news.

TB: Good news, I hope.

CH: We'll talk.

TB: ?

TB: ?

What the hell?

16

I was staring at my iPhone when the landline rang.

"Dr. Brennan," I answered by reflex, preoccupied with Charlie's cryptic text.

"Bones are ready." Hawkins.

That got my attention. "The hanging man?"

"Only ones I had boiling."

"Where?"

"Room two."

"Did you shoot pics?"

"Yup."

"Thank you, Joe."

Grabbing my mobile, I hurried from my office. Minutes later was re-garbed and back in an autopsy room.

A large Tupperware container sat on the table, one side marked with the case number MCME 224-22. I logged into the system, opened a file, and filled in what little data I had. Then I pried off the lid.

Hawkins might not be a talker, but the man was an ace at cleaning remains. The bones were now a glossy yellow-white and devoid of flesh. They lay neatly arranged, with the postcranial elements below, the skull and mandible resting on top, the latter in two pieces.

I spent about a half hour arranging what remained of Boldonado in anatomical order. Even before I began my detailed exam, I knew something was wrong. Still, I stuck to my normal protocol.

A skeletal inventory determined that all two hundred and six bones were present.

A bio-profile assessment confirmed my preliminary estimates for age, sex, ancestry, and height.

I started my trauma analysis with the skull, first using my naked eye, then an illuminated magnifying lens. Saw nothing noteworthy except for extensive tooth loss due to exceptionally poor dental hygiene. Boldonado was not a fan of regular check-ups.

Then, heart beating a little faster, I moved on to the jaw. The mandibular body had been fractured behind the canine on the left. The break was vertical and separated the jaw into two pieces. A hairline fracture was visible on the right segment, adjacent to the badly decayed second molar.

When I rotated the two pieces to view the broken surfaces straight on, each showed a "staircase" pattern, and each had beveled edges. I also noted what appeared to be a freshly fractured cusp on the right second molar. Both condyles exhibited pressure damage.

Crap.

I entered notes and shot close-ups from every angle.

Setting the jaw aside, I began with the postcranial skeleton, turning and scrutinizing every bone under the lens. Saw only arthritis and the healed fracture of the femoral neck. Until I began on the spine.

Each bone is a specialist. Different jobs, different shapes. That includes the vertebrae. The seven upper ones, the cervical, support the head and allow for neck mobility. The twelve in the chest, the thoracic, anchor the rib cage. The five in the lower back, the lumbar, create a curve to accommodate upright posture. The five in the pelvic girdle, the sacral, form the tailbone.

It was the sixth cervical that caused my heart to skip one of those accelerated beats.

But I oversimplify. The neck vertebrae do more than simply support the head. They also provide safe passage for arteries making their way to the brain. The arterial route involves a small hole, or foramen, in the transverse process, a tiny bone platform between the body of the vertebra and its arch.

MCME 224-22 had a vertical hinge fracture snaking across its left transverse process, on the medial, or body side of the foramen. I drew the bone closer to the lens. Twisting it this way and that, I spotted a hairline fracture on the lateral, or arch side of the hole.

Hinging. No healing.

Double crap!

The vertebral damage had involved force applied to fresh bone.

As had the jaw fracture.

All that trauma had occurred at the time of death.

I studied the vertebra, mind running plays.

C-6. Lower neck.

Fall? Falls can cause sudden excessive impaction. Such impaction can lead to vertebral fracture. But breaks due to falls are generally compressive in nature, and usually involve the vertebral body. This was a hinge fracture. Of the transverse process.

Strangulation? Strangulation most often affects the hyoid, a small *U*-shaped bone embedded in soft tissue in the front of the throat. Boldonado's hyoid was undamaged.

Whiplash? Not likely.

Blunt force to the head? Face? The chipped tooth and broken jaw were consistent with a strong blow to a living chin. Not so the damage to the vertebra.

I studied the C-6 again. The two tiny fractures set an alarm ringing.

I knew what the pattern suggested.

Didn't want to accept what it meant.

Before sharing my "case-cracking epiphany" with Slidell, I had to be certain.

I secured Boldonado's remains, then returned to my office, beginning to feel like a ping-pong ball. A ping-pong ball with cold fear in its belly.

Not bothering to change out of my scrubs, I dialed a number with an eight-four-three area code.

"Charleston County Coroner."

"Ebony Herrin, please."

"May I ask who's calling?"

"Temperance Brennan."

"Please hold."

Shortly, a different voice asked, "Well, how are you, Doc?"

"I'm good." The whole world seemed interested in my health.

"Glad to hear it."

After a brief exchange of obligatory small talk, I made my request. "I'd like to review my report on a case dating back at least fifteen years. Will my password get me into those old files?"

"Not sure. What's up?"

"I want to check out some trauma on a man named Noble Cruikshank."

"Way before my time. But whatever floats your boat. Give me your email, I'll get it to you in a few days."

"Any chance I could just log into the system?"

"That's not protocol."

"I worked the case."

After a thoughtful pause, Herrin provided a password. "Don't share that I did this."

"Gotcha."

Using Herrin's info, I logged into the CCC system and entered a name. The file popped right up. CCC-2006020285. I opened it.

Noble Cruikshank had rolled into the morgue at the MUSC,

Medical University of South Carolina, in 2006. A disgraced cop working as a PI, Cruikshank had vanished while searching for a televangelist's missing daughter. Eventually his body was found suspended from a tree, an apparent suicide.

I read the autopsy and anthropology reports. Viewed the photos. It all came back with crystal clarity.

While logging out, I noticed an odd thing. The file had been accessed three years earlier. Not protocol. And why review a case closed at that point for twelve years? Whose boat would that float?

I tried but could find no info on the other user. Made a mental note to ask Herrin who was allowed into the archives.

Then, anxious to talk to Slidell, I let it go.

A mistake I'd later regret.

At seven, I changed into street clothes and headed out. I passed no one else in the building. The parking lot held only the few cars driven by members of the night shift. I really needed to get a life.

Following up on that theme, I diverted to Park Road for takeout. Lame, but it was a start. The wait took longer than I'd hoped, but Portofino's made Birdie's and my favorite pizza.

A nasty surprise awaited me at home. In the dark it looked like a small round lump on the porch. Balancing the pizza box on the railing, I squatted for a closer look.

And felt fireworks explode in my chest.

A turtle lay propped against my door, head and limbs hanging loosely from its shell, eyes dull and cloudy in death.

"Goddammit!"

A light went on in one of the coach house windows. I didn't care. This time my neighbor had gone too far.

After burying the turtle in my garden, I shared the pizza with Birdie. By then it was cold. The cat didn't care. But, as usual, he insisted I remove the green peppers from his slice.

Every half hour I dialed Slidell. Either Skinny was busy or, more likely, he was avoiding me.

I had the same luck with Katy. And Mama. And Ryan.

Sensing my agitation, or drowsy with cheese and dough, the cat withdrew to the bedroom.

Slidell finally picked up around nine.

"You got nothing better to do than dog my ass?"

"Frank Boldonado didn't kill himself."

"The hanging guy."

"Boldonado was murdered."

"Go on." Not the avalanche of objections for which I'd prepared.

I described the trauma to Boldonado's jaw, said it was probably caused by a blow to the chin.

Slidell drew in air. I cut off his question.

"The damage was antemortem. That means it occurred to living, not dry bone. Living bone has collagen fibers which give it flexibility. The ability to bend explains why Boldonado's jaw fractures show beveling and overlap along the broken edges. Also—"

"So what? Some guy punched Boldonado in the face. Don't mean he didn't off himself."

I described the trauma to the C-6 vertebra.

When finished, I asked, "Do you remember a PI named Noble Cruikshank?"

I waited out a pause as Slidell considered the name.

"The drunk got booted from the job for pledging his soul to Jimmy B?"

"Yes. Noble Cruikshank died in 2006. His body was found in Charleston County hanging from a tree, a presumed suicide. Only it wasn't. Hold on. I'm going to text you a photo."

Finding a close-up of Boldonado's C-6, I hit send. In seconds I heard the image ping in on Slidell's end.

"See the fractures?"

"Mmm."

"You're viewing the left side of the sixth cervical vertebra."

"Don't start with no jargon."

"A lower neck vertebra. See how the left transverse process—the part that sticks out on the right side in the photo—shows a hinge fracture through the lamina closest to the camera, and a hairline crack through the lamina farther back?"

"Mmm."

"That pattern is classic for garroting, not hanging. Do you want me to explain what the differences are and why?"

"No. By garroting you mean strangulation?"

"Strangulation using a double noose with a side loop secured to a solid object."

"You put the noose around the vic's neck, then tighten it by twisting the object. That cuts off blood flow to the brain and air to the lungs."

"Exactly. A muscle originates where those fractures are, the anterior scalene, and that area is a pressure point for the carotid artery. Do you want me to explain why only the C-6 fractured?"

"Later."

"Homicide fits with what Quintal said about knots."

"You're saying someone clocked Boldonado, garroted him, then strung him up to make it look like suicide?"

"Yes."

"Who?"

"I don't know."

"Why?"

"I don't know. But it's exactly what happened with Cruikshank."

I waited out a very long, very deep silence.

No one voiced the thought.

It didn't need saying.

Cruikshank had been another one of my cases.

17

A *wind teases branches high overhead. The sound is scratchy, like dry sticks rubbing together.*

Forest surrounds me, black trees against a black background. I see no stars. No shadows. No hand raised up to test my eyes.

Though the darkness is impenetrable, I feel compelled to move forward.

A few steps, then I pause to listen. Save for the scraping branches, the silence is total.

I push on.

A strong gust whips my jacket and sends my hair flying. I am cold. So cold I can't feel my fingers or toes.

Foreboding takes hold. I'm desperate to escape.

I pivot to retrace my steps. Can't see my path.

I'm scared. Deep ice-in-my-belly afraid.

Frantic to find a way out of the woods.

As I alter my course again and again, sunrise begins to penetrate the gloom, softening the edges of the trees and lighting the gaps between them. The rosy crack expands upward along a fuzzy horizon, illuminating something on the ground to my left. Despite my fear, I veer toward it.

Five steps. Ten. The distance seems endless.

I must know what the object is. I try to hurry, but my feet won't respond. I feel as though I'm slogging through tar.

Then I am there.

It's a human form. Slowly, like a heavy velvet curtain rising to reveal a dark stage, the spreading dawn illuminates the body. The boots. The camos. The UVA sweatshirt.

The blond hair. The face.

It's Katy. Her eyes are closed, and her skin is a deathly translucent blue.

Dread sucks my breath.

I drop to my knees and place my fingers on her throat. They tremble.

I detect no pulse.

Terrified, I scream my daughter's name. No sound emerges from my mouth.

I watch Katy's features change shape. Her face swirls like an Edvard Munch painting. Soft creases form at the corners of her eyes and lips.

I feel confusion.

Relief.

Horror.

The corpse has morphed into me.

At nine the next morning, I was inside the Market at 7th Street, inching forward in the queue at Not Just Coffee. After waiting out customers with requirements more complex than Montgomery's at El Alamein, my turn finally came. I ordered a single origin pour-over and took it to a table.

I'd awakened early, still wired to bejeezus from my dream.

Needing an outlet for my pent-up energy, I'd thrown a quick glance out my bedroom window. Seen dead grass peeking through what remained of the snow. Thinking the streets would be back to normal, I'd bundled in a hoodie, joggers, mitts, and muffs, and set off on a run.

Bad idea. And poor prep. As though freed from its long, cloudy entrapment, the sun was shining with wild abandon. Within a mile I was soaked with perspiration and the meltwater splashing up from my Nikes. And sorely in need of caffeine.

So here I was. Uptown. At one of Katy's favorite morning haunts. Hoping for a sighting. Pathetic, I know. But she had talked about some "creep" following her. And she still wasn't answering her phone.

Perhaps to avoid a hovering mother?

I leaned back in the faux industrial chair. The metal felt cold through my soggy leggings.

Patrons swirled around me, some hurrying, some meandering. High-rise denizens out for donuts or bagels. Businessmen heading to offices. Mothers pushing strollers. None of the hubbub reached me. Two hours awake and I was still obsessed with the dream.

I'll lay it right out there. I dream frequently but very uncreatively. Most of my nighttime visitations are just reworked gibberish from my daytime intake.

But this little beauty had me freaked out. One didn't need a doctorate in psychology to understand my unconscious had conjured a vision of death.

Mine? Katy's?

My old Irish grandmother was a believer in omens. According to Gran, some folks were fey, meaning they possessed magical powers. Clairvoyance. Prescience. Call it what you will. Also according to Gran, our Emerald Isle peeps were the global champs.

I'm not sure I buy into Gran's thinking. Still, the dream did nothing to reduce my anxiety. Why had Katy slipped off the radar?

Screw dark omens. It was time to get my butt to the MCME.

I was downing the dregs in my mug when my iPhone rang.

Ryan.

"*Bonjour, ma chère.*"

"Hey." Smiling like a goof. "You back in Montreal?"

"Still in the islands."

"Nice."

"It was ninety-two today."

Sitting in my cold wet sweats that sounded pretty good. "I know how you love heat."

"Like a bookie loves an audit."

"Good one."

"Thanks."

"What's taking so long?"

"The boat owner OD'd on his own product."

"Wow. A whole new ball game."

"Premier league. How's life with Katy?"

"Interesting question. She's gone incommunicado."

"Oh?"

"I last saw her on Tuesday. Now she's stopped answering her phone."

Ryan's silence told me what he thought of that.

"I know," I said. "It's not that long and she's a grown woman." Mention the dream? Not a chance.

"Maybe Katy just needs some space."

"Maybe." From me? "It's just that she said she was nervous about some guy hassling her at the shelter."

"The place she volunteers."

"Yes."

"If it'll make you feel better, swing by her house, perhaps leave a note."

"And seem like a control freak?"

"Concern is not control."

We discussed the boat and its dead owner. The insect life in the hotel where Ryan was staying. His sun rash. I told him about Boldonado.

"When do you think you'll wrap up down there, island boy?"

"Soon." Then, in a bad Bob Marley imitation, he sang, "I am going home."

"Don't do that," I said.

"OK."

"Thanks for the advice, Ryan."

"*Je t'aime, ma chère.*"

"I love you, too."

I didn't go straight from the annex to the MCME. Following Ryan's suggestion, I diverted to Elizabeth. Katy's car was not in her driveway.

I rang her mobile. Knocked on her front and back doors. Peeked in her windows. Saw nothing. Got no response.

After banging one last time, I pulled out the emergency key Katy had given me and let myself in.

A jumble of mail lay just inside the door below the slot.

"Katy?"

Nothing but an eerie empty house silence.

"Katy?"

The refrigerator hummed. The heat kicked on. A floorboard ticked softly.

I moved from room to room, looking for signs of occupancy. Failing that, I returned to the foyer and checked the postmark on each letter. Curiously, one was from Charlie Hunt.

I scribbled a message, let myself out, and slipped the note through the slot. No point fingering myself for the B&E.

Anxiety is a powerful stimulant. Instead of calming my nerves, the empty house had made me jumpier than ever. Leaving Elizabeth, I detoured again, this time to the Roof Above men's shelter. It's where I'd picked Katy up the night of the blizzard.

First, I cruised the area looking for Katy's car. Not spotting it, I parked and walked back toward College Street.

Lacking a plan, I stood for a while on the far side of the street, scanning the action outside the shelter. Stalling?

Two men lingered near the main entrance, smoking and ignoring each other. One wore a green parka and fur-lined trapper hat. The other was in an overly large, extremely ratty plaid topcoat, rubber boots, and a bucket hat that looked like it belonged on a fisherman in Galway.

I fought an impulse to abort and proceed to the MCME. Instead, I crossed the pavement and entered through the front door into an empty lobby smelling of Pine-Sol, cooking grease, and unwashed clothing. A receptionist sat behind a glass barrier on its far side. Gaunt, bleached not quite to her roots, and wearing too much rouge, she looked like she'd been installed there since the sixties.

The receptionist's name was M. Zucker. She smiled at me all the way to the glass.

"How y'all doing?"

"Good," I replied. "You?"

"I'm doing so fine it's scary."

I ran through my spiel about Katy.

"Oh, no, no." Shaking her head and looking truly regretful. "I cannot divulge information about our volunteers."

After persuading M. Zucker that I really was Katy's mother, and that I really was concerned for her well-being, we spent some time commiserating on the difficulties of motherhood. Giving me a sly, mischievous wink, M. Zucker tapped her keyboard and checked her screen, then provided the answer I'd been dreading. Katy Petersons hadn't reported for a shift since Monday.

"Volunteers come and go as they please," M. Zucker added. "Perhaps your daughter needs some me time."

"Perhaps." I forced my lips into another conspiratorial girl-to-girl grin. "One other quick question. Do you know a man named Calvin Winkard? Winky?"

Mistake. M. Zucker drew back and squared her scrawny shoulders into rigid alignment. "I cannot, under any circumstances, share information on our clients."

"I understand."

Knowing further argument would be futile, I asked for the shelter's director. Was told the entire administrative staff was in a planning session and unavailable. Thanking M. Zucker, I left my card. She promised to phone should she see Katy.

Trapper Hat and Bucket Hat were still lingering on the sidewalk. I hesitated. Would I jeopardize Katy by approaching them? Put her at a disadvantage by breaching "etiquette"? I didn't know. I wasn't a psychologist. Or a detective.

Cut the crap, Brennan. What's the worst that could happen? They blow you off? Wouldn't be the first time.

One deep breath, then I walked over to the men. Trapper Hat tracked my approach with undisguised interest. His skin was mahogany, his eyes the color of week-old coffee.

Bucket Hat kept his gaze on his boots.

"Hey." Up close I could detect a familiar sweet smell wafting from the scruffy green parka.

Trapper Hat smiled, revealing more gaps than teeth. Bucket Hat kept his gaze down.

"I'm Temperance Brennan. I wonder if I could ask you gentlemen a few questions."

"Whooo-hee!" Trapper Hat stretched the word into at least six syllables. "You hear that, Wink mon? We be gentlemen." He drew a hit, held the smoke in, then blew a diaphanous cone up over my head.

Bucket Hat's gaze flicked up, just as quickly dropped. The movement involved a momentary cocking of his chin, but it was enough.

"Winky?" I asked. "I'm Katy Petersons's mother. You helped us with a chair the day she moved into her home."

"Whoo-hoo!" Trapper Hat chortled and began dancing an arthritic jig. "The little lady be looking for the Wink mon."

"Shut it, Eldon." Winky inspected me as he might a squashed turd on his boot.

Feet still shuffling stiffly, Eldon raised and waggled eight bony fingers, holding his joint between one thumb and pointer.

"Katy's a volunteer here?" I directed to Winky.

Blank indifference.

"She's a tall young woman with short blond hair? She's just gotten out of the army?"

I was certain Winky knew Katy. She'd snared him on moving day. She'd spoken of him later. Maybe. Still, I was hitting a brick wall.

"I'm concerned because I haven't been able to reach her for a while. Surely you remember her?"

Winky shifted his feet.

"I'm afraid she may have lost her mobile," I added, unsure what else to say.

That penetrated Eldon's reefer bliss. The snaggletooth smile disappeared in a blink. "Don't be putting no thieving on me. Nuh-huh. No way. Dis ol' boy didn't steal no phone."

Before I could clarify, Eldon pivoted and hurried up the street, skinny legs pumping gracelessly, arms swinging at his sides.

"Winky, please tell Eldon I wasn't accusing him."

Snorting, Winky lifted a boot to snub out his cigarette. The orange tip hissed as it died against the wet rubber sole.

"If you run into Katy, could you ask her to call her mother?"

"Yeah. I'll knock myself out." Thick with disgust.

What the hell?

Reaching into my pocket, I pulled out a card. "Or could you give me a call?"

Winky took the card. Dropping it and the stub into a coat pocket, he turned and followed Eldon up the block.

Discouraged, I debated with myself. Push on? Give up and proceed to the MCME? Katy was right about etiquette. This club was closed tighter than the Skull and Bones.

No one was going to talk to me. I'd tried. Katy was a big girl. Time to go to work.

Walking back to my car, hoping it was still there and intact, I passed a small coffee shop in a large brick building whose owners didn't waste money on power washing. Morning sun reflected off the shop's front window. Painted on the dingy glass were the words *Fresh Bean* and a promise of service 24/7.

I glanced inside with little interest.

Then stopped.

18

Eldon was seated at a table on the far side of the glass. The hat was off, leaving his kinky white hair plastered to his scalp. I watched him dip a triangle of toast into a mug, carefully tap the rim, then raise and nibble one crust.

No.

Yes.

I checked my watch. It was only ten. I could work late tonight. Again.

One last shot.

I pushed open the door. A small bell jangled.

Only one other table was occupied, two kids with nose rings and primary-colored hair, one red, one blue.

The old man didn't glance up as I approached him.

"Hi, Eldon."

His gnarled hand jumped, and the toast dropped. I noticed it was liberally coated with jam. He fished out the soggy wedge, then his eyes rolled up. He looked puzzled at first, then nervous as recognition engaged.

"I didn't steal no—"

"No one said you had."

Eldon watched blueberry jam ooze downward into his coffee.

"May I join you?" I asked.

He nodded, clearly wishing I wouldn't.

I took the empty chair. The marijuana buzz was gone as was the snaggletooth smile. Now Eldon just looked weary and old. Older than my first estimate, probably north of eighty.

A waitress appeared with a stainless-steel pot. Karlene. I ordered toast and turned my mug upright. Karlene filled it and withdrew.

Eldon sat silent, watching with hooded and wrinkled eyes. Their sclera was yellow, and a red cumulus rode the outer margin of the right iris, probably a harmless subconjunctival hemorrhage. Oddly, I wondered if the broken vessel worried him.

"You be looking for your chile," he said in a gravelly voice.

"I am." I smiled. "Though she's hardly a child."

We waited while Karlene delivered my toast. Added packets of butter and jelly. When she'd gone, I pushed the plate toward Eldon.

"Sorry I ruined your breakfast," I said.

"No need for you be treatin' ol' Eldon."

"I want to. Think of it as a peace offering?"

"I do like a good piece of toast come mornin'." Eldon helped himself.

"I'm Temperance Brennan," I said.

"I know. Eldon Poag may be on in years, but he ain't stupid."

"Mr. Poag, I—"

"Eldon." Peeling the lid from a tiny plastic packet of jam.

"Eldon, I'm just trying to be sure my daughter is all right. Winky knows who I'm talking about. Why won't he answer my questions?"

Eldon raised both brows. They were white like his hair and stubble. "Might be he do know her. But he got no idea why you askin'."

"I gave Winky my card. I'm not hiding anything."

Eldon dunked and chewed at his toast. The smell of pot and unclean polyester floated from him. And a hint of something more pleasant. Cinnamon? Ginger? Allspice?

Something that made me flash on Ryan.

"But who *are* you Miss Temperance Brennan with a business card? How's we to know you're this chile's mother? How's we to know you not meanin' her hurt? Or that you don't be heat?"

"Do I look like heat?"

"Winky and me, all we know is you come charging in here in your yuppie jacket and fancy boots and scarf, pokin' and pryin' and trying to shake this chile loose. You don't be a social worker and you don't look like you be needing one. Me, I can't figure where to put you. Winky he probably be thinkin' the same."

"You're right," I said, trying for humble. "I came on strong. It's just that I'm worried."

Eldon bit off another minuscule morsel.

"Worried about what, darlin'?"

Darling?

"Katy seemed nervous the last time I saw her. And she is *not* the nervous type."

"Nervous why?"

"Some guy's hassling her."

"That it?"

"She said he was weird."

"Weird be the name of the game on the streets."

As I told him an abridged version of the story—the army, Afghanistan, Katy's compassion for vets, her volunteer service at the shelter, the creepy guy popping up in odd places—Eldon swirled the dregs in his cup. When I stopped talking, he continued swirling. I suspected the dreaded blow-off was coming my way.

Eldon signaled for a refill. Karlene served us both. He thanked her. She was also darlin'.

"You thinkin' this stalker be Winky?"

"Why would you ask me that?"

Eldon shrugged. "Winky has his moods. How this man be lookin'?"

That took me a moment to decipher.

"Rough."

"That it?"

"My daughter said he occasionally eats at the shelter but never sleeps there."

Eldon nodded slowly.

"I think I know who be causing your girl hassle."

"Really?"

"I ain't giving no names. Don't ask that."

"Where can I find him?"

Again, the bony shoulders lifted and dropped. "The man I'm thinking, he won't go the night without drink, so he can't stay at the shelter. He just sorta drift in and out." Emphasizing the last with a wavelike movement of his free hand.

"Have you spent any time with this man?"

"Don't want to."

"Why not?"

"I avoid folks take joy in bringing others down. Nuh, huh. Done with that. Life be a short course and I'm nearing the finish line."

"Why does this man bring you down?"

Eldon set his mug on the table. The bloodshot eyes met mine.

"He sometimes be mean as a wharf rat."

"Is he violent?" Fearing the answer.

"We be goaded enough, darlin', we all be violent."

"Eldon, is my daughter at risk?"

Our gazes locked.

"Out on these streets, we all be at risk."

I tried Katy as I walked to my car.

Still no answer. Her mailbox was now full and refusing messages.

Not what I wanted to hear.

I wasn't in my office ten minutes when the landline rang.

Mrs. Flowers reported that Dr. Nguyen was doing a postmortem but wanted to speak with me as soon as I arrived.

Not what I wanted to hear.

I hurried to the main autopsy room, embarrassed at my late appearance.

Nguyen had stepped back from the table to allow Hawkins to lift the organs from a young woman's torso. Heart. Liver. Spleen. You know the players. Her breastplate, which had been removed following the initial *Y* incision, lay by her feet. Her eyes bulged purple and swollen below black pixie bangs. A small, round hole pierced her left temple.

"Suicide?" I asked.

"Maybe." Nguyen spoke through her mask, gloved hands held at shoulder height. "Your facial wounds look better."

"Thanks."

"This morning I had my second conversation with a very agitated deputy up in Burke County. Her second and third calls I did not take." With a rare hint of annoyance. "Deputy Santoya is anxious for a report on the bucket she sent to us."

"Topping my list." It hadn't been.

"Good. I will direct her future calls to you."

Hallelujah. "Anything else?"

"Nothing urgent. A man brought in a skull he discovered while cleaning his grandfather's attic."

"His story?"

"His grandfather ordered a truckload of gravel back in the fifties. The skull was an unexpected inclusion in the delivery. The old man kept it. The grandson wants it gone."

On the way to my office, I thought about that. Envied gramps. Wished I had someone to plow through the mounds of junk stored in the crawlspace under my roof.

Seated at my desk, I gathered forms for my personal hard-copy folder and logged onto the MCME computer system. Dug out then checked a line on the anthropology request form. The case had been entered as MCME 237-22.

After I opened an electronic file, my brain decided it was time for more coffee.

Really? The last thing my neurons needed was more caffeine. I was stalling.

Grabbing my mug, I headed to the kitchen.

As I poured, not as skillfully as Karlene, I contemplated my reluctance to tackle the bucket. Because the case came from outside our official jurisdiction? Why *had* it come to us from Burke County? Did Deputy Santoya's off-duty hours involve too much crime TV?

Was I simply unmotivated about viewing the remains of a chipmunk or squirrel? Perhaps someone's dearly departed pet lizard? Experience told me that's what I'd find in the fill.

Or did my foot-dragging spring from another source? Were the blasted id boys at it again? Whatever their issue, if they even had one, I needed a distraction. MCME 237-22 would keep my mind off Katy. And Nguyen off my back. Time to focus.

Back at my desk, I skimmed the pertinent information. *Date. Time. Responding officer. Summary of facts.*

The bucket was found by hikers in the Pisgah National Forest. Santoya caught the call. The next day she sent the bucket to us.

A few of the subliminal gang sat up.

I swiveled to the counter and unfolded the plastic sheeting for my first look. The bucket was blue plastic with a rusty metal handle. It was filled to its brim with concrete, not soil as I'd assumed.

The id gang was working itself into a dither when my mobile rang.

"It's Charlie." I knew that from caller ID. "Charlie Hunt."

"Hey, Charlie. What's up?" Desperately wanting to hear that he'd talked to Katy.

"I need to see you." The urgency in his voice surprised me.

"Aren't we on for coffee tomorr—"

"We need to meet today." Need. Not want.

"OK." Then, "Have you seen Katy?"

"No."

A chill began building in my chest.

"Does this have to do with her?"

"I don't know." Clearly trying to sound calmer than he was.

The chill spread. Raised the tiny hairs on my arms and the back of my neck.

"When?" I asked.

"Five tonight. The Caribou Coffee on Fairview Road. That'll be closer for you."

He didn't wait for my assent.

"And be careful."

Three beeps and he was gone.

WTF?

I sat picturing the kid I'd known in high school. The man I'd dated briefly a few years back. The kind eyes. The confident swagger. The ready flash of white teeth. This hadn't sounded like the Charlie Hunt I knew. And why did I need to be careful?

I checked my watch.

Two-ten.

Chill, Brennan. In three hours, you'll have answers.

I pulled on gloves. Challenging with unsteady hands. I was rotating the bucket when the landline rang.

Area code 828.

I figured Nguyen had been good to her word.

"Temperance Brennan."

"Dr. Brennan, it's Marissa Santoya. Yep. It was the go-getter cop up in Burke County."

"I'm examining your bucket now, deputy."

"Good. I have some additional intel for you."

"Yes?"

"Hikers found it in the Pisgah National Forest."

"I'm aware of that."

Her next words launched my stomach into a Simone Biles double-double.

19

"**W**iseman's View."

My mouth felt dry. I swallowed.

"Say that again."

"Wiseman's View. It's an overlook used for observing the Brown Mountain Lights."

"Off the Kistler Memorial Highway." Barely above a whisper.

"Yeah. SR 1239."

My mind was spitting flashbulb images. A remote trailhead. An outcrop. A shed.

"Had the bucket been tossed down the mountain?"

"Nope. You know the big snow we had on Monday? With some melting, the thing emerged, right on the ledge."

Not trusting my voice, I let her go on.

"Before shifting to Burke, I was over in Avery County. While there, I met a deputy named Zeb Ramsey. When the bucket made its appearance this week, I remembered a conversation I'd had with Ramsey several years ago. You know the guy I mean? He said you two worked a case together back in the day?"

"Yes."

"Ramsey talked about a pail of cement with a human head inside."

Close. The head had decomposed, leaving only an impression of its owner's face.

"Anyway, when this one showed up, also full of concrete, I called over to Avery. Ramsey's moved on, but they sent me the file. Damned if his story didn't track. You were named as consulting anthropologist so, thinking you might want to take a poke, I transferred this new bucket down to your office."

Santoya wasn't pushing for a quick turn-around. She had additional information that she wanted to share. Relevant information.

Terrifying information.

"Thank you, Detective. As I said, I'm examining it now."

"Much appreciated. Keep me briefed?"

"Of course."

Silence rolled from the mountains down to the piedmont. I broke it, sounding far calmer than I felt.

"Do you have any unsolved MP's up your way?"

"This is the high country, Doc. Folks go missing all the time. Mostly they show up."

"But not always."

"Not always. You find anything wonky in that concrete, you let me know what I need to do."

As we disconnected, my eyes drifted to the bucket.

Coincidence?

A coincidence the size of Colorado.

I punched Hawkins's extension and explained why I needed his help. Then I got a cart, lifted MCME 237-22 onto it, plastic sheeting and all, and rolled it to the other side of the building.

Hawkins was waiting in the stinky room, a clear plastic face guard in one hand. An array of tools lay on the counter at his back, suggesting we were about to attempt a vault heist.

Hawkins unwrapped the sheeting and took photos as I suited up.

"HDPE," he said when I returned.

I looked a question at him.

"High-density polyethylene."

"Is it common?"

"As spit on gum."

We donned our masks and face guards. Using what looked like long-handled pruning shears, Hawkins cut through one side and the bottom of the blue plastic. The HDPE. By pulling on the severed halves, he managed to slide the bisected bucket free of its contents.

I gave a thumbs-up.

After inspecting the newly exposed glob, Hawkins revved a small circular saw and, applying the blade in forty-five-second bursts, began what became a two-inch-deep cut from top to bottom on its right side. A powdery mist filled the air, coating our face shields, our hair, the sheeting, the tile, the cabinet glass, and the stainless steel.

The process was noisy and seemed to take forever. After repeating it on the left side, Hawkins killed the saw and picked up a chisel and hammer.

A zillion taps, then the glob finally split. Hawkins caught the two halves and gently laid each down, hollow sides on top. Nerves humming, I wiped particulates from my face shield and stepped to the table.

Inside the concrete was a hollow created with a life-size Joker mask. Apparently, the mask had been placed in the bucket, then the concrete poured in around it. Remnants of the brightly colored hard plastic remained, rimming the mold.

What held my attention was something placed in the empty space.

I've no idea how long I stood staring, trying not to inhale. Or maybe I was incapable of breathing.

Minutes. Hours.

Hawkins's voice finally penetrated.

". . . the flip *is* that?"

"A mold created with a Joker mask," I mumbled.

"Joker?" Dubious. "Like in Batman?"

"Yes."

"That a snapshot in there?"

"It is."

Reaching deep for a pocket of calm, Hawkins leaned over the table. "Heck, that's you. Outside on the steps."

He was right. The image captured me entering the MCME.

Hawkins scowled. "You know who took that picture?"

I shook my head.

Hawkins's gaze rolled from the objects in the concrete to me, brows furrowed behind the white-coated plastic.

"That don't seem right," he said.

"No," I agreed.

Hawkins straightened. "Going on five. Need me to do anything more?"

My eyes flew to the wall clock.

Charlie. Crap.

"I'm good. Definitely, go."

As Hawkins gathered the tools and stick-walked from the room, I fumbled for my phone, willing my fingers steady enough to punch the right number.

No answer.

Of course not.

After rolling the remains of the pail and its frightening fill to the cooler, I changed into street clothes, and left.

I hate being late. Not sure if that's a personality flaw or strength. My friends constantly advise me to chill. I can't. I dislike being kept waiting, find it rude. Assume others feel the same.

First the bucket, then my tardiness. Moving like a slug through, well, sluggish rush-hour traffic, did nothing to relax my frazzled nerves.

The Foxcroft East Shopping Center is located on Fairview Road, not far from the Charlotte Country Day campus. It was five-fifteen by the time I pulled into the lot. I scanned for Charlie's car. Realized I hadn't a clue what he drove these days. Only that it would be pricey and fast.

Caribou Coffee shares space with a UPS store. Neither had a single patron, making it obvious that I'd arrived first.

To my surprise, and apparently unknown to Charlie, the coffee-shop no longer offered inside service. Thanks, COVID. Unsure what he'd want, I ordered a sparkling green tea lemonade for myself and, despite the chill creeping in with the dusk, took it to an outside table.

Banning thoughts of Katy and Zeb Ramsey and buckets and concrete, I watched the action around me. There wasn't much to watch. A metal-mouthed kid and what looked like an older sibling departing the orthodontist, both looking sullen. A woman in a pants suit and pumps balancing a stack of Pizza Hut boxes. An elderly couple shuffling arm-in-arm toward the Novant Health facility. Only Foxcroft Wine Company and Ben & Jerry's appeared to be bustling. Vino and ice cream. A metaphor for our troubled age?

Time passed. No Charlie.

As I finished my lemonade, unbidden images of my daughter wormed through my resolve to stay chill. Katy slumped behind the wheel of a wrecked car. Lying off a hiking trail, her ankle broken. Shot by a junkie in a dark alley.

Stop!

I considered the coconut coffee jellies in the bottom of my cup. Thought about green tea. About jellies. About the rotten produce in my fridge.

I tried Charlie's mobile. Got voice mail.

It was full dark now and moving from chilly to cold. Carriage lights and lampposts glowed around me. Quaint. Tasteful. No garish neon here, no sir.

I checked my watch repeatedly. Five-thirty. Five forty-five. Five-fifty.

Had Charlie come and gone before I'd arrived? Annoyed by my lateness, had he split? Did he think I was a no-show?

After waiting for only fifteen minutes?

With slowly numbing fingers, I dialed Katy. Slidell. Ryan.

I tried Charlie's number again. Same result.

Why did no one answer my goddam calls?!

At six-fifteen, I went inside. The staff was tidying up to close. No, a very tall black man had not been into the shop earlier.

Instead of his mobile, I dialed Charlie's office number. Got an after-hours switchboard operator named Vickie. Vickie had no idea of Mr. Hunt's whereabouts. And refused to divulge such classified intel.

Had something come up at the last minute? A client emergency? Car trouble? Surely Charlie would have phoned to let me know.

Had something happened to him? A mugging? An accident? A heart attack?

The spectrum of possibilities ran from dark to horrible.

Charlie had seemed concerned about Katy. Had some tragedy actually befallen her?

Nope. Not going there.

Suppressing all distressing lines of thought, I tossed my cup and its jellies and walked to my car.

Still committed to not dwelling on unsettling notions, I decided to watch a movie. Birdie and I enjoy old classic films. I like comedies. He prefers Westerns.

After much surfing, I chose *Chinatown*. The cat was good with it.

Nicholson was having his nose reconfigured when my mobile rang.

Ryan.

I grabbed the remote and hit pause.

"*Comment ça va, ma chèr . . . ?*" Ryan's greeting was truncated by a loud hissing sound.

"I'm good. This connection is terrible. Where are you?"

". . . outer island. It has coconuts."

"Don't they all?"

"But no cell towers."

"How are you able to call?"

"An old lady is cranking a handle behind me."

"Funny."

"She definitely is. You don't sound good."

"Yes, I do."

"There. See?"

"Birdie and I are watching a movie."

"*Cool Hand Luke*?" Ryan named the cat's favorite.

I answered after another long burst of static. Ryan responded by impersonating Nicholson's closing line.

"Forget it, Jake. It's Chinatown."

"One of the great ones," I said.

". . . is. Now explain why . . . sound so wired."

I went at it in layers, peeling from the least to the most disturbing. Speaking when the crackling and popping allowed.

I started with the coffee meeting that wasn't.

"That's it? . . . guy stood you up?"

"It's out of character for Charlie. And why such urgency? Why did he have to see me today?"

"I'm sure you'll hear from . . . oon."

Next layer.

"I still haven't spoken to Katy. I went to her house, as you suggested. It appears she hadn't been there for days. I spoke to some folks at the shelter. It wasn't encouraging."

". . . ing how?"

"The guy who was following her may be bad news."

"Katy knows how to handle . . ."

"What if this prick grabbed her? What if she went running with no ID? What if—"

". . . makes you feel better, call around to the hospitals . . . sure she's fine."

I said nothing.

". . . you checked with your ex? Maybe he talked . . . her."

"Pete's in the Seychelles."

Ryan's response was nothing but static.

"I think Katy is suffering from PTSD," I said.

"Which means she's . . . enormous emotional turmoil. Flashing back to . . . you can't understand . . . not be making fully rational decisions."

"That's why I'm worried."

"She probably . . . time to herself."

Final layer.

Deep breath.

"Some psycho is imitating my old cases."

"What?" Sounding totally thrown. Or dubious. Or maybe he didn't catch my words.

"Copycat corpses." Keeping my sentences short to be understood.

"Are you serious?"

I laid it all out. Kwalwasser's eyeball and skull with the knife-pierced orbit. Sanchez's eviscerated torso. Boldonado's death by garroting disguised as a suicide by hanging. The bucket of concrete. Not sure how much detail made it through the sporadic popping and sputtering.

"Every one of these recent vics mimics remains I've worked in the past."

Ryan said nothing. Either considering my words or waiting for a patch of clean air.

"What was in the concrete?" he asked.

I told him.

". . . esus Christ! Any idea who this asshole is or why he's targeting you?" The question came through loud and clear. As did Ryan's anger.

"No." I'd thought of little else since seeing the snapshot in the concrete.

". . . Slidell."

"Why Skinny?" I asked.

". . . still working with the CCU?"

"Yes."

"He knows . . ."

The line went dead.

20

I awoke at seven-thirty and, before getting out of bed, dialed Charlie. Got rolled to voice mail. I left a message suggesting some urgency. After thirty minutes, a lot of coffee, and several more calls, I still hadn't connected with him.

A slapdash job with my Sonicare, then I ponytailed up and hurried to my car.

No need for navigation. I knew the way and was there in ten minutes.

Charlotte's city center is ringed by three districts that are largely residential. To show pride in their history, much of which was displaced at the time these low- and high-rise developments were proposed, the populace still refers to the neighborhoods by their original designations: First, Third, and Fourth Wards. Not sure what's happening in number Two.

I parked on the border between Fourth and First Wards. Walking along Church Street, I couldn't help thinking that Charlie's complex was a poster child for Charlotte's uptown revival. His unit was midpoint in a row of nine uber-modern townhouses. Party rooms and outdoor terraces on four, bedrooms on three, living and dining rooms, kitchens and dens on two, garages and offices underneath. Elevators to avoid all those pesky stairs.

City-center living with beaucoup amenities. And price tags that were an intergalactic voyage beyond my budget.

Hoping he was as much a creature of habit as *moi*, I checked under a rock beside the foundation to the right of the front steps. Bingo.

The key was obviously a survivor of many seasons in the elements. Rust and corrosion prevented it from fitting into the lock. No matter. The door was open.

That seemed wrong.

So did the dried footprints tracking from the porch into the foyer. Charlie was fastidious about his home. At least he'd been in his public defender years when we'd given dating a short-lived whirl. When we'd occasionally ended up here after a night out.

Had Charlie left that mud? Had a visitor?

"Charlie?" I called out, pausing just inside the door.

No answer.

"Charlie?"

Nothing.

I listened for sounds of a presence.

The place was silent as a tomb.

Call it intuition. Something felt off.

Wishing I had company, maybe a pit bull or a Doberman, I began looking around. The living and dining rooms were as I remembered, done in browns and creams, with artwork a mix of modern and old. An Indonesian mask. An African carving. A George Rodrigue blue dog print.

I moved to the kitchen, all stainless steel, granite, and natural wood. Saw no dishes on the table or in the sink. No garbage overdue for disposal.

It was clear Charlie's desire for cleanliness hadn't diminished. The place was spotless and smelled of wood polish and some sort of potpourri diffuser. And something else?

The refrigerator was bare of photos, Post-its, reminders, or lists.

I opened the door and checked a few labels. Not a single product was past its expiration date. How was that even possible?

I circled back and began climbing the stairs, noting the photo array as I ascended. Family gatherings. A ski trip. A beach outing. A sailing excursion. In most of the shots, Charlie sat or stood beside a willowy woman with long black hair and nutmeg skin. His wife, a victim of 9/11.

I looked away, saddened. For her. For him. For all the dreams that died that day.

Thinking Charlie might be on the terrace and unable to hear me, I continued up to the roof. No Charlie. He was also not in any of the bedrooms or baths on the third floor.

Was he below in his office, perhaps listening to music through earphones?

Opening the basement-level door released an unpleasant odor. The noxious mix of hydrocarbons was the faint undercurrent I'd been too preoccupied to identify upstairs.

Far from subtle down here, the nauseating scent was strong and coming from the garage. I recognized it immediately as fumes from the combustion of fossil fuels.

Using my scarf to cover my nose and mouth, I entered. The stench was almost overwhelming.

Charlie was at the wheel of his Porsche Panamera. Corrugated tubing ran from the tail pipe into the car's interior through the right rear window, the only one not tightly shut.

Charlie's eyes were closed, his head lying sideways on one shoulder. Nasal mucus and saliva crusted one cheek.

Get out! my reptilian brain screamed.

Touch nothing! my higher centers ordered.

Charlie! my limbic system bellowed.

I had to check.

Holding my breath, I used the scarf to open the driver's-side door. No pulse throbbed in Charlie's carotid.

My eyes grabbed a few more details. The engine was off, the starter in the "on" position, the gas tank empty.

That was it. Out of breath, tears streaming my cheeks, I fled the garage.

I waited in my car, feeling as dreary as the sky. The day was cold and damp, yet I hadn't the energy to turn on the heater.

A CMPD cruiser was the first to arrive, bubble lights flashing like fireworks on the Fourth of July. While one uniform positioned himself at the front door, the other hurried inside.

I tucked my fingers under my arms for warmth. Listlessly watched Charlie's home and its guardian pulse blue-blue-blue.

Next came a CSU truck. Then Hawkins and a tech named Sandford in the van, followed by Nguyen in her Mercedes.

Not far behind the MCME team were the first members of the press. I knew as word spread others would appear, eager to film and report on yet another human tragedy. Maybe get lucky and capture a shot of the corpse.

Ladies and gentlemen, children of all ages . . . I thought bitterly. How many times had I been a player in the grim circus? How many death scenes had I worked?

But this was Charlie. We were to have coffee yesterday.

A tremor built in my chest.

Charlie had killed himself. How was that possible?

I was palming tears from my cheeks when I sensed a vehicle pulled to my bumper. I glanced in the rearview mirror.

Slidell.

How did he know? Didn't matter. I was in no shape to deal with his attitude.

I stayed put.

Slidell got out and walked to my car. A gloved hand knuckle-rapped the glass by my ear. Resigned, I lowered the window, braced for an offensive Skinnyism.

"You OK?" he asked.

I shrugged.

"You knew this guy, right?" Cocking his jaw toward the pulsating townhouse.

I nodded.

"Sorry."

I turned to look at him, surprised by the subdued tone. Slidell's face was drawn, his eyes filled with compassion. I gestured that he should join me in the car. He did.

"What happened?" he asked.

I told him what I knew. Charlie's desire to meet earlier than planned. The no-show at Caribou Coffee. The unanswered calls. My cruise through the townhouse. Finding his body in the garage.

"It was my fault," I finished, prepared to be brutal with myself. "I missed the signs."

"What signs?"

"That's just it. I didn't see any."

"Don't sound like you."

It wasn't. I said nothing.

"You think this could be part of the whole clusterfuck?"

"What clusterfuck?" Having no idea of his meaning. Not really caring.

"You feel up to going inside?"

Oh, God.

"How 'bout we take a quick look, after that we talk," he urged gently.

Mind a turbulent mess, I nodded agreement. More self-brutalization?

Slidell and I walked to the short, sloping driveway. A gurney had been positioned at the top, body bag unzipped and ready.

The garage door was up now, the overheads on. Ditto every light in the townhouse.

Nguyen stood in the space between the Porsche and a set of wire wall shelves. Hawkins was beside her, shooting video. The metal death scene kit lay on the floor between them.

The Porsche driver's-side door stood open. Through it I could see Charlie, head slumped, upper arms hanging limp to the elbows, forearms crossed on his thighs, NBA fingers dangling between his knees. The floods on Hawkins's camera lifted the macabre tableau into surrealistic brightness.

A new tremor threatened. I fought it down.

"Doc," Slidell's way of announcing our arrival.

Hawkins kept filming. Nguyen looked over her shoulder, thermometer in one gloved hand.

"Detective, Dr. Brennan."

"What's the verdict?" Slidell asked.

"Probable carbon monoxide poisoning."

I said nothing.

"I'm seeing very little trauma," Nguyen added.

"Very little?" I managed to ask.

"Abrasions on the forehead, the left cheek and ear."

"From his head hitting the wheel?"

"Maybe."

"You're thinking suicide?" Slidell asked.

"I'll know more after the autopsy."

"The garage door was down when you arrived?" he asked me.

"Yes."

"Was the car hood up?"

"No."

"The vic have any grease on his hands?" This question to Nguyen.

"No."

Slidell scanned the small space. "No tools lying around."

"I agree, Detective," Nguyen said. "This doesn't look like an accident."

"Time of death?"

"Based on body temp, I'd put it at very early morning. But that's only a rough estimate."

"Refresh me. How long's it take to die by CO poisoning?"

"Not long."

Slidell scowled.

"Death can occur quickly. A level of one to three percent CO is normal, seven to ten percent in smokers. A level of ten to twenty percent will cause headache and poor concentration, thirty to forty percent severe headache, nausea, vomiting, faintness, lethargy, elevated pulse and breathing rates. With forty to sixty percent comes disorientation, weakness, and loss of coordination. With sixty percent, coma and death."

Slidell sighed. "How 'bout a ballpark?"

"Of?" Nguyen was inspecting one of Charlie's hands.

"How long you last."

"Inhaling air with a carbon monoxide level as low as point two percent can produce carboxyhemoglobin levels exceeding sixty percent in just thirty to forty-five minutes."

"That'll kill ya?"

"Very dead."

Slidell pulled a small spiral from his overcoat pocket, jotted something, then gestured with the notebook. "And we got that here?"

"Engine running, door lowered, windows shut. Definitely." Nguyen continued without looking up. "In as little as five to ten minutes."

"So he died soon after turning the key." I'd told Slidell what I'd seen in the car. And inside the townhouse.

"Assuming he turned the key," Nguyen said.

"Assuming that."

"And that he was breathing when he entered the car."

"And that."

"Which I suspect was the case. See this?" Nguyen lifted one of Charlie's hands.

Slidell eyed it from where he was standing. "That blood-settling thing? Because the fingers are hanging down."

"Yes. But I'm talking about the nail beds."

Slidell bent for a closer look. "They look pink."

"Yes again. Which suggests he was alive."

"Carbon monoxide, which is colorless, odorless, and tasteless, is an agent in auto exhaust. Highly toxic, CO combines with hemo-globin to produce carboxyhemoglobin, which blocks the transport of oxygen in the body."

"This carboxyhemoglobin kills you."

"Yes. And in doing so it turns your blood and tissues bright red."

I pictured the organs Nguyen would see when she cut Charlie open. The cherry red slivers of heart, kidney, liver, lung, spleen, and stomach she'd view under magnification.

"Remind me," Slidell said. "When does the blood-settling thing start?"

"Livor. Within two hours of death. Peaks in six to eight. But it's cold out here, which would retard the process."

"The livor in the fingers, that says no one moved the body, right?"

"Correct."

"And he ain't in rigor." Slidell pronounced it *rigger*.

"I see slight stiffening in the smaller muscles of the neck and face."

"So when did the guy die?"

"Rigor also starts in two hours. But that's variable. And the low temperature would slow that as well." Nguyen straightened. "I'll run a full tox screen."

"Looking for what?" I asked, knowing Charlie's abhorrence for drugs.

"Whatever he's got in him. People often self-medicate before killing themselves."

Slidell gestured to me that he was stepping outside.

As he trudged uphill, I took one last look at my friend. Slumped behind the wheel, he looked like a partier after a big night. I fought back the tears burning my lids.

When I exited the garage, Slidell was not on the drive. Rounding the townhouse, I spotted him on the front stoop. Talking to Donna Henry.

Henry nodded, flicked a wave, and disappeared through the door.

"What's your take?" I asked when Slidell joined me.

"No signs of forced entry. No note." The bed was made, the TV and radio were off. One set of tracks at the front door, large, probably his. No indications of a visitor."

I'd given him those details.

"There was a crystal tumbler on the desk in his office, clean. An open bottle of Chivas in one of the drawers."

I hadn't spotted the glass.

Slidell looked at his watch.

Cleared his throat.

Spoke words I'd never imagined him saying to me.

21

"I was right?" Certain I hadn't heard correctly.

"Yeah."

"About what?"

Slidell arced an arm toward the scene at our backs. "All this don't clang a dozen bells for you?"

"What do you mean?"

"You and me, we worked a suicide looked a lot like this. CO poisoning, homeowner dead at the wheel in his garage. Only it wasn't no suicide."

Suddenly, I did recall. The man's name. His ashen face. His crumpled glasses on the floor mat by his feet.

I'd been too close to this situation. Too distraught to note the parallels.

Not Slidell.

"Dr. Ajax," I said.

He nodded. Then, tight, as though the admission might cause his mouth to blister, "I think you're on to something. Boldonado. Kwalwasser. Sanchez. And there was that psycho art project in the bus."

"You believe I have a copycat?"

"I believe you got something ain't good."

At that moment, two things happened.

The gritty sound of wheels caused us both to turn. Hawkins and Sandford were rolling the gurney up the driveway. The body bag, now secured with mesh straps, held a very large bulge.

Icy pellets began stinging our faces.

"There's more." I started to tell Slidell about the bucket.

"Not here. I'm freezing my nuts off."

"Come to my place. I'll make coffee."

"That works."

Fifteen minutes later we were seated at my kitchen table. Slidell had made the expected cracks about my skills as a barista. Not using such an urbane term, of course.

Birdie was working Skinny's ankles. By some feline logic, the cat thinks the man is cool. Go figure.

Slidell blew across, then slurped his coffee. "Now. Slow your roll so I don't need to radio for an interpreter."

"Do you recall a case I did for Burke County a few years back?" Measured, though my pulse was racing. "A bucket of concrete that held a human head?"

"Bunch of whackos up in the mountains, right?"

"Yes."

"And there wasn't no head in there."

"But there had been." I swallowed. "On Thursday, a Burke County deputy sent another bucket to the MCME. Discovered in the same location as the previous one."

"That overlook?"

"Wiseman's."

"How the hell do you get yourself into thes—"

"Save it!"

"OK. Let's back up. When did all this start?" Taking out the spiral and a stub of pencil.

"My first hint was the eyeball."

"Pretty goddam good hint. Remind me. When was that?"

"The day Katy moved into her house. January 30." Saying it aloud made my stomach cramp.

Slidell wet the pencil on his tongue, made a note, looked up.

"Next was the head in the privy. Though, obviously the eyeball and the head are related. But the head had been discarded, the eyeball kept longer, then delivered to me."

"Kwalwasser," he said.

"Yes."

"Her head disappeared from the crematorium when?" Slidell asked. Birdie stopped working figure eights and began licking the water puddling around his shoes.

"Probably the same year she died, 2020. It was discovered missing during the investigation in 2020."

"And the stolen eyeball made you think of the kid got his organs snatched."

That and my nagging subconscious. I didn't mention the id brigade.

"Miguel Sanchez. He was found missing his liver, heart, and kidneys."

"When?"

"Why don't I pull up the files?" I suggested.

"Yeah. Do that."

I booted my laptop and, using my password, logged into the MCME system.

"Sanchez was three years ago," I said. "If he's part of the pattern, he died before Kwalwasser's head was stolen."

Slidell and I thought about that. Then he made a connection my overzealous hindbrain and I had missed.

"That kid found at Lake Wylie, what was his name?"

I looked at him blankly.

"No head? No innards?" Slidell prodded.

Images exploded. A gutted torso. A demonic symbol carved in flesh. A good man gunned down in the street. Memories from a time too painful to relive.

"Jimmie Klapec," I muttered, keying in the name. "But that was more than ten years ago."

The file was in the archives. I swiveled the screen so Slidell could read. The similarities between Klapec and Sanchez were frighteningly obvious.

More spit, more jotting. "Next was Boldonado."

"His death was a copycat of Noble Cruikshank," I said. "Garroting, then hanging to make it look like suicide."

"When did Boldonado go missing?"

I checked that file. "Also three years ago."

"Now this bucket thing."

"Yes."

"You crack the sucker open?"

"With Hawkins's help." I told him about the Joker mask and the snapshot of me inserted into the hollow.

Slidell scowled. "When was the pic taken?"

I shrugged. Who knows? "I've owned that jacket and those boots for a decade."

"Sonofafreakingbitch."

"Yeah," I agreed.

"The eyeball. The torso. The garroting. The bucket. You think this guy Hunt offed himself?"

"Maybe," I murmured, barely loud enough to be heard.

"You believe that?"

"Not for a second."

"Whoever's doing this knows way too much."

"Agreed," I said.

"We're shorthanded, so I can't put a tail on you, but I'll ask for drive-bys on your place."

"You really think I need protection?"

"Look." Barked more than spoken. "Hunt was your squeeze."

"He was *not* my squeeze. We dated a few times years ago."

"Whatever. If something's off with Hunt, this thing's gone personal. Taking pics of you, that's personal, too."

An icy arrow pierced my chest.

"I haven't heard from Katy since Tuesday."

Slidell had placed his palms on his knees to push to his feet. He held in that position, brows now furrowed deeply. "Is that unusual?"

"Yes. Though she's working through some issues right now."

A frozen moment, then he stood. Birdie skittered out of his path, slunk back to lick more meltwater from the floor.

"What do you plan to do now?" I rose.

"First off, I'll take a hard look at Hunt, check into his past, his associates, his clients, his financials. Then I'll circle back to Sanchez and dig up everything I can on Boldonado and his pal Smith. Maybe revisit Bus Acres."

"I'll try to find out who's been accessing ME files."

Slidell nodded once, short and quick.

"In the meantime, don't go out tripping the light fantastic."

With that, he was gone.

Slidell was uncharacteristically true to his word. He called around five that afternoon. And, characteristically, launched in without greeting.

"Big surprise. Smith ain't Smith. The Gaston County property is deeded to a Bobby Karl Kramden."

"Bobby Karl Smith. Bobby Karl Kramden. Guy's not too creative."

"You wanna hear this?" Sharp.

My upper molars reached for my lowers.

"Kramden served twice in the Gulf War, left the army after seven years on a section eight."

"I don't think that designation exists anymore."

"Whatever. The guy was mental. Based on Buspalooza, looks like he still is."

"PTSD?"

"Yeah. He sought treatment via one of the Veterans Affairs Departments in Gaston County—there are three—after six months gave up and fell off the radar."

"He owns the land where he's burying the buses."

"Kramden's grandfather, also Bobby Karl, bought the acreage when Hoover sat in the oval. That and a lot of other properties, homes, and businesses. Appears grandad was a depression predator. But his son, Benny, deeply into single malt, was not so good with figures. Over the years Benny lost everything but the hunk of dirt where Bobby Karl the younger is burying his buses."

"Kramden's a prepper?"

"Big time."

"That's what Cougar Piccitelli said."

"Boldonado's another story. A guy up the road from 'Bus Acres' said he was also a loner, touchy about his height, but otherwise a nice enough guy. Said Boldonado bought into Kramden's survivalist bullshit. That Bobby Karl let him hang around but treated him like a stray mongrel."

"Did anyone know where Boldonado lived?"

"No one knew zip."

"When was the last time anyone remembered seeing him?"

"Did you hear me?"

"So all we have is what Henry learned when she ran Boldonado's prints."

"Yeah. That the guy was a short, gimpy forty-two-year-old vet reported missing by his granny in 2019."

"And that someone garroted him and hung his body from a tree."

"And that."

22

I started awake.

The room was dark, not a pixel of moonlight sneaking through the shutters.

I didn't move.

Had I imagined a "thing going bump in the night"? Dreamed one?

I lowered my lids and listened.

Heard only the fluttering of my bewildered heart.

A few thousand beats, then, up close, another muffled buzz. Like distant cicadas on a summer afternoon.

Mental head slap. After switching to silent mode, I'd drifted off with my mobile beside me.

While excavating in the blankets, I heard another insect-like throb. Located the device between the pillow and the headboard.

Aware that voice mail was about to kick in, and still a bit groggy, I answered without checking caller ID. The screen showed the time as one-forty a.m.

This connection made Ryan's seem sharp as the White House hotline.

"...o...an you...me?" The voice was female, her words barely intelligible through the mix of static and background stir.

Katy?

Suddenly I was wide awake and totally focused. "I can't hear you. Disconnect and call again?"

"...ime."

"Who is this?"

"...eed your help."

"Katy? Is that you?"

"...es..."

"Where are you?" My pulse was now in overdrive.

"Steel Works International...Old Dowd Road."

I knew the place. A friend's family had owned SWI for decades.

"What are you doing there? Are you in trouble?"

"...now!"

Three beeps.

Dead air.

I sat a moment, heart hammering. A call after midnight does that to you.

I scrolled to check the incoming number. It was listed as unknown. Might Katy have used someone else's phone?

Without further thought, I flew across the room, threw on yesterday's discarded jeans and sweater, and hurried to my car.

Racing along I-277, speed limit be damned, my mind was crowded with questions, each elbowing and jockeying for primacy.

Had the caller really been Katy? The voice was so garbled I couldn't be sure.

If not Katy, who?

If Katy, what was she doing at a steel plant in the middle of the night?

Should I be charging out on my own? Easy one. Of course not. But no way I'd phone Slidell in the wee hours on a Saturday night. Sunday morning.

Newbie Henry?

Nope. Admittedly, it was reckless, but I'd assess the situation first. If it was merely Katy needing another winter storm rescue, no harm no foul. If it was something more sinister, I'd leave and call for reinforcements.

The defroster blew hard and the wipers slapped fast, both struggling to overcome the icy drops pummeling the windshield.

I knew the plant. Had visited only once, years back. Remembered it as a massive complex of low-rise buildings surrounded by concrete and bordered by swatches of lawn. Knew the Catawba River flowed somewhere off to the east.

I took Wilkinson Boulevard past the airport to Old Dowd Road. No planes were taking off or landing at that hour. Few cars were on the road. Probably due to the threat of black ice.

In minutes, I saw SWI on my left. Turning onto a small perimeter road, I made my way to the front entrance and stopped. Buildings loomed dark and empty on both sides of the car. Frigid beads pinged its roof and hood.

Now what?

Having no plan, I pulled to the end of the structures, turned right, and circled to the back of the property. Steel beams lay in piles around the acres of concrete, either awaiting fabrication or outbound transport.

Here and there sodium lamps threw down ill-defined cones of light, shimmery pink in the icy rain. A wet oval glistened on the pavement below each. In between, the night was dark as a crypt.

I scanned the lot.

Nothing moved. No one called out.

My eyes did another sweep, straining to pick out details.

The heater and defroster hummed. The wipers beat their steady cadence. Slushy drops sparked white in my headlights.

My gaze roved the mounds of steel and the gaps between. At last I discerned a shape in the mist, a dense cutout against the fleecy backdrop of forest beyond. Silent and still at the far edge of the lot.

More steel? A vehicle? An animal? All detail was obscured by darkness and the icy drizzle. If an animal, it was of extremely large parentage, and very still.

I crept several yards closer, instincts clamoring for retreat.

From my new position I could tell that the shape was, indeed, a car. Through its fogged and water-streaked glass, I could make out two silhouettes, the driver and a front-seat passenger.

As I wiped the windshield with the back of my hand to improve visibility, the other car's engine started up, the sound muted by my closed windows and the distance between us. Its headlights came to life, glimmering in the frosty drizzle.

The following sequence unfolded as if in slo-mo, the surrealistic tableau seeming to go on forever. In truth, the incident lasted less than a minute.

The car's passenger door opened. A figure staggered out, torso at an odd angle, as though propelled by a forceful shove.

The figure was slight.

A girl? A small woman?

The figure stood immobile, a covering molded tight to its skull and back. A hat? Hair?

A voice bellowed. I was too far away and too sealed off to catch the words.

The figure began to run, shoulders hunched low. When it had advanced about five yards, the car's headlights flared to high beam and its engine roared. The figure's head jerked around, swiveled back wildly. Then its skinny limbs began pumping, frantic to distance itself from the car bearing down.

I observed in disbelief as the vehicle gained speed and closed in on its helpless target.

Then, through the rain and closed windows, I heard sounds I will remember for the rest of my life. A muffled boom followed by a soft tumbling thud. Metal slamming flesh. A body dropping onto concrete.

Before I could react, the driver put the car in reverse. Nausea threatened as I saw its headlights judder up, then down with the movement of its wheels backing over its victim.

Then, tires screeching, the car fired across the lot. Breath frozen, I watched its taillights shrink to red dots and disappear.

My first impulse was to race to the girl. Maybe girl. This time I allowed common sense to prevail.

Taking my first breath since the horror began, I dialed Slidell. Henry. Neither answered.

I punched in 911, gave my location, and described what I'd seen.

"Do you need an ambulance?" the dispatcher asked.

WTF?

"No!"

"Does the presumed victim?"

Presumed?

"Yes!"

"Calm down, ma'am. Have you been drinking?"

"What?!"

"Have you consumed alcohol or drugs?"

"Jesus Christ! I just saw a hit-and-run!" Harsh. Even though I knew the dispatcher was doing her job.

"Are the victim's injuries life threatening?"

"She may already be dead."

"Did you get the vehicle's license plate?"

"No."

"Help is on the way. Do you understand?"

"Yes."

"Stay in your vehicle."

I followed that directive for about ten minutes, ears straining for the wail of sirens. Mind conjuring images of a girl bleeding out on wet concrete.

Adrenaline rushing to every cell in my body, I shifted into gear and crept forward. I'd gone maybe twenty yards when, to my shock, the Mazda's engine chugged, chugged again, then stalled.

Crap!

I pushed the starter. No response. I tried repeatedly. The damn car was dead.

Stay calm. Cops are on the way.

Trying to save my battery, I killed the headlights and wipers and leaned back to wait.

The car's interior slowly cooled. The outside world turned a blurry black peppered with fuzzy pink splotches.

My inside world went cinematic.

I saw blood. Mangled limbs. Skin white as bleached bone.

Screw it.

Throwing the door wide, I stepped out into the rain.

I'd gotten as far as the front bumper when the back of my head exploded.

Stars danced in my vision.

Then nothing.

I felt roughness beneath my cheek.

Heard people talking.

I raised my lids.

Saw a blinding white light.

I crooked an elbow to shield my eyes, tried pushing myself up with the other hand. Was restrained by a firm pressure on my back.

"Are you armed?" Deep voice.

What was he asking? My limbs were fine.

"Are you carrying a weapon?"

I shook my head. Pain slashed through every lobe of my brain.

"Are you drunk, ma'am?" A different voice, softer.

"What?"

"Have you been drinking?"

"No."

"I don't smell alcohol on her." Soft voice.

"I'm going to release you, ma'am." Deep voice. "Move slowly."

I rolled to my bum. Sat up and wiped icy gravel from my cheek. My fingers were numb.

A cruiser sat behind my car, engine running, doors wide, bubble lights flashing. Two cops hovered over me, dark profiles in the pulsing blue. One tall, one short. Tall/deep held a flashlight, mercifully now pointed away from my face.

My clothes and hair were wet, but no rain was falling. It was dark. The air was frigid and leaden with moisture.

What had happened?

Then it all came hurtling back. The racing car. The double beams. The terrified figure.

Boom. Thud.

"I saw a hit-and-run! Over there!" Words tumbling, arm jerking toward the far end of the lot. "It was intentional. A girl. I think a girl. Maybe a woman. She's hurt. Maybe dead."

Above me, the cops exchanged glances.

"What are you doing out here, ma'am?" Short/soft asked.

"What?"

"Why are you at this plant in the middle of the night?"

"I got a call. I thought it was my daughter."

"Why would your daughter be out here?"

"I don't know. I thought she needed me."

"Uh huh." Tall/deep. "Do you have ID?"

"In my purse. On the front seat of my car."

Short/soft moved off.

"How did you end up on the ground?" Tall/deep asked. "Did you fall?"

"My car died. I got out, then—"

I hadn't a clue what happened "then."

Short/soft returned and whispered something to Tall/deep. He responded with what sounded like, "No shit."

"Dr. Brennan?" Short/soft asked.

I nodded.

"Temperance Brennan?"

"What is this? Twenty Questions?"

"Do you need medical attention?"

"What I *need* is for you to call an ambulance for the girl who was run down!"

"There's no one else here," Short/soft said.

"What?!" Incredulous. "I saw the car hit her. I saw her body go airborne."

"Before circling back to check your vehicle and spotting you on the ground, my partner and I checked the whole lot."

There was a long, dead pause. Another shared glance.

"We saw no evidence of a hit-and-run."

23

"**A** potato." Fire was searing the inside of my skull, shooting flames into all the gray cells it held.

"Shoved up your car's ass." Slidell was eyeing me oddly.

"Someone jammed that"—pointing to the offending tuber lying between us—"into my tailpipe."

I was repeating Slidell's words, attempting to make sense of them. Attempting to jump-start my brain though the sun had barely cleared the horizon.

"Did that thump on the noodle affect your ears, Doc?" Slidell's attempt at levity?

"When? How?"

"Tailpiping ain't complicated and only takes a second. The perp must have circled wide, then crept up on your rear."

"The potato caused my engine to stall."

"It blocked exhaust from getting out and fresh air from getting into the combustion chambers." So *very* patient. "Game over."

I said nothing.

"Before you saw what you saw, maybe after, you didn't hear no

187

one messing with your car? Feel nothing?" Obviously Slidell wasn't convinced of my hit-and-run story.

The previous night's events existed as a fragmented muddle in my mind. I'd tried sorting and rearranging the pieces. With little success.

"It was raining. And dark." Defensive. "I was concentrating on the other vehicle."

"Tell me why you were out there. Exactly what happened, what you witnessed."

I did.

A slight hitch in his breathing, then, "The uniforms on scene reported no evidence of a vehicular impact. No skid marks. No broken glass."

"There wouldn't *be* any skid marks. The driver made zero attempt to stop. The hit was on purpose."

"They also reported no body and no blood."

"I saw it!" *Had* I? In the light of day, I was no longer sure. Such a cold-blooded act seemed impossible.

"You okay?" Again, that hound-dog look of, what, concern?

I nodded. Which made the room swirl.

"Where's my car?"

"Towed." Slidell jotted on a scrap of paper and slid it to me. "That's the garage. By the way, the cops said it was pure bliss driving you home."

I remembered snatches of my ride in the back of the cruiser. An argument about an ER visit. My protracted rant concerning the scene I'd observed. Tall/deep asking about keys to the annex, him squatting to turn over a rock. The stairs. My bed. Then nothing until Slidell pounded on my door early this morning.

"One of the cops recognized your name, that's why they brought you here and not to a loony bin."

"Seriously? Why a psych ward?"

"For observation."

I'd have rolled my eyes but knew it would hurt.

"I gotta ask." Slidell's tone was not quite gentle, but close. "You knock back a few last night?"

"What?!" Fine. As Katy would say, I'm an alkie. But it had been years since I'd had a drop. Why was booze everyone's first assumption. "No!"

Slidell raised a hand, palm toward me. "I had to ask."

No. You didn't.

"Did I leave an iPhone in my car?" Curt.

"Call that number. Have them check." Cocking his chin toward the paper. A beat, then, "Do you think the caller was Katy?"

"In retrospect, I don't."

"Could your hit-and-run vic be Katy?"

"No. The girl was small and rail thin." *Was* it a girl?

"Did you catch a plate number?"

"It was raining."

"Get a take on the car?"

"Compact, nothing fancy. Nissan? Ford? Toyota?" Vehicular detail is not my strong suit.

"Got any inkling who clocked you? Or why?"

"No."

"You think you were set up?"

"Of course I was set up!"

"Take a breath, Doc."

I did. Said nothing, wondering if the woman on the phone had purposefully imitated Katy. Or if that read had been drama of my making. Either way, the call had been a trap.

"Any clue why suddenly you're a walking target?" Slidell asked.

"No."

"Know anyone who would want to injure, not kill, you?"

"No."

"Suppose it's connected to all that shit with your old cases?"

"Gee. That never occurred to me." I knew I was being unkind to Slidell, but my head was hurting so he was taking the hit.

"Think about it," he said.

I had thought about it. Had come up with only one hideous possibility.

"Katy is still missing," I said after a brief silence.

"Missing? Or gone off for a while?"

"I haven't heard from her since Tuesday. In the past, that would be out of character for her. But she's not been herself lately. One minute she's all buddy-buddy, the next she seems to want distance between us. I suspect she may be suffering from PTSD. Still, should I file an MP report?"

"She'll go apeshit if she's chosen to bug out for some head clearing. I'd give it one more day." Seeing my expression, he added, "But I'll ask around, keep my ear to the ground."

I walked Slidell to the door because it seemed the polite thing to do. And I was already feeling guilty.

After downing two Advil, I went back to bed.

I awoke at eleven, head still throbbing so hard I was sure Metallica was practicing in my cranium.

Of course, I reached for my mobile. Of course, I didn't have it.

I lay for a while, poking at my incipient theory. If the awful notion had legs, where were the id guys?

Hunkered down to avoid the hurt blitzing their world.

In the light of day, my nocturnal memories seemed like a dreamlike montage in a Hitchcockian film noir. The inky black. The icy veil. The gauzy figure running for its life. What had I *actually* witnessed? Visibility was beyond lousy. What parts of my recollection were real?

Something or someone was run over. Twice.

I got up, showered, dressed, and went downstairs.

Using the landline, I called the garage. Got Carlos. Carlos went to check my car. Returned a month later to say no mobile was in it.

Crap.

I ate a bowl of Honey Nut Cheerios. Drank coffee. Took two more Advil.

Gradually, the pain in my head dropped from an eight to a six. But a generalized sadness filled the vacated space. A depression I didn't understand.

Feeling down and useless—the latter a state I was experiencing all too frequently lately—I booted my computer. And noted the date.

My baby brother succumbed to leukemia when he was three and I was eight. Following Kevin's death, my father, unable to cope with his grief, developed an unhealthy relationship with Jameson whiskey. Daddy was killed later that same year in what I now know would be called a single vehicle crash with ejection. His blood alcohol concentration registered a whopping 0.29.

My father's passing when I was so young profoundly changed my view of the world. The crash occurred on February 13. On each anniversary, a shapeless melancholy permeates my soul.

Fine. Sadness explained. Time to tackle uselessness.

Using the landline, I dialed the violent crimes unit. Gave my name, asked for Detective Henry.

"Dr. Brennan. How's it hanging?"

"Good," I said, not bothering to hide my irritation. The constant SoCal jargon was grating, and that expression was one I particularly disliked.

"Have you been in contact with Detective Slidell?" I asked.

"Not recently. No prog to report. What's up?"

I described the incident at SWI.

"Holy shit balls. Are you all right?"

"Dandy. We need to go out there."

"You said the team found zilch."

"It was dark. And raining. I want to run dogs over the lot. Can you get two for this afternoon, one cadaver and one tracker?"

"No handler will be wild about working on Sunday."

"As soon as possible."

"Roger that." Tone undisturbed by any hint of enthusiasm. "Chill till I bell ya."

Carlos phoned at two. The car was ready and could be picked up any time before four. I was surprised that a mechanic would be working on Sunday. Wondered if this involved some arrangement with Slidell. I thanked him and disconnected.

I was considering a call to Uber when Henry "belled" me. She'd secured a dog and handler for three p.m. Since the garage was on the way to Old Dowd, I asked if she'd mind dropping me there. She agreed. I would then meet her and the handler and dog at the plant.

Slidell's jotted address took us to a location behind an auto parts store and Jose and Juan's Taqueria. Both businesses were closed.

Carlos's garage was called, creatively, Carlos's Garage. It consisted of a low, cinder-block structure with a small office on the left and a single auto bay on the right. The building's exterior was painted pink and embellished with images of the Virgin Mary. I think. Maybe Saint Francesca Romana. Wasn't she the patron of drivers?

I thanked Henry and headed for what appeared to be the customer entrance. The hours of operation were posted on the door in Spanish. Carlos worked hard Monday through Saturday. Though Sunday was not on the schedule, he let me in promptly.

The car was purring. Carlos was beaming. The bill was stunning. Exiting, I made a note to query the impetus behind Slidell's choice of mechanic.

The SWI lot seemed even bigger under the woolly-white winter sun. It remained as deserted as in my memory.

Passing the main building, I spotted Henry's Explorer, beside it a blue and white Chevy SUV. Wire mesh covered the SUV's back windows. The words *Charlotte-Mecklenburg Police* ran along its side, and below that, in smaller letters, *K-9 Unit*.

Henry was talking to a burly guy with ruddy cheeks and one eye that refused to open as wide as the other. He wore a black knit cap pulled low to his brows, cargo pants, and a bulletproof vest. Under the vest was a long-sleeved tee. Under the tee were muscles that looked like something SWI had fashioned. Hanging from his person was enough equipment to outfit the Ecuadorian army.

Henry was in acid-washed jeans and a sky-blue puffer today. Her indigo cap, scarf, and gloves were in exactingly coordinated shades.

Both watched me get out and walk toward them. Henry was smiling. The handler wasn't radiating pleasure.

Henry made introductions. The handler's name was Michael Mortella. A spiral cord crawled to one of Mortella's ears from a radio clipped to his vest. A leather leash wrapped one of his gloved hands.

Mortella and I shook. His grip was a bruiser.

"I brought just the one dog." I heard Wrigley Field and Navy Pier in Mortella's speech. "Name's Vera. She's still in training. She was the only one available."

"How far into training?" I asked, wary.

Mortella shrugged. "Three weeks. She's a good nose. She'll do fine."

Great. A rookie. A full training course runs at least twelve.

"How about we take a look around first," I said. "See if we spot anything the cops missed in the dark."

"Sure," Henry said.

Mortella said nothing.

Both followed me to where I remembered seeing the hit-and-run. Joined in as I crisscrossed the concrete, eyes glued to the ground. No one found anything suspicious.

"You want I should get the dog?" Mortella asked, pointedly checking his watch.

"Let's do it," I said.

We walked back to our vehicles. Mortella unwrapped the leash and crossed to his SUV. Over his shoulder, I saw animated movement behind the wire mesh.

A word about canines on the job.

Patrol. Search. Rescue. Cadaver. Police dogs go by a variety of names and are trained for a variety of tasks. Some sniff out drugs, explosives, and other crime scene evidence. Some attack when commanded by their handlers. Some track living people. Some search for human remains. I'd requested a tracker or cadaver dog, one that specialized in the human scent, alive or dead.

Mortella opened the SUV's rear door and leaned in, I assumed to attach the leash to Vera's harness. A short command, then the dog jumped to the ground, tail wagging like a flagman's arm in a carnival parking lot.

Most police dogs are German shepherds or Belgian Malinois. Vera looked like a Rottweiler-spaniel mix. A big excited one.

Mortella walked Vera to Henry and me and spoke a command I didn't understand. Apparently, Vera did. The dog sat.

"This is Vera."

I glanced at Mortella. He gave a short nod.

Dropping to one knee, I offered the back of my hand for Vera's inspection. "Hey, girl."

The dog's eyes were chocolate orbs. After sniffing my scent, she lifted them to me, while simultaneously rotating the whiskers above. A quick glance at Henry, then a long, thin tongue dropped and hung quivering from one side of her mouth.

I rose and stepped back. "She scents human?"

"Something's out there, she's likely to catch it." Not exactly what I asked. "Conditions are good, there's enough breeze, concrete's still moist. And she likes the cold."

"What's her signal?"

"She goes batshit. Like I said, she's not fully trained."

Less than encouraging.

I glanced at the dog. She glanced at me, head tilting from side to side, crease between her eyes furrowing and unfurrowing.

"What's your plan?"

"I'll swing her around, bring her in downwind. She signals she's got something, I'll turn her loose."

"Will our presence bother her?" Henry asked.

"She knows you now. Your smell won't do nothing for her."

"Then let's roll."

"Vera," Mortella said.

Recognizing her name, the dog sprang up, spun a full circle, then froze, studying her handler's face intently.

Mortella wrapped the end of Vera's lead around his right hand, and we set off. Straining at her leash, the dog sniffed her way across the lot, exploring cracks and lampposts and items of interest only she could see. Smell.

We'd gone about a hundred yards when Vera tensed and began pulling even harder. She raised her snout high and jerked her head from side to side, nostrils twitching feverishly, testing the air in all directions.

Suddenly, the dog froze, ears forward and raised, tips trembling. A growl started deep inside her, low, then building, half howl, half whine. As it strengthened, I felt my own body go taut. A chill traveled my spine.

Mortella reached down and unclipped his dog's lead. Vera held, as though confirming her read, perhaps calibrating her position in relation to its source. Then she lowered her snout and inhaled several times. Exhaling sharply, she moved forward, to her left, forward again, her whole being focused on the ground in front of her.

Suddenly she stopped. The fur rose along her spine. Her flank muscles twitched.

Blowing out one last puff, she flew into a frenzy, lunging forward and jerking back in a circle, snarling and snapping at the concrete around her.

24

We searched that portion of the lot for one hundred and twenty-seven minutes, shoulder to shoulder walking a grid. Shoulder to knee in Vera's case.

We found not a single candy wrapper, hair elastic, glove, or key. Definitely no body. Vera calmed some, but not much. The dog was convinced a person had lain out there on that concrete.

Eventually, we shifted to the bordering woods. Gave that a go for another hour.

By six, we were all tired, and cold, and discouraged. Except for Vera. Though her tongue was hanging a bit lower, she was still as gung ho as at the outset.

When the pink lights began their nightly vigil, we decided to call it a day.

On the way home, I picked up far too much sushi and shared it with Birdie. We were both in bed by ten.

Despite my fatigue, I slept poorly. People I knew gamboled with unrecognizable phantoms in a ghostly performance without theme. Katy marched in a parade of faceless soldiers. Ryan sat with a woman on the deck of a boat, a tangerine sun dropping behind them. Slidell chased Henry into an abandoned building whose walls were covered with saintly images. A menacing figure stalked me on the grounds of Sharon Hall, its face obscured by darkness. And finally there was a twist on the culminating *Thelma and Louise* scene. In this one Daddy drives his car off a cliff and disappears into the ocean.

I woke many times, finally gave up and rose at seven. Birdie looked at me as if I'd cut off an ear.

The headache was gone, but my mood was similar to the day before. Inadequacy vied with melancholy for control of my emotions.

Was that mix a downgrade or an upgrade?

It was now a full week since I'd heard from Katy.

Burning with parental guilt, I reached for my mobile.

Damn!

Vowing to rectify the phone situation, I threw on sweats, clomped downstairs, and dialed on the landline. Katy's voice mail was still rejecting messages.

Call Pete? I knew what my ex would say. A variation on what Ryan had said. Katy's not a kid. She's an adult returning to civilian life after eight years in the army. She probably needs space to work through re-integration issues.

Why hadn't Pete noticed Katy's uncharacteristic silence? Right. He was in the Seychelles with his current squeeze.

Ryan. Damn him. Valentine's Day and nary a word. Big score for the melancholy team.

Screw chocolates and flowers and lacy hearts. Who needs that crap?

I opened my laptop and googled Roof Above. Checked the website, then punched in its number.

The lady who answered hadn't seen Katy in a while. Believed she'd chosen to take time off. Volunteers could do that, of course. Yes, she would ask around. Yes, she would deliver my message. The conversation was an M. Zucker reboot.

I stood staring at the back door. Saw Katy coming through it in her Virginia sweatshirt and jeans. Saw her on the day she completed basic training. Saw her at age fourteen at Camp Seafarer, her long blond hair damp with salt water and sweat as she reeled in and secured a jib. My sister Harry and I had gone to visit her one weekend. Upon seeing us, Katy had hopped onto the dock and run to throw her arms around me. We'd been so close in those days. What had happened? Why was she so unhappy now? Was it partly my fault?

I remembered a time following her graduation from university that Katy had disappeared for a week. I was crazy with worry. Turned out she and her roommate had gone spur of the moment to Yosemite.

But what if Katy hasn't taken time off? What if she's in trouble? What if she needs me?

Holy shit.

What if she's trying to reach me on my cell?

Racing upstairs, I threw on clothes and bolted.

I go to great lengths to avoid malls. Shopping is not my jam.

That said, SouthPark is a splendiferous consumer experience. Its vendors include Louis Vuitton, Coach, Tiffany's, Boss, Burberry, Neiman Marcus, and Gucci. And a billion other merchants targeting the less affluent.

The Apple store was crowded. Of course, it was. Apple stores are always crowded. I added my name to the queue and wandered, impatiently eyeing the iPhones, iPads, Air Pods, Apple Watches, and Macs. I was considering a remote that could probably operate my washer/dryer and Crock-Pot when my turn finally came. I bought a phone and left.

First Carlos, now Apple. I might have to look for a part-time job.

Figuring someone could help me configure my magnificent new device, I went directly to the MCME. Good call. It took a twenty-something tech named Xander all of fifteen minutes before he handed the thing back, connected and fully loaded with all my personal data. God bless the cloud. And Xander.

The phone icon showed seven recent calls. I had three voice-mail messages.

My mother had rung. She'd been "powerful blue" on the anniversary of her husband's death. I feel you, Mama.

My dentist's robot had called to remind me of an upcoming appointment.

Nguyen had news to share.

I checked my texts.

My breath caught in my throat.

Katy. Sent the previous day.

Sorry no contact. OOT backpacking with army pal. Going off grid soon.

She closed with a smiling emoji.

I thumbed in a response.

Call me please? Before you lose signal?

I watched for the three dots that would indicate she was typing a response. Nothing.

I read the brief message three times, simultaneously confused, relieved, and angry. Out of town? Where, Mogadishu? Why couldn't I reach her? Why hadn't she phoned? Did she really wish to be left alone? Why? Was her thinking so distorted that she had zero regard for my feelings? Could she be that self-focused? Could PTSD cause such a change in behavior?

Katy's texts tended to be detailed and, if anything, overly long. Why was this one so brief? So ambiguous? And who the hell was this army pal?

The landline cut short my speculation.

"Dr. Brennan." I'd asked Nguyen many times to call me Tempe.

"Yes," I said.

"Could you please come by my office in about an hour?"

"Of course."

"I have news that will interest you."

Her tone suggested the news would not be pleasant.

———

Nguyen was at her desk, hair in its usual bun, reading glasses midway down her nose. When I entered, she raised the half-moons to her head and leaned back in her chair.

"Dr. Brennan. Please have a seat."

I sat.

She watched me a moment with troubled eyes, saying nothing.

"Has a new anthro case come in?" I asked.

"You knew Charles Hunt, did you not?"

"Yes." Anxiety prickled my gut.

"You stated that you found his suicide surprising."

"I did." The prickle strengthened.

"Are you aware of any medical conditions Mr. Hunt may have had?"

I shook my head, baffled about where this was going.

"Any allergies?"

Flashback. Charlie on the cafeteria floor.

"He was allergic to peanuts. Carried an EpiPen at all times."

Nguyen nodded once, quick and short.

"Mr. Hunt experienced an episode of anaphylaxis shortly before his death."

"What?" I understood anaphylaxis but was struggling to make sense of what she was saying.

"His immune system mistakenly identified peanut protein as harmful and reacted violently, sending antihistamines—"

"But Charlie would never eat peanuts. Ever."

"The tox report says otherwise."

I just stared at her.

"And. Peanut residue was found in the Chivas in his office," she added.

"Are you saying Charlie was murdered?"

"I'm saying the manner of his death is suspicious."

"How so?"

"As I suspected, Mr. Hunt died of CO poisoning. But other factors may have been contributory."

"Go on."

"If untreated, his ingestion of peanuts would have triggered an accelerated heartbeat, breathing difficulties, light-headedness, confusion, anxiety, eventually loss of consciousness."

"Meaning?"

"Mr. Hunt was alive long enough to inhale a lethal amount of carbon monoxide, though perhaps not in full control of his faculties when he entered the car." Nguyen's deep brown eyes never left mine. "I have no way of knowing if he got behind the wheel by himself or with help."

Snap!

It came together with camera-shutter quickness.

Another car. Another suicide.

"Someone put him there," I said. "Charlie would never eat peanuts. And he would never kill himself."

A new collection of emotions seized me. None good.

Thanking Nguyen, I got to my feet, and strode to my office. After a trip to my wonky file cabinet, I picked up the phone.

A deeply breathed pause, then I dialed Slidell.

"Yo."

"It's Temp—"

"I know."

"Your clusterfuck just expanded."

There was a long silence on the line. Then, "Explain."

I lifted the first of the files, which I'd stacked in reverse chronological order.

"Sanchez. His murder mimicked the gutted torso that washed ashore at Lake Wylie." Next file. "Kwalwasser. Her head and eyeball mimicked a stabbing in Montreal." Next. "Boldonado. His garroting and hanging mimicked the death of Noble Cruikshank."

"We been through all this."

"Hear me out."

Slidell sighed.

"The bucket from Burke County."

"Yeah, yeah. That mimicked the kid went missing up in the mountains. Except for the novel Joker twist."

"And that snapshot of me we found in the hollow."

I could picture Slidell's jaw muscles jackhammer bunching and relaxing.

"And I think your instincts are right about Charlie Hunt."

Slidell said nothing.

"When we were at Charlie's townhouse you mentioned an ER doc who died by CO poisoning in his garage a few years back?"

"The pedo." Resigned? As though he knew what was coming?

"Yes." Though the situation had been much more complicated than that. "He was a person of interest in a cold case I was working. Anyway, the guy's death wasn't a suicide. He'd been drugged, then placed in his car with the engine running."

I could sense Slidell's grip tighten on his mobile.

"I just met with Nguyen. She received the tox report on Charlie Hunt. He had peanut protein in his system."

"So, what, we're looking for Mr. Peanut? Didn't he die in a crash?"

Knowing Slidell's sarcasm stemmed from a deepening mix of anger and fear, I ignored it. "Charlie had a severe allergy to peanuts. Avoided all contact with them."

"Don't mean—"

"Remember the bottle of Chivas in his office?"

"Let me guess." Zero flippancy now. "The booze was spiked with peanut."

"Yes."

"I'll be goddamned."

I was silent for a moment, steeling myself to go on.

"The killer's been at this a while. Planning and staging his little horror show. Sanchez. Kwalwasser. Boldonado. But I wasn't getting it, wasn't seeing the connection to me. To my old cases. So he's grown impatient."

"The sicko's bringing it home." Slidell's breathing sounded low and steady. Dangerous.

"Yes." I swallowed. "Now he's murdering people I know."

"Like I said in your kitchen, that's personal."

25

The sun rose and set twice. Temperatures warmed slightly.

My neighbor, Alasdair, treated me to two more turtle tirades. And a crudely painted sign on a stake in my yard. *A Child Abuser Lives Here.*

I received no text or call from Ryan. CNN reported on a tropical storm in the Caribbean, so I figured it had hit Saint Martin. Or he was somewhere at sea on a boat.

Except for her sole cryptic message, Katy also remained "incommunicado." I tried keeping my mind on other things, but now and then thoughts of my daughter jabbed me like needles. Where was she? The Appalachian Trail? Cape Lookout? A Hilton Head spa? What was she doing? Slidell had his hounds out, but so far no sightings.

Wednesday morning, I kept the dreaded dental appointment. Learned my gums were healthy, my teeth structurally sound. Finally, some good news. I departed the office with the same sense of euphoria I'd felt as a kid leaving the confessional. Free!

The elation was short lived.

Arriving home, I saw Alasdair planted in the spot where his sign had been. His movements suggested rage fueled by an abundance of caffeine. And mental issues.

I turned off the car's engine, got out, and crossed the yard, circling my neighbor as widely as possible. He followed me to my door, snapping and flapping his arms.

Even inside, I could hear his harangue.

Jesus. How to deal with this nut job? His insults were getting meaner and his threats were escalating.

Sure, I could continue refusing to engage. But he'd keep coming at me. Was a trifling garden sculpture worth it?

No. I'd be the grown-up.

"You win, asshole." To the empty kitchen. "The turtle comes in."

I made myself a smoothie for lunch. Yogurt, almond milk, peaches and blueberries, with a pinch of protein powder tossed in for health. It wasn't bad.

While drinking my wholesome concoction, I retrieved the turtle from the garden and set it in the sink. Then, smug with proper nutrition and sparkling dentition, I headed out to find a replacement.

Blackhawk Hardware offered a variety of choices. Rejecting all gnomes, St. Francis, Buddha, and an angel supporting birds on her outstretched arms, I chose a snail with an exceedingly friendly smile. What could be scary about that?

From the garden center, I swung by Katy's home. The house was as quiet and undisturbed as on my first visit. More mail piled in the foyer.

I was now seriously worried. And convinced that the call luring me to SWI hadn't come from my daughter. Despite Skinny's reluctance, I considered filing an MP report.

And where the hell was my phone? Did my attacker have it? Had he cracked the password and accessed my personal information? Before I'd deactivated the old device, I'd dialed my number repeatedly, never gotten an answer.

Little comforted by the smiling snail, I went to the MCME, hoping for a call from Slidell. Mostly, to stay busy.

Also, I had an idea.

Thankfully, no new request forms had landed in my in-box. I checked a contact on my spiffy new phone and dialed, hoping the number was good.

Two rings, then a male voice answered, familiar as my Midwest childhood. "Dr. Dobzhansky."

"J.S. It's been so long I wasn't sure if you still used this line."

"Tempe?"

"The one and only."

"Oh. My. God."

John Samuel Dobzhansky was my first love. We met as counselors at Camp Northwoods, maintained the romance that summer and the next. Then J.S. went north to school, and I went to the U of I, then to Northwestern. He majored in psychology; I trained in anthropology. I married Pete, J.S married twice, divorced twice. Years later, after Pete and I split, we reconnected at an American Academy of Forensic Sciences meeting, considered a fling, decided the old spark wasn't there.

I specialize in the compromised dead. J.S. specializes in sexual predators. Happy stuff. Better colleagues than lovers.

"Are you still with the lab in Illinois?" I asked.

"Nope. I'm in DC now. Profiling for the F B of I. What's happening in the world of bones?"

"Funny you should ask. I'd like your take on something."

"Of course, you would." Faux hurt. "The only reason you ever call is to pick my brain."

I ignored that. "I've had some puzzling cases crop up. There's no common MO, but I think they're related."

"MO isn't fixed, at least not with sexual predators. I once profiled a guy who used a different kind of weapon at every scene."

"I don't see a sexual component in these deaths."

"Fair enough. But no serial offender remains static. For one thing, there's a learning curve. These guys figure out what works and what doesn't, and they improve with practice. Also, there are all kinds of random variables that can impact the best-laid plans. A knife blade breaks. A dog starts barking. A neighbor shows up. The perp must improvise. Some are better at that than others."

"I don't think it's that, either."

"Is there a signature?"

"A signature?"

"A unique pattern. Most repeat criminals develop one because, once a plan works, they stick with it, thinking it will lower their risk of getting caught. But with violent, repetitive offenders there's something else operating. In a word, anger. Their anger leads them to fantasize about violence, and eventually they act out their fantasies."

"They evolve rituals for expressing the rage."

"Exactly. Maybe to control or humiliate the victim. But the victim isn't really the point. Their age, gender, appearance may be irrelevant. It's the need to express the anger. I profiled one guy whose victims were both male and female and ranged from thirteen to eighty-four."

I didn't interrupt.

"Important questions: How does the perp encounter his victims? Does he know them? Is his approach verbal? Physical? Does he torture them? Sexually assault them? Mutilate them? If so, does he do it before or after he kills them? Does he leave items at the scene? Take items away? You still there?"

"I'm listening."

"And?"

"I think there is a ritual. And I agree that the victims don't seem to be the point."

"Go on."

"I don't think sexual sadism is operating here."

"What is?"

"Who knows? Jealousy? Revenge? Resentment? Hatred? Good old anger?"

"Directed toward whom?"

"Me."

"What?!"

I laid it all out. Kwalwasser's eyeball and head. Sanchez's gutted torso. Boldonado, garroted and hung from a tree. The Burke County bucket. Charlie Hunt, dead of peanuts and CO. Then I explained the parallels to my previous cases.

I waited out a long pause. A slow expulsion of breath.

"I hope you've reported all this to the cops."

"I have."

"Please keep your head up. Sometimes serial offenders get bored and try to up the ante."

"Listen, my daughter was discharged from the army recently. I think she may be suffering from PTSD." I swallowed. "I haven't heard from her in a week. Should I be worried?"

"Is that normal for her?"

"I'm not sure what's normal lately."

"I'd try very hard to find her," he said.

"Thanks," I said, trying not to show the anxiety that at that moment had me vowing to do just that, Katy's possible annoyance be damned.

"Keep me updated."

"I will."

I sat gripping the phone so hard my metacarpals bulged white. I jumped when my mobile rang in my hand.

"Dr. Brennan. I'm so sorry to keep interrupting you like this." Nguyen's somber tone raked my already frayed nerves. "I am performing an autopsy, and, sadly, I think you must view this young woman."

Dear God. Not Katy!

"What happened to her?" Barely masking my fear.

"When you get here." Brisk and clipped, but with a terrifying note of compassion.

I bolted.

Racing across the lobby, I ran into none other than Slidell, his scowl as deep as the Mariana Trench. I wondered if he, too, had been summoned to the autopsy.

Oh, God. Why?

When I pushed open the door, Nguyen's back was toward us. She was staring down at what lay on the stainless steel. Two feet splayed outward at the far end of the table, the skin cinnamon brown, the toenails a fiery red.

Relief flooded through me. It wasn't Katy. Guilt followed swiftly. I was spared, but this girl was someone's daughter or sister or wife. Some family would be changed forever.

I couldn't tell if Nguyen had yet cut her *Y*. She was standing motionless, regarding the body.

Shielding it from me? From Slidell? From the many who'd poke and probe and photograph and dissect?

Odd thought. But true. The cold process had begun. Slidell and I had been asked to take part.

I scanned the room. X-rays glowed on a computer screen. Cranials. I knew the tech would also have taken a full-body series.

A pair of boots sat on one counter, black suede with fringe and faux gems rimming the top. Caked with mud.

And small. Maybe size five. Tiny feet striding in big cowgirl boots.

Clothing hung from a drying rack. A denim dress. A brown corduroy jacket. A pink cotton bra. Pink cotton panties with little red dots. A locket in the shape of a sunflower.

Looking closer, I noted that the sunflower split down the center. The words *Tú eres mi sol* were inscribed on a disc below the petals.

Slidell walked to the rack, spread his feet, interlaced his fingers, and dropped his hands low over his genitals. A quick nod to Nguyen, then he assessed the clothes and the body, his frown neither softening nor deepening.

I stepped to the table. And felt my heart shrivel. Sweet Jesus. Who could be capable of such cruelty? Why?

Squelching such reactions, I kicked into scientist mode.

First rule: No emotion. Leave sorrow, pity, and outrage for later. Anger or grief can lead to error and misjudgment. Mistakes do your victim no good.

Second rule: No preconceptions. Don't suspect, don't fear, don't hope for any outcome. Observe, weigh, measure, and record.

Nevertheless.

I looked at the bruised and distorted young face and, for a moment, pictured the girl alive, connecting the clasp of her locket behind her neck. Walking along a bleak stretch of road.

Running across a dark parking lot.

Heart hammering.

Headlights blinding.

"It appears to be a hit-and-run." Nguyen's voice snapped me back. "The victim appears to be in her late teens, perhaps Hispanic. She hasn't yet been identified."

Nguyen crossed to the monitor, her expression somber.

I joined her. Using a gloved finger, she pointed at a defect located approximately mid-shaft in the left collarbone.

At two ribs inferior to it.

Shifting to the next film, she ran the finger down the arm, over the humerus, the radius, the ulna. The hand.

"Yes," I said to her unspoken question.

She brought up the pelvis. No need to point.

"Yes," I repeated.

A frontal view of the skull. A side view.

Wordlessly, I returned to the body.

The girl lay on her back. Nguyen hadn't yet opened her torso and, except for the bruises, abrasions, and odd angles of the limbs due to fractures, she might have been sleeping. The hair haloing her head was long and dark.

Sudden flashback.

Focus, Brennan.

I gloved, masked, and examined the ravaged flesh, ghostly pale and cold to the touch. I palpated the arm, the shoulder, the hand, the abdomen, felt the underlying damage evident on the X-rays in glowing black-and-white.

"Can we turn her over, please?" My voice broke the stillness.

Nguyen stepped to my side. Together we tucked the slender arms tight to the girl's body and rolled her by the shoulders and hips.

My eyes traveled the delicate spine and the double mounds of the buttocks. Took in the tread marks imprinted on the flesh of the painfully thin thighs.

"This is a patterned injury," I said, indicating a discoloration on the girl's right shoulder. Maybe five inches long, the hematoma appeared as a series of dashes. "Any idea what may have made it?"

Nguyen shook her head.

I looked at Slidell. He glanced at the bruise but said nothing.

"May I see the CSU photos?" I asked, stripping off and tossing, not so gently, my latex gloves and mask.

Nguyen collected a bound collection of five-by-sevens from the counter and handed it to me. Frame by frame I viewed the desolate spot where the girl's body had been found.

The photos told the same story as the corpse.

This was no accident.

26

"This girl was murdered."

"Yeah." Slidell was still scowling, his mouth compressed into a tight, bitter line. "That part I got. Explain."

I gestured him to the monitor and brought up the X-ray showing the left arm bones. Using a pen, I pointed to the humeral shaft, four inches below the shoulder joint.

"See this dark line?"

"Umh." Slidell was peering at the gray-and-white image.

I indicated the hand. "Note the medial and distal phalanges."

"Don't go all jargony on me."

"The finger bones."

Slidell leaned in and studied the illuminated fragments at the tip of my pen.

"The middle phalanges should look like small pipes, the distal ones like tiny arrowheads," I said. "They underlie the fingertips."

"Looks like all that's crushed."

I brought up a cranial X-ray.

"There are no skull fractures. But note the mandible, especially the mental eminence."

Slidell made a noise in his throat.

"The chin," I explained.

"Fine. Her chin's broken, her arm's broken, and her fingers are smashed. How's that add up to murder?"

"The tread marks on her thighs tell us this is a vehicular death. But it's no regular hit-and-run. The victim wasn't strolling along the side of the road. Not hitchhiking on the shoulder. Not waiting for a bus. She was struck square in the back."

Nguyen nodded glum agreement.

The id guys were raising a clamor. I tried to ignore them.

Slidell continued staring at the film.

"Picture this," I said. "She's walking, maybe running. A car comes at her from behind and plows into the backs of her legs."

Slidell said nothing. Nguyen kept nodding.

"She goes down hard, arms outstretched. Her chin hits the pavement. She's forced beneath the chassis. The left tires roll over her left hand, crushing her fingers."

"How the f—"

"Then." I indicated a second tread mark, this one angling across her back, just above her waist. "That's where the vehicle backed over her."

"You sure about this?"

I gestured an upturned palm at Nguyen, who began speaking.

"In an auto-pedestrian accident, typically, the victim is slammed onto the windshield or thrown sideways and outward, resulting in injuries to the head, upper torso, or legs," she said. "This victim has no cranial or thoracic trauma consistent with a windshield impact or rapid deceleration angled to the left or right."

"Where are you putting PMI?" I was asking Nguyen about post-mortem interval.

"To be safe, three to five days. Lividity is fixed. Air temp dropped into the thirties every one of the past three nights, never got out of the forties during the days. Rigor—"

"Whoa, whoa. Back it up, Doc." Slidell pulled the ubiquitous pencil and spiral from his pocket and began taking notes.

Nguyen indicated the body. "Notice the dark mottling on her belly, the fronts of her thighs, the undersides of her arms, and the right half of her face?"

"The flesh turned purple 'cause the blood settled when her ticker stopped pumping. You push your thumb in, it goes white, yeah?"

"For a while." Nguyen simplified. "After about ten hours the red blood cells and capillaries decompose sufficiently so blanching no longer occurs. That's the case here."

"And rigor?" As usual, Slidell pronounced it *rigger*.

"When the body arrived, rigor had come and gone."

Sweet Jesus.

Slidell raised both brows in question.

"Rigor usually ends after a few hours or several days. Again, the cold weather would have slowed the process."

Slidell looked like his thoughts were going somewhere else. Somewhere dark. "So, she died days before she got here."

"Yes," Nguyen said.

"Who found her?"

"A trucker pulled over to relieve himself, spotted the body, dialed 911. She arrived at the morgue a little after ten this morning."

"What's the guy's name?"

"Gordon Halsted. His statement is in the police report."

Barely breathing, I studied the scene photos again. The first series showed an empty stretch of two-lane not different from what I'd pictured in my mind. A narrow strip of gravel and dead vegetation ran each side of the road, yielding to dead underbrush as the ground sloped downward.

The next series focused on the body. The girl lay on her back, hem of the denim dress hiked up onto her thighs. Her right leg twisted outward from her hip at an impossible angle. Beside the foot, not on it, was one of the black suede boots. The left leg lay straight, the foot crooked unnaturally toward one side. Both arms were flung high and outstretched above her head.

Bands of anger and sadness squeezed my chest. I forced a deep breath.

The next several photos drew closer. The girl's face looked ghostly white against the backdrop of oil-darkened gravel and black winter vegetation.

A thought cut through my dread.

"She has no outerwear. No jacket, scarf, gloves. But it's been cold the last few days."

No one replied.

I moved on, through close-ups of the battered face, the crushed hands, the sad little boots.

Slidell finished jotting. Punctuated his note with a tap of the pencil. Then, "So lemme get this. The kid's running—"

"Or walking," Nguyen cautioned.

"The bumper slams the back of her thighs. She goes down. Her chin smacks the pavement. Her arms fly out. The vehicle rolls over her, crushing her fingers, then reverses and gets her again while she's down."

The id brigade was screaming now. A young girl. Three to five days. A double hit. I knew they were right.

Nguyen nodded.

"So what killed her?"

"When I open her skull, I'm certain I'll find subdural, subgaleal, and intracerebral hematoma accompanied by massive edema in the parieto-occipital region."

Slidell's brows furrowed deeper.

"A blow to the head caused bleeding into her brain."

Slidell thought about that. "The kid's hit from behind and goes belly down with her brain busted bad. Maybe she's dead at that point, maybe not. Then the asshole backs over her to finish the job."

I see violent death on a regular basis. I know the cruelty and stupidity of which humans are capable. And yet, every time, the same question.

How?

How could someone run down a kid on purpose?

The others watched me cross to the counter and pick up one of the boots. The boots she wore as she walked her last steps on earth. Despite my best effort, a tear broke free and trickled a warm path down my cheek.

Many males are embarrassed in the presence of strong female emotion. Most have mastered the art of nonreaction. The unneeded cough. The shifting feet. The averted eyes.

Slidell went to his fallback, the pointless wristwatch check. Then, "We'll have the clothing tested, for particulates, whatever."

I flipped back through the crime scene photos.

Stopped on a close-up of the crumpled body.

Sonofabitchingbastard!

"Have you looked through all of these," I asked, pulse thrumming because of what I'd just realized.

"I eyeballed them."

"Look at this." I tapped the pic I was viewing.

Slidell stepped to my side.

"Notice something off?" I asked.

Slidell got it right away. "The purple is on her belly side." He pivoted slightly to view the body behind us. "At the scene, she's lying on her back."

I turned to Nguyen. "Did the trucker turn her over?"

"He stated that he hadn't."

"She wasn't hit where she was found," I said, my insides snapping around.

"Could she have died as early as Wednesday night?" Slidell asked.

The pathologist spread her hands, palms up. "It's possible," Nguyen said.

Slidell's question triggered the soul-chilling flashback I'd been avoiding. A figure in the darkness, a silhouette backlit by double beams closing fast. Lungs burning. Heart hammering. Legs pumping.

Was it really possible?

Ten minutes later Slidell and I were in my office drinking a watery brown liquid that resembled coffee.

"You're thinking this is the vic I saw run down at SWI?" I asked.

"I'm thinking a lot of things. You got any idea who lured you out there?"

I shook my head. "Might my presence have been coincidental?"

Slidell looked at me as though I'd suggested ants invented radar.

"Do you think this girl's death was staged for my benefit?" Wanting to hear his answer. Not wanting to hear it.

Slidell shrugged.

"Let's think outside the box." I could feel my hands shaking. Knew the coffee wasn't helping. "If not at SWI, where might she have died?"

"Rabbit Hollow? Mars? My aunt Fanny's garden?" Anger leaked between the gaps in Slidell's words. "How the hell would I know?"

"If not for my benefit, *why* was she killed?"

"Same answer. A spurned lover? An irate pimp? A panicked motorist scared of doing time?"

"Why dump her there? Beside that two-lane?"

"It's remote, there's little traffic."

"Which suggests a local familiar with the roads."

"Or someone who passes through regularly."

Our eyes met. A trucker?

"I'll run this Gordon Halsted."

"Find ou—"

"I'll lean on him till I know every time he farted."

On and on. Back and forth.

Who was she?

Who killed her?

Why?

Question after question. No answers.

I told Slidell about my trip to SWI with Henry, Mortella, and Vera. Described Vera's lack of training. Her keen reaction.

As I spoke, Slidell's brows drew even closer.

"Why use a rookie?" he asked when I'd finished.

"She was the only dog available."

Slidell said nothing.

"What?" I asked, seeing his expression.

"That don't track."

"What don't—doesn't track?"

"I haven't met Mortella. But every handler I know is streaking his jockeys wanting to work his mutt. They live for that shit."

"It was Sunday."

"Maybe." Sounding unconvinced.

Before going our separate ways, Slidell and I agreed on a plan. While he submitted the girl's clothing and personal effects for trace analysis, I'd review old cases, looking for parallels to this hit-and-run.

Slidell said he'd have Henry do a missing persons search. I said she should begin with an age range of eighteen to twenty-five. Based on hair and skin color, and on the locket, I suggested she enter an ethnic association of Hispanic.

Throughout the meeting with Nguyen and our subsequent conversation, it never occurred to me to ask Slidell why he'd been at the MCME. In retrospect, I think Skinny was pursuing a theory. A theory supported by the upside-down lividity.

Like me, Slidell suspected that the girl's death was another in the grisly chain of copycat murders.

I spent the rest of the afternoon and early evening assisting Nguyen. Soft tissue dissection confirmed the trauma pattern we'd seen on the X-rays.

Birdie was asleep when I arrived home. As I entered the bedroom, he looked up from his spot between the pillows, blinked, then lowered his head back onto his paws.

"Hey, Bird. Sorry. It was another long day."

I scratched behind his ears. The cat stretched his neck and front limbs, either enjoying or ignoring the feel of my touch.

I dumped my clothes in a pile on the floor, let my hair down, and took a quick shower. Then, exhausted, I threw back the covers and dropped into bed.

I fell instantly into a dark void. No ghostly apparitions, no melodramatic reenactments. Just dense, deep nothing.

Then my heart was pounding and my eyes were wide open. Adrenaline was demanding action and I didn't know why. The transition was dizzying.

The digits on my phone glowed one twenty-four. I lay in the dark, breath frozen, straining to know why my sleeping brain had gone to high alert.

Birdie wasn't with me. Why? He was not a night prowler. Had his ears detected something abnormal? Had mine?

Body still rigid, I listened harder. Caught only my heart hammering against my ribs. The annex was eerily silent.

Then I heard it. A soft *crick* followed by a muted tapping. I waited, not moving, not breathing. The glowing digits soundlessly ticked off time. Ten seconds, twenty, a full minute. When I thought I might have imagined it, the sound came again.

Crick. Tap tap tap.

Had someone broken into the annex? I knew all the ordinary squeaks and hums and groans of the place. This was a stranger, an acoustic misfit.

Turn on the lights? No. I was familiar with the layout. Darkness would provide an advantage.

Easing back the covers, I slid from the bed and, thanking last night's laziness, snatched up and slipped on yesterday's clothes.

Avoiding any boards I knew would give me away, I crept across the bedroom.

The hallway was pitch black. Inching to the top of the stairs, I paused, questioning my conviction not to keep a gun in the house.

I heard nothing.

I started down, eyes wide, stopping every other tread to test the silence.

I was crossing the dining room when I heard it again.

Crick. Tap tap tap.

The noise was coming from the kitchen. Inhaling in ragged little gulps, I stole forward and inched the swinging door further open. Palm sweaty on the wood, I peered through the crack. The night was moonless, the kitchen as dim as the upstairs hall.

No boogie man leapt from the shadows.

Crick. Tap tap tap.

Birdie is white. The kitchen was black. I picked him out of the gloom, body coiled, tail twitching in nervous little flicks. His eyes were fixed on the door.

Another *crick tap tap* came from outside. The cat's ears went flat, and a snarl rose from his throat, low and primal. He held a heartbeat or two, then pivoted and shot from the room.

Birdie's flight unnerved me. I stood paralyzed, searching my mind for a rational sector.

Run! The usual warning came up from my hindbrain.

What the cat heard is outside. The logic guys countered. *If someone is inside, your escape is through that door.*

If someone is outside, don't allow him a way in!

I glanced over my shoulder. The warning light on my security system glowed evenly. There'd been no breach.

The noise is outside. What Birdie heard is outside. Take a look but don't open the door.

Seemed reasonable.

I scanned the kitchen for a weapon. It wasn't exactly an armory.

Tiptoeing to the counter, I slid my utensil drawer open and felt for a steak knife. Fingers tight on the handle, I angled the blade backward, dropped my hand, and crept toward the door. Shoulders flattened to the wall, I craned around to peer through the glass.

The shapes in the yard were teased from obscurity by the single yellow bulb glowing on my back porch. The magnolia tree, the holly bushes, the smiling snail. All seemed natural. No lurking figures. No shadowy ripples. The only movement the occasional leaf winking light then dark as it tossed on a breeze.

"Where are you, you bastard?"

My voice sounded gritty, like sand through a sifter. I tried to swallow. My mouth was too dry.

I watched for a few more moments. The scene within my limited field of vision didn't change.

The wind gusted slightly.

Crick. Tap tap tap.

I jumped and almost cut myself.

The sound was right at my ear. Created by something in contact with the door?

Emboldened by knowing the security system hadn't been breached, I disengaged the alarm, tightened my grip on the knife, and turned the knob.

An object arced toward the door, then settled against the exterior wood.

I stepped onto the porch to see what it was.

Too late, I heard footsteps. Saw a large form in the darkness.

Whirling to bolt back inside, I caught lightning quick movement in my peripheral vision.

Arms wrapped me, pinning my own to my sides.

27

Thirty minutes later my adrenals were still in hyperdrive.

And I was still dumbfounded.

Ryan stood across the parlor, watching me sip my chamomile tea. He'd searched inside the annex and outside on the grounds. He'd talked to the patrol team doing their drive-by.

CSU would come in the morning. They'd look for tire treads, footwear impressions. They'd dust for prints. I knew they'd find nothing to suggest the identity of my uninvited visitor. They hadn't with the eyeball.

Ryan had explained his wee hours arrival. Weather. Delayed flights. Two no-show Ubers. Coming down from near hysteria, I'd missed most of it.

I did catch the part about the failed Valentine's Day surprise. The apology for his recent lack of communication. Something about toppled cell phone towers in Saint Martin. Or somewhere.

Ryan's hair was disheveled, the lines and creases in his face deepened by fatigue. But then, I wouldn't have been mistaken for Sandra Bullock.

For every alcoholic, no matter the years or decades sober, there are times when the body craves booze. Or wine. Or beer. Whatever your preferred poison. This was one of them. But I wanted more than a drink, I wanted a whole bottle of Pinot Noir. Or Cab. Or Merlot. One I could pour from until the blessed ruby liquid was gone.

Forget it, Brennan. The cork's staying in.

The object lay on a side table by my chair, now sealed in a Ziploc bag. I couldn't look at it. Instead, I watched Ryan. He wore jeans and a teal polo. Good choice. The colors complemented his eyes like a blue spinnaker against a summer sky.

Eventually, the tea kicked in. Or maybe it was Ryan's presence. My heartbeat slowed. My skin relaxed on my flesh.

"I'm sorry," I said. "I overreacted."

"You didn't. Of course, you were scared. Some goon jumps out of the dark and grabs you? It was a stupid move."

"I'm glad you're here." Not disagreeing with his assessment.

Ryan crossed to me and lowered his face to mine. The blue lasers almost stopped my heart. "I couldn't wait to hug you."

I raised both arms and wrapped his neck. He pulled me to my feet. I felt the roughness of his stubble on my cheek. Inhaled the familiar scent of male sweat and sandalwood soap, a hint of something island spicy.

My eyes drifted to the Ziploc. To the sunflower locket inside. To the inscription visible through the clear plastic. *Tú eres mi sol.*

No. Not now.

I allowed Ryan to take my hand and lead me upstairs.

I awoke to the smell of coffee. Bacon?

Momentary confusion.

Recall.

Ryan.

Romping away my distress.

My stomach did that little flippy thing.

I threw on a robe and a smile and hurried downstairs.

Ryan was at the stove wearing jeans and a long-sleeve tee that said *Be You Bravely*. His hair looked largely unchanged from last night. He turned, a small tong in one hand.

"*Petit déjeuner, madame?*"

"Damn right, I want breakfast." Taking a place at the table. Which was set with mats, napkins, napkin rings, and all.

Ryan served plates of scrambled eggs, bacon, toast, and what I think he meant to be grits. I hoped the expiration date on the package had been within this century.

We were adding salt and pepper when Slidell showed up. I buttered my toast. Ryan got up to let him in.

"Christ on a crawdad, Doc. Let me see it."

My eyes rolled to the baby blues. Ryan retook his place opposite me. Obviously, he'd phoned Skinny.

"It's in the parlor," Ryan said, never breaking our gaze.

Slidell blustered out of the room, back in, Ziploc in hand.

"Would you like breakfast?" Ryan asked around a mouthful of eggs.

"No." A crumb rode Slidell's upper lip, like a tiny biscuit caterpillar clinging to a leaf. I guessed he'd already downed a McMuffin.

"Pull up a chair," Ryan said.

Slidell kept pacing. "There's a psycho out there got you in his crosshairs."

"Calm down," Ryan said.

I said nothing.

Slidell shifted his ire to Ryan. "This mutant's worked your girlfriend into whatever degenerate fantasy he's spinning for himself."

Girlfriend?

"We'll get him," Ryan said.

"Fuckin' A," Slidell snapped.

The intensity of Slidell's emotion surprised me. Did his anger stem wholly from concern for my safety? Or from frustration over failing to catch the "mutant"?

Slidell mistook my silence for belligerence.

"I mean it, Doc. This guy's wiring is twisted. You can't pull any more of your stunts."

"Stunts?" Annoyance sharpening the edges of my response.

"I don't mean this." Flapping a hand at the Ziploc.

Slidell and I glared at each other. Both knowing what he *did* mean. Both knowing he was right. Which increased my sense of vulnerability. Which increased the annoyance.

"This prick's stalking you," Slidell said. "He knows where you live. How to get in."

"He's never come inside."

"He hooked a dead girl's goddam locket on your doorknob!"

"You have *hers*." Petulant. And unnecessary. "This one is a duplicate."

"Jesus F Christ!" Slidell whipped back to Ryan, wired into tomorrow. "Did she tell you what this freak's been doing?"

"We were just getting to that."

Ryan bunched and tossed his napkin. Crossed his right ankle onto his left knee. His legs stretched almost the width of the table. Slidell removed his overcoat and leaned against the counter.

An hour later, all of us afloat on coffee, Ryan had the whole story.

"All these recent remains mimic cases you worked in the past?" Ryan's expression was now as dark as Skinny's.

"Yes," I said.

"What about the hit-and-run?"

"I'm not sure if that fits in, though my guess is we'll find that it does."

"Got any idea who would do this?"

I shook my head, again feeling weak and exposed. And dependent on others for my safety. On these two. And hating it.

"Boldonado, the man found hanging in the state park, he ran with the bus guy?" Ryan was organizing data bytes in his head.

"Yes," I said. "Bobby Karl Kramden. They were both vets. According to Cougar Piccitelli, Kramden uses the alias Smith."

"Kramden and Piccitelli are preppers?"

"Survivalists. Whatever."

Slidell jumped in. "Kramden's pinups are a who's who of serial killers. All the pretty boys. Dahmer. Bundy. Gacy. Ramirez."

Ryan's eyes met mine, looking like chips from a frozen lagoon. Then he turned to Slidell.

"Surely you've followed up on this skeeve?"

"Yes, but I'm CCU, pal. A detective named Henry did most of the digging, a newbie with Homicide/ADW. She found nothing suspicious in Kramden's background."

"So violent crimes is looking into this?"

Slidell waggled a hand. Yes and no. "Until Hunt, all we had were cold cases and a prepper with a sicko hobby."

"And a stalker who leaves eyeballs."

"And that."

Ryan said nothing for a very long time. Then he asked me, "Does this complex have surveillance cameras?"

"Each unit is responsible for its own security," I said.

"I don't suppose you have video surveillance?"

"I have a Ring doorbell system." Immediately regretted my snippiness.

"Awesome." Glancing at the door, puzzled, then at me. "Where is it?"

"In its box in that drawer by the sink."

"*Sacre bleu.*"

"My next-door neighbor has one."

"The psycho Scot?"

"No. His unit is in the main house. Walter lives in the coach house. Perhaps his camera captured something."

"Here's my proposal," Ryan said. "First, Tempe and I talk to Walter about viewing last night's footage, see if we can spot her early-morning visitor. Meanwhile, Skinny gives Kramden another look. Then we discuss following up on the crematorium and on Sanchez."

As Ryan let Skinny out, my memory cells unspooled a montage of Kramden's board. Like a quick zoom lens, my mind's eye zeroed in on one headline. On an article published in 2013.

Suddenly, I was on fire to get to my laptop.

It took me no time to find and review the file. MCME 580-13.

A teenage girl had been run down and left to die on Rountree Road in south Charlotte. The crime scene and autopsy photos brought it all back.

The girl's long blond hair, dark at the roots. Her ravaged face. The tire treads scoring her pale flesh. The dark and lonely stretch of two-lane. The little pink purse lying down the embankment.

The girl had arrived at the MCME as an unknown. I'd given her a name. Slidell had caught her killer.

Sweet mother of god. It was true.

Ryan returned to the table and tossed down his mobile. One glance at my face told him something was wrong.

"What?" he asked, laying a hand on my shoulder.

"I saw a woman murdered, Ryan. I was lured to SWI to witness her death."

"It's not necess—"

"That woman died because of me!"

My front teeth clamped onto my trembling lower lip.

Don't cry. Don't you dare cry.

"This bastard is upping the ante," I said, borrowing the phrase J.S. had used. "He's getting more aggressive."

"That's how I read it."

I raised both brows in question.

"He's been killing for a while," Ryan said, pensive. "Sanchez. Boldonado. You just weren't noticing. Now he's making sure that you do. Murdering your friend. Murdering a woman while you watch."

"That's what Slidell said. What about Kwalwasser?"

"Snatching a head from the crematorium may have been opportunistic."

"The bucket?"

"His notion of a playful threat."

"Playful!?" Way too bitchy.

"Poor choice of words."

I didn't disagree.

I brought up a shot of Rountree Road. The spot later identified as the probable point of impact. The embankment. The little pink purse.

"Look at these, Ryan. What do you notice?"

Ryan dragged his chair beside mine, dropped into it, and studied the images. "No skid marks."

"What else?"

"Is that a smear of paint from the vehicle?"

"It is. There were also a few fragments found on the pavement. And yet, in the SWI parking lot, nothing. Not a speck."

"You said it was raining."

"Still."

A beat, then Ryan asked, "Have you tried to determine when all this started?"

"Kwalwasser died in 2020. Her head was discovered AWOL later that year. Boldonado was reported missing in August 2019. Sanchez turned up in a dumpster at Christmas 2019."

"So, this chain began at least three years ago. Can you think of any triggering event around that time? A dispute? An argument?"

"My asshole neighbor moved in."

Ryan raised both brows.

"Alasdair Campbell. The psycho Scot."

"Anyone else?"

"I recently crossed paths with a former student who seemed to hold a grudge."

I told him about Terrence Edy.

"Anyone else?"

"There's a homeless guy I think was stalking Katy. He was very hostile to me."

I told him about Winky Winkard.

"Jesus, Brennan."

"Don't go there."

"Could any of these people be this hateful?"

I shrugged. Who knows?

"Call your next-door neighbor?"

I did. Walter said we were welcome to view the video anytime.

As things turned out, it was good that we did.

28

"I see you!"

The tinny voice startled Ryan, despite a warning that my neighbor was quirky.

"Hi, Walter." I gave a five-finger wave.

"Three-D motion detection and head-to-toe video," he chirped. "No one sneaks up on this old boy."

The door opened before we reached it. Walter stepped out and pointed to his roof. "Cameras, lights, action!" He was wearing a track-suit perhaps purchased from a meth dealer in the eighties, purple with turquoise chevron stripes. His toupee was new. And not custom fitted.

We followed Walter inside, across a faux Persian rug to a living room furnished with dark mahogany pieces upholstered in bright emerald velvet. Green patterned drapes.

Walter gestured at a sofa outfitted with enough throw pillows to stock a Bed Bath & Beyond, all in variations on the verdant motif. Forest. Kelly. Something a decorator would probably call moss.

After clearing space, Ryan and I sat.

Settling into a wing chair, Walter raised one polyester-clad arm and waggled what looked like an iPhone 13 Pro. "My nephew wired the system for me. It's state of the art."

"Impressive," Ryan said.

"You would be the oft-mentioned Canadian cop?" Walter asked.

"I would."

"You're supposed to be French."

"*Je suis, vraiment.*"

"Not bad." Walter pointed a finger pistol at Ryan, mimicked blowing smoke from the barrel. Two of his digits sported rings the size of bagels, one sapphire, one ruby.

"I didn't catch your last name," Ryan said, smiling.

"What?" Walter gave a flirty wink. "Are you considering asking me out on a date?"

Ryan winked back.

Walter turned to me. "So you think we had a prowler, sweetheart?"

I nodded.

"As do I." He said it with sudden conspiratorial intensity.

"Really?"

"I was up late last night watching *Saturday Night Fever*. John Travolta is absolutely marvelous. Have you seen it?"

Ryan and I nodded.

"Anyway, Travolta was dancing in these gorgeous platform boots when my phone signaled motion on the lawn. I remember thinking that the chiming blended well with the music."

"Did you look outside?"

"Not necessary." Proudly. "I viewed the action right here on my mobile. Saw nothing amiss. Since there was no follow-up warning, I figured it was a deer, maybe a dog passing by. Or the wind. She was blowing up a tizzy last night."

"When did this happen?" I asked.

Walter swiped twice, tapped several times on his screen. "At 1:09 a.m."

"Do you still have the video?"

When Walter looked up, the hairpiece shifted position. It wasn't a good shift. "Indeed, I do. For sixty days." Beaming. "*And* I can share it."

"Could you send it to me?"

"I surely could, darling. Though I fear you'll see naught."

Ryan and I spent the next half hour watching footage of the outside of my neighbor's home. And mine. Though Walter's cameras were focused on his two entrances, the one above his side door caught the patch of grass between the coach house and the annex.

The video was in color—Walter had boasted with pride—but the previous night had been moonless and gusty. It was like viewing the world through murky water. All movement was wobbly and in shades of gray.

We saw the prowler simultaneously, hurrying toward my unit with a quick, determined stride. The sequence lasted a total of seven seconds before the figure disappeared off frame.

The time stamp said 1:09 a.m.

"What did you see?" Ryan asked after we'd rewound and replayed the footage again and again.

"The face was totally obscured."

"That's what you *didn't* see."

"He's tall. Maybe six feet."

"How do you know?"

"I estimated as he passed in front of the magnolia. I know that tree is eighteen feet high."

"He?"

That surprised me. "Did you see something to suggest otherwise?"

"Just keeping an open mind. What else?"

"Baseball cap."

"Baseball?"

"Jesus. Fine. He or she is wearing a brimmed cap of indeterminate affiliation."

"What else?"

"I saw a flash when his left hand moved."

"A weapon?"

"Or a laser beam. Or a Batman ring."

Ryan looked at me.

"Just keeping an open mind."

After fifteen more run-throughs, we gave up. The totality of our knowledge of the intruder was as follows: a tall human in a cap carrying or wearing something shiny who may or may not have left a locket on my doorknob.

Now we were getting somewhere.

Slidell called as Ryan and I were sharing a lunch of ham and Havarti sandwiches. He was going to think we did nothing but eat. Well, almost nothing.

"I got nature boy here."

"Sorry?"

"Kramden." In the background, I heard voices, the scrape of chairs, the clump of feet.

"He's at the station?"

"No. I'm treating him to pancakes at the IHOP."

"He agreed to come in?" I asked.

"Not exactly."

I let my silence act as question.

"He thinks the roust is about permits."

"When will you interrogate him?"

"I'll let the squirrel sweat an hour, then it's bombs away."

———

The CMPD is headquartered in the Law Enforcement Center, a geometric hunk of concrete facing off with the Mecklenburg County Courthouse across the uptown intersection of Fourth and McDowell. Ryan and I arrived shortly before two. We presented IDs, then rode the elevator to the second floor, the location of every detective unit.

The elevator smelled of sun-warmed nylon and wool and a late lunch being carried in a grease-stained bag. A meatball hoagie? Conversation focused on an upcoming Hornets game.

Slidell had already called to have Kramden brought to an interview room. So far, no interviewee. This did not put Skinny in a cheery mood. Nor did the sludge passing as coffee in the CCU. While waiting, everyone knocked back a mug. Skinny's agitated pacing did not put *me* in a cheery mood.

The desk phone rang at 2:23 p.m. Kramden was in place. Sound and video were up and running.

We trooped down the hall. Slidell split off into interrogation room 2, gestured us to the adjacent door. Knowing the routine, Ryan and I stepped to the one-way observation mirror.

Kramden, all angles and scowls, sat motionless in a scarred wooden chair at a gray metal table, booted feet spread, knees splayed, arms crossed on his chest. An athletic cap rested low on his forehead. I put his height at somewhere around six feet. His attitude at two exits past hostile.

Kramden was staring at the floor. Or his genitals. Hard to tell. He glanced up when Slidell entered. The logo above his bill looked like a red circle with a cross in the center. I couldn't make out the lettering.

Piccitelli told us the man's face was damaged. Still, I wasn't prepared.

A scar snaked south from Kramden's right temple, then cut east toward his chin. Puckered and permanently discolored, the stitching had not been done by a skilled plastic surgeon. Perhaps not by a doctor at all.

Ditto the eye lost to the IED. The upper lid, drawn down and sewn to the lower, was a translucent violet spiderwebbed with veins.

Over time, the rearranged tissue had collapsed into the empty orbit behind it. The scraggly half-brow topping the repair diagonaled upward sharply, creating a look of perpetual surprise.

Slidell tossed a thick folder and a yellow legal pad onto the table. Through the speaker their landing sounded like a thunderclap.

Kramden shot to his feet, good eye bombing the room, every fiber ready for a fight. Or flight.

Slidell's face flushed and his body coiled.

Kramden raised a hand palm outward. It was shaking. "Sorry, man. Loud noises mess with my head. I'm cool now."

"Sit your sad ass down, you fuckwit." Slidell was still shaken but trying to hide it.

Kramden sat.

"You've got problems, Bobby Karl."

"Who don't?" Embarrassed by his overreaction, Kramden was quickly moving back to belligerent.

"That's hilarious. I make a comment, you come up with a one-liner quick as a wink."

"I don't need no permit for my buses."

"You sure about that?"

"Check it out. You're a cop."

"Another sidesplitter. You ever think of doing stand-up? Maybe use a stage name, like Smith?"

If Slidell's knowledge of the alias surprised Kramden, he didn't let it show. The wonky eyebrow helped.

Slidell dropped into the remaining chair, slipped a pencil from his shirt pocket, and poised it over the tablet. "Tell me about Frank Boldonado."

"I don't know nothin' about Frank Boldonado."

"Wrong answer."

"Only one I got."

"Talk about Cougar Piccitelli."

"What about him?"

"He claims you and Boldonado hung tight as tits on a goat."

"Look, I may have met the guy. We aren't buds. We're both just planning for the day."

"What day is that, Bobby Karl? The one the Piggly Wiggly don't get its beer delivery?"

"Go ahead. Laugh. But when the sky's on fire and the air ain't fit to breathe, I'll be warm and my belly will be full. Don't come begging for shelter."

Slidell used an old interview tactic. Throw your subject off guard by attacking from multiple directions.

"Dahmer. Gacy. Bundy. You got a hard-on for killers, Bobby Karl?"

The damaged face darkened.

"For murder?" Slidell pushed.

"You can't bust my chops for appreciating history." Kramden's left hand never stopped moving. It stroked his jaw, thumbnailed the arm of the chair, brushed nonexistent fuzz from his nose. Below the table, one knee pumped nonstop.

"History?" Slidell scoffed.

"True crime. It's all over the airways."

"Let's discuss murder."

"Can I have a smoke?"

"No."

"That ain't how this is supposed to play."

"Murder," Slidell repeated.

"What about it?"

"Where's Boldonado?"

"Hell if I know. I'm just trying to survive, man."

"In your little foxhole for Armageddon."

"You got a problem with that?"

The two men glared at each other, radioactive with loathing. Then Slidell opened the folder and, one by one, spread prints across the scarred tabletop. Though I couldn't see them, I knew what the images showed. Kwalwasser's eyeball and skull. Sanchez's mutilated torso. Boldonado's hanging body. The bucket. Charlie Hunt. The hit-and-run girl.

Kramden leaned heavily onto both forearms. I noted that his right hand, now visible, was missing three digits. He rotated an image with his left, looked at it, then quickly away. His Adam's apple made a round trip of his throat.

"I need a smoke bad."

Slidell jabbed a finger on the photo of the mummified man.

"Frank Boldonado?"

"The guy dropped by the bunker a few times." Kramden's bravado was showing serious fault lines. "We drank a few brews. Caught some Jets action. Then he stopped coming around. End of story."

"When did you last see him?"

"It's been years. Two? Three? I swear, that's all I know."

"And the others?"

"Never seen them in my life. Fuck. Seriously? An eyeball!"

Slidell tucked the prints back into the folder.

"Where were you last week, Bobby Karl?"

"What day?"

"All of 'em."

"Doing field training."

"Field training? What are you, special ops?"

"Suck my dick."

Slidell slid the tablet to Kramden. "Write it all down. Names, addresses, dates. Where you been. Anything has to do with this prick Boldonado. You *can* write?"

Kramden scribbled with his good hand, then lay the pen on the table. "You want, I'll take a lie detector."

Slidell grabbed the tablet, rose, and headed for the door.

"What about me?" Kramden asked, now flustered. "Can I go?"

"Don't plan no European invasion."

We met Slidell in the hall.

"Impression?" I asked.

"Guy's a sniveling weasel." A pause, then: "You think he could be the mope who conked you when you made your Marvel hero move by the buses?"

"I don't know," I said curtly. "I never got a good look at him."

"You'll cut him loose?" Ryan asked.

"Got nothing to hold him on. For now."

Ryan and I were pulling in at the annex when my mobile rang.

"It's J.S.," I said.

"Your profiler pal?"

"Yes." I put the car in park, the call on speaker.

"Hi, Tempe. It's J.S. I've been considering our conversation."

"And?"

"The more I think about it, the more this guy sounds like a nasty piece of work. Extreme violence. Tremendous anger. I think he'd grown impatient that you weren't recognizing, or discovering, his handiwork, so he taunted you with the eyeball. Hard to ignore a body part on your doorstep. Now that he has your attention, he's growing more aggressive. I really don't like this new twist, killing not some random stranger but your friend."

I glanced at Ryan. His eyes were dark, his lips set in a grim line.

I told J.S. about the phone call and the incident at the SWI plant— how I'd seen a woman murdered. I added that her hit-and-run death also mimicked one of my old cases.

"If that *was* his doing, the violence is escalating," he said. "And the intervals between killings are growing shorter."

I'd thought of that.

"Here's the thing that worries me most. When taking down your friends or luring you to witness his brutality is no longer enough, he may switch his focus to you."

I'd thought of that, too. And a possibility that terrified me even more.

"What about Katy?" It came out trembly. I felt Ryan take my free hand.

"You still haven't heard from her?"

"I received a text last Monday. But somehow it didn't seem like her."

"How so?"

"It was very short. And she didn't wish me a happy Valentine's day. Both those things were out of character for Katy. At least, for the old Katy."

There was a moment of silence before J.S. spoke again.

"This type of indirect, orchestrated vengeance isn't common, but I have seen it. His acts are almost theatrical in nature. Does that pattern tell you anything about who this bastard might be?"

"Some 'innocent accused' who resented my testimony?" I offered, hooking air quotes with my sarcasm. "Some next of kin who disagreed with my findings? Some waiter who thought my tip was stingy? Who the hell knows? It's America in the age of rage."

J.S. ignored my outburst. "Now that this individual has your attention, he probably intends to raise the stakes."

That night we learned just how high those stakes would go.

29

While Ryan caught up on his backlog of emails, I did a Google search using the key phrases *sunflower*, *pendant*, and *Tú eres mi sol*. I learned that the locket could be purchased from many online vendors, including Amazon.

Deflated, I added the descriptors *Charlotte* and *jewelry*. Was given links to two stores. Both were located on Wilkinson Boulevard.

I dialed the first, Hermosa. Got a recording saying the number had been disconnected.

I tried Mis Joyas. A heavily accented voice answered, sounding like decades of unfiltered Camels.

"*Mis joyas. Si no lo tenemos, no lo necesitas.*"

"*Buenos noches,*" I said. "*Me alegro de que todavía estés abierto.*"

Unimpressed with my Spanish, the voice switched to English. "*Cariña*, this shop always open. What I can do for you?"

"I have an odd request."

"Like I said, we don't have it, you don't need it."

"I'm not looking for jewelry. I need information about a possible sale."

I heard a deep inhalation followed by an expulsion of breath. Pictured a stream of smoke rising from corduroy lips.

Several beats passed. I was expecting a hang up when the voice spoke again.

"You a cop? I don't talk to cops."

"No. My name is Dr. Brennan." I left it at that. No need to mention the ME or the morgue.

"Doctor, eh?"

"Yes."

"So, this not about taxes?" Wary.

"Definitely not."

"Yolanda González here. My son owns the *joyería*. If my arthritis is good, I work the register."

"I'm curious about a locket shaped like a sunflower. Inside are the words *Tú eres mi sol*."

"Your accent not bad. For a gringo."

"Thank you, Yolanda. The locket?"

"*Sí*. We sold some of those. Don't stock them no more. Too pricey for most of our customers." Followed by an indecipherable snort.

"Do you keep records of your sales?"

"The bigger ticket items."

"Could you check to see who bought the lockets?"

"I could."

Pause.

"Would you?"

"Why?"

"I found one and want to return it to its owner."

"The thing ain't *that* valuable, *cariña*."

"I know. But I own a piece of inexpensive jewelry that has great sentimental value to me. I'd be heartbroken if I lost it." Lame. But the best I could do.

"That's sweet. Hold on."

A receiver rattled against a hard surface. An eon passed. The receiver rattled again.

"I thought there was more, but I found just the two. You ready?"

"I am."

"Kamila Ochoa. She come in one day because of me being here. Bought a locket last September for her granddaughter."

"Do you have contact information?"

"Got a phone number but she won't answer."

"Oh?"

"She's dead. Found her floating like a big guppy in her tub."

Alrighty.

"I'm sorry."

"Sold the other to a fellow named Juan Gato. I remember thinking his name fit because he looked like a cat."

"Do you have—"

"Write this down."

Yolanda gave me a phone number and address. I wrote them down.

"*Gracia—*"

A male voice barked in the background.

The line disconnected abruptly.

At five-thirty, Ryan and I were standing on the broad front porch of a faux colonial at the far end of Sugar Mill Road. Redbrick, white trim, black shutters.

Dusk had already handed off to night. Streetlights were casting cones of light at intervals along the block. Windows were glowing yellow.

Gusts of wind teased the ties on my jacket. A listless rain was falling, sullen that the ground was too cold for percolation, too warm for accumulation.

I looked around as we waited for the door to be answered. So did Ryan.

The neighborhood was typical working class, the theme repeated again and again all over America. Nondescript ranch and split-level homes. Flags at the doors. Bikes on the lawns. Sheds in the backyards.

Beyond the house to which Yolanda's address had sent us, the street ended in a cul-de-sac. Beyond the cul-de-sac was a greenway running both sides of Little Sugar Creek. Cars and pickups waited on drives or sat parked at curbs.

I was poising my thumb for a second go at the bell, when the door opened as far as a brass chain would allow. Two eyes appeared in the crack, maize with bright jade flecks. The eyes peered down at me from an impressive height.

"Mr. Gato?" Ryan asked.

The eyes shifted to Ryan. Held.

"Juan Gato?" he asked.

Nothing.

"*Señor Gato*? *El detective y yo tenemos algunas preguntas.*" I took some liberties with Ryan's current status.

"I am Juan Gato. What is it you and the gentleman wish?" The English was perfect, the voice melodious enough to record the works of the bard.

"We're interested in a locket you may have purchased."

I scrolled to an image on my phone. Gato bent to study it. Straightened.

"Yes?"

"You recognize the locket?" I asked, unclear of his meaning.

"I purchased it as a gift," he said. "For my cousin's daughter. She turned eighteen this year and had earrings like that so I bought it to match."

"May we come in?" Ryan asked, somber.

"Is there a problem?" The yellow eyes widened. "The *joyería* appeared to be a lawful enterprise."

Ryan gestured toward the door. Gato closed, then opened it wide. We followed him into a foyer with a crystal chandelier hanging from the ceiling and black and white tile covering the floor. A clear acrylic bookcase rose on one wall.

The crystal sparkled. The tile gleamed. The books were organized by color and height.

The living room was down a short hall and through an archway on the left. Through an identical archway on the right, what had been a dining room now served as some sort of work area. Long folding tables lined all four walls, each piled with documents, manuscripts, and reference volumes. A chair angled awkwardly from one position, as though unexpectedly and quickly vacated.

The parlor held no sofa. Six upholstered wing chairs formed a semi-circle around a white brick fireplace *sans* logs, grate, or mantel. The palette was earth tones, the art geometric. There wasn't a speck of dust or a coffee ring anywhere.

We took places at opposite ends of the semi-circle. Gato was wearing a burnt orange sweater and tan slacks that hung somewhat baggily on a pair of long legs. His hair was black and wiry, his face oddly smooth. He could have been forty or sixty.

Wordlessly, Gato steepled his fingers and touched the tips to his lips.

Ryan and I exchanged glances. He nodded discreetly. I took over.

"Your home is lovely, Mr. Gato."

"You have not come for advice on interior design."

"Is that what you do?"

"I am a translator." Wrongly anticipating my next question. "I have been a US citizen for over twenty years. I can produce documentation."

"We're not here concerning your immigration status."

"Then please spare me any small talk and get to the purpose of your visit."

"I found you through Yolanda at *Mis Joyas*."

"So you said."

"Sadly, the owner of the locket I showed you was killed in a hit-

and-run two days ago. I work for the medical examiner. We have not yet confirmed the young woman's identity."

As I spoke, Gato's attitude transformed from aloof to dismayed. His face sagged and his shoulders curled in on themselves.

"I am so sorry," I said. "If you're willing to view another photo, we could use your help."

Gato nodded, face now pale as the fireplace brick.

I opened a facial close-up and held out my phone. He took the device and studied the screen.

"*Dios mío.*" Softly. "It is Andrea-Louisa."

"Andrea-Louisa?" I prompted.

"Andrea-Louisa Soto. She came to America from Chile to improve her English. She's been in this country less than a year."

"Where was she studying?"

"CLI. Charlotte Language Institute. It's a private school on South Boulevard. Andrea-Louisa's father is a surgeon in Santiago, quite wealthy. He didn't want his daughter to come here. He felt it was unsafe. She insisted. He finally relented and agreed to support her."

"Where was Andrea-Louisa living?"

"An apartment in South End. I'm not sure the name. One of those complexes with a ridiculous one-word appellation."

"May we have contact information for Dr. Soto?"

Gato got up and strode through the arch. Returned shortly and read us an address from his phone.

"Thank you, sir. Until the ID is official, it's probably best to say nothing to Dr. Soto. The ME may contact him for a DNA sample."

Ryan and I rose to leave.

As we passed into the hall, a random question popped into my mind.

"Has anyone else questioned you about Andrea-Louisa?"

"No."

I said nothing.

At the door, Gato turned, gave us a doleful look. "It appears my cousin was right. America was not safe for Andrea-Louisa."

We stopped for chicken at the Roasting Company. I chose dilled lima beans and cheese grits for my sides. Ryan went for a double order of garlic mashed potatoes.

We'd just begun eating when Ryan asked, "Why did you ask Gato if he'd already been questioned?"

I'd wondered the same. "I found the necklace online, then the jewelry store. Yolanda had a record of Gato's purchase. Gato gave the locket to a young woman fitting the victim's description. It was all so easy. Why hadn't someone already done that? Why hadn't Slidell?"

"Because he's CCU?"

"Detective Henry?"

"You said she's a newbie."

"That's Slidell's portrayal. Henry's been in Charlotte for several years."

"Before that the LAPD?"

"Yes."

"Ask her."

"I will. After I brief Nguyen."

"The chief will be pleased to have a name."

"She will."

We ate in silence for a while. Ryan broke it.

"Did you catch the possible link?"

"Link?" I hadn't.

"Andrea-Louisa's language school is on South Boulevard. You said Miguel Sanchez lived at the Beacon Hill Apartments."

"Off South Boulevard." Pointing a triumphant finger at Ryan. "Potential info for victim profiling?"

Ryan grinned.

"Nice detecting, *monsieur.*"

"*Merci, docteure.*"

While Ryan drove, I phoned Nguyen. She was, indeed, pleased, and promised to follow through with the ID. I didn't envy my boss her heartbreaking conversation with Dr. Soto.

Drowsy on poultry and cheesy starch, I wasn't in the mood for confrontation. Decided the call to Henry could wait until morning.

I'd just dropped my mobile into my purse when it rang. Sang, actually. I'd changed the ringtone to Joe "Bean" Esposito. "You're the Best." Yes, I'm a nerd.

I considered letting the call go to voice mail, but at the last minute dug for the phone, hoping the caller might be Katy.

It wasn't.

I'd never heard Slidell so distraught.

Rightly so.

His news was appalling.

30

I clicked to speaker phone.

"Don't talk. Listen. I gotta go ten-six."

"Seriously?"

"A kid's missing. The powers that be have lassoed every available butt for a task force."

"Even CCU?"

"What part of *every* needs explaining?" Too much stress and too little sleep were turning Skinny even more churlish than normal. "Everyone's in—the state boys, the feebs. A special agent name of Mitch Byrd is in charge. Mitch *Turd* is more like it."

"What's your problem with Byrd?"

"The guy's got a bug up his ass over a homicide we worked eight years ago. Turd played the angles wrong and I called him on it. Dick-wad hates my guts and the feeling's mutual."

"Surely the two of you can get along for this."

"Screw Byrd. I'm taking orders from Mangiorotti."

Captain Julian Mangiorotti headed the CMPD detective division. Knowing that the feud with Byrd was typical Skinny, I had no interest in learning details of the squabble.

"When did the child vanish?" I asked.

"Yesterday morning." I heard engine sounds in the background. A turn signal clicking.

"Any chance it's a runaway?"

"The kid's eleven."

"A noncustodial parent abduction?"

"Gee. We never thought of that."

Easy, Brennan.

"When was the last sighting?"

"At 0740, the kid was walking south on Quail Hollow Road toward Beverly Woods Elementary. Never made it. I'm meeting Detective Dimwit to canvas at the school. You'd think—"

"I have news," I said.

"Not now."

"Ryan and I got a probable for the hit-and-run vic."

"No shit." Grudgingly interested.

"The ID's not positive, but it looks good for an eighteen-year-old Chilean temporarily in the States on a student visa. Andrea-Louisa Soto."

A car door opened. I heard grunting, the scrape of Skinny's substantial derriere.

"Later."

Slidell disconnected.

No "good work," "nice job," "well done."

Pure Skinny.

"Detective Dimwit?" Ryan asked.

"Henry."

"Why does Skinny dislike her?"

"He's Skinny."

We rode in silence for a while, listening to the wipers and the icy *tic-tic-tic* of the drops they were chasing. Ryan spoke as we pulled in at Sharon Hall.

"I guess that answers your question about Henry's failure to pursue the locket lead."

I looked a question at him. Invisible in the dark.

"Her butt's been lassoed."

"Good point." Maybe. She'd had two full days to follow up on the thing.

Crossing from the car to the annex, Ryan and I both waved toward the patrol unit in the circle drive. The silhouette at the wheel may or may not have waved back. The headlights created two sparkling shafts piercing the rain.

Birdie greeted Ryan with a sequence of warm ankle rubs. Ignored me.

Ryan made me tea, grabbed a Fat Tire for himself. We settled on the sofa in the study.

My mood had nose-dived with Slidell's call. I'd worked too many missing-child cases. So often, the outcome was tragic.

And the pesky id voice was back.

What was its bloody point now?

I couldn't sit still.

Ryan suggested a movie. Birdie was all in. I let them choose. They picked *Legally Blonde*.

Throughout, I chewed a cuticle on one thumb. Ryan repeatedly, but gently, lowered my hand from my mouth.

When the closing credits began rolling, I suggested we contact Slidell to see if the child had been found. Ryan shrugged. Whatever. As before, I switched to speakerphone.

"Yo." Slidell picked up with his usual greeting.

"Yo," I said.

"Yo," Ryan said.

"That you, *monsieur*?" Slidell pronounced it "miss your."

"It is," Ryan said.

"How was the canvas?" I asked.

"These morons couldn't find their own assholes without a diagram." Dishes clattered in the background. Utensils. "They're teaching our kids?"

"You hate kids."

Slidell either missed or chose to ignore that.

"If anybody ever needs a talking dildo on legs, I know just the guy. This twerp principal."

"What did you learn?"

"Jackshit."

A woman queried Skinny on coffee. He answered in the affirmative.

"Brief me on the case," I said.

Heavy sigh, then pages flipped in a spiral.

"The kid's name is Olivia Lakin. White female, age eleven, with freckles, and carrot-red hair, braided."

A spoon clinked against china. I waited, knowing Skinny used at least two pints of sugar.

"Weight eighty-two pounds, height fifty-six inches. Mother, Sheila Lakin. Father, Dennis Lakin. He's a pinstripe at Bank of America. She's a receptionist at some old folks' home down Park Road."

"The Cypress?"

"Sounds right. The mother says the kid was wearing denim coveralls, a blue-and-white-polka-dot blouse, pink sneakers, a green puffer jacket, and a green wool cap."

Two loud slurps.

"The sub carried or wore a navy and lavender Mackenzie unicorn backpack."

I noticed that Skinny was doing the usual cop thing, depersonalizing by avoiding use of the child's name. The kid. The sub.

"What now?" I asked.

"We keep looking."

"Call with updates?"

"Why?"

"Because I care."

"Eee-rrg."

After disconnecting, Ryan and I climbed to the bedroom. Following an interlude during which my brain entertained only happy thoughts and admitted no subliminal messages, Ryan fell asleep with dizzying speed.

I did not.

My mind played images of a pigtailed girl shivering in a cold February rain. Frightened. Alone.

Or worse, not alone.

I lay in the safety of my bed, familiar objects shaping the shadows around me, Ryan's body lean and strong at my side. The warm cocoon wasn't enough to relax me.

I tried one of those sleep mantras.

Nope.

I tried another.

I focused on Birdie's purring. Ryan's soft snoring.

Slowly, reluctantly, my mind yielded.

Then my eyes were wide open.

Joe Bean was crooning that I was the best.

I reached for my phone. The screensaver clock said four forty-nine. Ryan's breathing suggested he was also awake. Of course, he was. Calls in the wee hours are never good news.

After much fumbling, I managed to answer.

Beside me, Ryan hiked his pillow to the headboard, sat up, and leaned against it. Again, I used speakerphone.

"Mm," I said.

"You listening? Am I wasting my time here?" Slidell's exhaustion was clear but saturated with some fiery new emotion. Fury? Bloodlust?

"I am." Over-annunciating to sound fully awake.

"We found the kid's backpack."

Slidell's words sent adrenaline fluttering through me.

"Where?" I asked.

"Patch of woods off Rea Road."

The pesky neurons went apeshit.

Feeling me tense, Ryan took my free hand.

"How did you find it at night?" I asked.

"The freakin' thing glows in the dark. Some local spotted it while looking for her cat. Thinking a kid had lost it and would catch shit at home, the good Samaritan called it in. Henry went to collect it."

I said nothing.

"It looks bad," Slidell said.

More nothing.

"It ain't just the daytime snatching and chucking the kid's backpack at a place some distance from her school. Byrd had Henry check the contents for anything that could clue us to the sub's location."

"And?" Impatient.

"Besides the usual school crap, the pack held a black leotard and tights, pink cotton underwear, and a pair of those wonky rubber shoes."

"Blue Crocs." I felt nauseous.

"Yeah. The mother says they don't belong to her kid."

A nuance in Slidell's tone told me he'd recognized the same horrific connection I was now seeing. The link my subconscious had suspected before Slidell's dreadful news.

"Now what?" I asked.

"Now some of us keep busting ass on the streets while others squeeze the usual charm parade."

I knew what Slidell meant. Teams would continue searching alleys, garages, ponds, fields, properties, and places kids were known to hang out. Meanwhile, others would question parents and relatives, friends, friends' families, neighbors, babysitters, doctors, dentists, coaches, those at Olivia's school, church, community center. And, his favorite, registered sex offenders. Beginning at the center and working outward, they'd interview anyone who'd had the slightest contact with the little girl.

"It's him, isn't it?" I could barely speak.

"Yeah."

Ryan looked at me with raised brows.

I shook my head.

He squeezed my hand.

"Do you really think he'd go that far?" I asked.

"I'm going to get this son of a bitch." Slidell sounded murderous.

"Keep me—"

"Yeah, yeah."

Slidell was gone.

Ryan didn't ask. I was grateful for that.

It took several minutes to wrap my mind around this new development. Several more until I was calm enough to lay it out for Ryan. During that time, he made mint tea. Like Gran, Ryan sees brewed herbs as the panacea for every ill.

We sat, backs propped against the pillows, Ryan's arm wrapping my shoulders. I talked. He listened.

"You're up to speed on this copycat situation, right?" I knew he was. We'd talked of little else. The unnecessary intro was a soporific for my anxiety.

"I am."

"Slidell and I think there's another victim. A child."

"*Tabarnak.*"

It was Quebecois Ryan's go-to cuss. I ignored it and continued. "As you just heard, Olivia Lakin has been missing for almost twenty-four hours. She's eleven years old. Yesterday morning she was abducted while walking to school."

Ryan sipped his tea.

"What you don't know is that Olivia's profile matches that of another girl killed years ago. Elizabeth Ellen 'Lizzie' Nance was also eleven. She was taken in broad daylight while walking home from a ballet class."

"You and Slidell worked the case?"

"Yes."

Synapses fired in my brain, bringing memories of the whole horror show. The massive media coverage. The hundreds of volunteers answering tip lines, posting flyers, searching woods and lakes near Lizzie's complex. To no avail.

Two weeks after Lizzie's disappearance, decomposed remains were found in a nature preserve northwest of Charlotte. My mind flashed images of the small body lying supine among the dead leaves, feet together, arms tucked to her sides, hair haloing her little white face.

Lizzie's corpse had been carefully arranged by the hands of her abductor.

I experienced a tickle of the same rage I'd felt back then.

"Did you catch the kid's killer?"

"We did. But not until years after her death."

Deep breath. Then I shared the final terrifying element.

"Lizzie's satchel was found in a wooded area off a rural two-lane. Last night, Olivia's backpack was found in a wooded area off Rea Road."

"A rural two-lane?"

"Not rural exactly, but sparsely developed suburban. Inside the backpack were a black leotard and tights, pink cotton underwear, and blue Crocs. Olivia's mother says those items don't belong to her daughter."

I swallowed.

"Lizzie Nance died wearing a black leotard and tights, pink cotton underwear, and blue Crocs."

31

S lidell and I agreed that the ballet clothing in the backpack was meant as a threat to me. That Olivia Lakin's disappearance was linked to the other copycat murders. That the perp was escalating.

Three points of concurrence. Might have been a record.

Skinny asked that I meet with his task force first thing in the morning. And that I come prepared.

At seven-forty a.m., Ryan and I entered the Law Enforcement Center and rode to the second floor. This time the elevator was empty save for an elderly cop with a belly two sizes too large for his uniform shirt. Wordlessly, the three of us watched the digits light up, then darken.

The task force had taken over an entire floor at the LEC. As Slidell had reported, several outside agencies were helping the CMPD, including the FBI. Preoccupied with orchestrating a triple homicide investigation, Captain Mangiorotti was letting SAC Byrd call most of the shots.

Skinny's nemesis assumed that the child was the victim of a sexual predator, and all effort was being expended in that direction. Though Skinny had pitched his alternative theory, Byrd didn't believe that the kidnapping was part of a vengeance scheme directed at a nerd forensic anthropologist.

Neither Byrd nor Mangiorotti was thinking copycat or serial killer. Or at least no hint of that possibility was contained in the statements being grudgingly released to a frenzied press. The last thing the mayor and the police chief wanted were the eyes of the national press zeroing in on their town.

Slidell wasn't buying into the sexual predator "horseshit." He'd requested and been given a small team of his own. Why? Pain in the ass that he is, Skinny is a legend at the CMPD. Charlotte's own Dirty Harry Callahan. And, oddly, the chief of detectives likes him. Or wants to avoid his tantrums. Whatever. Mangiorotti gave Slidell his own team and license to follow his instincts.

Slidell's operation was housed at the far end of the hall. The room wasn't huge, but big enough. A half dozen chairs sat haphazardly scattered at the back. Three corkboards stood at the front. Collapsible tables lined both side walls, one with laptops, the other with phones. At that hour, every line was silent.

Two uniforms occupied each table. O'Reilly. Papadopoulos. Roosevelt. Chan. Looked like a hometown United Nations.

Slidell and Henry were discussing items on the leftmost board. Henry's outfit of the day featured shades of blue and an appropriately accessorized sapphire and diamond band on one finger. The alternating stones sent off a big-bucks vibe.

The missing task force members, more beat cops I assumed, were busting ass on the street.

Ryan and I crossed to Slidell and Henry. They turned at the sound of our footsteps.

"Yo," Slidell said.

"Yo," Ryan said.

Jesus, I thought.

"Dr. Brennan." Henry sounded tired. "Good morning."

"Good morning."

"There's coffee in the CCU."

"I'm good," I said, eyes shifting to the display at Henry's back.

Topping the first board was a school portrait of Olivia Lakin. The child sat smiling directly into the lens, hands crossed on a railing to her left. Her sweater was pink, her blouse a lacy mint green. The coppery hair was tied back with avocado bows.

Below the photo was a timeline of Olivia's last-known movements. A map indicating her usual routes to school. Photocopies of interview notes.

"Any news?" I asked.

"No." Slidell sounded like he might have slept a few hours. His appearance suggested the nap had taken place at the station. His hair was spiking on top, lying flat on one side. His face looked as wrinkled as his shirt, his five o'clock shadow dense enough to hide small mammals.

"Post what you got, recent cases in the middle, old on the right," Slidell instructed me, cocking his chin at the two empty boards. Turning to the UN, he said, "You guys. Heads up. You'll want to hear this."

"Chronology's tough," I said, opening my briefcase and selecting a file. "Some of the copycat bodies weren't discovered right away. With others, we didn't see the link for a while."

I thumbed several pics onto the center board. All were scene or autopsy shots.

Behind us, the four uniformed cops went quiet. I sensed them watching and listening.

"Miguel Sanchez, age nineteen, street name Scrappy. The day before Christmas 2019, Scrappy's ear was discovered nailed to a tree outside his Beacon Hill apartment in South Charlotte. At the—"

"How 'bout we keep it short?" Slidell cut me off.

Okeydokey.

"Three days later, the rest of Sanchez turned up in a Wendy's dumpster. He was missing his liver, kidneys, and heart."

I opened a second, much older file, stepped to the last board, and posted another set of photos.

"These are the remains of a young man found near Lake Wylie in 2008. The victim had been killed, decapitated, and disemboweled."

O'Reilly winced. "They catch the skeeve who did that?"

"Yes," I said, not wanting to elaborate at that moment.

Everyone studied the Sanchez and Lake Wylie remains. The parallels between them were undeniable.

I selected a third and fourth folder and removed two sets of pics. The first featured the eyeball. The second showed the privy skull, knife projecting from one socket.

"This was actually the body that started it all," I said, thumbing the new prints onto the board below those of Sanchez. "At least from my perspective."

"Body part," Henry corrected, a bit too blithely for my taste.

"Veronica Kwalwasser died of natural causes in 2020. Sometime in the year following her death, her head was stolen from the Happy Trails crematorium, eventually discarded in a privy behind MiraVia at Belmont. One of Kwalwasser's eyeballs was kept and frozen, then left at my home this past January thirtieth."

"Christ," O'Reilly whispered under his breath.

I stepped to the board bearing my old cases and tacked up a photocopy of a story that had appeared in a Montreal tabloid called *Allo Police*.

"Years ago, I stabbed a serial killer in the eye to save my life."

"Don't mess with her," Ryan said, perhaps to break the tension in the room.

I gave him The Look.

"The murders got a lot of press at the time." I added, "In Canada."

"How would the killer find media about a case from so long ago and so far away?" Henry asked.

Slidell snorted. Not a pleasant sound. "Nothing ever dies on the Weird Wide Web."

"You think Kwalwasser was symbolic?" Henry asked. "An eye for an eye?"

"I hadn't thought of that." Why hadn't I? "Maybe."

New folder. New pics.

"On February seventh, Francis Leonardo 'Frank' Boldonado was found hanging from a tree in Lake Norman State Park. He'd been reported missing in 2019. My skeletal analysis determined that Boldonado had been murdered by garroting."

Board three. Another old case.

"In 2006, a PI named Noble Cruikshank was garroted, then hanged to make his death appear to be a suicide."

Fourteen eyes moved between the Boldonado and Cruikshank pics. Again, the similarities were unmistakable.

Next, I tacked up shots of the bucket sent to me by Deputy Santoya. Added close-ups of the Joker mask Hawkins and I found inside the hollowed-out concrete. A copy of the snapshot showing me on the steps of the MCME.

"This bucket was discovered a little over a week ago in the Pisgah National Forest in Burke County."

Stepping right, I posted photos of the bucket found in Burke County in 2015. Added images of the head-shaped mold inside the concrete fill.

"The copycat bucket is clearly a taunt," Ryan said, voice now tight.

"Or it could just be a prank?" Henry suggested.

Ryan and Slidell both looked at her. She shrugged.

I could hardly bear to view the next series of images. Charlie Hunt at the wheel of his Porsche. In a body bag. On stainless steel at the MCME.

"Charles Anthony Hunt died of CO poisoning in his garage this past Friday night, an apparent suicide."

Everyone waited while I drew a deep breath.

"Toxicology screening showed traces of peanut protein in Charlie's system. He was severely allergic and fanatically careful, checking labels, querying waiters, carrying an EpiPen. He would never, under any circumstances, eat anything containing peanuts. Especially in his own house. Peanut residue was detected in a liquor bottle in Charlie's home office."

Up went photos of another suicide that wasn't.

"In 2008, this man, an ER physician, died of CO poisoning in his garage. Toxicology screening picked up chloral hydrate in his system. It was later established that the doctor hadn't knowingly ingested the drug."

I moved on to the last set of files.

"Andrea-Louisa Soto, an eighteen-year-old Chilean national, was murdered in an intentional hit-and-run last Saturday night." I posted Andrea-Louisa's photo. It showed a teenaged girl with light brown skin and long black hair.

"Ara, last name unknown, was a fifteen-year-old Afghan national murdered in an intentional hit-and-run in 2013." I posted Ara's photo. It showed a teenaged girl with light brown skin and long blond hair, dark at the roots.

The room was deathly quiet as I added my last pair of images to the collection of old cases. A school portrait of a young girl smiling into the lens. A small pale body surrounded by yellow tape, limbs and hair posed by the hands of a killer.

I gazed at the face I'd studied so many times. At the dusting of caramel freckles. At the long brown hair, center parted and woven into braids. At the sparkling green eyes so hopeful and full of life. A life denied her by a psychopath.

I swallowed.

"In 2009, Lizzie Nance was abducted in broad daylight while walking home from a ballet class. Her body was found in a nature preserve northwest of town. Lizzie was murdered when she was eleven years old."

The similarity in MO was indisputable, the resemblance between Olivia Lakin and Lizzie Nance striking.

"Same race, same age, same body size, same hair style," Slidell said, voice controlled. In cop mode.

"No bangs, no glasses, no braces," Ryan said. "Things common in kids that age."

"I don't know," Henry said, sounding dubious. "That describes a lot of kids. So do freckles and braids."

Slidell stared hard at the images, a tiny vessel throbbing in his temple. "This psycho has gone too far."

"Think it's another threat?" Ryan's face was without expression or humor. "Or would he really harm the girl?"

"Don't matter his intent. No one grabs a kid on my watch."

I didn't point out that, being retired, Skinny has no watch.

"From this moment, we think about nothing but nailing this prick." Slidell turned to me. "Tell me again. Who'd you finger as possible perps?"

"I didn't really see all of those people as serious—"

"Just gimme the names."

I listed those I'd mentioned earlier: my bitter former student, Terrence Edy; my angry neighbor, Alasdair Campbell; the murder-besotted prepper, Bobby Karl Kramden; the hostile homeless vet, Winky Winkard.

"I did some interviews at the shelter," Henry said. "Couple guys said Winkard was bad news."

"Write down the goddam names," Slidell barked.

I did. As I scribbled, was reminded of bossy Yolanda at the *joyería*.

Slidell handed the list to Papadopoulos. "By lunch, I want a report on every skin cell these jerks ever shed."

Papadopoulos took the paper, handed it on, and began tapping keys.

Slidell turned to Chan and O'Reilly, the pair manning the phone lines. "You two go through the doc's files. Same focus."

"Skin cells." O'Reilly snapped a two-finger salute.

"Cross-check anything even hints of a tie to Lakin."

Ryan, Slidell, and Henry left to help search for Olivia. I stayed in case questions arose with regard to my old files.

Papadopoulos, Roosevelt, and I booted computers. Save for an occasional question, the only sounds in the room were the clicking of keys, the rustling of paper, the squeak of a metal chair, the ringing of a phone.

Calls came in with regularity, some rolled from the main number, some direct to our dedicated line. Olivia was on a train heading for New York. In a shed behind a home on Radcliffe Avenue. At an urgent care center in Indian Trail. On a spaceship zooming toward Venus.

Every time my mobile buzzed, my pulse went stratospheric. I snatched it up, hoping for one of two things. The child had been found. Katy was safe. No such call.

People think police investigations proceed at breakneck speed, with car chases, and takedowns, and gun battles in the street. Not so. Most of the work is tedious and involves plowing through records, phone logs, and surveillance tapes.

Three hours later, we were still eyeballing screens and perusing hard-copy files when Papadopoulos broke the silence.

"I've been playing around, poking at this guy Kramden."

"The prepper," I said, glancing up from my screen.

"Yeah. He owns the land where he's burying the buses."

Slidell had already learned that. I didn't say it.

"He drives a 2010 Ford Fusion registered to a Charlotte address. I found a deed says Kramden owns the property. It may not have come up in previous records searches because the deed's under the name B. K. Kramdan. I'm guessing that's a typo."

Not particularly exciting. But his next words were.

"The address is on Sharon Hills Road." He read off a number. "That puts it six doors down from the Lakin home."

"That can't be coincidence!" Too loud. I knew it could be just that. Or that the misspelled name might not be an error. Still, I was totally jazzed.

"Good catch," I said, grabbing my phone.

Slidell answered on the third ring.

"Yo."

"Any news?" I asked.

"No."

I told him what Papadopoulos had discovered.

"Sonofabitch," he said.

"Yeah."

"Enough to get a warrant?"

"Enough to try."

Forty minutes later he called back, sounding sufficiently irked to eat his own dog.

"The idiot judge says she needs more."

"Jesus. The guy is fixated on murder, knows how to butcher animals, was associated with Frank Boldonado, and lives down the street from the missing child."

"Can't mention that we know about Kramden's little hobby. We entered his bus without paper."

"Crap."

"Keep digging."

We kept digging.

Roosevelt learned that Terrence Edy had served a short stint at Belmont Abbey College after flunking out of UNCC. With equal academic distinction. And that he'd been a counselor for one summer at Camp Pine Tree. In Burke County. In the Pisgah National Forest.

Chan discovered that after an honorable discharge from the army, Calvin "Winky" Winkard spent eight years with the Phoenix PD.

Then Papadopoulos uncovered an unsettling fact.

32

"There's another thing, perhaps relevant, perhaps not," Papadopoulos said. "During his interrogation, Kramden mentions he's a Jets fan. I played with that, figuring something might kick loose in New York. Dead end. The guy's a biscuit buff."

O'Reilly, Roosevelt, Chan, and I regarded him blankly.

"Guess we've got no hockey fans in the crowd. Kramden is NHL, not NFL. He follows the Winnipeg Jets, not the New York Jets."

"He's Canadian?" Chan asked.

"I'm working on that now."

"How did you think to go that route?" I was impressed. And wondering why neither Slidell nor Henry had.

"Look at this."

I dragged my chair right.

Papadopoulos brought up a poor-quality photo of Kramden seated in the interview room at the LEC. I assumed it was a still taken from the surveillance video. He zoomed in until the pixilation started getting dodgy.

"Look at his cap," Papadopoulos said.

I did. Enlarged, I could see that the fuzzy letters at the top of the circle spelled "WINNIPEG," those at the bottom "MB." The *X* at the center was formed by two crossed cannons.

"You mentioned stabbing some perp up there, how it made the papers. So I thought the Canadian angle was worth a poke."

This time I phoned Ryan.

"*Sacre bleu*," he said.

"*Oui*," I agreed.

"A Canadian link could explain the eyeball."

"My Montreal case got national coverage."

I also passed on the info about Winkard and Edy.

In less than an hour, Ryan appeared in person. Partly news. Partly hunger. He arrived with enough hoagies to feed Lithuania.

As we ate, Ryan briefed us on what he'd learned via a contact at the RCMP. Bobby Karl Kramden's mother, Everjoy Amand, was Brokenhead Ojibway, a First Nations tribe in Manitoba. Everjoy was now dead, but her sister Zinnia, age eighty-two, was alive and widowed and living in a retirement home in Alberta.

"Is she sharp?" Chan asked.

"As a straight edge. And eager for conversation. Zinnia said Bobby Karl grew up in the States and spent time in the US military. She wasn't sure which branch. She *was* sure that he came out of service a very bitter man. Disfigured, half blind, and disgusted with the US, he moved to Manitoba. A few years there, and he grew disillusioned with Manitoba and aimed his nose south."

"Could she pinpoint his time in Canada?" I asked.

"She wasn't certain when he arrived, but she knew when he left. It was the year her youngest turned thirty. She has six. Bobby Karl didn't stay for the celebration. Zinnia still holds that against him. And the fact that he killed her dog."

I raised both brows in question.

"He left in 2000. She said all the Y2K daftness turned him snake crazy."

"Her words."

"Yes. She also said he was a shameful excuse for an Ojibway."

"Sounds like Zinnia doesn't care for her nephew."

"She described him as a cruel man at war with his soul."

"Why did he kill her dog?" Roosevelt asked, voice curdled with disgust.

"It snapped at him, so he decapitated it with a machete."

"Christ almighty," O'Reilly said.

"Zinnia remembered that Bobby Karl was once a person of interest in a rape investigation. She didn't recall details. Said he wasn't charged but figured the lout was probably guilty."

"Does Slidell know all this?"

"Yeah. After talking to my colleague in Manitoba, he thought he had enough to sell it to the judge."

Moments later Skinny thundered into the room.

"Success?" Ryan asked.

Slidell gave a thumbs-up.

"Which location?"

"Both. According to your Mounty friend, the rape in Canada involved a fourteen-year-old kid. That jangled her honor's bells. As we speak, a unit's hitting Kramden's crib on Sharon Hills. You up for a surprise drop-in at bus haven?" The invitation wasn't directed to me.

Ryan bunched and tossed his sandwich wrapper. Stood.

So did I.

"No way, Doc. This could get nasty."

I spoke slowly and firmly. "Kramden suffers from PTSD. Katy may also suffer from PTSD. She aspired to help vets, so the two may have crossed paths. Besides, I'm fluent in nasty."

With that, I beelined for the door.

The road seemed even steeper than I recalled. But today was warmer, the dirt trail muckier. I could sense Slidell's irritation at the coating being applied to the sides and underbelly of his precious 4Runner. Wondered why he hadn't taken the other road.

Three cruisers sat idling at the top of the last rise. Nothing stirred in the valley below. No vehicles were present near the mound or bus pit.

Slidell got out and explained the game plan. The first unit headed downhill and circled to the back of the property to block Kramden's fleeing from the rear. The second positioned itself at the front. The third rolled to a stop beside the entrance.

Slidell re-took the wheel and we descended, SUV lurching, tires spitting mud. At the same spot as last time, Slidell shifted into park and turned to me.

"Your ass stays—"

"—put until the place is cleared. Got it."

The men alighted and walked toward the stairway leading down into the buses. Both were strapped, Ryan's weapon in a shoulder holster, Slidell's at the small of his back. Both unzipped their outerwear with the same fluid movement.

Simultaneously, the front doors of the visible cruisers opened. The four uniforms got out and stood behind them.

All was still. No chirping birds, yapping dogs, crackling radio, whining generator.

"Police!" Slidell called out.

Silence.

"Bobby Karl Kramden. This is the CMPD. We have a warrant to search these premises."

More silence.

Slidell circled a finger in the air, pointed at the nearest cruiser, then toward the stairs. The two uniforms donned protective gear, drew their weapons, and crept forward, an advance team to check for trip wires, flash bombs, or any sort of booby trap. For a bad guy with an AK.

I heard no yelling. No gunshots.

Hinges rasped. Metal slammed metal.

Minutes later, a lot of minutes, one of the team signaled all clear. Slidell and Ryan hurried down the stairs.

Seconds crept by with glacial slowness. Minutes.

Realizing I was going at the thumb cuticle again, I slipped my hands into my pockets and watched, willing someone to emerge. Slidell leading a handcuffed Kramden. Ryan carrying a child, her tiny arms clinging to his neck. No one appeared.

When I thought I could take it no longer, Ryan's head came bobbing up the steps. His hand rose to wave me forward. I bolted.

Descending the narrow treads, I passed one of the advance team heading topside.

"Any sign of the Lakin kid?" I asked.

He shook his head glumly.

"Kramden?"

"Negative."

"Nothing?"

"Oh, there's something."

We hurried in opposite directions.

Slidell was in the first bus speaking by radio with the Sharon Hills unit. His flushed face and animated tone told me the search of that property had also yielded nothing.

Ryan was in the second bus, examining two papers lying on the makeshift desk. I joined him.

"The cop said you found something?"

"You're not going to like it."

I glanced down. The papers were actually maps, the kind passengers used to study while offering suggestions to frustrated drivers. Usually with both parties lost and irritated.

The smaller scale map showed both Carolinas. The edges were perforated, so I guessed it was torn from a spiral bound atlas.

The larger scale map was of Charlotte and the surrounding area. On it were features such as streets, parks, schools, and waterways, each category highlighted in a different pastel.

Slidell joined us, bringing with him the smell of sweat and outrage. "The other place is clean. No vehicle, no Kramden, no sign of the kid."

"You'll get him," Ryan said.

"You can take that to the bank." To me, "Don't touch nothing."

Gesturing irreverently to Slidell, I leaned over the desk. And noted that both maps were marked with pencil-drawn *X*s.

I focused on the city map. An *X* marked Lake Wylie to the south, the Charlotte Motor Speedway in Concord, Greenleaf Avenue. On the larger map, *X*s indicated the small town of Earl in Cleveland County, Lumberton in Robeson County, Wiseman's Overlook in Burke County, all in North Carolina. In South Carolina, Charleston had scored twice.

What the hell?

As in a supercollider, particles slammed together in my mind.

My scalp prickled.

Many of the pins marked sites involved in my old cases.

"Where did you find these?" I gestured at the maps, pulse pumping overtime.

Ryan hooked a thumb at a cardboard box with a pile of papers beside it. Removing a pen from my pocket, I began sifting. The collection included hundreds of photocopied news stories and court transcripts.

"Did you check this stuff out?" I asked without turning.

No response.

I looked at Slidell. He refused to meet my gaze.

I returned my attention to the pile.

No way!

Using the pen, I rotated a sheet of scrawled notes to verify that I really was seeing the tail end of a familiar logo.

I was. *Allo Police.* A photocopy of the feature dating back decades. The story I'd tacked on the board in Slidell's task force room. I'd refused to grant an interview, but the paper had proceeded without my input. A string of dead women. A break-in at the anthropologist's home. Her escape after defending herself with a knife. Names. Places. Dates. It was all there. Even a pic of me entering the courthouse to give testimony at a trial.

My mind popped the same question Henry had asked. How had an ancient story from a Montreal tabloid found its way to this bus?

More important, why?

Barely breathing, I scanned other photocopied articles. Many were from the Charlotte *Observer* and the Charleston *Post and Courier*. Others had appeared in publications I couldn't identify. All involved violent deaths, many in North and South Carolina. Some I didn't recognize. Some I remembered vaguely. Some I recalled in vivid detail: 2006: a killer stalking the streets of Charleston; 2008: a mutilated cadaver lying on the shore of Lake Wylie; 2010: a war hero misidentified; 2011: remains discovered in a dump near the Charlotte Motor Speedway; 2013: a young woman killed in a hit-and-run; 2015: bones found below a mountain overlook; 2020: a corpse mutilated by feral hogs; 2021: decomposing bodies tossed ashore inside a medical waste container.

Again, I whipped toward Slidell.

"Where's Katy?" I could barely form the words. "Does this maniac have Katy?"

Slidell stormed out, his bellowed orders floating in his wake.

"Issuing a BOLO for one Bobby Karl Kramden, AKA Smith. White male, six-footer missing one eye. Anyone spots this douchebag, he goes in the cage. And I need eyes on two locations twenty-four/seven." Slidell provided Kramden's two addresses. A staticky response sputtered back over the radio.

Ryan studied me with the bluer than blues, then pulled me close and kissed the top of my head.

An unfamiliar sensation was sweeping through me.

I had no idea what to do.

What to feel.

Only fear.

33

Ryan agreed to a drop by at Katy's house. If she'd returned home since I'd last been there, again she'd taken care to leave no sign.

After departing Kenmore Avenue, we grabbed burgers at the Five Guys on Central. Ryan ate both mine and his. And all the fries. I had no appetite.

Our next stop was Roof Above. The thermometer was flirting with thirty and an ice-water wind had ridden in on the dusk. Only one man was smoking outside the shelter, a chunky twentysomething with blond dreads and skinny jeans several sizes too skinny, given his poundage.

Dreads watched as Ryan and I walked toward him, not hostile, not welcoming. Not anything. A metal ring winked from one brow when his head moved.

"Hey," I said when we drew close.

"Hey." Dreads sucked smoke into his lungs, exhaled it in an impressively sharp-edged cone.

"Nicely done," I said.

"Practice," he said.

"You crashing at the shelter?"

"Dining. I heard the chef just earned his third star."

"Good one." And not a response I'd expected.

"Thanks."

"Do you come here often?"

"Now you offer me a beer or mixed drink?"

Dreads was right. My question sounded like a clichéd pickup line. And he was doing a good job of parrying my lame overtures.

I introduced myself and Ryan. Dreads didn't offer a name. Remembering etiquette, I didn't inquire.

"You into the Lil Wayne thing?" I asked, referencing the bleached dreads.

"I'm into the Socrates thing," he said.

I had no response to that.

"Plato, Aristotle, Descartes, Kant."

"Beware the barrenness of a busy life," Ryan said.

Dreads took another long drag and blew the smoke skyward. No cone. "Cogito ergo sum."

"Too much thinking can get a guy into trouble," Ryan said.

"So *that* explains the lightness of my wallet." The hint of a smile. "*Sum* Hersh Bender, a grad student of very limited means."

"Cadging a free three-star meal?" Ryan guessed.

"Conserving my metaphorical bread."

I explained to Hersh about Katy. He gave me a vague look that could have meant anything. After pausing for a beat, he drew smoke into his lungs, then dropped and crushed the butt with his heel.

"I can picture the woman you're talking about. Nice looking. Tough. Someone said she was army. Never spoke to her, though."

"When did you last see her?" *Calm, Brennan.*

Hersh wagged his head. The dreads danced. "Sorry. I only hit this place once every couple of weeks. The conscience thing and all."

"Do you know a man named Calvin Winkard? Goes by Winky?"

"I see that dude coming, I go the other way."

"Why?" I prodded.

"Don't like him."

"Why?"

"Don't know."

"When did you last see Winky?"

"Don't know."

Ryan crossed his arms. "The only true wisdom is in knowing you know nothing."

"Socrates." Jabbing one chubby finger toward Ryan. "You're grooving, man. Sorry. Time to bounce. Got a seminar on existential philo at seven."

Hersh shoved his hands into his pockets and started up the street, shiny denim sculpting his sizable buttocks. Six paces out, he stopped and turned back.

"I *do* know something." Again, the pointing finger. "The last time I saw your daughter she was with another chick. I remember thinking they both looked buff, and that I should get my fat ass to a gym. I was outside smoking, like tonight, caught a few phrases as they passed by. PTSD. VA. EMDR. I figured they were army buds."

"When was this?" Heart now thundering like hoofbeats.

"Probably the week before last. But it could have been earlier. Time is but celestial motion."

"Can you describe the other woman?"

"Not really."

"Tall, short, fat, thin?"

"Tall. But then everyone looks tall to me."

"That's it?" *Easy, Brennan.*

"It was cold. Both were wearing hats and scarves."

With that, Hersh left for his class.

Ryan and I entered Roof Above. The lobby smelled exactly as it had on my earlier visit: Pine-Sol, cooking grease, and unwashed clothing. And was equally empty.

M. Zucker sat behind her glass barrier. She smiled at seeing me, but not as broadly as on our first encounter.

"You still looking for your daughter?" she asked, angling her brows to look appropriately sympathetic.

"I am."

"Still haven't seen her. But I did ask around. Seems no one has." The brows dipped lower. "I'm sure she just needs time to herself."

I asked a few more questions, then, knowing further probing would produce nothing, I repeated the same request as on my initial visit. As before, M. Zucker promised to phone should she see Katy. As before, I left my card.

We were almost at my Mazda when Ryan's mobile rang. He clicked to speakerphone and held it between us.

"We got us a whole new ball game." Slidell sounded simultaneously furious and jazzed. "The Lakins just got a ransom call."

Ryan and I looked at each other in shock.

"That doesn't fit the pattern," I said.

"Tell that to the scumbag who dimed 'em."

"What's the demand?"

"Two hundred thousand. The usual horseshit. Further instructions to follow. Don't call the cops or the kid's toast."

"Yet the parents contacted you," Ryan said.

"Daddy. After strenuous argument with Mommy."

"How are they doing?" I asked.

"How do you think they're doing?"

"Their phone is wired, right?"

"Yeah. But the incoming number will trace to some burner at the bottom of Steele Creek."

"Now what?"

"Byrd's got guys sitting at the house. Now we wait."

"It makes no sense," I said, buckling my seat belt, still reeling from Slidell's bombshell. "Could Olivia's abduction be unrelated to the copycat killings?"

"Anything's possible," Ryan said.

"Olivia's parents aren't wealthy. Could the ransom demand be an attempt to throw us off?"

Ryan shrugged. Who knows?

We were discussing other possibilities when Ryan's phone pinged to indicate an incoming text. He glanced at the screen. Seconds later, the device rang. He answered, this time did not go to speaker.

I recognized Slidell's blustery cadence but couldn't make out his words. Listening to Ryan's monosyllabic responses, I felt miffed that he wasn't including me in the conversation.

"A tip came in on the main hotline," Ryan said, after disconnecting.

"Classified intel?" Dripping with sarcasm. "I lack proper clearance?"

Ryan considered that for a moment. Then, "Slidell asked me not to use speakerphone."

Slidell's request didn't surprise me. Ryan's compliance did. I said nothing.

"A female caller said the Lakin kid is at a construction site off Highway 51 in a town called Matthews. She claimed to have witnessed a kid with braids and matching Olivia's description being led into a trailer by a scruffy gorilla in a baseball cap. Her turn of phrase."

"Colorful." Chilly. "When did she see this?"

"Ninety minutes ago. She continued on to her condo, saw Olivia's picture on the evening news, decided to call 911."

"Is the tip credible?"

"Byrd thinks so. Slidell agrees."

"Matthews isn't far. Let's go."

"No."

"No?" Swiveling to face Ryan.

"Slidell also asked that I take you home. I know you'll be pissed, but I agree with him. If Olivia is at that location, this could—"

"Yet it was okay for me to accompany you to Kramden's compound. Why bar me now?"

"You have no official reason to be on scene for a takedown."

"Nor do you, *monsieur*."

"Slidell had me deputized."

"He can't do that." I had no idea.

"He can. And did."

The red-hot Kilauea rage threatened. I held my tongue.

"Look, Tempe. This probably isn't Skinny's call."

We rode in silence the rest of the way, the air between us charged with anger. Slidell's SUV was idling in the circle drive by the annex. Skinny was outside his vehicle, talking to my tail through the open window of her cruiser.

Shifting into park, Ryan rotated to face me. I felt the blue sizzle of his eyes on the side of my face. The light touch of his fingers on my neck. I shrugged his hand off with a sharp shoulder jerk.

Then I did what I do when my temper is blown. I went too far.

"Pull your head out of your ass, Ryan. If it weren't for me, all you'd know about this case would be the tidbits *I* chose to share."

"Tempe—"

"Screw you."

I got out, slammed the door, and strode toward my porch.

Normally, my temper cools as quickly as it flares. Not this time. I felt betrayed on two levels.

Slidell doubted my ability to function outside the lab, an attitude I'd come to expect. But Ryan? How could Ryan side with Skinny in excluding me? In devaluing my competence? Did he really believe I'd do anything to endanger myself or a victim?

And Olivia was still missing.

And Kramden was still out there.

I paced for a while. Worked the thumbnail. Of course, neither helped. Birdie kept his distance, alarmed by the maelstrom of emotions radiating from me.

Sleep was out of the question. Besides, it was only seven-fifteen. Food didn't appeal. Neither did waiting by my phone.

I considered options. TV? Novel? Laundry? Shower?

Deciding a bubbly soak might be the best antidote for my rattled nerves, I drew a bath as hot as I thought I could stand.

Twenty minutes later, my skin was crimson and every muscle

had seceded from my body. I was slipping on sweats when I noticed that a voice message had landed on my mobile.

Figuring the caller was Ryan, and eager for news, I clicked on.

Detective Henry had phoned to check on my well-being.

My newly acquired composure self-destructed.

"Goddamfreakingsonofabitch Slidell!" The device hit the mattress, ricocheted, then rebounded off the dresser. "Freaking hell!"

I sat on the bed and ran through Taylor Swift lyrics in my mind. *Oh-oh. You need to calm down.* It took the entire song, but the old trick worked.

More serene, I retrieved my phone and dialed Ryan. He answered, voice barely above a whisper.

"Can't talk."

"Tell Slidell to lose the big daddy act."

"What?"

"I don't need a guardian."

"Meaning?"

"He put Henry on me."

"I doubt that."

"Is Henry part of the operation?"

"Not here at the trailer. She's with one of the search teams in Charlotte."

"What's happening where you are?"

"Surveillance. Can't light the place up if there's a chance the kid's inside."

"Anyone present?"

"There's a truck parked beside the trailer. The overheads are on inside. Gotta go."

"Be safe."

"Always."

I sat there, antsy as hell, the subliminal voice at it again. Intangible as smoke, steady as a beeper.

What had re-triggered it? Fear for Olivia? Guilt that I was ground zero for the whole ugly mess?

Or was my id whining about something more immediate? The snub by Slidell? The argument with Ryan? The call from Henry? The fact that she was out being useful while I was home sitting on my ass?

A tiny blip jiggled the needle.

Henry?

If not at Slidell's bidding, why *had* Henry phoned me? To share new intel?

Unlikely after eight on a Saturday night. Besides, Henry was busy searching playgrounds and dumpsters, praying she wouldn't find a child's corpse. Praying she would?

Unlike me. Sitting vigil with a cat.

Hour after hour, the phone didn't ring.

To occupy my mind, I chose an utterly inane activity. After testing dozens of ringtones, I programmed my mobile with the theme song from *Bonanza*. What could go wrong with Pa and the boys by my side?

I was heading upstairs when a tune rolled off the Ponderosa.

It was well past eight.

On a Saturday night.

34

"No joy," Ryan said.

Silence as he and I shared the same thought. Olivia had been gone for more than seventy-two hours. We both knew what that meant.

"She's still alive," I said with more conviction than I felt.

"Yeah."

"What happened at the trailer?"

"When a uniform let loose with a megaphone, a guy fired out looking like he'd just junked his jeans."

"The scruffy gorilla."

"Yeah."

"Not Kramden."

"No. He showed ID as Earl Franklin Quail. The kid with him was Erla June, Quail's ten-year-old daughter."

"What were they doing at a construction site on a Saturday night?"

"Quail's the project foreman. He's divorced and this is his visitation weekend. Erla June wanted to see where daddy works. Quail figured what the hell."

"Another dead end."

"Sadly . . ." A pause, then, "Henry just reported in. Her team's been working a wooded area surrounding a pond off Green Rae Road. No joy for them, either, and she sounds like hell. I think she's about to be ordered 10-10."

"Tell her *mercy buckets* for the call, but I'm swell on my own."

"If our paths cross, I'll thank her for you."

Another moment of empty air passed between us. I heard Ryan's breath on the receiver, night sounds behind it.

"Sanchez. Kwalwasser. Boldonado. Hunt. Soto. Lakin. We have five bodies and a missing kid and absolutely no physical evidence," I said. "No prints. No tire tracks. No hairs or fibers. No body fluids. No skin cells. No touch DNA. No paint smears or glass particles at the hit-and-run scene or on Soto."

"What's your point?"

"Isn't the *absence* of evidence evidence in itself?"

"Meaning?"

"Could Kramden—"

"Or whoever."

"Or whoever have experience with decontamination procedures? Maybe he worked at a lab or a hospital? Or he's knowledgeable about cleanup? Maybe he was employed by one of those disaster rehab services?"

"Not bad, Brennan. I'll tell Skinny. He can have his team work that angle."

It took thirty minutes and several calls west to an earlier time zone before Ryan phoned back. Officer Chan had surfaced an interesting fact.

"Calvin Winkard—back in the day he didn't go by Winky—served most of his time with the Phoenix PD as a member of its crime scene unit." I could read Ryan now. He sounded amped.

"No shit," I said.

"Winky probably swabbed plenty of that."

"Hilarious. What else?"

"Mangiorotti green-lighted Slidell to issue a second BOLO, this one for Winky. So far, no sightings. We're heading to Roof Above now to check the guy's tent and ask around at the shelter."

I didn't envy M. Zucker her upcoming encounter with Detective Delightful. Suspected she'd be more forthcoming with Slidell than she'd been with me.

Restless and needing to do something, I nosed around on the internet. Learned there were dozens of disaster restoration services in the Charlotte area. My surfing turned up way more about damage from water, fire, and bodily fluids than I wanted to know.

Then, needing to stay busy, I fiddled with dates, organizing the copycat cases, not in the order in which they'd come into the morgue, but in a chronology of death. Who died when?

Boldonado went missing, and presumably died, in August 2019. Sanchez was murdered in December 2019. Kwalwasser passed in August 2020, and her head was swiped later that year. Hunt and Soto had been dead only a week.

Were there other killings we'd missed? Before Boldonado? During the long gap between Sanchez and Kwalwasser?

What we *did* know was that the first copycat killing took place three years ago.

Mental head slap.

Boldonado's death mimicked that of Noble Cruikshank. The Cruikshank file had been accessed three years back. By whom? I'd meant to follow up with Herrin, had totally forgotten.

I checked the time. Nine-forty. Too late. A call to the Charleston County coroner's office would top my morning's agenda.

More time passed with no further word from Ryan. At eleven, I gave up and went to bed.

Sleep fought me. Or I fought it.

I was finally drifting off when the id boys yipped a new warning. A comment by Slidell.

Was that the wisdom they'd been tendering all along?

Whatever.

I added their concern to the morning's list.

SUNDAY, FEBRUARY 20

Ryan slipped into bed sometime after midnight, departed before dawn. No pile of rumpled clothing attested to his brief presence. I think he put on the same jeans and BYLT hoodie in which he'd spent the previous day.

I found brewed coffee and a half bag of donuts in the kitchen. Silently thanking Old Blue Eyes for both, I chose a honey glazed, filled a mug, and sat down with the portable.

I was on hold several minutes before Herrin picked up. Again, we exchanged pleasantries.

"As you know, I recently asked to see a fifteen-year-old file. Is it unusual to want to review material from that far back?"

"Yes. But it happens."

"I know you permitted me access because I worked the case, but normally who's allowed to request a file?"

"Anyone can ask—cops, family, PR, general public."

"PR?"

"Court-appointed personal rep."

I thought about that. "Might law enforcement request a file years after their involvement?"

"Could happen. If the agency is reopening the case."

"Why?"

"New detective, family asking for a reinvestigation, file getting rolled to a cold case unit, whatever."

"The case I asked for was solved, the file closed."

"That's a bit unusual."

"How would a law enforcement request come in?"

"Usually via phone or email."

"What about from family or the public?"

"We ask them to put in writing what they want and their reason for wanting it. Same deal, email or snail mail."

"And they get a copy that easily?"

"Some things are public record, like the coroner's report. As you know, that's a short, thumbnail sketch of the investigation. Anyone can have those. Other info is available only to the legal next of kin, PR, or via subpoena."

"Autopsy, tox, anthro, odont reports, and so on."

"Correct."

"How are copies supplied?"

Herrin sighed slightly. I think I was exceeding my question quota. "Either via mail or email or by personal pickup. Except autopsy photos. Those must be collected in person or sent by certified mail."

"Can you do me a solid?"

"Another?"

"Sorry, but it's important. Someone requested the Cruikshank file three years ago. Can you pry loose a name, maybe an address for that person?"

"Okay," said Herrin with what sounded like less than wild enthusiasm. A pause, then, "There's no such thing as a free lunch."

"Name your beverage of choice." Assuming Herrin's last two comments were hints. They weren't.

"We usually charge a fee for copies."

"Payable by credit card?" I asked, catching the drift.

"I'll have to check about procedure back then."

"But there might be a trail there?"

"Uh-huh."

"Hot diggity damn."

After disconnecting, I ordered two bottles of Taittinger Prélude Grand Cru sent to the office of the CCC.

Discussing Cruikshank got me thinking about Boldonado. I pulled up the dossier and studied the autopsy photos. Spotted a detail I hadn't noticed before.

The phone was still warm when I dialed Ryan. Got his voice mail.

Crap!

Unable to sit still, I decided to view my neighbor Walter's video again, hoping for a detail I might have missed. I was on my fourth run-through, slo-mo advancing, then rewinding my nighttime caller, when hooves thundered beside me. Hoss? Little Joe?

Again, Ryan's voice had a quality I couldn't read. It was ragged with sleep deprivation, yes, but now sparked with a frisson of something else.

"Slidell's BOLO generated a call from upstate. Guess who's in the can."

"Just tell me." Wanting to get to my news.

"Mr. Calvin Winkard."

"Where?"

"Raleigh."

"On what charge?"

"When collected, inebriated, from the stoop of an unhappy homeowner, Winky was found to be the proud possessor of twenty grams of blow." I heard Ryan drink, then the sound of a can being crushed. Guessed he was high on caffeine.

"He's looking at six to twelve months," I said.

"Yes, ma'am. I hear tell that's a class-one felony in these parts."

When Ryan is stressed, or overcaffeinated, he often relieves tension with his version of a Gene Autry imitation. Sometimes Roy Rogers. He was doing that now. I made a mental note to change my ringtone.

"When was Winky busted?" I asked.

"Seven sundowns yesterday, ma'am."

"Stop that."

"Okay."

I calculated the time interval.

"I talked to Winky a week ago Friday. He blew town the next day. He couldn't have abducted Olivia."

"No, ma'a—"

"Everything points to Kramden. Kramden's our guy."

"Skinny and I may have a line on the varmint."

"Seriously? You didn't open with that minor tidbit?"

"I thought you'd want to know about Winky."

"I want to know about Kramden."

"A Circle K cashier claims a man bought a boatload of crap in his store last night."

"Well, hallelujah. Case closed."

"Shall we talk later?"

"Sorry."

"*Said* cashier called 911 to report that the man looked like the guy they're showing on TV. His name is Randall."

"The man was missing one eye?"

"The customer, not Randall."

"Thanks for the clarification." Rolling both of mine.

"Randall said the man bought six bottles of Fanta orange soda, six ice cream sandwiches, and three bags of sour cream chips. According to Olivia's mother, those are the kid's favorites. The man also purchased a pink hairbrush and some sort of kids' shampoo."

"Holy bouncing crapballs. Where's the Circle K?"

"Two miles east of Kramden's bus complex."

"Does Byrd know about this?"

"Yes. He thought it was weak. And they've had their own tip saying the kid's being held at a compound on Sledge Road, out by the airport. Some registered pedophile. I don't know the details. Byrd thinks the info's credible so he's focusing his manpower on that for the moment."

"What now?"

"Skinny and I are heading back out to the buses."

"Byrd is good with that?"

"He thinks it's a waste of time. But Slidell phoned Mangiorotti. He told him to have at it."

"I'm in."

"Nope."

"I'm going crazy here, Ryan. This is torture."

"Even if I agreed, he—"

"I can be helpful."

Silence.

"Which is Kramden's dominant hand?" I demanded.

"What?"

"You don't know, do you?"

"What's your point?" Ryan was asking that a lot.

"He's a lefty. The preference may be compensatory since he's missing three digits on the right."

"So?"

"You know Célia Quintal at the LSJML. Right?"

"The knot lady."

I briefed Ryan on what I'd learned from Quintal. Chiral knots. S and Z images. The fact that the S variety is more common. The fact that the S variety is weakly associated with right-handedness.

"The noose on Boldonado's neck was made with a Z image knot," I concluded.

"Suggesting the person who tied it was left-handed."

"Yes."

"Kramden is left-handed."

"Exactly."

"That's hardly conclusive."

"No."

"And it doesn't mean—"

"It means I observed a detail and made a connection that you and Slidell missed."

"I doubt that argument will fly with Skinny."

"Tell him if he cuts me out, I'll go on my own." Not really, but I was bursting my skin with pent-up energy.

"Or that one."

"If Olivia is in one of those buses, she'll be terrified. The last thing she'll need are you two charging in like storm troopers."

"I'll call you back."

He did.

"Saddle up, podna."

"Yippee kiyay!"

For the second time in two days, I was heading to Gaston County.

35

February has a way of messing with North Carolinians. One day we're pulling on mittens and boots, the next we're sniffing the buds on our pear trees.

Based on the previous week, I dressed for cold. Crossing to Slidell's SUV—not his own, so I assumed another CMPD issue— I realized my mistake. The sky was immaculate, the sun going for a personal best. Once buckled in, I checked the weather icon on my phone. The fickle mercury was expected to dance around in the sixties.

Slidell and Ryan were similarly overdressed. Both were in unzipped leather jackets and had shed their gloves and scarves. Both wore aviator shades and faces as droopy as month-old produce.

I sat in back. While driving, Slidell explained the op. Thinly.

Three cruisers would assemble by the road leading down into the far side of the valley. We'd descend by the usual route, led by two more cruisers and a small-unit SWAT team. Preoccupied with the potential takedown on Sledge Road, Mangiorotti hadn't objected to Slidell's request for extra manpower. The feds had already commandeered most of the cops with body armor anyway.

At Slidell's command, all would engage. Fast. The surveillance cameras would be taken out. I would remain in the SUV until Kramden was in cuffs or Slidell gave me the go-ahead.

"Capiche?" Skinny twisted to ask, not so gently.

"And if I see the suspect, you know, running away or something? Like on our first visit?" A bit snarky, but Slidell's brusqueness was grating.

"You see Beyoncé on a tricycle your ass stays in this crate."

"We should leave her a handheld," Ryan said.

Slidell nodded.

Ryan lifted a radio from the floor by his feet, adjusted a dial, then passed it back. My squinty eyes dared him to query my knowledge of portables. He didn't.

We made record time. Sunday traffic was light. The flashing bubble lights helped.

As our team assembled on the little knoll, Slidell and Ryan donned bulletproof vests. Then everyone observed the valley below.

A blue Ford Fusion was parked by the stairs leading down into the buses. No one was visible. Nothing moved. I wondered if Kramden could possibly be fool enough to return here knowing of Slidell's previous bust. Perhaps he hadn't been back until now? Perhaps he felt the compound was the last place the cops would suspect? A hide-in-plain-sight mentality? Perhaps he had nowhere else to go? The house on Sharon Hills was also under surveillance.

Through my handheld, I listened to the exchange between Skinny and those across the valley.

"B unit up?"

A lot of clicks came back.

"A?"

More clicks.

"Remember. No Lone Ranger shit. There could be a kid in there." Deep breath, then, "Let's get this pussbag."

The cruisers roared downhill, followed by the SWAT team in

their tricked-out Humvee. We brought up the rear, rocking so hard I had to brace with both hands.

As Slidell threw the SUV into park, the doors on the other vehicles flew open. The members of the SWAT team scuttled to their positions, Colt M4 carbines trained on the bus pit. Ryan and Slidell ran, hunched low, Glocks at the ready.

As before, an advance team rushed into the buses first while, simultaneously, a cop drew his weapon and blasted the front security cameras. Gunfire told me the same was happening in the rear. I wondered why the cameras had been left intact last time. Had the search warrant required a nondestructive entry? Did the possibility of Olivia's presence now make property damage acceptable? There was no one to ask.

Slidell, Ryan, and two uniforms convened by the stairs, bodies tense as barbed wire. Ryan laid a hand on the hood of the Ford, testing for heat. Shook his head.

Time seemed to freeze.

At last, two words spat from the device in my lap. "Premises secure."

Slidell and the others thundered down the stairs.

Minutes crawled by.

Eyeballing the Ford, I thought about Andrea-Louisa Soto. Was it the car that ran her down at SWI?

I thought about Charlie Hunt. Frank Boldonado. Were we about to encounter their killer?

I thought about the first time I'd cooled my heels like this. I'd been goading Slidell today, but what if I *did* see someone trying to escape? Easy. I had the radio now. Besides, Skinny's directive or not, I wouldn't repeat my idiotic behavior.

Again and again, I checked my watch and worried my thumbnail raw.

My mind circled back to the figure I'd seen on that first trip. Was it Kramden I'd chased into the woods? If not Bobby Karl, then who?

I tried recalling details. Came up with little. Pumping legs. A hoodie. BO.

Twitchy with impatience, I scanned the woods rimming the valley. I could trace the figure's path toward the trees and identify the stretch into which it had vanished. But where had it appeared? I closed my eyes to envision the scene.

My lids opened wide.

Yes!

Suddenly, I was *en fuego* to talk to Slidell and Ryan. I tried the radio. Got no response.

It took a lifetime until one of the uniforms emerged to signal me forward. Mae Pitluck. I'd worked with Mae before. Liked everything about her but the cloying smell of her cologne.

I sprinted to the stairs. Took them two at a time.

Slidell and Ryan were in the first bus, both flushed and breathing hard. Pitluck was off to one side. Skinny was letting the world know his level of unhappiness.

"—little snake slithered into some goddam pit. His piece-of-shit car's sitting outside."

"Maybe he went off with a friend?" Pitluck ventured.

"Kramden look like Mr. Popularity to you?" Slidell's inability to control events had him light-years past polite.

"I have an idea."

Three heads swiveled my way.

"I've been thinking about the day I chased the guy in the hoodie—"

"One of your more spectacularly stupid moves."

I ignored Slidell. "He seemed to pop up full-blown at midfield, hauling ass for the trees."

"And?"

"How did he materialize so suddenly?"

Ryan got it right away. "You're thinking tunnel."

"Or isolated hidey-hole, set off by itself. That would explain why he'd feel safe coming back here."

"Why didn't the asshole rabbit today?" Slidell asked.

"A freaking SWAT team has the place in their crosshairs."

Slidell's brows plunged as he labored through options. Then he bellowed into his handheld, telling unit B to report for a search of the eastern half of the valley, unit A to maintain their twenty at the buses.

After ordering Pitluck to secure a K-9 unit, Slidell headed for the steps. Ryan followed. I fell into line, figuring Skinny was too amped on adrenaline to bother about me. I was wrong.

"Your ass goes back in the car," he threw over one shoulder.

"No."

"What did you say?" Whipping off the aviators and turning to point them down at me.

"I'm trained in archaeology. I know how to organize a surface survey. Do you?"

Slidell looked at Ryan. Ryan shrugged.

"Holy fucking fucksville!" Jabbing his shades into place, Skinny exited the stairway and stomped toward the vast expanse of ground between the buses and the trees.

Topside, I met with unit B, described the way in which the search would proceed, and indicated approximately where I'd first noticed the runner. Then we began walking the field, shoulder to shoulder, six feet apart.

A cop on one end of the line ran a metal detector over the ground. Useless and annoying. The damn thing never stopped beeping.

Plodding along, head down, eyes raking the field, I kept seeing outcomes, one uglier than the next. Olivia, terrified and alone in the dark. Chained to a bed. In pieces in a bag at the bottom of a lake. Whitewash pale in a shallow grave. The sunniness of the day contrasted sharply with the dark path my mind was traveling.

We worked our sad drill for what felt like hours, reversing direction each time we reached the trees, nothing breaking the silence of focused concentration. Of collective dread.

At some point the dogs arrived. A voice I didn't recognize addressed them as Toots and Stan. I glanced up. Toots and Stan were both shepherds, one brown, one black. On a command from their handler, the dogs set off, noses sending sporadic puffs of air rustling the ground cover.

Branches were casting long spidery shadows from the edge of the forest when Toots alerted by sitting and staring pointedly at a patch of earth. Ryan and I hurried to the spot. The metal detector was brought in to sweep the area. The beeps sputtered, then merged into one long wail.

"Shovels!" Slidell yelled.

Pitluck's partner hurried to a vehicle. Sackler, I thought. Maybe Stickler.

"Dig where?" Pitluck looked to Slidell.

"Ask the goddam dog."

The handler ordered Toots away from the spot that had interested her, assuring the dog that she'd "done good." The excavation had barely begun when metal clanged metal. More shoveling and scraping, then a rectangular outline appeared in the soil below the scrub vegetation.

Everyone watched the spades hack double time. Soon a manmade object came into view, nailed boards with hinges running on one side. An escape hatch or back door?

A booby trap?

"Back!" Slidell's shout was raw-edged and far too loud.

As the rest of us withdrew, the advance team, still in gear, ran their paraphernalia over the boards.

I'm not good at waiting. I'm especially not good when anxious for a child. For my daughter. For anyone defenseless against the violence of another.

Blood thundered in my ears. Sweat rolled down my back.

Finally, a thumbs-up.

"Flip the goddam thing!" Slidell ordered.

Using their blades, two diggers found a gap opposite the hinges, and levered hard. The planks flew back and landed with a soft *whump*. The sun was low now, sending little light into the freshly revealed wound in the earth.

Maglites came on, their beams arrowing through the subterranean gloom. The illumination exposed a pit maybe eight feet square, roughly hewn beams, a hard-packed floor, three dirt walls. The fourth side opened onto hollow blackness.

"There. A ladder. On the floor." Pitluck had her light focused on an object against the east wall.

"Someone get down and set the fucking thing up," Slidell commanded.

Ryan moved toward the pit.

"Not you." Skinny pointed to Sackler/Stickler. "You."

Sackler/Stickler reattached his flash to his belt, crouched and jumped. Another cop joined him. Together they propped and steadied the ladder.

One facet of Slidell never changes. He turned to me and said exactly what I thought he'd say. Or at least a variation of what I expected.

"You leave this spot, your ass goes to jail. Got it?"

Wanting no delay in Olivia's rescue, if she was down there, I didn't argue.

So, I waited, pacing and gnawing my own flesh. As before, willing Ryan to emerge with Olivia's tiny arms circling his neck.

A lifetime later a man emerged, a redheaded girl pressed to his chest, her thin wrists blanched with the effort of grasping each other.

The girl was Olivia Lakin.

The man was Bobby Karl Kramden.

As Slidell closed in tight behind Kramden, the others scrabbled from the pit and surrounded them. I saw tense readiness, but no drawn weapons.

Stone-jawed, Slidell looked to me, then tipped his head toward Kramden.

Shocked that Sackler/Stickler and the other uniform had left Olivia with her captor, and not wanting to alarm the child, I approached carrying one of those stuffed bears cops keep in cruisers for such occasions. Smiling, I moved in what I hoped was a reassuring manner.

"Hi, Olivia," I ventured, Mary Poppins cheery. "We've been looking for you."

Olivia tightened her hold on Kramden. Tears ran down both her cheeks, and one of his.

"I have someone who'd like to meet you." Waggling the bear.

Jesus! Was I blowing this? Was a stuffed animal an insult to a preteen?

"It's okay, sweetheart. You're with us, now." I spread my arms and took a few steps closer.

Olivia squeezed her eyes tight and buried her face in Kramden's shirt.

"Your mom can't wait to see you. She's missed you so much."

Olivia's body tensed into a knot.

"That's it. We're done with this horseshit." Slidell cocked a thumb at Pitluck. "You. Help the doc."

Pitluck joined me and together we gently pried Olivia's fingers from her wrists. Kramden didn't fight us, but the child's strength and determination were remarkable.

Murmuring a steady stream of reassurances, I wrapped Olivia in a blanket and carried her to the back seat of Pitluck's cruiser. The trembling in her small body made my heart ache.

I was stroking the girl's shoulders when she let forth a wail that sent ice down my spine. Following Olivia's sightline, I saw Slidell shove a cuffed Kramden into the rear of a van, slam the doors, and whistle to the driver.

All my life I'll remember that vehicle flashing past, that mangled face peering out. That expression—the saddest I have ever seen, before or since.

Through the cruiser's open car door, I heard Slidell call to Ryan.

"We got the sick bastard."

Ryan said nothing.

"Do you believe the freakshow he had going down there?"

36

livia Lakin suffered no sexual or physical assault.

Following her rescue and Kramden's arrest, the child expressed concern for her captor and repeatedly asked to see him. Stockholm Syndrome? Genuine affection? A pediatric psychologist was sorting that out.

Both Olivia and Bobby Karl told the same story. Though a seemingly impossible pairing, the two considered themselves pals. The friendship started when Olivia, out of pity, asked her scarred neighbor about the flowers he was planting in his front yard. Caught off guard, and unused to kindness, Bobby Karl showed the child his garden, then offered her Oreos. Occasionally, unknown to the senior Lakins, Olivia would pedal or walk up the block to discuss horticulture and share cookies with the lonely old man who lived all by himself.

On the day of her disappearance, recognizing Bobby Karl at the wheel of his car, the child waved Kramden over to ask for a ride to school. Why not? She'd done it before upon such chance sightings. When Kramden proposed a prank on her parents, Olivia happily agreed.

According to Olivia, the bus complex was "awesome sauce" and "her ugly neighbor" was gentle and kindhearted, like the "BFG." I didn't quite get the BFG thing, later learned it was a reference to the "big friendly giant" in a kid's movie based on a book by Roald Dahl. For Olivia, the whole outing was a grand adventure.

According to Bobby Karl, the ransom idea was spur of the moment. He needed money. Olivia was in his car. He planned to keep her very briefly, then release her unharmed, payout or not.

Kramden was charged with abduction of a minor, kidnapping, and a number of related crimes. Slidell insisted he was also guilty of desecration of corpses, concealing evidence of death by dismembering or destroying human remains, and three counts of first-degree homicide. Lacking a theory on Kramden's motive for the copycat murders, Skinny failed to persuade Mangiorotti on the additional offenses, but was encouraged to pursue his investigation and allowed to question the prisoner.

While freely admitting to the kidnapping, Bobby Karl was adamant in his denial of the killings. The harder Slidell pressed, the more firmly Kramden held fast.

Mangiorotti ordered CSU teams to toss the buses in Gaston County and the house on Sharon Hills Road in Charlotte. Forensics experts started the backbreaking task of analyzing every shred of potential evidence.

In tandem with members of the main task force, Slidell's team bulldozed through Kramden's present and his past—relatives, friends, neighbors, and known associates. They investigated any purchase he'd ever made, any argument he'd ever had, any bill he'd ever paid, any prepper gathering he'd ever attended. You get the picture.

Kramden was assigned a public defender and locked up in the Mecklenburg County jail awaiting arraignment. Slidell grilled him daily. Henry and the others discovered nothing linking Bobby Karl to Sanchez, Kwalwasser, Hunt, or Soto.

Ryan headed north.

I turned to new cases. Remains unearthed by a beagle named

Florence in her owner's crawl space. A mandible fished by middle schoolers from an abandoned septic tank.

WEDNESDAY, FEBRUARY 23

Three days after Kramden's arrest, Henry strode into my office, an uncharacteristic grin on her face.

"You won't believe this. It is totally bitchin'."

"Believe what?" I asked, covering my annoyance at the constant lingo.

"I went back to Kramden's bunker and found something the search team missed." Clearly pleased with herself.

"Lay it on me." Take that, lingo queen.

"The kid's earrings."

I was lost.

"*Tú eres mi sol.* Andrea-Louisa's wee baubles."

"Inside one of the buses?" I asked, incredulous.

"Outside. I can't believe—"

"Didn't CSU check the surrounding area, the trash—"

"They were in a plastic sack tucked under a rock in the woods. That's probably why CSU missed them. Did I mention that a friendly forest creature had fortuitously clawed the bag out into plain sight? And that I have the eyes of an eagle?"

"Have you told Slidell?"

"Yes, ma'am. Doc."

"This burns Kramden's story."

"To the ground."

"Good work, Detective."

"Thanks." Henry turned toward the door, reversed, a frown creasing the over-tanned face. "Sorry, I should've asked. How's it going with your kid? She back in the loop?"

"Katy is hardly a kid." Keeping my voice absolutely neutral, I added, "She'll get in contact when she's ready."

"Damn straight."

After Henry left, I pondered her news, wondering at the gumbo of emotions vying for attention. I felt elation, sure. Henry had found physical evidence linking Kramden to a copycat victim. But the happiness was tempered by something else.

Uncertainty?

Why?

And why the edginess every time I encountered the woman? Was it chemistry? Was my sister Harry right? Are there some folks your gut is simply predisposed to dislike?

Gnarly.

I turned back to Florence's bones.

The big shocker came the next day.

THURSDAY, FEBRUARY 24

"Yo." Slidell's greeting was almost a growl.

"Detective." The screen on my iPhone gave the time as seven forty-four a.m. Birdie and I were still in bed.

"Kramden's alibi checks out."

"What alibi?"

"Him being out of town."

My groggy mind slogged back to the interview room. To Kramden's interrogation.

"He claimed he was away doing some sort of field training," I said.

"Yeah. The squirrel was making prepper whoopee up in Nags Head."

"When Hunt and Soto were killed?"

"You on something, Doc?"

"I'm trying to get this straight."

"Kramden couldn't have done Hunt or Soto." Slidell spoke very slowly, as though explaining the basics to a dull recruit. "He was in Nags Head, a shit ton of miles from Charlotte."

"He never left the Outer Banks?"

"Not according to fourteen of his survivalist pals."

"But Henry found Soto's earrings near Kramden's buses."

"Yeah." Slidell had no theory on that.

"Maybe someone planted them there?" I suggested, not really believing it.

"Who?"

I had no theory on *that*.

"Now what?" I asked.

"Now they hold Kramden for kidnapping the Lakin kid and we keep slinging a net for this copycat prick."

I got up, fed Birdie, and set off for work. Halfway there, a text pinged in on my phone. At the first red light, I glanced at it.

Your new creature is an abomination. Finlay is distraught. I am done with forbearance. AC.

Happy day. My lunatic neighbor, Alasdair Campbell.

At the MCME, I filled my coffee mug and helped myself to a cinnamon frosted from an open Krispy Kreme box in the kitchen. Then I went to my office and spread plastic across my work counter.

The septic tank mandible was interesting. Retaining four upper and two lower molars, all with gold crowns, the jaw was definitely human. I asked Hawkins to shoot X-rays.

While awaiting the radiographs, I mulled over the two most recent developments in the copycat murders: Soto's earrings and Kramden's alibi.

If not Bobby Karl, who was mimicking my old cases? What was his motive? His plan going forward? How did Andrea-Louisa's earrings end up hidden near Bobby Karl's buses?

Booting my laptop, I opened the file I'd created on Saturday. Timeline.docx. Slowly, I reviewed facts I'd reviewed a zillion times.

Veronica Kwalwasser passed in August 2020. Her head was stolen, eventually tossed into a privy, sans one eye. The missing eye was frozen, then left on my porch last month. Had her head also been frozen for a while? Had both been taken as part of some hellish plan? Or was the snatch opportunistic? Did the desecration of Kwalwasser's eyes mimic my stabbing a perp in Montreal? The info was public knowledge, the incident having been reported in *Allo Police* and other rags.

Frank Boldonado disappeared and presumably died in August 2019. His death by garroting and hanging mimicked that of a PI named Noble Cruikshank. The story had received little coverage. But three years back, someone accessed the coroner's file on Cruikshank.

Miguel Sanchez was murdered in December 2019. His death mimicked that of a young man found mutilated, decapitated, and eviscerated at Lake Wylie. The local media had reported on the case.

Charlie Hunt was incapacitated, then placed in his car with the engine running to stage his death as a suicide. That situation mimicked the killing of an ER doctor in 2008. His death had received some press coverage.

Andrea-Louisa Soto was mowed down in a hit-and-run, her body then transferred to a different location. Her murder mimicked that of Ara, an Afghan girl recently arrived in the US. I was unsure if Ara's murder had made the news. Made a note to run a search.

I went for more java and pastry. Back in my office, I reached for the phone. My call was answered right away.

"Charleston County Coroner's Office."

"Ebony Herrin, please."

"May I ask who's calling?"

"Temperance Brennan."

"Hold please."

I finished half the coffee and all the donut before Herrin picked up.

"Sorry about the wait." The coroner offered no explanation for the delay.

"I'm wondering if you managed to determine who accessed the Cruikshank file."

"I was about to ring you."

Right.

I heard paper rustle. A lot of paper. Then a chair squeaking as

Herrin leaned back. "My clerk found a photocopy of the request form when she pulled the hard-copy file. The form was submitted in person. Filled out with handwriting that suggests someone in the possum family."

"Possums aren't known for their elegant cursive."

"The paper is creased and smeared to Kansas and back."

"What happened to the original?"

"Before my time."

"Why wasn't the request entered into the system?"

"Same answer."

I waited out a long silence. Pictured Herrin struggling to decipher the info on the page before her. Info clearly not studied before my call.

"The request may have come from law enforcement. Looks like that box is checked. I think. Maybe."

"Did the applicant sign the form?"

"Just initials. OSA? Maybe OSH? Heck, it could be DSA?"

"Who handled the request?"

"Reggie Pudding. Man took a lot of grief because of that name. Never lost his cool."

"Does Pudding remember the transaction?"

"Reggie's been retired over a year now. Surely do miss him. He was one conscientious son of a gun." Another pause, this one accentuated by a short squeak. "Reggie left a note in the file saying he'd given out a photocopy of the coroner's report. As I've explained, anyone can access those."

"Will you shoot me a pic of the form?"

"Can do. I hope your eyes are better than mine."

They weren't. No way I could decrypt the scrawled initials. The smeared checks. The only thing clear was Mr. Pudding's meticulous autograph. All the squinting and magnifying gave me a headache.

Frustrated, I returned to the septic tank jaw, wrote a report, and called Ari Leshner. The dentist penned me onto his calendar for the following Monday.

With an epic headache blooming, I finished with the crawl space remains, wrote a report, and dialed Florence's owner to say the beagle could have her bones back. They'd belonged to a member of *Sus domesticus*. Domestic pig.

Driving home, I was again in a mood to be ruthless with myself. All this time and what had I accomplished? What did I have? Victims' names and their dates and causes of death. Links to old cases. Cold, cold cases.

Harsh admission. Grating as she was, Henry had contributed more to the investigation than I had.

37

At the annex, I popped two Advil, lay on the study sofa, closed my eyes, and allowed my thoughts to free-range. They thundered like mustangs crossing a prairie.

Leading the charge was my dislike of Henry. The woman had rubbed me wrong from the moment we'd met. Why? Her ability to dress with more aplomb than I could afford—the designer outfits, the pricey leather, the flashy jewelry? The California lingo? Her height? Her youth? Was I capable of such pettiness, or was my antipathy justified? Based on paranoia? On Harry's gut chemistry theory?

Searching for the source of my animosity, I roped in my horses, one by one.

Fact: Slidell disapproved of Henry.

Big deal. Skinny disapproved of most people.

Fact: Henry had entered my office and, uninvited, handled a picture of Katy and Charlie.

Big deal. The pic was on full display.

Fact: Henry had put no effort into researching Soto's locket.

Big deal. Her butt had been lassoed to search for Olivia Lakin.

Fact: Henry arrived in Charlotte about three years ago.

My crazy neighbor, Alasdair Campbell came into my life three years ago.

Sanchez and Boldonado—the earliest of the copycat cases—dated to three years ago.

Notre-Dame burned down three years ago.

Big deal.

Fact: Not every case that had been mimicked was public knowledge. Some of the deaths may have received zero coverage. Ergo, the copycat killer had access to insider intel?

Henry was a cop.

Big deal. The CMPD had more than two thousand employees.

Fact: A member of law enforcement may have accessed the coroner's report on Noble Cruikshank.

May have. The form was almost illegible.

Henry was a cop.

Like two thousand others.

An idea took shape in my pain-addled brain.

A name floated up.

"What do you think?" I asked Birdie when he hopped onto the sofa.

The cat began licking his toes with a diligence I had to admire.

"I agree," I said. "One must be thorough."

I searched my contacts. Brown, Micaela. A decade my junior and my counterpart in LA, Mickey and I had tossed back a few in my drinking days. Quite a few. Though booze was now history for me, Mickey and I still got together whenever we could. I'd hit the Perrier. She'd throw down shots of tequila.

Three rings, then a raspy Whoopi Goldberg voice answered.

"Goddam, Brennan. How the hell are you?"

"Perfect today, better tomorrow." Except that my frontal lobe was exploding.

"Hot damn, girl."

"Got a favor to ask."

"'Course you do."

"You still consult to the coroner and the LAPD, right?" Rubbing circles on both my temples.

"I'm at the morgue as we speak. Got a body turned up on the roof of a twenty-story high-rise. Birds and rats opened a buffet, couple of felines bellied up. How the hell do cats climb that high?"

"Perseverance."

"What's your favor?"

"I'm hoping you can get the inside dope on a detective who left the LAPD several years back."

"His name?"

"Her name is Donna Henry."

"What's the deal?"

"A detective I partner with gets a bad vibe."

"You'd like to put a cork in his whining."

"Assuage his concerns."

"Your timing is superb, my friend. I'm heading over there shortly. I'll ask around, see what pops."

"Much appreciated," I said. "Are you coming east any time soon?"

"Not if your pasty Irish ass is there."

"Love you, too."

Next, I dialed Slidell.

"It's me."

"Mm." He couldn't have sounded less enthused without serious pharmaceuticals.

"Something you said has been bothering me."

"I'm working here, ya know."

"It's related to Henry."

"You gotta be shitting me."

"When I described the search with Mortella and Vera at SWI, you said every handler you know is eager to work his mutt, Sunday or not. So why would Henry agree to use an untrained dog?"

"Because she's a fucknozzle twit—"

"Why do you dislike her?"

"In my humble, Henry's carrying a badge someone else oughta have."

Hearing radio static, voices, a barking dog, I asked, "Where are you?"

"Sugar Creek Park. Captain got a credible tip some wanker's been waving his weeny at kids."

"Nice alliteration."

"Eeh."

"Why you?"

"Why not me?" Bristly.

"You're CCU."

"He and I was chewing the fat when the call came in. Figured I could sit here as well as anywhere, so I volunteered."

Flash recollection.

"When I told you that Henry went to Asheville to investigate a credible terrorist threat, you sounded surprised."

"Yeah. So?"

"Why?"

"Hadn't heard any scuttlebutt."

"Normally you would?"

"Word usually gets around. Not always."

"Can you find out about that incident?" I scrolled through Notes. "She was up there on Tuesday, February 8."

"You think I got nothing better to do than pester folks on account of your whims?"

"Did you tell Henry that Katy has gone incommunicado?"

"And have her sniffing around where she don't belong? Fuck no." Long suffering sigh. "I'll call you when I can."

He did. Within the hour.

"Henry was 10-10 that day."

"Off duty."

"Yeah."

"Why would she lie to me?"

"Because she's a douchebag."

Mickey got back to me at seven. Her report was confusing at best.

Following our conversation, I phoned Slidell. Got voice mail.

I phoned Ryan. Got voice mail in French.

I made a grilled cheese sandwich and ate it with a Peach-Pear LaCroix sparkling water chaser. Birdie joined me. He likes the buttery crumbs.

After clearing the dishes, I phoned Slidell again. Paced. Cursed the weeny waver.

When the headache had throttled back a bit, I printed Herrin's pic, got a magnifier from my briefcase, and resumed my efforts at deciphering, rotating the page and raising and lowering the lens.

Readability had not improved over the past two hours. Every edge was fuzzy and black streaks obscured most of the content. I guessed the original had been moved as the photocopy was still in process.

Birdie came and went.

Twenty minutes of straining and squinting, then I leaned back and rubbed my protesting eyes. Christ. What was I hoping to gain?

The name of the person who'd requested the Cruikshank file.

Right.

Retrieving the lens, I focused on the initials. Could come no closer than Herrin. Just as I decided the trio were OSA, I changed my mind to OSH, then DSA.

Frustrated, I gave up.

Birdie woke from his nap and began cleaning his ears.

Excellent suggestion. Approach from a different angle. Or return to a previous one that hadn't proved fruitful.

Booting my laptop, I opened the file on every old case mimicked by the copycat murderer. The serial killer I stabbed in the eye in Montreal. The kid decapitated and eviscerated and tossed ashore at Lake Wylie. The man garroted, then hanged to suggest a suicide. The man whose detached head was encased in a bucket of concrete. The doctor poisoned and placed in his running car. The Afghan girl killed in a hit-and-run. Thank you Skinny for sending me the full jackets on each.

For the next several hours I plucked details like a mother fine-combing her kid for lice. Victims, witnesses, cops, places, dates—no entry was too obscure, no fact too seemingly unimportant or un-related.

Slidell didn't call. Ditto Ryan.

Shortly after ten, Birdie left for good. I soldiered on, the head-ache still a miserable companion.

I'd finished two files and was well into the one on the Lake Wylie torso when a signature on a witness statement caught my eye.

I read the entire interview.

Read it again.

No way. Couldn't be what I thought.

I was staring at the screen when glass shattered somewhere in the house.

My alarm began wailing.

38

Birdie was crouched three treads down from the upstairs hall-way, eyes wide, ears flat, nose testing the air. Below him, the first floor was cooling fast.

When I entered the parlor, a million distorted versions of myself bounced from fragmented glass blasted inward onto the couch and carpet. Among the shards lay my friendly garden snail.

"Sonofafreakinbitchbastard!"

Birdie whirled and shot out of sight.

Glass crunching underfoot, I crossed to kill the alarm.

"You've gone too far, you psycho prick!" I shouted into the sud-den silence, then strode to the kitchen to get my phone. Not seeing it, I double-stepped up to my bedroom.

No mobile.

I was ripping another expletive when strains of the Ponderosa floated up from below. Racing back to the kitchen, I found the thing under my discarded sweater. Answered too late.

I listened to Ryan's message. *Ships in the night. Miss you,* chère. *Phone me back.*

Sorry, buddy.

I punched in 911. Amped on adrenaline born of fury, my thumbs hit wrong. I tried again. Connected and reported the attack.

Then I waited. Ten minutes. Fifteen. I knew vandalism would be low priority. Still.

I was rummaging for plywood in the attic when a fist pounded the kitchen door.

Finally. Those who serve and protect.

I raced downstairs. Passing the parlor, I glanced through the newly fractured window. Spotted no cruiser. Assumed the cops had pulled onto the driveway behind my car.

Entering the kitchen, I saw a single head beyond the door's small square of glass, dark against slightly thinner dark. A head sitting on a tall body. A head not wearing a peaked cap.

Flash memory of a similar scene. Katy?

My asshole neighbor come to follow up with more vitriol?

I shouted loud enough to be heard outside. "I'm done, Alasdair. This time I press charges."

"Hey, Doc. You okay in there?"

"Detective Henry?" I queried, shocked that a detective had been sent to answer a complaint about property damage.

"Just me. Not your eyeball freak."

Was that supposed to be funny? I didn't laugh.

"You have some kinda sitch going here?" Henry asked.

"Hold on."

I crossed to release the dead bolt, then cracked open the door.

Henry was all in black—wool jacket, jeans, mid-calf Uggs. Her lipstick stood out ebony against the over-tanned skin.

"They sent a detective?" I asked, bewildered.

"I was cruising on Selwyn and heard the property damage call go out over the radio. Being just a block over, I told the dispatcher I'd swing by. Didn't know it was your place until I got here. So what's this about a rock-chucking prowler?"

"My volatile neighbor."

"Volatile. Good one. You want to give me a statement, then we can scare up something for a temporary patch job?"

I didn't.

A thought was beginning to form. Was I being paranoid? Phone still in my hand, I pressed a speed dial button and dropped the device into a side pocket of my cargo pants. Though the ringer was silenced, if Slidell answered, his voice would still be audible. Unless Skinny was canny enough to stay mute and just listen.

As I turned my head to track where Birdie's frightened meow was now coming from, I heard the door slam inward behind me and hit the adjacent wall with a loud crack. A throaty expulsion of air. Thudding boots.

Before I could pivot, hands shoved my shoulders and I pitched violently forward onto my knees. My arms were wrenched backward. Cold steel mashed my left, then my right wrist.

Air rearranged behind me.

The world exploded into a million nanopixels.

Went dark.

I felt hard-packed soil beneath one cheek. Grit.

The scent of moist earth filled my nose. Of things left underground far too long. Decaying paper. Rotting fabric. Dead vegetation.

I opened my eyes to pitch black.

Raised my head. Felt nauseous and laid it back down.

Lowered my lids.

I tried reaching out to explore my surroundings. Chains *snicked* and one hand dragged the other. I was on my belly, wrists bound behind me in what felt and sounded like cuffs. The distorted joint angles and immobility had taken their toll on my arms. The movement shot fire from my elbows to my shoulders.

I tried moving my feet. They, too, were shackled.

How long had I been here? An hour? A day?

Where was "here"?

I dragged my last conscious recollections into alignment. The broken window. The snail missile atop the shattered glass. Henry in the doorway. My quick look away from her intense stare to wherever Birdie had located himself . . . and then the attack in my kitchen.

Henry's attempt at humor fired up from my cache of recent memories. Her insensitive quip about the eyeball. What the hell? Of all the stored images, why that scene? No matter. The flashback nudged two other data bytes lying dormant in my id. One by one, the pair roused and snuck through the keyhole into my forebrain.

Christ! Why hadn't I had this epiphany earlier?

Suddenly, it all made sense.

The phone! Barely breathing, I rolled toward my right side. Felt hardness against my thigh. My mobile was still in my pocket. Functioning? I had no idea. Less how to access it.

Easing back onto my stomach, I strained for other telltale noises. Overhead, I heard the muted cadence of a TV. Closer in, the steady *plunk plunk plunk* of dripping water.

My own ragged breath as consciousness ebbed away.

When I opened my eyes again, my body was in the same position. I was shivering and chilled to the core, my clothing a damp shroud wrapping my skin. All ten fingers were numb. From cold? Lack of blood? I wiggled them as best I could.

As before, the movement made me queasy. I fought the wave of nausea, determined not to black out again.

Two things had changed while I'd been out.

Twenty feet off and eight feet up, a slash of light lifted the top few risers of a staircase from the gloom. The railings were wooden, the treads covered by a filthy rubber runner.

The TV had gone silent.

Shout for help?

Why not? Activity might hold the hypothermia at bay.

I raised my head. Which hurt like hell.

"Hell-o!"

I heard a soft *skitching* off to my left. Pictured beady red eyes and long naked tails.

Crap!

"Help! Anyone? I'm down here!"

Pain ricocheting through my skull, I called out until my throat felt raw. To no avail.

Exhausted, I lowered my head onto the dank floor and listened for movement above. For scurrying feet on my level. A basement?

Ten minutes. Two hours. An eternity.

Finally, hinges creaked, and the slash of light went trapezoid.

Boots entered my field of vision.

Black Uggs.

Black jeans.

Blond hair.

"Detective," I rasped, trying hard to camouflage my fear.

"Doc." The ebony lipstick had faded, but the malevolence in the smile was undeniable. "Rough night?"

"I've had better."

"I'll bet you have." Henry's features were distorted by the light angling down across them. "Can I help you up from there?"

Not waiting for an answer, she strode forward, unlocked the ankle cuffs, and yanked me upright. Both arms screamed and my knees buckled. My feet were dead weight.

Wasting no time on compassion, Henry dragged me toward the stairs and shoved me into a lawn chair on the far side. I had to double over to avoid smashing my senseless hands against the rusty metal at my back.

"Sorry." Faux pity. "Did that hurt?"

Before I could respond, she unlocked the cuffs and, with them, secured my right hand to the right side of the chair. Moving like lightning, she clamped my left hand onto a second pair pre-attached to the chair's left side. Again, I was helpless due to my own ineptitude.

"Not that you're going anywhere." Henry drew her Glock and waggled it in my face, so close I could smell the lubricating oil she used to clean it. I wondered if she was also packing the backup .380 ACP, the sap, and the knife.

Sudden terrifying thought. Did this lunatic have Katy? Was my daughter in this house? I was scared. Scared with a life-passing-before-me-end-of-days fear.

You still have the phone. No way my dialed call would still be live. No matter. Talk. Buy time.

Deep breath.

"I spoke to a friend in LA today," I said, powering over my hoarseness.

Henry stared at me, feet spread, right hand on one hip. Glock firm in the other.

"She said rumor has it you made detective only because you have an uncle high up in the ranks."

The stare didn't waver.

"She also said you left the LAPD under less than cordial circumstances."

Henry's brows dipped ever so slightly.

"That you weren't fired but were asked to leave. That you were promised a good record only if you resigned and went quietly."

"Gold star for your friend."

"She said word around the shop was that you were nuts. That you capped a homeless guy in an alley."

"That shoot was ruled good."

"That's what she said. But by then the department had had it with the drama. And the uncle with the stripes refused to intervene."

"You believe her story?"

"I think it's probably bullshit." I didn't.

Plunk. Plunk. Plunk.

Keep her engaged.

I recalled my sudden epiphany during my first brief period of consciousness.

"You made two mistakes, you know."

"Yeah?"

"Back when all this began you referenced Kwalwasser's eyeball being left on my back porch. I'd told you only that the thing had turned up at my home. I let it go at the time, figuring Slidell had shared that detail with you. He hadn't."

"And the other?" Grudgingly curious.

"Last time we spoke in my office you asked about my daughter. I never told you Katy was missing."

Henry's lips tightened, but she said nothing. I kept talking.

"I ran through my old files, again. The deaths being mimicked by the copycat murderer. Cruikshank. Aja—"

"You making a point?" Henry snapped.

"An old white woman, a black male, a Hispanic teen, a middle-aged white guy. Death by stabbing, hanging, poisoning, hit-and-run. Smart. No common victimology, no common MO. Took us a while to see a pattern."

"No shit."

"You tampered with Olivia Lakin's backpack while transporting it uptown. Why? That had us fooled for a while. The similarity to Lizzie Nance."

"Just messing with you."

"How did you know about Lizzie's ballet clothes?"

"God bless the net, source of all rando intel."

"I know why you're doing it." Despite the cold, I was perspiring. I was desperate to wipe the sweat from my face.

Henry shifted her weight. I tried to read the shadow show sliding across her features. Failed. Kept talking.

"I found the interview you gave in the Lake Wylie torso case in 2008." I didn't mention that the discovery occurred only seconds before Henry lobbed the snail through my window. Or that I'd always wonder how things might have gone had I had time to process the intel.

"Hot damn, the doc's a detective."

"You were dating a guy named Asa Finney back then. He was a self-proclaimed witch who went by the name Ursa. That was before your family relocated to California."

The Glock came up, the steel tunnel of death leveled on me.

Easy, Brennan.

"I get why you're angry," I said. "You were a high school kid. You weren't a witch, still Finney was your boyfriend. He was gunned down in his own front yard. It was tragic. But why target me?"

"You're the badass forensic scientist. The mighty and exalted Dr. Temperance Brennan. And you revel in that."

"I—"

"Asa hadn't harmed anyone!" Henry spit the words with such venom that her saliva misted my face. And the gun. "I loved Asa and you took him from me!"

"It wasn't like that."

"Yeah?" The way she bit off the word conveyed venomous loathing. "You're in denial, bitch! You and your fucking pals got it all wrong and that got Asa killed! You're right. I was just a kid. But I knew that you had to pay."

"Why me?"

"You fed the cops your junk science—"

"I never—"

Consumed with rage, she'd stopped listening. "—and I knew that just capping you would never even the score. I vowed to be patient and take you for the full ride. To rip from you the two things you love most in life, starting with your precious career."

Henry cocked her left arm high, the one holding the Glock. Unable to defend myself, I twisted sideways as far as possible and braced for the blow. None came.

Moments passed.

When I turned back, the gun was gone and Henry was scrolling through options on her phone. The cast-off glow sparked an irregular band on her left hand.

Dots connected. The sapphire and diamond ring. The flashing object on Walter's surveillance video.

Henry's eyes rolled up, dark with murderous intent.

With insanity.

"You get why I'm angry? Really, Doc? No! You! Do! Not! But you will." Henry thrust the device close to my face. "Numero dos."

A fuzzy video was playing on Henry's screen, the lens panning across a woman chained to a pipe leading down to a tangle of blankets. The woman appeared to be sleeping.

Dead?

The camera reversed, slowed, then stopped. Zoomed in.

The woman's features morphed into a recognizable pattern.

Panic ripped through me.

The scene mimicked my nightmare cinema of death.

The woman was Katy!

39

"**P**lease!" I begged with hopeless desperation. "Don't hurt my daughter!"

"But the young lady is my pièce de résistance." Henry's voice was thick with hatred. "I've been working up to her all these years. And this time the great doctor gets to observe."

"Katy has done nothing to you."

"Like Asa did nothing to you. Or to that poor kid carved with Satanic symbols, then gutted and dumped into Lake Wylie. Asa was a kind and gentle soul. A healer."

Henry was right. Asa Finney was an innocent misjudged for being different. Investigators had taken far too long to recognize that, and it had cost Asa his life.

"Asa would disapprove of such vengeance," I said.

Something complicated skittered through Henry's eyes. Then she stepped forward and backhanded me hard across the face. As my head snapped sideways, my optic nerves registered a terrifying tableau. A night-darkened window, high on a wall. Below the window, two gaping holes in the floor, a mound of dirt beside each. Pre-made graves?

My left parietal cracked concrete. Dizziness overtook me, and black clouds threatened in the corners of both eyes.

No!

Awash in pain and fear-induced adrenaline, I bucked my torso and wrenched my wrists wildly. The cuffs wouldn't break. I thrashed harder. The cuffs wouldn't break.

Did the chair move ever so slightly?

Henry kept smiling her deranged smile.

I continued struggling with my bindings, frenzied as a wild beast caught in a trap. Pale grooves appeared on my wrists, oozed red as the metal bracelets cut deeper and deeper into my flesh.

Never easing up, I watched Henry disappear into the shadows. She returned with a wire attached to a wooden peg at each end.

Sweet Jesus!

The garrot that killed Frank Boldonado?

Henry dragged a second chair to a position facing mine, draped the garrot across its back, turned and fixed me with another icy grin. "You'll have the best seat in the house, Doc."

With that, she withdrew again.

Footsteps. Somewhere in the cellar a door opened. I heard fabric swish, a thud, then grunting, like someone struggling under the weight of a heavy burden. A minute later—maybe several, I'd lost all track of time—Henry emerged from the shadows, hands hooking Katy's armpits, dragging her motionless body across the slick floor.

Katy's eyes were closed, her head lolling uncontrolled on her chest. Her skin was ashen.

I felt my heart explode.

"No!" I shrieked. "No!!"

"Save it for the show, Doc."

Breathing hard under the strain of moving her one-hundred-and-thirty-pound captive, Henry lugged Katy to the empty chair and, lacking a free hand, kicked the garrot to the floor, out of my reach. Emitting a final Maria Sharapova–level grunt, she heaved my daughter up, then double-shackled her as she had me.

Did the restraints mean Katy was alive? Or were they simply to hold her lifeless body in place?

I looked at my daughter, slumped like a rag doll, vulnerable and helpless.

"Katy!" I screamed. "Katy! Wake up!"

"Save it. She can't hear you."

"For God's sake. Don't do this."

"After all those years planning? Ha!"

"It's true," I said. "You're sick. Stop now and we can get you help."

With an exaggerated tooth-baring smirk, Henry pivoted and swept a hand toward Katy. "Heeere's Johnny!"

God, no! Please no!

Henry bent to snatch the garrot by one of its pegs, straightened and began circling toward Katy's back, carefully staying out of my reach.

Or so she thought. Under the guise of irrational thrashing and flailing, I'd been hitching my chair forward millimeter by millimeter.

Now!

Planting both feet, I thrust hard against the floor while swinging my upper body like a pendulum gone mad. The chair tottered, then toppled sideways with a metallic crash. I shoved wildly, lurching myself jaggedly across the floor.

Startled by the noise behind her, Henry whirled, realized her mistake, and tried yanking the full length of the garrot clear of my reach.

Too late.

Moving with a quickness I wouldn't have thought possible, I scooted onto the wire, grabbed the retreating peg with one cuffed hand, and tucked it under the arm of the rusty chair encasing me.

Henry reacted with a swiftness equal to mine. Springing forward, she attempted to right the overturned chair and its occupant. Keeping my head tucked and my torso curled, I kicked out whenever she drew close enough for a foot to connect. Again and again, I struck flesh, occasionally bone.

Frustrated, Henry snarled and scampered out of my field of vision.

As seconds passed, the only sounds in the basement were the dripping water, Henry's panting, and the booming of my own heart. Nothing from my daughter's direction.

I remained coiled and ready, chained to my tumbled mooring.

Time seemed to stop.

Plunk. Plunk. Plunk.

Boom. Boom. Boom. Boom.

Something clattered to my right.

Panicked, I raised my gaze to Katy.

Henry leaped the chair, flexed one leg, and kicked me hard in the throat. The sudden blow sent my jaw up, my lungs into spasm.

Tears ran my cheeks.

Breathe!

My burning lungs took in no air.

"Let it go!" Henry shrieked.

I refused to yield the shaky grip I had on the garrot.

Breathe!

The black clouds began to gather again.

Breathe!

"Do it! You're finished! This *will* happen!" A note of hysteria now sharpened Henry's tone.

I refused to acknowledge her commands.

I refused to acknowledge the searing fire in my chest and throat.

I tried to inhale. Felt the tiniest easing. Tasted the first molecules of oxygen.

"You have a gun," I managed to croak. "Shoot me."

"No! No! No! This has to go down *exactly* as planned." Henry now sounded like a madwoman. A madwoman caught in a crazed delusion. "You die. Then the truth of what you really are, of your arrogant judgments and the pain they've caused, will be revealed to the world."

"I won't watch," I said. "You can't force me to be a player in your sick theater."

That seemed to catch her by surprise. Then, "Good idea about the gun. What say I cap one of your knees, then get you back into your front-row seat? You refuse to view the performance, I cap the other."

Icy fingers ran my spine.

What to do? What to say?

Before I could act, Henry grabbed the chair by its back and wrenched it upright. My eyes took in an arcing kaleidoscope of grays and blacks interspersed with spots of color. The concrete walls. The two pits. The green of Katy's shirt. A flash of blond hair.

Stepping to face me, Henry drew the Glock and pointed it two-handed at my knees.

"Got a fave, Doc?" Waggling the weapon back and forth. "Righty or lefty?"

"If you harm my daughter, you will spend the rest of your life behind bars."

"That's a stupid threat. I will anyway."

"Or worse." Pure acid.

Henry shrugged.

Smiled her deranged smile.

Ratcheted back the slide on the Glock.

Aimed it fixedly at my right leg.

I glared, hating Donna Scott Henry as much as I've hated any other human being.

Henry inhaled. Spread her feet.

I closed my eyes. Braced.

Fleeting thought. Does a bullet hurt? Does shock blanket the initial pain?

I heard a pop.

Shattering glass.

Raised my lids.

Henry's arms were down, the Glock gone. A small circle glistened dark on the right side of her forehead, blood streaming down from it toward her right ear.

Henry's eyes were open, her lips shaped into a lopsided oval.

The expression held as its owner pitched forward onto the floor.

I must have looked as shocked as my suddenly dead tormentor.

My iPhone said 3:41 a.m.

I was calmer now. More rational than when they'd first brought me out of the basement, screaming and demanding a report on Katy.

I scanned the scene through an open door of Slidell's 4Runner, a cold compress wrapping my neck.

An unlit road fed the isolated cul-de-sac, empty fields flanking it on both sides. Only one house occupied the little dead-end circle. One enormous oak, winter bare. One nonfunctioning streetlamp.

My first reaction had been creative but irrelevant. The isolated court looked like a set awaiting breakdown after shooting a scene for *The Grapes of Wrath,* maybe an episode of Ken Burns's Dust Bowl series.

I know. But my head had taken multiple blows.

The home was one-story—not a ranch, bungalow, mid-century, or craftsman. Not anything with sufficient style to warrant a name. It just looked old.

My battered brain was still trying to untangle what had happened inside those walls while around me the usual crime scene three-ring played out.

Shagbark Court—I'd heard that shouted—was a hive of activity. Patrol units had shot into it and stopped at random angles, their headlights piercing the darkness, their flashers strobing blue. Unmarked cars and SUVs, later arrivals, sat behind the ragged semicircle of cruisers, other vehicles along the curbs lining the street.

Uniforms mingled with plainclothes detectives and CSU techs. Some shouted orders, others shouted back, others conversed in clusters of two or three. Journalists strained behind yellow tape stretching across the street, frustrated at being held fifty feet back from the action. Everyone seemed tense.

The ambulance had screamed off before I was brought up from the basement, taking Katy to the nearest hospital before I could join her. Leaving me furious and fuming.

The ME van had left for the morgue, Henry's body strapped to a gurney in the rear.

The SWAT team had departed in their Humvee.

I was glad Slidell had been called away from my side. His repeated insistence that I be checked by medics hadn't been helping my head.

I thanked whatever gods were looking over me that Slidell had been dogged in pursuing every lead in the copycat murders.

Having found that the sketchy gardener at MiraVia alibied out and recalling a comment the security guard, George, had made about a previous 911 call from the facility, Skinny had pulled the old B&E report. Henry was listed as one of the responders. Inspired by this finding, he did similar digging on the Happy Trails crematorium "sitch." Found that Detective Henry had also been involved in that investigation.

Slidell had also listened to his gut.

Feeling more and more vindicated in his distrust of "the newbie," Skinny had called the LAPD and received essentially the same report that I'd gotten from Mickey. Henry had made detective due to nepotism, was unstable and had been forced to leave the job.

Slidell got the speed dial call from my pocketed phone as he was researching Henry's home address. Though he couldn't make out "a goddam word" being said, he ordered a check on the annex, then secured backup and raced to Shagbark Court.

A uniformed cop approached me. Fortner.

"I understand you need transport to Atrium Health Pineville?"

"I do."

I rose, shakily, and followed Fortner to his patrol car, again thanking that pantheon of unknown deities.

And Slidell, who'd said my statement could wait.

There was only one question that needed answering at that moment.

How was my daughter?

40

Two weeks passed.

Spring sashayed into the Carolinas, a-bumping and a-grinding with bunnies and butterflies and baby birds. The seventy-degree days encouraged the redbuds and dogwoods to green-light their blooms, the snowdrops and crocus to venture aboveground.

On a sunny Saturday afternoon, Katy and I were in her garden, clearing dead vegetation from a clutch of daffodils struggling to make their appearance. A mockingbird high up in her magnolia had a lot to say.

To the right of the daffodils, a solo tulip stood tall and oddly alone. I wondered. Had the property's previous occupant planted just one bulb? Had this renegade blossom offended its garden mates? Had it survived a winter its brethren hadn't?

Katy was yanking with vigor, her face flushed, her tee damp with the effort. Her pile of discarded vines and runners was much larger than mine.

Too much time spent pondering the bulbiferous loner?

I like tulips. I liked thinking about this one. Or was I using my curiosity regarding the rebel flower to avoid pulling weeds?

To avoid thinking about Henry and her psychotic need for vengeance?

I still had flashbacks to that night in the basement. The terrifying ride to the hospital. The endless hours in the ER waiting room. The final word that Katy would recover. The overwhelming relief.

Katy continued to suffer flashbacks, too. Hers involved a different time and place. Different players. A psychotherapist was helping with the PTSD—a treatment called EMDR, Eye Movement Desensitization and Reprocessing. Katy had explained the process, but I'm not sure I fully understood. Something about accessing traumatic memories while simultaneously focusing on an external stimulus, like moving your eyes. Katy was "rolling with the campaign." Whatever "the campaign" was, she was improving.

My daughter recalled little from her time with Henry. They'd met right after Katy started at Roof Above. Henry had visited the shelter to inquire about a robbery suspect, undoubtedly fictitious. They'd hit it off—a cop and a former soldier—subsequently shared craft brews and wings at the Moosehead Grill on Montford. Then nothing.

Tox testing found Versed, a benzodiazepine, in Katy's system. Henry had probably laced her beer during that Moosehead meal. After hauling her prisoner to the farmhouse, Henry had kept her sedated via intranasal delivery.

The drug had wiped Katy's memory as clean as a wet sponge washes a whiteboard. Versed will do that for you. Good for colonoscopy patients. Not good for crime vics.

In retrospect, we figured Henry had been tracking me for years, but had finalized her plan for Katy's abduction the day she saw the photo on my desk. My idiot disclosure that my daughter volunteered at a men's homeless shelter played right into her hands.

Smart move, Brennan.

Goosed by comments from *moi*, my daughter had been trying to stay open to letting new people into her life. Henry had taken advantage, stalked, and eventually kidnapped her. Ironically, in the days prior to the abduction, Katy's PTSD had been causing her to interpret my concern as smothering. Thus, she'd been refusing to take my calls.

"How about a break?" I asked, swatting at a bee divebombing my hair.

"What about leave no weed behind?"

"I called for regrouping, not full retreat."

"Lemonade?" Smiling.

"Sure."

As Katy disappeared into the house, I settled in one of the rickety lawn chairs on her porch. A lawn chair not dissimilar from the one to which I'd been cuffed. A bit newer, less rusty.

Nope! Happy thoughts today!

Katy returned with two frosty glasses, a lemon wedge riding the rim of each.

"What are you, Martha Stewart?"

"I see myself more as the Trisha Yearwood type."

"Did you chill these in the freezer?" I asked, incredulous.

"I did."

"I'm impressed."

"And I'm impressed you installed your Ring doorbell system."

"Thanks." Half true. The previous week, I'd started, finally given up and hired an electrician. She didn't need to know that.

We sipped in silence for a while. Katy spoke first.

"Shagbark Court. What the hell is a shagbark?"

"I think it's some sort of hickory."

"Do we have them in Charlotte?"

"I think so. They were common around here once."

Thanks to Slidell, we'd learned that the lone home on Shagbark Court had begun life as a farmhouse a century back. Which explained the labyrinthine earthen-floored cellar. Coal room. Furnace room. Tool room. Canning pantry.

Shagbark Court was to be the starting point for a housing development that never went forward. Renfro Farms, named for the original owner of the acreage. Surveys had been done, streets laid, pipes, whatever. Then, three years back, the money ran dry, and the project went belly-up.

Knowing her client sought isolation and low rent, a realtor had suggested to Henry that the old house might be available for lease. It was. Henry had signed on the dotted.

"Ryan was right," Katy said, eyes closed, face tipped skyward to take in the sun.

"Don't tell him that."

"From uptown, Shagbark Court is a straight shot down South Boulevard. Or up it if you're heading into Charlotte."

I knew where she was going. When I offered no reply, she forged on.

"Ryan noted that Sanchez had lived on South Boulevard, and that Soto's language school was located there. He nailed it. Henry probably prowled that stretch for vics."

"Slidell ordered a second canvas of the businesses along South Boulevard. Turns out Boldonado used to hang at a dive bar called The Thirsty Grub."

"Dive bars are trendy now," Katy said.

"Not this one."

"What else did CSU find at Shagbark?" Katy dropped her chin and swirled the ice in her glass.

We hadn't talked about that. Until now, she hadn't asked.

"Each item will be listed on the evidence log," I said, then took a very long swig.

Reacting to my evasiveness, Katy turned my way. "Seriously, Mom? You think I can't handle a full sitrep?"

I set my chilled glass on the brick at my feet.

"Surgical equipment. Rope. A freezer that yielded human hair and skin cells. Hundreds of news stories on me and my old cases, going back years. I'm sure the tech guys will find a motherlode of incriminating info on her computer. Being a cop, Henry also had access to inside intel. There's some of that—police reports, specialist reports, coroner's reports."

"And the gun and garrot, of course."

"Guns. And a knife and a sap."

"Probably what she used to hit you on the head."

"The lady liked to be armed."

"So, no surprises." Katy sucked the juice from her lemon wedge.

"One. Sort of. Look at this."

I handed over my phone and showed her a CSU image Slidell had forwarded to me. Pictured was a lighted magnifier lamp, much like the one I use at the MCME. Below the lamp was a slotted tray holding a Ziploc bag full of long grain white rice, and another containing a wad of polymer clay. Filling the remaining slots were a vial of magnifying oil, a Micron fine-tipped pen, and tiny stoppered vials.

Katy frowned at the assemblage, baffled. Or maybe her face was puckered from the straight hit of citrus.

When her eyes rolled up, I said, "She was into rice grain art. This is her kit."

The frown held. Then understanding dawned.

"Henry was a miniaturist."

"She belonged to some sort of miniaturist club or society. Got into the hobby via therapy when she was a teen."

"Henry was in therapy as a kid?"

"After the move to California her parents sensed that something was off."

"No shit."

"That explains the GPS coordinates on Kwalwasser's eyeball." I stated the obvious.

"It surely do."

"Don't call me Shirley. Did I tell you that her full name was Donna Scott Henry?"

Katy raised her free hand in a "so what?" gesture. Then her eyes widened. "It was Henry who asked the Charleston County Coroner for a copy of the Cruikshank file. She signed the form with her initials. DSH."

"Wish I'd figured that out earlier."

There was another long silence. Except from the mockingbird.

"What's happening with Kramden?" Katy asked.

"He'll do time for kidnapping Olivia Lakin. And he confessed to tackling me outside his bus bunker. Claims he was defending his property. I'm not inclined to press a complaint, but if Slidell has his way something may come of that."

"The kid went willingly and Kramden didn't hurt her," Katy said.

"That drops the kidnapping from a Class C to a Class E felony." I suspected Katy's concern stemmed from knowing Kramden was a vet with mental issues. "That means he's facing fifteen to sixty-three months. He's out on bail, and could cop a plea, bringing his jail time even lower."

"Here's something that's been bothering me," Katy said. "Why did Charlie want to meet with you earlier than originally planned? You said he was adamant."

"I don't know. Maybe he'd uncovered the truth about Henry? Maybe he'd learned that she was buddying up to you? Maybe he'd managed to score tickets to a Hornet's game? We may never know."

"How did he cross paths with Henry?" Katy asked.

"Slidell's team found an entry on Charlie's office calendar for last February 3. The name Henry, D."

Katy thought about that.

"So Henry knew who Charlie was well before seeing us together in that photo in your office. Maybe even met with him."

I nodded.

"How did Henry know about Charlie's peanut allergy? That would hardly come up during a legal consult."

"Good point. Henry was a looker. And calculating. She probably came on to Charlie, they shared a meal, yadda, yadda."

"Did you say 'yadda, yadda'?"

"I did."

Katy rolled her emerald greens.

"Charlie must have let her into his home that night. They ended up in his office, she slipped the peanut powder into his scotch, Charlie drank it, she didn't—"

"Yadda, yadda."

"You show promise," I said.

"Thanks."

A full minute passed until Katy spoke again.

"Another thing I don't get. Why was Henry so goddam theatrical? I mean, why all the complicated mimicry? Why not just cap your ass and be done with it?"

I told her what Henry had said about depriving me of the two things I love most in life, my daughter and my work.

"So kill me, then destroy your reputation," Katy said.

"I think that was her plan."

"That seems like such friggin' hard work."

"My profiler friend, J.S., talked about violent repetitive offenders acting out of anger. About them developing fantasies, eventually rituals to express that anger. I think the copycat murders were Henry's ritual."

"Sick."

I couldn't disagree.

"Will you answer *my* one lingering question?" I asked.

Katy looked at me but said nothing.

"Who was the 'creep' stalking you?"

Katy sighed. "I guess it doesn't matter now that he's locked up. It was Winky. I doubt he meant me any harm. He's just a lonely old vet with no one in his life."

"Speaking of which, how's it going with your project?"

"Charlie's partner is great. His name is Storey, but I can get past that. Storey's helping me set up the trust, structure the foundation, yadda, yadda. I've put in a bid on a piece of property and I'm about to hire a design firm."

Katy had come out of her ordeal more determined than ever to establish a charity for homeless vets. She planned to name the organization the Aaron Cooperton Foundation, and the shelter the Charles Anthony Hunt Center. The venture had already cost me *mucho*.

"Have you bought your pavers?" Katy was selling memorial benches and walkway pavers starting at $1,000 a pop.

"Four," I said. "In the names Miguel Sanchez, Veronica Justine Kwalwasser, Francis Leonardo Boldonado, and Andrea-Louisa Soto."

"That's a nice gesture, Mom."

"How's it going with your applications?"

Katy had decided to return to school to earn an MBA. She planned to run the foundation herself and wanted the skill set to do it right.

"It's pure hell. I feel like I'm in high school again."

"Speaking of pure hell, shall we get back to the weeds?" I asked.

Katy saluted, then stood.

I drained my glass and we headed down into the garden.

ACKNOWLEDGMENTS

Many people shared their time and expertise with me during the writing of this novel. Their kindness and generosity helped make *Cold, Cold Bones* a much better book.

The Charleston County coroner, Bobbi Jo O'Neal, RN, ABMDI, answered questions concerning the functioning of her office. Lorri Ayers, MD, advised on the effects and modes of delivery of various narcotics. Hannah Jeter, LCMHC, explained the use of EMDR (eye movement desensitization and reprocessing) in the treatment of PTSD. Detective Matt Hefner offered details on the workings of the Charlotte-Mecklenburg Police Department. Bill Rodriguez, PhD, DABFA, was my go-to colleague for the latest breakthroughs in the forensic sciences.

I owe an enormous thank-you to my editors: Rick Horgan in the US, Laurie Grassi in Canada, and Bethan Jones in the UK. You are an amazing team.

I also want to acknowledge all those who work so very hard on my behalf. At home in the US, Nan Graham, Ashley Gilliam Rose, Jaya Miceli, Brian Belfiglio, Abigail Novak, Brianna Yamashita, and Katie Rizzo. On the other side of the pond, Ian Graham, Suzanne

Baboneau, Harriett Collins, Rich Vlietstra, Polly Osborn, and Gill Richardson. In the great white north, Kevin Hanson, Nita Pronovost, Felicia Quon, Adria Iwasutiak, Jillian Levick, and Rebecca Snoddon.

I am grateful to Deneen Howell, my legal representative at Williams & Connolly, LLP. Thanks for dotting all those i's and crossing all those t's.

Melissa Fish checked zillions of facts and dug scores of details from earlier Temperance Brennan stories.

Paul Reichs offered sound at-home editorial advice.

Skinny kept me company curled in the chair opposite my desk. Turk, not so much.

There are many others too numerous to name. If I failed to mention you, I apologize.

I send out a big virtual hug to all of Tempe's loyal followers. Hopefully, this time around, we may see one another at signings and other events. If our paths don't cross, we can meet via what Slidell calls the "weird wide web." Until then, visit my website (KathyReichs .com), like me on Facebook (kathyreichsbooks), and follow me on Instagram (@KathyReichs) and Twitter (@KathyReichs). You are the reason I write!

If this book contains errors, they're solely my fault.